Praise for the novels of L*** ***

"With typical Ker*** ************* ***** to the author's stunni** ********* *** **su- ality with strong, ***** ********** ** a seemingly impossib** *** ******** *Library Journal*

"Subtly nuanced characters, exquisitely sensual love scenes, and a plot laced with dangerous suspense and perilous secrets all blend brilliantly together. . . ."

—*Booklist*

"An exquisite tale of revenge, honor and redemption. This spellbinding story ensnares you with passionate characters caught in a tangled web. Kerstan reaches new heights in sensuality and storytelling with this keeper, which enthralls straight to the dramatic climax."

—*Romantic Times*

"If you can only read one book this fall, make it *The Silver Lion*." —*Contra Costa Times*

"*The Silver Lion* is a passionate, intriguing, utterly engrossing tale that will captivate readers from the first page to the last." —Romance Reviews Today

Heart of the Tiger

"An unforgettable romantic adventure. Don't miss it!"
—*USA Today* bestselling author Susan Wiggs

"Exotic adventure, dangerous intrigue, seductive passion . . . a superbly written story of revenge, redemption, and romance." —*Booklist*

"Deeply conflicted, honorable, and effectively rendered protagonists combine with a darkly intense, complex plot to create a beautifully written novel."—*Library Journal*

"Exquisite style and unparalleled prose . . . brimming with emotion, danger, and mystery. . . . [A] perfect 10."
—*Romance Reviews Today*

continued . . .

"Lynn Kerstan is a master storyteller. I highly recommend this passionate, heart-tugging story of the triumph of love over evil." —AOL Romance Fiction Forum

"Lynn Kerstan's talents continue to reach new heights as she explores all aspects of the human heart: the good, the evil, and the passionate." —*Romantic Times*

The Golden Leopard

"Exquisitely written . . . extraordinarily well-developed characters, stunning sensuality, and a few surprises. A truly exceptional, potentially award-winning romance."
—*Library Journal*

"Readers won't be able to put down Kerstan's emotionally captivating and highly dramatic adventure."
—*Booklist*

"This is a must-read by a marvelous talent."
—*Romantic Times*

"An exotic, absolutely riveting tale of suspense, adventure, and a love too strong to be denied. Enthralling from the first page to the last."
—Romance Reviews Today

"A passionate love story that is also an adventure story. . . . I loved it. . . . delicious . . . an extremely fun book." —All About Romance

"A new star in the tradition of Mary Balogh, Lynn Kerstan moves onto my personal shortlist of must-read authors. . . . Snappy, fast-paced, entertaining, [and] wonderfully witty." —*The Romance*

and others

"Lynn Kerstan beautifully renders this historical period and then adds . . . a quest, an assassin, and a few surprising twists that kept me turning the pages with eagerness. Her bold characters are well drawn, their dialogue sharp and their motivations intelligent. . . . A must read from a marvelous talent."
—Historical Romance Reviews (Top Pick)

Dangerous
Deceptions

Lynn Kerstan

A SIGNET BOOK

SIGNET
Published by New American Library, a division of
Penguin Group (USA) Inc., 375 Hudson Street,
New York, New York 10014, USA
Penguin Group (Canada), 10 Alcorn Avenue, Toronto,
Ontario M4V 3B2, Canada (a division of Pearson Penguin Canada Inc.)
Penguin Books Ltd., 80 Strand, London WC2R 0RL, England
Penguin Ireland, 25 St. Stephen's Green, Dublin 2,
Ireland (a division of Penguin Books Ltd.)
Penguin Group (Australia), 250 Camberwell Road, Camberwell, Victoria 3124,
Australia (a division of Pearson Australia Group Pty. Ltd.)
Penguin Books India Pvt. Ltd., 11 Community Centre, Panchsheel Park,
New Delhi - 110 017, India
Penguin Group (NZ), Cnr Airborne and Rosedale Roads, Albany,
Auckland 1310, New Zealand (a division of Pearson New Zealand Ltd.)
Penguin Books (South Africa) (Pty.) Ltd., 24 Sturdee Avenue,
Rosebank, Johannesburg 2196, South Africa

Penguin Books Ltd., Registered Offices:
80 Strand, London WC2R 0RL, England

First published by Signet, an imprint of New American Library,
a division of Penguin Group (USA) Inc.

First Printing, November 2004
10 9 8 7 6 5 4 3 2 1

PUBLISHER'S NOTE
This is a work of fiction. Names, characters, places, and incidents either are the product of the author's imagination or are used fictitiously, and any resemblance to actual persons, living or dead, business establishments, events, or locales is entirely coincidental.

To Pat Potter and Tara Taylor Quinn
for their inspiring dedication to Romance Writers of
America,
but mostly for the privilege of being their friend.

Chapter 1

Jarrett, Lord Dering, rode his astonishing good luck the way he rode an enthusiastic woman. He gave it all he had.

On this particular night, desperation sat in the saddle right along with him. He'd sold or pawned nearly everything he owned to fund one last gamble, and his only ally in the rash venture was Lady Fortune. But she had ever been a fickle mistress, betraying him more often than not. He could scarcely believe the giddy wench had opened her arms and claimed him for her own.

Masking intense concentration with a relaxed smile, he reviewed his count of the deck, calculated the odds, and nodded. The other players leaned forward, watching avidly as the dealer laid a card faceup in front of him.

Six of hearts. He flipped over his hole cards. A twenty, good enough to beat the dealer's nineteen. The eight men at the round baize-covered table were playing an elimination version of vingt-et-un, with heavy betting and a large pot to the winner of each round. For the last four rounds, that had been Jarrett.

Lord Beaton, brows arched, gathered up the cards

while Jarrett raked in the banknotes and vowels. "If I didn't know better, Dering, I might think you'd marked the deck."

"Fetch another, then." Jarrett never cheated unless he was playing against cheaters, and tonight the company was relatively honorable. In fact, he was probably the most disreputable guest invited to Lady Hazeldon's ball. To spare his hostess any second thoughts, he had proceeded directly to the room set aside for gaming and remained there all evening.

While the dealer shuffled for the next round, a servant came by with a decanter of brandy. Jarrett picked up his glass before it could be refilled and strolled over to a window. If he was to keep winning, he had to remain sober and appear indifferent to his success, the way he appeared indifferent when he lost. Sangfroid meant everything for an aristocrat forced to make his living on the turn of a card.

A wise fellow would take his leave now, while he was well ahead. He'd won enough to pay his immediate debts, even to redeem some of his possessions from the pawnbroker. And for the last few minutes his nose had been itching . . . nearly always a sign of impending trouble. But Lady Fortune had cradled him tightly between her thighs, humming a Siren's song. He scented victory.

Not to mention that this could be his last chance to come about. The Season was drawing to a close, and when the others left for their country estates, he'd be slumming in the London hells for chicken stakes or swallowing his pride to accept invitations he could never return.

His decision made, he turned from the window and felt a change in the overheated room, as if a breeze had wafted in. Heads swiveled to face the door. There, a petite young woman in a simple, elegant gown was smiling up at Lord Greville and offering her wrist for his salutation.

Julia, Duchess of Sarne. Almost as famous as Princess Charlotte, although *infamous* was a more accurate term for Her Grace. Jarrett had encountered her a dozen times, kept a wary distance, and watched her charm every man who let himself be drawn into her orbit. Most did.

She wasn't the only woman in the gaming room. Four dowagers were playing whist in the corner, and two ladies hovered near the gentlemen at the hazard table. But the light seemed to have shifted in her direction, and all the interest as well. Realizing that he was gawping right along with the others, he took a sip of brandy and made his way back to his chair.

The initial two cards were already dealt. Jarrett noted his poor holding, then glanced up at the duchess. She was wandering in the direction of the table, her apricot-colored hair gleaming under the crystal chandeliers. By the time he requested another card and got precisely the one he needed, she was standing across from him, a little behind Golsham's chair, her head slightly tilted as she watched the play.

Three men, tying for worst score, were eliminated, and not long after, Jarrett claimed another round. His turn to deal. He shuffled with practiced ease, Beaton eyeing him suspiciously and the duchess's gaze on the mound of winnings in front of him.

"Do you never lose?" she said.

"I lose rather too often, Your Grace." He offered Golsham the deck for a cut, and to Jarrett's surprise, the duchess reached by Golsham's arm to lift a quarter-inch's worth of cards.

"What are the stakes, sir? The usual for social gaming, or the sort you gentlemen play for at the clubs?"

Golsham covered her cut with the rest of the deck. "Not high enough," he said, his voice slurred. "The game's not int'resting. We need a prize. Something rare. Something . . . irresistible."

General laughter from the men, who knew the duchess's reputation. Jarrett took the cards and began to deal, wishing the lady would wander off again. She looked . . . He could not say. Too excited. As if she tiptoed on the edge of a razor.

"Do you refer to me?" she asked, placing a hand on the back of Golsham's chair. "I might consider it. But I do not wager myself alongside shillings and pence. The game must be for high stakes all around."

"One hundred guineas to open?" Beaton suggested smoothly.

Frowning a little, she plucked a flute of champagne from the tray of a passing servant. "Is this a game of skill? I do so appreciate a skillful man."

Jarrett saw his night's winnings about to vaporize. Someone ought to cart Golsham away, and Beaton, and the capricious duchess as well.

"Too high for me," said Freddy Pryne, pushing back his chair. "And if I won the prize, m'betrothed would have my ears for garters."

Go! All of you! Teeth gritted, Jarrett completed the deal. His own cards totaled a respectable eighteen, so he'd live for at least one more hand. Glancing up, he saw the duchess regarding him from green eyes flecked with gold.

By God, she was having them on. He was sure of it. She'd play her teasing game a few more minutes, pronounce herself bored, and go in search of better entertainment. The men would laugh as if they'd known her intentions all along, because what else could they do? The Duchess of Sarne, everyone said, was a law unto herself.

Relieved, he put in another hundred guineas and dealt the next hand. Two men eliminated, four to go. The losers mourned their fate in good-humored misery. The duchess laughed.

The room went suddenly cold.

Near the door, silence fell and rippled like a wave in their direction. Watching the duchess, Jarrett saw her go still. She didn't turn, but the color had washed from her face.

He took up his brandy glass and stole a look at the tall, imposing man who had just come in. Near-black hair lightly sprinkled with gray, rigid posture, an air of total command. The Duke of Sarne.

He spoke to people without appearing to notice them, moved in the direction of the table without seeming to be aware of its existence. Jarrett knew Sarne was scarcely older than his own thirty-two years, but he seemed to have lived a great deal longer than that. A doomed family, everyone said. Cursed. The Sarnes had rarely been seen the past several years, spending most of their time in the north. And in mourning.

Except for the duchess, who had come alone to London and taken the city by storm.

As the duke neared the table, Golsham caught sight of him and lurched to his feet. "Look here, Your Grace."

If Jarrett could have reached across the large table, he would have shut Golsham up with a fist to the jaw. But it was too late. Sarne paused, turned his head slightly, lifted an arrogant brow.

"We're playing for the duchess," Golsham said, his

words mushy from drink. "There's an empty chair, if you want into the game."

Sarne flicked a glance at his wife. "Why would I wager for what is already mine? If, to be sure, I happened to want it. Do proceed, gentlemen. Don't let me spoil your fun."

He moved on by, the chill he cast over the room reaching all the way to Jarrett's spine.

"You heard His Grace," said the duchess lightly. "Someone ought to be dealing. Or is there no one here who wishes to escort me home tonight?"

Immediate protests from everyone, saving only Beaton and himself. She was playing her game in earnest now, Jarrett could tell. She intended to see it through.

He wanted no part of this. His legs stiffened, preparing to lift him up and carry him away. And then, with a smothered oath, he settled back again. Trapped, dammit. He wasn't so ungallant as to subject her to a second humiliation by scarpering. Not that she hadn't come asking for trouble. But if she strayed, and clearly she did, a block of ice like Sarne gave her ample reason for it.

With luck—he couldn't believe he was now hoping for *bad* luck—he might lose the next hand. That would free him to leave in a gentlemanly manner, with most of his winnings intact. *Go away,* he ordered his suddenly faithful mistress, but Luck smiled and gripped him all the tighter. Soon only Jarrett and Beaton remained in the game.

And behind the empty chair, fingers white as she clutched the back of it, the Duchess of Sarne gazed on him with a look he could not interpret.

He could still withdraw. He could even deliberately lose, although that would be hard to conceal in a game of vingt-et-un. And he didn't want to lose, not with banknotes, guineas, and signed vowels piled high in the center of the table.

Sarne had left some time ago, apparently unconcerned about the outcome. And when you came right down to it, the duchess wasn't the first adulterous wife to offer herself to Jarrett at the end of a party. Where was the harm, after all?

Besides, he didn't want to send her home with Lord Beaton. He couldn't think why. Nothing wrong with the fellow that he knew of. Beaton was handsome enough, rich, well-spoken. All in all a better prospect, even for one night, than an impoverished viscount.

"You wished for skill," Beaton was saying to the duchess. "But there is so little required in the simple game we have been playing. With the battle come down to single combat, would it amuse you if Dering and I made a contest of it? Something more worthy of our prize than the luck of the deal?"

With Beaton setting the terms, Jarrett knew he might as well bid that pile of money good-bye. Through the roar of disappointment in his ears, he heard the duchess's voice, but not her words.

Then Beaton said, "Chess, don't you think? A true test of a man's ingenuity, and his endurance."

"Also an interminable bore for a spectator," Jarrett pointed out. "And where would we find a board and pieces?"

That was taken care of with annoying ease, and soon he was sitting opposite Beaton at a small marquetry table in the center of the room. The duchess accepted a chair between them, propped her elbows on the table, and rested her chin on her folded hands. She looked alert as a squirrel. Around them, at least thirty people jockeyed for a view.

They had agreed to three minutes for each move,

with Freddy Pryne keeping time. Beaton drew white and began with a standard opening, his expression bland, smugness in his eyes. Clearly he fancied himself a master.

Jarrett played most games well, but chess was not a favorite. It proceeded too slowly, and while he was waiting for an opponent to move, he generally lost a degree of concentration. The speed of this particular match worked to his advantage, he supposed.

But he required another advantage as well. As the conservative early moves were taken, he let his gaze wander to the onlookers. He beckoned for a servant to top off his glass and took a long drink. Safe enough. By the time he felt its effects, the game would be over. And he watched the duchess, who appeared to be studying the game and wasn't.

Her unhappiness curled around him like smoke.

He'd begun the match wanting to win the money and fairly sure he would not. But as her misery settled over him, he could not mistake her silent plea. He felt it all the more when she was looking at Beaton, a flirtatious smile curving her pretty lips.

The timekeeper had to point out that Beaton had taken a move and that most of Jarrett's three minutes had already ticked away. Quickly, he sent a pawn into a trap and saw it snatched away.

He made a show, then, of buckling down, even as he drank more deeply and tried to start his own flirtation with the duchess. If he won, it would be on the wings of theatrics and a gambler's hunch . . . assuming a hunch had the kindness to appear.

Beaton, he noted with pleasure, had failed to seize the first advantage given him. Instead, he continued with a plodding strategy designed to produce inevitable victory. Pure logic, no flair.

Jarrett took a pawn, lost two more. Then he lost a knight and a bishop. Attrition was sucking him down a hole. The time had come.

He reached in the direction of his remaining bishop, which could not move in any way to his advantage. Paused as if rethinking the action. His fingers edged toward his queen, because the obvious strategic moves were all hers. The timekeeper said, "Five seconds." Startled, he jerked his remaining knight to a hopeless position.

Beaton, concealing what was surely glee, claimed the knight with his rook. Jarrett, concealing his own glee, seized Beaton's rook with a daringly aggressive move.

Three minutes didn't allow a methodical thinker like Beaton to work out the nature of the attack mounted against him. He took the logical next action, lost another piece, and within ten minutes watched Jarrett's black queen gently topple his white king onto the board.

The relief that passed across the duchess's face was all the reward Jarrett needed for his skillful maneuver. That and the money, of course, not to mention his own appreciation of his brilliance.

Beaton, looking puzzled at the outcome, offered his hand. Freddy Pryne, who had taken custody of the winnings from the card table, handed over a thick stack of folded banknotes and vowels. Jarrett slipped them inside his jacket. There were guineas as well, a lot of them. While Beaton took polite leave of the duchess, Jarrett looked around for a container. He was about to pull flowers from a vase when the duchess spoke from behind him.

"Use this."

He turned to see her holding open a delicate mesh

reticule threaded with gold and silver, studded with gemstones and pearls. "It's quite strong," she said. "And empty. A servant carries anything I might have need of."

After a moment, he began loading it with coins until it was swollen as a melon. Those that wouldn't fit went into the pockets of his tailcoat. A gamester without a valet to protest could get away with stuffing his pockets.

"Come along, then," said the duchess. "We shall take leave of Lady Hazeldon while my carriage is brought around."

"But—"

"You needn't look so unhappy, my lord." She arched one brow, very much the way her husband had done. "Or do you fear that being seen in my company will tarnish your reputation?"

"Hardly that. But I assumed you to be playing out a jest, Your Grace. When the chess game ended, did not *your* game end as well?"

"My game, Lord Dering, has only just begun." She handed him the reticule. "Appear pleased, if you will, but not too eager."

Pockets clinking, he found himself trailing behind her like a dinghy as she sailed from room to room. Deliberately making a spectacle of them both, he thought. And looking for someone, but not Lady Hazeldon. She intended to troll him past her husband.

Sarne had left, though, or was successfully evading them. Everyone else eyed them with knowing smiles and whispered from behind cupped hands when they walked by. Word of the outrageous wager had spread from the gaming room. By tomorrow morning, it would be common gossip throughout London.

When the duchess finally abandoned her plan to

thumb her nose at the duke, they settled across from each other inside her extravagant crested coach. Outriders in midnight-blue-and-gold livery escorted them, and bewigged servants rode atop the carriage and on the platform at the rear of it. Lanterns inside the compartment cast a golden glow over the duchess's pert face.

She could not be more than five-and-twenty. Probably younger than that, and deceptively fragile in appearance. She was looking beyond him, or through him. Desperately unhappy, he could tell, determined to conceal it, and using him to do precisely that. He ought to have minded more than he did.

The brandy he'd drunk to mislead Beaton was settling in, fuzzing his brain. And he was in a splendid mood. He had *won*! For the first time in a long time, he was plump in the pockets. And in the reticule, which sat on his lap like a fat kitten. What's more, he would soon be in bed with a beautiful woman.

Well, probably not. To his considerable regret. As they drew closer to St. James's Square, he kept expecting her to put him out on a street corner. But she kept not doing it.

"You were correct," she said at length. "It was a game, to begin with, and then it became more than that. I was unfair to drag you into my private war. But I'll not keep you long, sir. Only a few hours, if you are kind enough to indulge me."

"I am at your service," he said, as any gentleman would. "But I suspect your intentions are not so carnal as you have led everyone else to believe."

She blinked. "How could you tell?"

"That a woman does not want me to make love to her?" He didn't think she would relish the truth, and he'd no right to intrude on her private misfortunes.

"You will think me vain to say so, but the few women disinclined to welcome me to their beds rather stand out from the crowd. Sadly, you are one of them. But now that we are out of public view, why carry on with the masquerade?"

"Because a gambler always pays her debts. Or appears to. By sending you away, I am behaving dishonorably, and I do not wish anyone to know it."

"Then drop me at the next dark corner. I will say nothing of this."

Her slender fingers dug into her skirts. "You must come home with me. Someone may be following."

That was possible. Newshounds lurked outside fashionable parties, hoping to nip off a bite of scandal. "Very well. But if you don't mind, I shouldn't like to run into the duke."

"He never stays at Sarne House when I am in residence.. And he wouldn't object, in any case, to your being there."

"Give me leave to doubt that, Your Grace. No man is indifferent to a trespasser on his property. One fine morning, I'm apt to find myself at the point of his sword."

Her laugh, too brittle, came on cue. "He couldn't be bothered, I assure you. But I think he does keep track of my . . . activities. For Sarne, information is the air he breathes. He requires to learn everything, as if knowledge of people or circumstances will grant him control of them."

"Most people, I have observed, cannot even control themselves. So I am to enter the house and be shuffled out through the mews?"

"If you don't object, I wish you to stay a few hours. You can enjoy Sarne's library and brandy, if not his wife, and a servant will bring you some supper. At dawn you will be shown the back way out."

"Oh, the front way, I should think. We would not be ashamed, would we, to have done what we are not going to do?"

This time her laugh was genuine. "I am so full of pride, sir. That has always been my undoing. Leave by whatever direction you wish. But if you go out the front, be sure your waistcoat is unbuttoned and your cravat untied."

"Indeed. And I'll be smiling."

"May I count on you, then, to tell no one what really occurred?"

"I will say only that I have never spent so memorable a night." He leaned forward, took her in a light embrace, and brushed a kiss on her lips. Her fragrance, at once subtle and seductive, sent a rush of desire through him. "Or ever held in my arms so enchanting a woman. Are you quite sure, Your Grace, that this is all we will share together?"

"I am." Gently, she restored the distance between them.

Moments later the coach drew up in front of the impressive town house. He put his arm around her waist while they walked to the door, but when it closed behind them, she immediately stepped away. "Raxley will show you to the library now. Keep the reticule as a souvenir, if you like. And you will always have my gratitude for your kindness."

She started up the sweeping arc of the staircase, paused, and turned. Her remarkable eyes shone as she looked down on him. "I am in your debt, Lord Dering. If ever you require a service of me, I shall do all in my power to grant it."

Chapter 2

Woozy from overindulgence in the Duke of Sarne's brandy, the best he'd ever tasted, Jarrett stumbled from his bed in the early afternoon, managed to shave and dress himself, and rang for the porter.

He rented the top floor of a three-story house on the fringes of respectability, where Grimple—when he was sober—played dogsbody to all the tenants. Most times, including this one, Grimple failed to respond. But he'd fetched the morning post, Jarrett saw when he went into the sitting room.

On top was the usual collection of bills, which he added to the stack that had been accumulating since he was last in funds. It seemed a long time ago. There were invitations as well, which he put aside, and a perfumed letter from a persistent widow who had been trying to rekindle their affair. Later he would contrive a polite reply.

For now he had collections to make and his bank to visit. Then, if his luck held, he'd be on time for his regular Thursday afternoon entertainment.

Just inside the tiny foyer, a square of white on the uneven floor caught his attention. A dropped letter?

He picked it up. Expensive stationery, he could tell, with his name—only his name—printed in thick black ink. This hadn't come through the post. The seal, black wax and unusually large, was stamped with something he could not identify. An eagle rising off the top of a bush, perhaps. Not an insignia he recognized.

With some impatience, he broke through the seal and opened the single sheet of paper. The writing had a forceful quality. His gaze fell on the first words and could not move beyond them: *You are summoned . . .*

Sarne. It had to be. Cold sweat beaded on his forehead. Dukes, it seemed, did not dispatch their seconds to arrange an affair of honor. The same way, he supposed, that a man could never fight a duke and win, no matter the outcome of the duel itself. He wondered if "Which of us can run the fastest and farthest?" would qualify as choice of weapons.

When his breathing steadied, he wrenched his attention to the rest of the letter.

> *You are summoned, for your failures, your guilt, and your debts, to undertake a mission that will test your every claim to character and courage. Expect danger to the point of death. Should you succeed, the benefit will go to others.*
>
> *To learn what is being asked of you and how to proceed, take supper at the New Moon chophouse in Billingsgate tonight at nine o'clock.*

No signature. But then, a man luring another man into a trap would hardly identify himself in writing. It seemed that Jarrett Dering was too commonplace a fellow to be called out by a duke. He was to be slain by hired thugs or, if Sarne had a merciful streak, merely pounded into sausage.

The summons went into the trash basket.

His errands accomplished, Jarrett spent the rest of the afternoon tormenting himself at Tattersall's Repository.

The nags he might have afforded had been first on the block, and only the prime goers, what few were on offer this time of year, remained. He wandered from stall to stall, speaking with the handlers, testing his evaluations against theirs. Horses were his first, greatest, and only love. From boyhood he had read everything he could find about them, hounded stablemen for equine lore, sneaked rides on temperamental mounts he was forbidden to go near.

Spent far too much time at a neighboring estate where racehorses were bred and trained, and look where *that* had got him.

But the horses weren't to blame. He liked them all, whatever their flaws, although his pulse invariably leaped when he came upon a steed like the one being groomed in the courtyard. The large bay, deep-chested, coat gleaming over perfect musculature, was an opera on four legs. The big head swung toward Jarrett. Intelligent brown eyes measured him up.

Jarrett, temptation curling his toes, calculated the likely price. Auctions were hard to predict, especially in London, where rivalries sometimes drove the bidding far beyond a horse's value. But if he was still on Lady Fortune's good side, she might slip him a bargain. Why shouldn't he have what he most wanted? After last night's success, he could even bear the cost of stabling and feeding.

But not if he paid his debts, which he was determined to do. And not if he refurbished his wardrobe, an overdue necessity for a man of his class. And not if he laid up funds for the hard times. A gambler required a stake for the next game, and the one after that.

He felt, sometimes, as if a whirlpool had caught him in its spin. He couldn't breathe, couldn't escape, had no choice of destination.

He gave his vanishing dream one last, regretful glance before leaving Tattersall's. Reality might be an appalling nuisance, but it couldn't be ignored. The horse would not be his.

He found a chophouse a long way from the one he'd been summoned to and celebrated his unaccustomed solvency with rare sirloin and a bottle of good claret. He stopped by his club, read the newspapers, and broke even at ecarte before taking a hackney to his lodgings. It occurred to him that most of his evenings passed in similar fashion, without the expensive wine and the luxury of a ride home.

Grimple had remembered to light a pair of colza lamps. They glowed from the mantelpiece, casting golden light over the sitting room with its worn carpet and tatty furniture. It looked as it always did. But something was wrong. Out of place.

Not that his few possessions had a place of significance. Most belonged in the rubbish bin. He flipped through the afternoon post, stacked where Grimple always left it, but found only the usual bills and invitations. No mysterious summons—second notice—to an obscure destination.

Then he spotted the problem. In summer he left open the bedchamber door to encourage an air flow between the front window and the back. Now it was closed. Might the aggressive widow have come in person to press her case, and herself, on him? She wouldn't be the first female to slip uninvited into his lodgings. Grimple was easily bribed.

Well, what better way to end his day of celebration than in the embrace of an imaginative lover? He was not, he hoped, so drunk as to have rendered himself incapable. Tossing his hat and gloves on a chair, he crossed to the bedchamber door and swung it open.

His gaze went first to the side table, where a single candle cast a small circle of light. He looked to the bed and the faded blue counterpane that lay across it, flat and undisturbed. Then he saw the tall shadow beside the bedpost.

"Hullo," said a friendly voice. "You needn't kick up a dust. I'm not here to murder you."

"Glad to hear it." Jarrett tried to think if anything weaponlike lay within reach. "Who the devil are you?"

"M'friends call me Jordie." He was leaning against the bedpost, arms folded and feet crossed at the ankles. An unthreatening pose if ever there was one.

Which meant, as any saphead could tell, that Jordie was a threat of the first order. Jarrett fisted his hands and prepared to spring.

Something hard poked him in the back. "Don't be impetuous," advised another too-friendly voice. "Yes, it is a pistol. I'm a terrible shot, but at this range, even I couldn't miss."

Jarrett held still. "Sarne's messenger boys, I take it."

"If the duke means to call you out for dallying with his wife," Jordie said, "I expect he will deliver the challenge himself. My, oh, my. *Such* a scandal. The story has reached even my innocent ears. But we are not here on that account. And really, Dering, these theatrics would have been unnecessary if you'd just taken yourself to the New Moon like a good lad."

The gun pulled away from Jarrett's back. "Shall we go into the next room," said the man holding it, "and make ourselves comfortable? I am unaccustomed to late hours."

Not much to do but trundle along to the sitting room and take the chair pointed to by the man with the pistol. He was, Jarrett saw, soberly dressed, brown-haired, of average height, and near his own age. Altogether unremarkable, in the way of a clerk or a solicitor.

Jordie, on the other hand, had the cheery face of a young aristocrat fresh off an Oxford cricket pitch. Older than that by a decade, Jarrett would guess, somewhat taller than the pistol-wielding clerk, with powerful shoulders and sun-streaked hair.

A gambler soon learned to size up his opposition. Jarrett, without pleasure, reckoned both men to be quite other than what they seemed.

Jordie dropped onto a chair and stretched out his legs. "Let's get to it, then. Why did you refuse the summons?"

"I've a better question. Why should I trot off to a chophouse on account of an anonymous letter?"

"You're *not* guilty?" A light brown eyebrow went up. "*Not* a failure?"

"That's my concern. And who do you think *you* are? The Spanish Inquisition?"

"Something like, without the thumbscrews. Will you pay the debts you owe from what you just won?"

Jarrett had heard of militant Methodists and other stern-minded groups that ran about preaching repentance in brothels, gin shops, and gaming hells. Apparently they were now calling at private residences.

"Whatever you were going to say to me at the New Moon, say it fast. Then get the hell out of here."

The clerk, standing at the fireplace, regarded him sadly. "Jordan does not mean to offend," he said. "It is your lack of curiosity, I think, that has set him off. Without an inquiring nature, you'll not suit our purposes."

"That's good news. So why are you still here?"

"We thought," Jordie said amiably, "that you might wish to go to Paradise."

"Not immediately, thank you. And there are, I understand, rules of admission. It happens I've broken nearly all of them."

"He does not refer to the ultimate paradise," said the clerk. "We're talking about the one in the Lake District."

"Ah." The anvil on Jarrett's chest, the one making it difficult to breathe, lifted slightly. "What red-blooded man doesn't want to go there? But from what I hear, the admission standards are even stricter than those up yonder."

"Just so." Jordie drummed his fingers on the arm of the chair. "We have had considerable difficulty selecting the proper guest for this party. Despite your disreputable character, a definite plus in these circumstances, you were too publicly penniless to qualify. But after last night's spectacular triumph, followed by an act of incredible folly, I believe an invitation can be secured. We are proceeding on that assumption."

"There is a degree of urgency," the clerk said. "It must be weighed against caution, to be sure, but we have no time to waste."

"You are speaking," said Jarrett, "as if I had some notion of what you are talking about. An invitation to Paradise sounds delightful, but the message I re-

ceived this morning was a trifle more ominous. You
sent it, I presume."

"Not directly." The clerk withdrew a folded sheet
of paper from his coat and brought it to Jarrett. It
bore the creases of having been scrunched up and
thrown away. "The letter is from Black Phoenix."

"You won't have heard of us," Jordie said. "And
you'll not hear much about us even now. Robin—
that's all the name he likes to give out—and I are a
small part of . . . What shall I call it? An informal
confederacy, with a few continuing members and an
increasing number of ad hoc participants. Most, like
yourself, are called to perform a specific task."

Jarrett tapped on the sheet of paper. " 'Expect danger to the point of death,' it says. I don't imagine
people are queuing up to join you."

A pause. Then Jordie said, "Few assignments carry
this level of risk. Perhaps you are not up to it."

"On the other hand," the clerk said softly, "what
has a man in your circumstances left to lose?"

Jarrett glanced down at the paper, at the words that
seemed to have gone on fire. *You are summoned, for
your failures, your guilt, and your debts. . . .*

Jordie, like a golden angel of retribution, smiled be-
nevolently. "There is no penalty for refusal. Save only,
I should imagine, regret."

Jarrett swore under his breath. How he lived his life
was nobody's business. Who had ever given a damn,
anyway? "What is it you *do*, precisely? Are you connected with the government?"

"Dear me, no. More like entrepreneurs, unofficial
as field mice. When a crime is done at the highest
levels of society, the authorities generally cannot, or
will not, interfere. In such cases, we sometimes step
in to see that right is done."

"Most boys cease playing at Knights of the Round Table when they are sent off to school."

"But not all." Jordie's expression darkened. "However, our motives are not your concern. You are summoned for this one endeavor only. If the reports we have received are exaggerated, you will enjoy a few weeks of sporting, gaming, and assorted dissolute pleasures in company with your fellow rakehells. If you find the reports to be accurate, you will procure incontrovertible evidence for a trial. Failing that, you will do whatever is necessary to close the gates of Paradise."

Jarrett rubbed the heavy parchment paper between his thumb and forefinger. "You're going to have to be more specific than that. What do you imagine is occurring there?"

"You'll learn nothing more at present," said the clerk. "Your associate, who is already in place, will make contact with you upon your arrival. Meantime, there is groundwork to be laid. Tomorrow night, play hazard at The Devil's Bones. Stop after you have won a thousand pounds. Saturday night, take supper at Boodles and allow Lord Fairstone to entice you into a game of whist. Then accept his challenge at piquet. The cards will be marked, but deal and play as if unaware of it. Fairstone will see to it you win the rest of the stake allotted you for this mission."

"That includes the bay you admired this afternoon at Tattersall's," Jordie said. "If we have procured the invitation, you will ride north on Monday. Instructions will be provided as you require them."

Thousands of pounds to be dished into his hands? The magnificent bay would be *his*? Almost, Jarrett was tempted to leap into the boiling oil with both feet.

"Nice carrots," he said. "Now tell me about the sticks."

Jordie pointed to the letter. "Danger," he said airily. "Death. It's all right there."

"You're a clever fellow," said the clerk. "We chose you precisely for your habitual pursuit of folly, but self-preservation should keep you this side of disaster."

"Do I get to keep the horse?"

Jordie rose. "Black Phoenix pays only those expenses necessary to accomplish our purpose. But if your performance is exceptional and effective, perhaps we'll let you buy the nag for a moderate sum."

"One thing more," said the clerk. "Under no circumstance, now or in future, are you to make reference to Black Phoenix or indicate that you know anything of us."

"Or the undertaking," Jordan said, "or anyone you meet in the course of it. The consequences of indiscretion would make you wish we were, after all, the kindly Inquisition."

"And the consequences of refusal?"

"Do think it over, there's a good chap. Unlike most of our recruits, you have an entire day to consider."

Both men were heading for the door. Jarrett jumped up to go after them. "How do I inform you of my decision?"

"Follow our instructions," said the clerk in a sharp voice. "If you appear at the Devil's Bones tomorrow night, we'll assume you're in the game."

He continued on his way, but Jordie paused on the landing just outside the door. "Sometimes the backroom contrivances get a little out of hand. I am too well-known for there to be any point withholding my identity. Major Lord Jordan Blair"—he gave a slight, mocking bow—"at your service. Do remember what I said. Compromise our mission or the Black Phoenix fellowship, and I will personally see that you regret it."

Jarrett shrugged and closed the door in his face.

If they'd wanted his help, they should have let him keep the horse.

Chapter 3

Even in the gloom of a damp twilight, Jarrett could tell that the gates of Paradise weren't the least bit pearly. In fact, they were constructed of heavy wrought iron carved into fanciful gilded vines that spelled out PARADISE across the arching top. A close look at the iron vines weaving among the twisted columns revealed that each was capped with the fanged head of a serpent. This was a welcome to Paradise as imagined by Lucifer, after the fall.

The two young men hurrying from the round towers on either side of the gate wore neat maroon livery and looked eager to please. One rushed off in the direction of a nearby building while the second, wielding a large key, opened the gate and stepped aside to let Jarrett ride through.

"Lord Dering." The gatekeeper bowed. "Such unfortunate weather. I trust your journey was not unpleasant. We had expected you earlier today."

"I took a wrong turn," Jarrett said, entering Paradise with a lie. He'd got himself deliberately lost for most of the afternoon, scouting the territory in the vicinity of his destination. "Several, actually. No sense of direction."

"The landscape is indeed puzzling and can be, in some places, quite dangerous. Most of our guests take care not to leave the estate without an escort. Ah, here is Reeves, who will accompany you to the manor house. Enjoy your stay, my lord."

The other young man, now mounted, rode up and handed him an open umbrella. "Your luggage arrived this morning, my lord. We took the liberty of unpacking and seeing to your wardrobe. Shall we expect your valet, or would you prefer us to make arrangements for a personal servant?"

"I'm partial to good service," Jarrett said, his experience of it a distant memory. "But I dislike anyone hanging about."

"Then your needs will be seen to without intruding on your privacy. Please follow me, my lord."

The ride took about fifteen minutes. Despite the rain, Jarrett glimpsed small paths curling off the road and leading to tree-sheltered cottages, all of them a good distance from the traffic and from one another. Then the road straightened, with lime trees arrayed on either side like an honor guard, and he saw at the top of a gentle rise a tall greystone house, crescent-shaped and surrounded by terraced gardens. It could have been the home of a respected gentleman, and perhaps it had begun that way. Light, softened by the drizzle, filtered through the windows. A tracery-and-glass conservatory was set at one end, and at the other, a one-story square that looked to surround a courtyard. Stables and outbuildings, Reeves explained, were located in the back, out of sight.

Servants rushed down a half circle of marble steps, one to take his horse, another to carry his umbrella, and a third to lead him inside. The circular entrance hall, floored with buffed marble, was ringed with carved pillars. Set between them, pedestals held painted urns or Grecian statues. Two staircases descended like wings from a balconied landing, and on the wall beneath it, he saw a life-size painting of a woman.

It first drew his attention because the rich colors and dramatic pose seemed out of place in this pale, classical setting. The woman, her black hair severely scraped into a coil at the back of her head, was poised at a three-quarter angle, looking over her shoulder. She wore a long-sleeved scarlet dress that encased her tightly from the neck to a point just above her knees, where it erupted in a cascade of black and red lace ruffles. He couldn't see her face. She was holding a fan, provocatively spread to conceal all but her eyes. A startling blue, they seemed to look directly into his.

"Gaetana," said a jovial voice from behind him.

Startled, Jarrett swung around.

The man, short, rotund, and hairless, showed both rows of teeth as he smiled. "Our newest attraction. She will perform tonight, I believe."

"Gaetana means 'Gypsy,' does it not?"

"So I am told. She came to us by way of a traveling theater company that chanced to be playing in Windermere when we had a spate of poor weather. A bad year, this one, for sunshine. We hired the company to perform for our housebound guests, who had no patience with their Shakespeare but were soon enraptured with the lady. When she had a falling-out with the company manager, we invited her to stay on."

More than he wanted to know, Jarrett thought, suspecting the man had a private interest in the actress. "You are the owner of this establishment?"

"Oh, my, no. Merely the host, at your service. Do come into the salon, Lord Dering, and warm yourself with a glass of wine."

When Jarrett was settled in a chair, a glass of wine in hand, the steward flipped open a Moroccan leather folder.

"I'll not keep you long, my lord. In early days, we used to indoctrinate our guests on their arrival, describing all the amenities of Paradise and most of its attractions. They found the lecture tedious, so now we provide a written sample of our offerings and leave the gentlemen to seek recommendations from their fellow guests. I am, by the way, Mr. Miles Fidkin. Fidkin to everyone but the servants."

"You are in charge?"

"On the premises, yes." A flash of impatience in his brown eyes. "As we speak, a supper and a hot bath are being prepared for you. Your cottage is the most remote of our private residences, but you'll have a splendid view of the lake."

"There is no accommodation here at the manor?" An investigator, Jarrett reckoned, should be close to the center of activity.

"Sadly, no. You'll not mind, though. Our evening activities take place in a compound overlooking the lake, halfway between here and the cottage. In this folder is a map of the property, along with a list of the most popular recreational activities. If you do not find what you are looking for, you have only to ask."

Jarrett nodded. "I was pleased, of course, to receive the invitation and lost no time accepting. But it did not specify the length of my welcome, nor the tariff."

"Both," said Fidkin, "are indefinite. Within limits, you may remain for so long as we profit from your stay. There is no cost for lodging, food, drink, or service. We make up the difference by charging substantial amounts for sports and entertainment, and we claim a percentage of all wagers."

"But a bet can be made at any place or time. How would you even know of it?"

"I've a better question. Why would a gentleman risk expulsion, or forfeit the chance of another invitation, merely for an off-the-books wager? Money does not change hands here. You will sign for everything, including the markers we provide at the gaming tables. And within a fortnight of leaving, you will have paid us in full."

"Of course." Jarrett set down his glass. "Are the games honest?"

"We cannot guarantee it. But the house, I assure you, is strictly neutral, and our guests carefully selected."

"Not to mention that your profit is assured, no matter who wins or loses."

"Exactly." Fidkin looked pleased, as if a puppy had just fetched a stick. "Paradise, Lord Dering, opens its gates only to sophisticated gentlemen capable of managing their own affairs. We provide a service—*many* services—without passing judgment on your choices, or on your behavior. Unless, of course, you spend no money."

"How about women? Do you provide those?"

"Whatever you fancy can be had, for a price. But it grows late, and a carriage is waiting to take you to the cottage. If you are not too weary, perhaps you'll wish to join our other guests this evening at the Pleasure Dome."

"A fanciful name." Jarrett rose, stretched, and took the folder Fidkin was holding out.

"Indeed. Plucked, I am told, from a poem. Of all things!"

"I should like to read it one day."

"Then we must procure you a copy," said Fidkin with the smile that never seemed to leave his face. "In Paradise, your whim is our command."

Mellowed by a steaming bath and a good dinner, Jarrett set out on foot just as the sun was disappearing over the hills on the other side of the lake. Herne Water, according to the map. No village or house lay within miles of the shoreline.

"That's because the lake is cursed," he'd been told by the polite young man who pressed his shirt and cravat. "It's where they brought witches for the testing. Bound them hand and foot, they did, and tossed 'em in the water. If the creatures stayed afloat, it had to be the devil kept them up. Being proven witches, they were taken out, dried off, and burned. The ones that sank were innocent, but they drowned. Their bones are scattered across the lake bed, and after a bad storm, we find a scatter of them washed onto the bank."

"Something to look forward to," Jarrett had said, earning himself a curious glance.

The water looked peaceful enough now, the calm surface reflecting the crimson and gold of a brilliant sunset. Like paint on a coffin, he thought, imagining the accused women sinking into a muddy grave.

Like them, he had been dragged from his own unsettled existence and summoned to this place of testing. *For your failures, your guilt, and your debts,* said the letter, as if he were expected to recognize what sins Black Phoenix had charged him with.

And he did, of course. It seemed that all of England, or at least the portion of it he regularly encountered, knew precisely what had caused him to be cast out of his family and into icy waters. As for failures, what man could claim to be free of them?

But guilt? He'd done what he had to do.

Regarding his debts, he'd gritted his teeth and paid nearly all of them before departing London. Soon enough, his holiday ended, he'd again be scrounging at the gaming tables for his next month's food and lodging. Better dressed, though. He was a gentleman, by God, and well-favored to boot. A new wardrobe was an investment he'd not even tried to resist, and if he did say so himself, he looked uncommonly fine.

The path curved around a thick copse of hazels and birches. Far to his left, lights shone where the manor house must be. He sucked in delicious breaths of crisp, clean air. Why sully Paradise with thoughts of gloom and doom? He'd examined his conscience quite thoroughly on the ride north, trying to figure out why he had been chosen to do a good deed, and more to the point, why the hell he'd accepted.

No sensible answer had yet pushed its way forward. Because he had been bored. Because he had nothing better to do. Because he would have his expenses paid during the slow summer months. Because he would escape the muggy city into the countryside. Not good enough reasons to risk danger and death, but how was a man to make an intelligent decision without knowing what was expected of him?

He was in no particular hurry to find out. It wasn't often that he could afford to live down to his reputation, so until someone put an end to his fun, he meant to enjoy himself. In that spirit he'd meandered north by slow stages, staying at the best inns, ordering the best wines, and imagining himself on a leisurely tour

of his imaginary estates. Tonight, if not forestalled by
the appearance of his associate, he would find out
what Paradise charged for an evening of bed sport.

The path arced back toward the lake and ran alongside it for a time. The twilight breeze cooled his face.
Two horsemen were coming his direction, pausing at
intervals to ignite the torches that lined the path. Another stretch of woodland, and when he emerged, the
path began to climb a long, gentle hill. At the top, on
a promontory about fifty yards above the lake, the
Pleasure Dome glowed with lights.

There was an actual dome, in fact, resembling a
large round hat sitting on a much larger mushroom
cap. The last rose and gold rays of sunset painted the
window glass and the chimney pots, the tracery and
the tiled dome topped with a statue of some sort.
From this distance, he couldn't tell what it represented.

A wide, roofed veranda edged every part of the
building he could see. Men in groups of three and
four were clustered there, talking and laughing.
Among them, he presumed, was the man who would
tell him what the devil he was supposed to do.

He recognized most of the guests lounging on the
veranda, only because they had at one time or another
attended the same party or sat around the same gaming table. As he mounted the stairs to the main entrance, a thin young man with a pocked complexion
and prominent ears broke away and loped in his
direction.

Good God. Not Royce Meacham. Black Phoenix
must have been scraping the bottom of the barrel.
The second son of a wealthy baronet, he was always
hovering around, never part of any circle but trying
to make it appear he was. The older ladies invited

him because he was full of the latest gossip. And for all his gangly physique, he danced well.

Come to think of it, Meacham would make an ideal conspirator, if he had only to report what he saw and heard. Coming face-to-face with him at the top of the stairs, Jarrett contrived to look pleased.

"Let me show you around," Meacham said after an effusive welcome, and for the next twenty minutes he led Jarrett through a large dining room beginning to empty of its patrons, into a larger gaming room filled with tables, chairs, and surprisingly few men. When Jarrett remarked on it, Meacham said, "Every spot will be filled later. After the performance."

Then it was upstairs, where a passageway marked the circumference of the dome and opened onto smaller rooms for dining and what Meacham described as "private entertainment."

"With implements," he added. "Or, well, whatever you can imagine. Not my cup of tea, but I've watched a time or two. Some rooms have peepholes. The men inside know it. They want to be watched."

Was that all there was to Paradise? Jarrett wondered as they went across a short bridge to the second level of a smaller building. Orgies and assorted perversions?

Apparently so, because Meacham had brought him to where the whores plied their trade. "It's called Xanadu, which don't mean anything in English. You can take the ladies elsewhere on the property, but here's where you rent them."

He'd come to the right place, then. "How do I go about it?"

"Now? It's almost time for Gaetana. But if you must, take those stairs down to the showroom. I'm for the theater."

Which ruled him out as the other Black Phoenix puppet, Jarrett decided. Even the most inept conspirator would be seizing this opportunity for some scheming. It also ruled out his own plans for a night of self-indulgence, what with having to make himself available for the real Black Phoenix emissary. With a shrug, he followed Meacham back across the bridge.

Chapter 4

The sounds of laughter and music grew louder as Jarrett and Meacham came to a foyer where several men were gathered around a set of wide double doors. One of them broke from the group and approached the new arrivals.

"Lord Dering," he said, bowing. "My apologies for the inconvenience. We are unusually crowded tonight, so I have ordered extra tables and chairs to be brought in. While not so comfortable as the others, they provide an excellent view. Will you mind waiting here for the time being?"

"Not at all." Jarrett recognized on his lapel the discreet gold stickpin Meacham had described, the insignia of an upper servant. "Is there wine to be had?"

Two of the men were already being led inside, leaving a place by the door. Jarrett wandered over, propped his shoulder against the casement, and looked into the theater. A perfect miniature of a lavish opera house, it was oval in shape and lined with velvet-draped boxes. Crystal chandeliers hung from the gilded ceiling, and Turkey carpets covered the raked floor. Small tables holding decanters and glasses were set among the captain's chairs, all of them occupied.

On the stage, goat-footed satyrs cavorted with saucy shepherdesses while a leering Hercules set about seducing a unicorn. Except for a surprisingly good orchestra in the sunken pit between stage and forestage, it was the sort of farce one might see at a second-rate London theater. The audience, equally unimpressed, was entertaining itself with talk and, at more than one table, a deck of cards.

Jarrett turned his gaze to the boxes, surprised to recognize a few of the women seated there. "Is that Lampert's wife?" he asked Meacham, who had come up beside him.

"That's her." Meacham handed him a glass of wine. "She's the only leg-shackle I've seen here, but there's usually one or two mistresses brought along. Coals to Newcastle, says I."

The performance had reached some sort of climax involving a pair of live sheep and a great deal of screeching. Nymphs were binding Hercules with garlands of daisies, and a Pan on stilts tossed bits of colored paper and sequins into the air.

Jarrett was wishing he'd remained at Xanadu for a little personal entertainment when the glimpse of a familiar face rocked him on his heels. She was seated beside a tall man in a box very near the stage, their chairs pulled back into the shadows. He hadn't noticed her at first. But when she leaned forward for a moment, exposing her profile, there was no mistaking his beguiling, devious, utterly wicked sister-in-law. What the devil was she doing here?

Despite the racket coming from the stage and the laughter from the audience, which was finally getting into the spirit of things, he could hear the pulse thudding in his ears. He had seen her only once since leaving home, when he returned for his father's burial, and that had been once too often.

Applause, then, and Meacham tugging on his sleeve. "They're setting up the tables in front now."

Directly across from Belinda. *Damn.* But she'd probably seen him by now. She missed very little. "Let's wait for a place on the left side," he said. "I'm left-handed."

The explanation was good enough for Meacham, who set out immediately in that direction. After a moment, Jarrett pulled himself away from the door frame and began to weave through the scatter of tables and chairs. What, after all, could she take from him now?

"I say, Dering! I've been telling m'friends about the wager. On the run from Sarne, are you? Bad idea, coming to the Lake District. He's got an estate here."

Without pleasure, Jarrett acknowledged Lord Golsham, who had been one of the players in competition for the duchess. Three men were seated with him, two of them laughing at his weak jest while the other, narrow-faced and unusually pale, regarded Jarrett speculatively.

"Has he, indeed?" said Jarrett. "May I?" He picked up the decanter in front of Golsham and refilled his glass. "I suppose I ought to be frightened. Is dueling one of the featured entertainments here?"

"What kind of entertainment are you looking for?" asked the pale man.

"After the duchess," said Golsham, "what could he possibly want? Is she as good as everyone says, Dering?"

"No words could describe her."

"Surely the usual words would suffice," the pale man said. "In the dark, are not all women much the same?"

"More than likely." Jarrett felt like a specimen being delicately probed with a scalpel. "But I've made it a hobby to find out for myself . . . one woman at a time."

"And your conclusion?"

"None as yet." He might as well give the surgeon something to find. "Except that I grow increasingly difficult to please. Perhaps the ladies are at fault, but to be fair, my tastes are something out of the ordinary."

"Ah. Mine as well. No doubt we shall encounter each other during one of our extraordinary pursuits. I am Carrington, by the way."

Jarrett recognized the name. "Honored, to be sure," he said to the marquess with a bow. "If you will pardon me, gentlemen, I must find my place before the lights are extinguished."

Servants had lowered the chandeliers and begun snuffing the candles while other servants went from table to table, turning the keys of the colza lamps. He found his way to a ladder-back chair near the stage, hard to miss with Meacham standing beside it, waving both arms. If Belinda hadn't spotted Jarrett before, she knew his precise location now. He sat, Meacham to his right, with a table between them just large enough for a decanter of wine and a saucer of cheese.

As the theater darkened, the sounds dimmed as well. Anticipation vibrated in the warm air. Jarrett put down his glass, folded his arms, and waited with the others.

The silence endured for what seemed to him a long time. This close to the stage, he was aware of movement. A faint squeak when something was lowered from the flies. The soft padding of shoeless feet on wood, the harder beat of leather, the swish of fabric.

His own breath, irregular as he held it to listen for other sounds.

And then, as if the sun had begun to rise in a fog-shrouded sky, pale golden light crept up behind a filmy, near-transparent screen that had been lowered across the middle of the stage. It revealed the outline of a tall figure wearing a long hooded cape and standing perfectly still.

From somewhere, the sound of a somber chord plucked on a stringed instrument. And then a voice, clear as rainwater, singing in a language Jarrett did not recognize. The haunting sound resonated like a summons to an ancient ritual. The melody, primitive, mournful, defiant, was the passion of a woman about to bury her fallen lover, or to kill him.

Like the others, he sat motionless and enthralled until the song was finished, and afterward. The spell broke only when the cloak, uninhabited, rose into the air and vanished.

Nicely done. He dabbled in illusions and sleight of hand, and while this bit of trickery was no more than fabric attached to strings and drawn up into the flies, he appreciated the theatricality of it.

The silence in the audience held. The men's appetites were whetted, their curiosity on edge. The light had slowly dimmed, and once again, the theater lay in darkness, waiting.

On fire!

No. Another illusion from behind the transparent curtain. Flames licked up a backdrop of some sort, too flat to be real. And a violin began to play, picking up the melancholy tenor of the first song and transforming it into a dance. A second violin joined, and from behind the screen came the metallic clang of finger cymbals.

This time a swing descended, bearing a female with her skirts flaring out and her long legs crossed at the ankles. She counterpointed the violins with the cymbals, her arms and hands shimmying in the air, her body illuminated from behind by red-gold flames.

Gaetana, and before she had so much as shown her face, a hundred men were entirely in her power. When the swing was still too high for safety, she sprang free of it and landed barefoot on the wooden stage with scarcely a thump. The rhythm changed, became slow, deliberate, like the tide moving in. Like the blood pulsing through his veins. Jarrett's hands fisted. Sweat gathered hot on his nape. A Gypsy at the campfire, fire-lit and untamed, she writhed in an ecstasy of her own as the tempo inexorably picked up speed. His heart pumped in concert with it. So did his breathing. Passion cut loose and spun out of control. In the enthralled imaginations of the men, she twirled and leaped in the demanding frenzy of a woman driving to climax.

And then the fire appeared to engulf her. With another theatrical trick, she was gone.

But still no applause, Jarrett noticed when his heartbeat, breathing, and selected portions of his anatomy had begun to subside. Perhaps even the most drunken and idiotic of the guests understood that silence was the greater tribute.

Or perhaps it wasn't over. No one had raised the wick on a lamp or ignited a candle. The theater, like a church on Good Friday, waited dark and sacrilegiously expectant.

When the music struck up again, lively and piquant, so did lights from both sides of the stage. From where he was sitting, he could see the vertical strips of lights in the wings focused on the transparent curtain, now opaque because it was lit from the front. And where the two halves of the screen met, a gloriously long leg with a scarlet ribbon encircling its upper thigh made itself visible.

A war could be fought over a leg like that.

"I have everything I need," she sang in French, "save a vegetable for my pot-au-feu."

Her fire pot. He knew immediately where this song was going.

"A long vegetable. A firm vegetable, one that can endure the heat and keep its form. A king among vegetables. Nothing else will satisfy me."

"I've got one," called a slurred voice from the back.

She feigned interest, moving downstage, striking a pose, pretending to search the audience.

Shields flipped back from the wing lights, now intensified by polished reflectors, giving Jarrett a close look at Gaetana's sable hair, loose and rippling down her back, and her smooth complexion above a neck of surpassing beauty. Her eyes, fringed with long black lashes, were blue as polished lapis lazuli.

She sang another flirtatious verse about the object of her desire and what she meant to do with it, the lines clever and the rhymes inventive. He noticed that her accent was not that of an Englishwoman speaking French.

None of his concern. He settled back, enjoying the way she manipulated the audience. Her Gypsy costume was modestly designed, but the slit in the long ruffled skirt provided teasing glimpses of those glorious legs.

Which began of a sudden to move, seemingly midair, across the orchestra pit. Another illusion. Tilting his head, he saw the narrow bridge of glass on which she stepped before reaching the curved forestage and jumping lithely onto the floor not six feet from where he sat. Still singing her ribald song, she went the other direction, flirting with the men she passed, eluding their hands, ruffling their hair.

Jarrett turned on his chair to watch her. Perfectly in control, she planted her hands on her hips and leaned back to evaluate this chap's cucumber, that one's carrot, or the other's string bean. She wove among asparagus and celery, leeks and parsnips and squash. By now the men had caught onto the refrain and were joining in.

He knew most of these fellows, by reputation if not personally. In no case did she single out for teasing a man whose pride outpaced his sense of humor, or one who was too shy to welcome the attention. She had chosen her targets with care, meaning that information about the guests had been provided her. Paradise left nothing to chance.

She was moving in his direction now, slipping past outreached arms, brushing her fingers against a shoulder or a cheek. Pausing at the box nearest him, she sang to the men seated there what appeared to be the last verse. In all the market, no vegetable would do.

Then she spun around, lifted her hands in pretended surprise, and flounced directly up to him. Her knees touched his—she was that close—while she began another verse, more scurrilous than the others.

All the women, she sang, recommended him, but that only meant he was woefully shopworn. Yesterday's goods. Could anything of worth remain in him now? She must find out.

Next he knew, she had planted herself on his lap. The chair wobbled. Instinct sent his hands to her waist. But she caught his wrists and pushed them down, so that his arms dangled beside him like wet cravats.

She wriggled, and he responded predictably. She squirmed, his breathing picked up, and he wondered if he could finish his part in this scene without embarrassing himself. It occurred to him she was still singing . . . something about rising to the occasion. Yes, indeed.

Then she leaned forward, her hands on the back of the chair behind his neck, and as laughter erupted after a particularly witty line, he heard an urgent whisper at his ear. "When I stand, come after me. Seize hold of my breasts."

A role he was willing to play, of course, along with a few others she hadn't cast him for. But if she didn't hold still, dammit, the consequences would be left to nature. He felt her body tense, poised to move, and prepared himself. Heard her sing something about a fine soufflé expanding to fill its container, and more, and then . . . and then . . . collapsing like a pricked sheep's bladder.

A roar of laughter. A sharp pinch on his neck and she was up. The pain drew his attention from where it had been. He remembered his task, lurched after her, closed his hands on full, firm breasts.

"Salaud!"

Something sharp struck his calves. At the same time she pushed with both hands at his chest. Off balance, he lost his hold on her and toppled backward, landing hard on the chair.

Except that the chair had begun to drop shortly before he did. So while he was, in a fashion, seated, he'd ended up with the ladder-back and his own back flat on the floor. The fall, he was quite sure, had hurt him a damn sight more than it affected the chair.

Hoots and derision from the audience for him, mingled with cheers for the triumphant Gaetana. Through a haze of pain and sexual frustration, he saw her curtsying from the stage, blowing kisses, and dancing off to music from the pit. The stage lights abruptly shut down.

Almost immediately, lamps on the tables began to glow, illuminating the theater. Meacham was leaning over him, a look of concern in his prominent eyes. He offered a hand.

Jarrett took it, swung his knees and backside off the chair, and allowed himself to be towed upright. That chair had been helped on its way before he landed against it. He turned immediately to the men seated at the table behind him.

"It was the lady," Lord Warrant said, grinning. "When you took your weight off the chair, she hooked a foot under one of the legs and started it on its way. Then she pushed you after it. Neat trick, eh?"

"Effective, certainly." Jarrett brushed himself off, took his wineglass from the table, and remembered with taut fury that Belinda had witnessed his humiliation. Looking over at the box, he saw her leaving through the private door, her escort beside her with a proprietary hand at the small of her back.

A man who had spent the last decade clinging to the edges of society knew how to conduct himself in almost any circumstance. Gritting his teeth, he meandered from group to group, making himself pleasant, abiding the good-humored insults, pretending to enjoy them. In fact, he was in no position to do otherwise. Between his supposed success with the Duchess of Sarne and his decided comeuppance by a Gypsy dancer, his fellows could hardly resist singling him out for ridicule.

"Is that why I was seated in front?" he asked Meacham as they left the theater. "Because I'm new and hadn't seen the act?"

"No one has seen what she did tonight. She was hired on after I came here, and I've never missed a show. Not even the Shakespeare. Serves you right, Dering, for putting your hands on her."

"A lesson now engraved on my backside. Do you suppose they'll let me play cards standing up?"

He tossed dice instead, lost three hundred pounds, and reckoned that his luck was entirely out. Not even Xanadu could tempt him. And since the Black Phoenix associate had failed to appear, he might as well give it up for the night and make a fresh start in the morning.

But first he had to run another gauntlet of jokesters, through the series of gaming rooms and the tavern with its polished mahogany bar trimmed with polished brass, and finally to the entrance where several men waited for transportation back to the manor house. He'd rather have slipped by them unnoticed, but the Marquess of Carrington was already turning to greet him.

"The Gypsy's plaything," Carrington said, his narrow, pale face and glittery eyes putting Jarrett in mind of a martyr-saint in one of those spooky El Greco paintings. "My landau has room for one more. Will you accept a lift to wherever it is you are staying?"

"Very kind, to be sure, but I've just spent four days in the saddle. I believe I shall walk, with a fresh breeze to air out my head and the moon to light my way."

"How very bucolic," said Carrington, flipping open a jeweled snuffbox. "Before you set out on your hike, my dear fellow, tell me this. Will your *hobby* direct you to find out if the Gypsy is indeed unique, or merely a predictable female with a temper who requires a man to discipline her?"

Jarrett pretended to give it some thought, wondering why Carrington kept tossing out this particular bone for him to chew on. Why the marquess had the slightest interest in an obscure viscount's opinions about any subject whatsoever.

"What I have concluded about Gaetana," Jarrett said, bowing to signal his imminent departure, "is surely obvious to everyone who witnessed tonight's festivities. The lady is a superbly talented performer, and a damnable pain in the arse."

Chapter 5

Wearing the black trousers and shirt contrived by her dresser, Kate was indistinguishable from the tree trunks as she flitted from one to the next, avoiding the patches of moonlight filtering through the canopy of leaves. She had tucked her inconvenient hair into a knitted cap that reached down to cover her face, with narrow slits for her eyes and mouth. It had a tendency to slip around when she perspired, as she was doing now. Summer conspiracies had never suited her.

The inner clock marking the time since she left her lodging near the manor house warned her to take better cover. She found a clump of bushes beside an oak and crouched down. A night bird called from directly overhead, startling her. Then the sound she was listening for, hoofbeats moving in her direction.

Her destination, a cottage located about a hundred yards from where she waited, was the last stop on the servants' rounds made every hour between three of the morning and seven. She knew every day's schedule, just as she knew where every guest resided and which ones demanded extra attention.

The rider slowed as he came near the turnoff to the

cottage. If a lantern had been raised, he would take the path, receive the guest's request, and see that it was speedily fulfilled.

A pending request from Lord Dering would scotch her plans. Gloved hands curled into knots, she waited for the night sounds to tell her what was occurring. The hoofbeats got louder. The pace slowed as the rider found the angle from which he could see the pole and the lantern, were it suspended there. Then the horse moved on, picking up speed.

Now she tuned her clock to the first hint of dawn, perhaps half an hour from now. That gave her ten minutes alone with Dering, fifteen if he made a nuisance of himself.

As she'd expected, he had left the windows open to catch the cool breezes off the lake. Most of the cottages were alike. This one was set in a small clearing, and on the side nearest the lake, all the trees had been removed to allow an unbroken view of the water. There would be a terrace there, she had been told, and a garden. A faint light flickered in the parlor, but the other rooms lay in darkness.

Moving quickly and quietly, she came to what she expected was the bedchamber window and peered inside. The curtains had been left open. Moonlight streamed into the room, illuminating the top portion of a bed. She adjusted her recalcitrant hood, put one leg over the sill, and let herself in. Immediately she slipped into the darkest corner and waited for her eyes to adjust.

No movement from the bed. The sound of heavy breathing, not quite a snore. He was lying on his stomach, face turned away from her on the pillow, arms spread out on each side. A sheet covered the bottom half of him just to the point of decency. A little below it, actually. The swell of taut buttocks curved into a narrow waist, and above that stretched a surprisingly well formed back.

She wasn't pleased. Experience had taught her that the most troublesome males were those with reason to be vain. She had hoped the fine physique she couldn't help but notice during her performance owed most of its excellence to padded coats and rolled fabric in the breeches. Men forced to rely on artifice were much easier to control.

This one had fallen easily enough when she tumbled him over the chair, but for the upcoming encounter, she could not depend on simple tricks and surprise. She slipped the knife from its sheath on her calf, tiptoed on her felt-wrapped shoes to the side of the bed, and took a deep breath. Then, in silent and coordinated moves, she clamped one leather-gloved hand over his mouth and set the point of her blade against the side of his neck.

He came awake instantly, muscles tensed, breath held.

"Hush!" She let him feel the knife. "Do nothing to draw attention. I am from Black Phoenix."

When he raised splayed hands from the bed to signal compliance, she let go her hold on his mouth. A cough from his lordship, and a dry laugh. "You Phoenix fellows are great ones for dramatic entrances."

"Hold it to a whisper, fool!"

"Someone might be listening?"

"I am. For the sound of a horse. For birds that sing just before dawn. We haven't much time."

"Knife," he reminded her. "It has rather all my attention."

She put it away and moved to the other side of the bed, the direction he was facing. But when she got there, he was already upright and stuffing pillows between his shoulders and the wooden headboard. A shaft of moonlight caught him like a focused stage beam, limning him in silver. It illuminated rumpled hair, long eyelashes, and a mouth curved in amusement. It also carved out the impressive muscles of his arms and chest. Unless she stayed alert, he could easily overwhelm her. She wished she had kept the knife in hand.

"If you now feel safe enough to converse intelligibly," she said, "let me begin."

"Not before you remove that absurd mask. It's distracting, and I already know who you are."

"How?" She had whispered the entire time. Her breasts were bound, to create a male silhouette if glimpsed at a distance. Men were commonly found in places where she went and was not supposed to be.

"Your scent."

"I wear no scent."

"Nonetheless."

She wanted to argue the point. Which was absurd, so she rolled the mask portion of her hat to her forehead. "We have perhaps fifteen minutes now. It is important you understand the circumstances. Our greatest difficulty will be to communicate without raising suspicion. In the ten days I have been here, no solution presented itself until this morning, when Mr. Fidkin told me that Paradise has found it necessary to alter the terms of my employment. It had been understood that I would be a performer only, unavailable to the guests. But several of them have demanded I be put on offer."

"Xanadu?" he said after a moment.

"Not that. Common whores are easily come by. Although it is not advertised, those who visit regularly or who are especially favored have learned the unofficial motto of Paradise—'Whatever you want can be had, for a price.' Mr. Fidkin was apologetic, but with gentlemen insisting Paradise live up to its promise, he had no choice. I am fairly sure he expected me to refuse and take my leave. Instead, I laid out terms for a new contract."

She looked toward the window. The three-quarter moon hung low in the western sky, appearing almost to sit atop the fells. She must hurry. "Tomorrow night I shall be put on auction. There have been two others since I arrived, both featuring girls being sold for their virginity. Perhaps that was true. Certainly they were young enough."

"Are you?"

"I am eight-and-twenty."

He smiled, acknowledging her evasion. "Will you be expensive?"

"Probably. But at any cost, you must make the winning bid."

"I think you'll be extremely expensive. Well worth the price, to be sure, but it hardly matters. If you are an object of contention among several men, the bidding will be driven by pride and the spur of competition. I've seen it happen at Tattersall's, even when the horses in question were nothing out of the ordinary."

"I'll refrain from whinnying, then. Bid as high as you must, sir. Black Phoenix provided you with ample funds."

"Yes. But here's the thing, Gaetana. Is that your real name?"

She could scarcely see him, now that the moon had nearly set. "Use it. The others do."

"There is a problem. Less than a fortnight ago I was known to be drowning in River Tick. Then I won a well-publicized amount at cards, and later, as you say, Black Phoenix arranged funding. But it was all done in public, with much comment about my new-found fortune. Phoenix wanted it known I was suddenly plump in the pockets, but in consequence, my entire worth has been computed to the last filed coin. I dare not bid above that amount."

She had ticked him down as a wastrel and a cockscomb, but perhaps he was a trifle less stupid than she'd been assuming. "I had not understood the precise situation," she said, finding it difficult to admit even that small miscalculation. "When you rode in alone, without a carriage or even a valet, I feared the worst."

"What? That I had been robbed?"

"That you had gamed away your entire stake. I did take precautions, as a matter of course, but I cannot say they will be effective. Tonight's buffoonery was meant to set up a quarrel between us. Now we must hope it becomes a factor in the auction."

"You mean the song? Kicking the chair from under me?"

"What else?" She looked again at the window, seeking traces of dawn in the sky.

"I reckoned it was part of the act. Or that you were in bad humor. Or that someone had paid you to humiliate me."

"Who would do that?"

He made a motion, indecipherable as all his expressions and motions had been since moonset. "Several I can think of."

"That is your problem to deal with . . . *after* our mission is accomplished. Whatever their fantasies, I doubt most of the gentlemen wish to take me into their keeping. Here, money buys the flawless, deferential service that few of them enjoy at home or in society. They prefer compliance to challenge. They wish to live like petty monarchs, however briefly. Do you understand?"

"In part. They suspect, probably with cause, that they couldn't measure up to you. But in an auction, blood may run high. Men may behave foolishly. And at the end, two or three of them will be determined to prove themselves bold enough to buy you and strong enough to tame you."

"You're getting close to the idea," she said. "Generally, the guests expect no more than self-indulgence and entertainment. Perhaps they would enjoy watching you try, and consistently fail, to master the female who sent you to the floor. Then they could boast of how they would have handled me to better effect."

"*Taming of the Shrew,* you mean? Kate and Petruchio?"

The sound of her name brought her up short. To hide her confusion, she rose and pulled the knit mask down over her face. "Something of the kind. If you have a trace of imagination or initiative, put it to use tomorrow night. One more thing. Mark the time now. Do you know how to summon a servant?"

"Raise a banner in daylight, a lantern at night."

"When I have been gone ten minutes, put out the signal. Tell the servant I injured your back at the theater. Ask for opium."

"Laudanum?"

"Or powder. Say you prefer to measure it yourself, into brandy or wine. Give the impression of long experience. Leave evidence that you're ingesting it."

"Are you saying I should not?"

"If you are unable to control yourself, we'll not use this ploy." She slipped a vial from a pocket in her breeches and set it on the dressing table. "But if you can maintain a degree of sobriety, these eyedrops will make it appear you are quite otherwise. Now I must go. Do whatever it takes, my lord, to purchase me."

He was on his feet as well, the sheet wrapped around his waist. Behind him, through the open door to the next room, a lamp glowed. "And if I fail? What happens then? Will you leave?"

She was already at the window, one leg swung over the sill. "How can I? My mission is here. We can neither of us go—can we?—until it is accomplished."

"I agreed to come," he said. "I understood it could be dangerous. But no one made clear why, or what is expected of me."

"Tomorrow, after the auction, we shall be free to discuss it."

"At which point I reserve the right to change my mind. Or at any time, for that matter. I haven't signed my life away."

"Nor have I. But so far, no one is asking for my life. Only my virtue, and if I must whore myself, I will."

Her heart gave a lurch. Steadied. *At any cost,* she reminded herself. "But then we'll be left with the original problem—how the two of us are to meet and work together. Be clever tomorrow night, Lord Dering. Everything now depends on you."

Chapter 6

The next day Jarrett went exploring. Not on his own—that would have looked suspicious—but following the advice of the young man who delivered his breakfast, he took himself to the wharf located near the Pleasure Dome and spoke with the master of boats.

The best way to get an overview of the landscape, it seemed, was to go out with the sportsmen's yacht, which made a circuit of the lake every two hours. He was just in time for the next departure. About a dozen men were already aboard, along with servants carrying their fishing tackle, their rifles and powder, their climbing gear, baskets of food and drink, everything a gentleman might require while enjoying his favorite sport.

Jarrett found a spot near the prow, marking how long it took to get from place to place in the light morning wind. He had sailed a bit, more than a decade earlier, and would have relished the chance to do so again. But for transportation, he'd do better to rely on a dinghy.

The yacht set out to the west, and he enjoyed the view for several minutes before two fellows he'd never met came up to join him. It was their last day, and they were more than glad to provide a running commentary about Paradise, the landmarks, and the best ways to spend one's time. The glances, the touches of hands, the way each hung on the other's words, told Jarrett they had come here to spend their own time together.

They disembarked at the second mooring, on their way for some climbing at Cripple Crag, whatever the devil that was. Too bad. He had quite liked them.

Much more than he did the three boors who came forward shortly after. Already well in their cups, they were on their way to fish the far eastern reaches of the lake, with heavy wagers on who would hook the largest trout. Invited to place his own bet, he politely declined.

"Saving your blunt for the auction, eh, Dering?" That was Golsham, apparently impossible to evade after the Duchess of Sarne incident. "Mean to get a bit of your own back, I daresay."

"I've no idea what you are talking about." Jarrett propped his elbows on the teak railing and rested his chin on his hands. "What's being auctioned?"

"Gaetana. High bidder has exclusive use of her for a week. You didn't know? The bill is posted everywhere."

"Not in my cottage, nor on this boat. But never mind. I wouldn't pay tuppence for that virago."

A nod of agreement from one of the men, a laugh from another. Golsham, like a dog with his yellow teeth on a bone, wouldn't let go. "Wilder than the duchess, you think? But then, a Gypsy would have no refinement."

"I wouldn't know." A thought came to him, risky and probably useless, but he'd only a few hours to plant curiosity and gossip. "I do know about bad-tempered bitches. One of them stole my inheritance. So you have the right of it, sir. I'd enjoy punishing the Gypsy for her insolence, but the devil is, I cannot compete with the fat purses. As for the rest, I didn't travel all this distance to put a woman in my bed. Paradise has other, less commonplace attractions. Or so I am told."

"Tell Fidkin what you want," said a plump man with a sunburned face. "Have you a taste for shooting? We'll disembark shortly and be driven to a private reserve. I'm sure there are guns to spare."

"Perhaps another day," Jarrett said, glad to turn the subject. "What sort of reserve? What is your quarry?"

Not long after, when the shooters were gone, he returned to the prow with a tankard of ale. It had been difficult to mix the opium powder and brandy that morning, surreptitiously pouring out nearly all of it in the woods and leaving just enough in the glass to indicate what he'd supposedly drunk. Devils had been driving pitchforks into his back since the Gypsy upended him, and he'd given serious thought to easing the pain with a little harmless medication. After all, he didn't require to be clever until eleven o'clock that night.

But he was already distracted by the banquet of pleasures laid out before him, indifferent to the task Gaetana was taking so seriously, and not terribly curious to know what it amounted to. She interested him, of course. But she had entered his life already despising him, before he'd even had the chance to disappoint her. Still, he probably owed her the courtesy of a sober hearing. And—he kept trying not to think about it—he must make sure she did not fall into another man's hands tonight.

"You should be wearing a hat, sir."

Jarrett turned to see a dark-haired young man, slim and rather pretty, holding out a wide-brimmed straw hat with leather ties to secure it against the wind.

"I didn't mean to disturb your solitude, but you were speaking earlier with Lord Sindley and must have observed his scarlet complexion. Yours will be the same, I fear, if you remain uncovered in the noonday sun."

"I cannot take your hat," Jarrett said. "But thank you."

"Oh, it isn't mine. These are available for guests who come aboard with bare heads. I look as if I'd burn to cinders, I know, but I never do. And nearly all my time is spent tramping about outdoors."

"Dering." Jarrett took the hat, shook the young man's hand, and adjusted the straps.

"John Gilliam. Generally unnoticed in company. Third son of the Earl of Hargrove and a horrid disappointment to the family."

Jarrett knew precisely what that was like. "Because you go wastreling around Paradise?"

"Hardly that. My visits here represent the only times I've succeeded in pleasing them. Mother would never admit so much, but Hargrove is delighted that I have been showing an interest in manly pursuits."

"Sports? Or drinking, gaming, and whoring?"

"All of those. There's already a son in the church, you see, and the heir has dutifully married and got about siring his descendants. But my interests are confined to the things my father most abhors—books and learning. He believes they will unman me, or have already done so, and imagines I can be cured only by periodic doses of dissipation."

"And have you been?"

"Like everyone else at Paradise, I indulge fantasies and obsessions. But in my case, those amount to fossils and rocks. Every day I explore the fells, collecting specimens and sketching maps. The two gentlemen you were speaking with earlier enjoy climbing, so we often made our treks together. Indeed, we had engaged to climb this morning, but when I saw they would prefer to be alone, I said I wasn't feeling quite the thing and begged off."

"You can't go on your own?"

"It isn't safe, really. Most days there are larger, organized groups with servants and a guide. I suppose I shall have to join them in future. And find some other way to spend the money that will preserve my welcome here. My two friends were kind enough to conspire in a gambling ploy that suited us all."

Jarrett, astonished, looked over at him. They were side by side, forearms on the railing, the wind cooling their faces. "To pay your tariff, you deliberately lose wagers?"

"We bypassed the actual gaming, which I would find tedious, but yes. I don't drink, sail, fish, or shoot living things. As for the ladies, there's a young woman in Surrey whose family does not measure up to my father's standards, but I still hope to marry her one day. We have pledged our love and fidelity. So you see, there is little for me to spend money on at Paradise, other than fake gaming."

"And what would it require to become the man who wins your fake wagers?"

Gilliam grinned. "You wish the job? Father will be rapturous, my keeping company with the infamous rake who thumbed his nose at the Duke of Sarne."

"Devil it, is there anyone in England who hasn't heard that story?" Jarrett grinned back. "It's not often my bad reputation serves as a recommendation."

"Except, I imagine, to the ladies. Shall we strike a deal? I've already lost half the amount my father usually pays for these excursions, so don't expect more than fifteen hundred. And I prefer to lose it gradually, right up until my departure five days from now. In return, I would ask a service of you."

"Certainly." For fifteen hundred pounds, there was little Jarrett wouldn't agree to. "What is it?"

"Come climbing with me a time or two. The easy ones, with guides and servants. Is that a terrible imposition?"

"I think you wonder if I'm up to healthful exertion," Jarrett said with a laugh. Gilliam could be useful, he was thinking, in more ways than as a source of funds. "Agreed. And if you have no plans for the afternoon, I intend to go riding. Will you come along? Show me the neighborhood and its attractions?"

Gilliam nodded, his flushed cheeks betraying his pleasure.

The yacht dropped anchor while three small boats came out to pick up the fishermen. Then, with only the crew for company, Jarrett and Gilliam were returned on a brisk afternoon wind to the Pleasure Dome.

As they drew close enough to see the windows glittering in the sunlight, Jarrett picked out the long expanse of lakeside woodland that marked the location of his cottage. That morning, while taking his breakfast on the terrace, he had noted the tip of an island some distance to his right, a fuzzy splash of green in the morning haze. The lake was dotted with islands, most of them little larger than a tennis court, but as the yacht passed by this one, he was surprised at its breadth. Densely forested, the island appeared to be unpopulated.

"Hecate's Isle," Gilliam said. "Last time I was here on holiday, the body of a young boy washed up on its shore. Rumor said he had gone eeling at night, as some of the local residents do, and got himself in trouble. I never heard what the authorities decided, except that the boy was unknown to anyone in the area. The island is said to be cursed. People claim to hear strange noises coming from it, and there are reports of smoke rising from the interior. Superstitious lot here in the north."

"I've arranged with the boatmaster for a dinghy," Jarrett said. "Perhaps one day I'll paddle over and have a look."

"You should ask Fidkin about that. I'm told the island is privately owned, and that trespassers are unwelcome."

"Who would know I was there?" Jarrett said. "The witches?"

Chapter 7

In the gaming room where John Gilliam was earnestly losing the first installment of his promised donation, Jarrett had made sure his chair provided a view of the ormolu clock on the mantelpiece. Nearly ten o'clock. One hour more to wait.

They had little company. Most of the guests had already taken themselves to the theater, where some sort of musical performance was going on. But all of them, or so it seemed to Jarrett, had stopped by his table at dinner, or by the table where he and Gilliam were playing piquet, to ask about his plans for the auction. Would he bid? How high would he go to have Gaetana in his power for a week?

Bad jokes, worse puns, insults cloaked as jests . . . The Gypsy had been right. They wanted an event—a *confrontation*—at the auction, with, he supposed, a series of farces to follow. And he had been cast as the fool.

A role he should have down pat by now. But if the bidding went over three thousand pounds, as it was bound to do, even a star turn by Edmund Kean wouldn't secure the prize. A miracle would be required, and he didn't expect miracles in this godforsaken place.

Gilliam, at least, was enjoying himself. The only difficulty was to keep him from losing too much, too fast. After a time, Jarrett showed him a few card tricks and taught him a fairly simple one to impress his father with. And the clock ticked on.

"Dear me," said the Marquess of Carrington, pausing by the table, his lips stretched in what, for him, passed as a smile. Jarrett had seen corpses with more color and expression. "I could scarcely believe what everyone is saying . . . that you have no intention of bidding on the Gypsy."

"For once, the rumors are true. Did you want her for yourself?"

"A common trollop? But she has asserted herself above her station, and I shouldn't mind seeing her disciplined. You seemed the man to do it. Perhaps you do not wish to take the trouble."

"I don't mind trouble." With a smooth gesture, Jarrett fanned the deck of cards across the table. "I merely object to paying for it."

"You are something of a disappointment to me. But you do have a fine eye for horseflesh. I'll make you a generous offer for the bay."

That afternoon, when Gilliam was showing Jarrett around the area south of the estate, they had nearly been driven off the road by a brass-trimmed carriage. Before the shade was snapped down, Jarrett had glimpsed Carrington's long, pale face through the window. "Banshee is not for sale," he said. "I'm practicing fidelity."

Carrington appeared to be studying his eyes. Then, with a nod, he took his leave, and shortly after—at Jarrett's request—so did Gilliam.

Fifteen minutes until the auction was scheduled to begin. He located a deserted retiring room, refreshed himself, and took a moment to examine his eyes in a looking glass. The pupils were contracted, looking unnaturally small, an effect of the eyedrops Gaetana had given him. He hoped Carrington had drawn the intended conclusion.

Stepping back, he considered his costume. The mirror showed him a proper, formally attired gentleman, stamped out like nearly all the other gentlemen who would be there tonight. He made several unorthodox adjustments, swiped his fingers through his hair, and made his way to the theater.

In the vestibule, the upper servant who had been there the previous night smiled and bowed. "Lord Dering. Just in time. Shall I find a place for you inside?"

"That won't be necessary. But I'd be glad of a large brandy." Jarrett found a spot near the door where he could see inside without attracting notice. Light poured from the chandeliers, presumably so that the auctioneer could make out the bidders, and below the darkened stage, the orchestra was playing a cheerful song. Guests milled around, voices loud with drink, the humid air charged with anticipation. No wives tonight, nor mistresses. He looked to his right, to the second box from the stage where his sister-in-law had sat witness to his dethronement. It was empty.

When other matters settled a bit, he would attempt to discover if she was still on the property, and the identity of the man who had accompanied her.

A change in the music then, a sound of announcement. The shutters were pulled back from the wing lights and footlights. Mr. Fidkin, his bald pate gleaming, strode to the front of the stage.

"My lords. Gentlemen. Welcome to a most special

evening. Please take your seats so that we can get under way."

The servant returned with Jarrett's brandy, a generous glass filled to the top, and conveniently left on some other errand. Jarrett swallowed about half the drink, awaiting his cue and hoping he'd recognize it when it came.

Fidkin was speaking again. ". . . expect the best of everything in Paradise. Perhaps nothing has been so exceptional as the young woman whose beauty, talent, and spirit have enlivened our theater. Now, by popular demand, she has agreed to make herself available to one of you."

Cheers and whistles, as if the men were getting the news for the first time. Servants moved among the tables, refilling glasses and replenishing the cheese plates and nut bowls. Jarrett pulled his lucky gold guinea from his waistcoat pocket.

"As befits a woman of her quality, she does not offer herself unconditionally."

Groans and hisses from the crowd.

Fidkin waved his hands. "I quite understand your sentiments. But were she everyday ware, you would not be gathered to compete for her services. And when she came to us at Paradise, we offered her certain considerations in turn. They include the contract that governs this arrangement, which is designed only to protect her from a few of the more *unusual* predilections some of our guests delight in. You would not, I think, wish her permanently damaged."

No protest this time, beyond a little grumbling.

"The high bidder will have Gaetana's exclusive attention for one week. She will not perform in the theater unless he wishes it. Beyond the few understandable restrictions, she agrees to obey his every command and indulge his most urgent desires." A broad smile from Fidkin. "In fairness, I must warn the gentleman who wins her. There is great likelihood that she will make it impossible, in future, for any other woman to satisfy you."

Laughter, more cheers, and someone shouting, "Enough talk! Bring her on!"

A grand gesture from Fidkin as he stepped out of the way, a fanfare from the orchestra, a change in the stage lighting. Jarrett found himself holding his breath.

He had expected . . . well, he didn't know what he had expected. Not the masked, trousered conspirator with a knife at his throat, certainly. The haunting, disembodied singer from behind the scrim . . . no. Perhaps the tempestuous Gypsy dancer, or the flirtatious minx on the swing. More likely the taunting coquette who had plunked herself down on his lap, mocked him, aroused him, and overturned him.

Who the devil was she? They had met only twice, and briefly, but already she had shown him a half dozen women who might represent her true nature. And probably did not.

Onto the stage, imperious as a goddess, came a different woman altogether. All the light seemed to gather where she stood, robed in a dark blue gown that flowed over her like water. Belted at the waist with a silvery rope, gathered at her shoulder with silver clasps, it left her arms bare and revealed nothing else. At the same time, the silken fabric hinted at every treasure it concealed.

She turned, graceful as the dancer she was, in a gentle circle. Her hair, sleeked back from her face, was caught in a thick braid that fell to just below her waist. When she came around again to face the audience, her chin went up the barest notch. *Here I am,* she appeared to be saying. *What am I worth to you?*

More than I will ever have, Jarrett thought with a shot of regret.

A sound like the wind—air released from a hundred male throats—echoed the sound coming from his mouth. And then he saw her gaze, entirely detached before that moment, slide to the place where he had been sitting when first she saw him.

"Oh, too predictable, my dear," he whispered, squeezing his lucky coin.

Fidkin waited until the initial impact of her appearance had peaked before moving again into the light. "Only a man of great mettle would dare claim her," he said. "And he must have a fortune to match his courage. This is a once-in-a-lifetime experience, gentlemen, for the extraordinary one among you who can stay the course and claim the prize. Let the bidding commence!"

He wasn't here!

She ought to have expected it. A man of questionable reputation, they had told her, who would be welcomed by the other guests. And why not? He was exactly like them, an irresponsible lout who cared nothing for his duty.

So now she would be sold to one of these oglers, their heated gazes like sticking plasters on her breasts and the jointure of her thighs.

It didn't signify, she supposed. Dering would have been a useless ally and an irritant. What she required was the luck to be purchased by a man of limited physical stamina and few wits who might leave her to her own devices much of the time. Clearly she was going to be handling this job alone, and she couldn't be sorry for it. If she had learned anything in her life, it was to do what she had to do without relying on anyone else.

She looked into the middle distance, seeing nothing, becoming the character she had chosen to play to-night. A patrician Greek lady, abandoned by husband and family, she was being sold to pay their debts. At her feet, the rabble milled around, remarking on her endowments, assessing her worth. She heard jibes, boasts, and occasionally an insulting bid. They wished to draw this out, make of it a spectacle. What fun would it be if someone hauled her away betimes?

The shame, the dishonor of it, burned in her veins. She felt debased, lower than a person, less than an animal. Years ago she had chosen to surrender her identity, but had not understood that what she'd left behind could be ripped from her again and again.

She could bear it, though. After all, she had come here prepared to die. More than willing to die, in fact, if death would balance the scales. She hadn't consid-ered that dying might be a lesser sacrifice than the one she faced.

The lessons kept coming, each one harder than the one that came before. There was to be for her no absolution without penance, no redemption without punishment.

"A thousand guineas," someone called.

The lights of the chandeliers blurred. *What if I fail? What then?*

"Eleven hundred!"

"Don't be a nodcock, Lorrick. What use have you for a woman?"

"Twelve hundred." The bidder sounded elderly. That would be good.

"Fourteen."

But what can I learn on my own? I will not be permitted to go anywhere of interest. This could all be for nothing.

A sound, different from the others, originating in the back of the theater. A change in the atmosphere, as if windows had swung open. With difficulty, she let her eyes focus.

Insouciant as a cat, Dering was weaving among the tables, making his way toward the stage in no great hurry. As the men became aware of a stir, they turned to see what was going on.

He was impossible to miss. He wore no jacket, and amidst the dark, formal coats of the others, his white shirt and gold-embroidered white waistcoat stood out like a snowball in a coal bin. As he meandered closer, she saw that he'd loosened his neckcloth and removed his starched collar. His brown hair, overlong and a little disheveled, shone in the light. He had a glass in one hand and something small and golden in the other.

She had to admire the showmanship of his entrance, and the timing. The bidding for her had so far been desultory. Most of the participants, joining in because it was the fashion of the moment, would soon drop out.

Now the cat had come to stroll among the pigeons. He looked indifferent, expensive, and confident, as if certain that everyone had gathered solely for his amusement. In turn, they looked eager to see what he would do next.

Mercifully, the prey had been all but forgotten. She regathered her wits and prepared herself to take on a new role, pretending to ignore him while watching for her cue. What was it he had said last night? Something about *The Taming of the Shrew*. Yes, he could be Petruchio, swaggering into Padua to claim a bride.

She knew Kate's role. Had acted it often enough, but never opposite a Petruchio with the slightest chance of mastering her in any world that was not the play. Tonight—if her guess was on the mark—she and Dering would be improvising a comedy with higher stakes than he knew. And she wanted to match him. Anticipate his moves and best him. Cross the finish line at least a step ahead of him.

How absurd it all was. Only five minutes earlier she had mentally dismissed him as a fribble. Now he'd made a grand entrance in his shirtsleeves, and she could scarcely wait to cross swords with him.

A man, his face in shadows, spoke as Dering passed his table. "Come to claim her? Don't think she'll be yours so easily. You'll have to best me."

Dering paused, glancing over his shoulder. "At what?"

"There is only one game here tonight, sir. Money, and who is willing to spend more of it for a harlot."

"By all means, Sheffer, carry on with the festivities. I am here for a little entertainment, no more than that. How does the bidding stand?"

"Fourteen hundred," Fidkin said, holding up his slate. "But we've only just started."

"My God." Dering turned to look at her, eyes wide with astonishment. "You expect more? She's devilish overpriced as it is."

Kate knew a direct challenge when it stared her in the face. Smiling, she moved downstage to where the lights converged. "A man accustomed to tuppenny bawds," she said sweetly, "is hardly a good judge of quality."

Laughter. The men would be on her side, she knew, just so long as it took to pull Dering into the game. He was laughing as well.

"He's had a duchess," someone informed her loudly. "Isn't that right?"

"If you are referring to my most *recent* duchess," Dering said, "I won her at chess. But most transactions are more straightforward. Indeed, why would I pay for a woman when so many of them leap into my bed without charge?"

"I cannot account for women who overrate you and undervalue themselves." She stepped out onto the glass bridge. "Be sure I am not among them."

"Nor I!" from a man with more enthusiasm than logic. "Sixteen hundred!"

The bids came quickly for a time, and as they tumbled over one another, Lord Dering ambled toward an empty box to her left, coming close enough for her to see what he was carrying in his left hand. It appeared to be a coin, which he effortlessly passed among his fingers from one to the next, thumb to pinkie and back again, like a golden fish darting between strands of seaweed.

Skilled hands. He probably used them to cheat at cards and dice.

At the moment he was signaling his lack of interest in the auction, and in her. Was it her turn to speak, to launch the next exchange? She felt light-headed. Bewildered. She thought, for the first time, that he might be someone she could rely upon.

"Three thousand," called a firm voice. Lord Sheffer, staking his claim.

Kate went cold. She knew his reputation. If he won the auction, she would probably have to kill him.

Dering had settled himself on the railing, planted

his shoulders against the carved wooden pillar that divided the box from its neighbor, and raised his feet onto the rail. Not Petruchio, she thought. Now he was Puck, lounging on a tree branch, watching Bottom and the other befuddled characters stumble through their midsummer night's dream. The coin danced through his fingers. A smile curled his lips. Nearly everyone was watching him.

Do something! Or was it her turn? She could think of nothing to say, no challenge to issue. The import of what awaited her left her breathless. Witless. No one would risk Sheffer's temper by contesting his bid. In a short time he would lead her away, and then she would be truly lost.

"Three thousand," said Dering, conversationally. "And one."

Voices rose as the men remarked to one another. He was in the bidding. Or was he? It could not have been a serious offer.

"We do not play with children's numbers here," Sheffer said, striking the flat of his hand against the table in front of him. "Advance the bid properly, like a gentleman, or stay out of this."

"I'll have to stay out, then," Dering said, his voice mournful. "And here I'd finally summoned the pluck to do battle with the Gorgon. But never say I failed to play the gentleman, sir. What more can a gentleman offer than everything he possesses?"

"He can keep silent, if he has no more to offer than a guinea."

"What say you, Gypsy?" Dering's gaze fixed on her. "Would you have me for a golden coin?" And then he sent his coin into the air, spinning as it arced across the distance between them to land on the narrow bridge, precisely at her feet.

She stopped herself from looking down at it. *Well played, sir.* Planting her hands on her hips, she gave him her fiercest glare. " 'Is it your will to make a stale of me among these mates?' "

He grinned. " 'Where two raging fires meet together, they do consume the thing that feeds their fury.' "

Good heavens. He did know the play. Even the lines. Well, one of them, but the one he'd chosen resonated to her bones. God knew she was a raging fire. But she was also a competent actress, one who had, for the moment, forgotten all that Shakespeare wrote for his Kate to say. Except, " 'Where did you study all this goodly speech?' "

His teeth flashed. " 'It is contempore, from my mother-wit.' "

"Give me leave to doubt it, sir. A few witticisms filtered into your dreams while you were sleeping through a play."

A weak riposte, she knew, that got a more appreciative laugh than it deserved. The audience, most of them, wanted to see this drama unfold to the last act. But the end was already determined. Dering could bid no higher, and Sheffer was not a man to back away.

As if to prove it, he rose and jabbed a finger in the direction of the stage. "Five thousand!"

Gasps at the amount and murmurs of conjecture from the audience, who would know even more about Lord Sheffer than she did. A few faces turned in her direction, and on them, she read pity.

" 'From all such devils,' " said Dering, "good Lord deliver us.' "

It wasn't clear which devil he referred to, since he was gazing meditatively at the ornate ceiling. For all his engagement with the proceedings, and the outcome, he might be counting the gilded cherubs. She wanted to pick up his damned gold guinea and fling it in his face.

But Kate was stealing away. She could not endure this. Not as herself. The role of the patrician Greek woman slipped over her again. Despairing, mute, stiff with pride, she awaited her instructions.

The theater had grown unnaturally quiet. She became aware of a stir in the vicinity of Lord Sheffer's table. Nearly everyone but Dering was looking that way, trying to hear what was being said. She made out a figure leaning over the table, apparently speaking to Sheffer. The men who had been seated with him were no longer there.

Fidkin came up behind her, stopping at the edge of the stage. "It is over, I expect. A good take, even better than I'd hoped for. Management will be pleased. You have made the necessary arrangements?"

She nodded, her mouth too dry to speak. A few of her things—she had only a few—were packed. Her dresser, Mrs. Kipper, would see them delivered to her owner's lodging. A great heaviness anchored her in place, muffled her thoughts. She dared not let them venture past the moment she was taken from the stage and into his possession.

The next she knew, the Marquess of Carrington was approaching the stage. Sheffer she hated, for what he was and what he was capable of doing, but Carrington she truly feared. As he gazed up at her with his fog-colored eyes, she recognized that he had not the slightest interest in her as a woman. But he might take pleasure in dissecting her, she thought, by way of a biological experiment.

"Lord Sheffer and I have come to an arrangement," he said, his voice soft and touched with amusement. "The bid made prior to his shall stand."

Fidkin made a wheezing sound. "My lord. A bid of five thousand pounds has been recorded. We can accept no less."

"Oh, I'd not deprive Paradise of its profit, nor the young woman of her satisfaction at being so greatly valued. All that remains is for Lord Dering to accept my offer."

Dering, his brandy glass cradled between his hands, glanced over at them incuriously. "Good God. You want to put *me* up for auction now?"

"Sixpence!" called a man seated near enough the stage to hear the exchange.

The marquess, his ash-blond hair tied back in an old-fashioned queue, gave the man a quelling smile and turned to Dering. "Do you want her, sir? Or was your bid the gesture of a coward who knew it would not stand?"

Dering appeared to consider the question. "An impulse, I think. Caught up in the moment, and the next moment tossed onto the shore like . . . like witch's bones."

"Ah. You've attended the local gossip. But you haven't answered my first question."

"Which was . . . ? Oh, yes. Do I want her? Not particularly. Well, I should like to bed her, of course. But the price is high, and the satisfaction fleeting."

"Because in the dark, all women are much the same?"

Laughing, Dering swung his long legs off the railing, rose, and stretched. "I won't admit to that. Not yet. But I can't imagine any one of them is three thousand guineas' worth of difference. If you are trying to do me a kindness, sir, I thank you. But let Sheffer have her. She can keep my golden guinea as a souvenir."

What was he doing? Kate held herself like a statue, scarcely breathing, her head pounding with rage. How could he walk away like this, away from his duty? Away from her?

"Are you not a sporting man?" Carrington's soft voice purred the insult. "I am challenging you to a game. It will cost you your original bet to play, and my ante will be the remaining two thousand guineas."

"That hardly seems fair." But Dering, who had clearly been about to depart, took a thoughtful sip of his drink, turned, and rested his hips on the railing. He was willing to listen.

"You get the use of the woman for a se'nnight. That must be worth something."

Dering shrugged. "What's the game?"

"I am curious to know if your impressive reputation is founded on anything more substantial than gossip and puffery. And, of course, the wish of your fellows to imagine that one of their own can master any woman he chooses. Is that possible, do you suppose?"

"Certainly, if he is careful to choose only the women he can master. You think I'll not be able to manage this one?"

"I neither know, nor care. I wonder only if you will pay a great deal of money to prove that you can."

"No." Dismissively, as if swatting a gnat. "Permit me to borrow your words, Carrington. I neither know nor care what others think of me. And I would pay nothing whatever to buy anyone's good opinion. Not even yours."

Kate saw the marquess's eyebrows go up. "My opinion has some interest to you?"

"That would be overstating it. *You* interest me, because we appear to have at least one thing in common. We do as we like, and the rest of the world be damned."

"Just so. Would it not be diverting, then, to play my little game? This is what I propose. On the seventh day, I shall sit in judgment of this impudent whore. If she has learned fear and obedience as befits her sex and station, then I shall acknowledge your mastery and return to you the funds you expended to enter the contest."

"As the sole judge, and the only one with anything to lose, will you not set impossible standards?"

"What would be the point? Under those circumstances, I could not enjoy the game or its outcome. The prospect of losing is what seasons the stew, although it does help, I admit, to have a fortune that makes this trifling wager of no significance."

"It is of great significance to me, sir. If losing means I must cover your two thousand—"

"No, no, my dear boy. I don't want your money. Your forfeit will be the mockery and scorn of your peers. But since you have lived with that for a decade, a bit more derision will not greatly concern you."

Kate, with so much riding on every word of this negotiation, was brought up short by the notion of the supremely self-assured viscount spending the last ten years as an object of ridicule. It was unimaginable. Except that he showed no reaction to Carrington's sly insult, which was more telling than a denial would have been.

"And *your* forfeit?" Dering inquired.

"None. I shall rejoice in your triumph, publicly at least, and acknowledge you a clever fellow, which it will not trouble me to do. Besides, I shall already have got from you what I once asked, only to be denied."

Silence. Kate, watching Dering's face, detected the barest change. A tightening of the jaw, a nearly imperceptible narrowing of the eyes. Whatever Carrington was talking about, Lord Dering did not want to surrender it.

"All of this," he said, waving a hand, "to get possession of my horse?"

"It's a fine horse."

"Not that fine. There are probably ten better in your stable right now. You want him because I wouldn't sell him."

"Exactly. You see how ennui has corrupted my sense of values. How difficult I find it, with each slowly passing day, to entertain myself. I am become like a child, wanting what is forbidden, demanding what is denied me. But I mean no harm, sir. Only consider. Neither of us stands to lose anything he cannot afford. I've more money than I can spend, and your reputation is long since evaporated. Whatever the outcome, each of us wins something we want, if not greatly. You will ride the woman, and I shall ride your horse."

Carrington made a flamboyant gesture, quite unlike his usual restraint. "Oh, and our friends here will have the pleasure of choosing sides, laying wagers, and watching the proceedings. Even Paradise will profit, I have no doubt."

And me? Kate felt like a volcano about to erupt. *What about me?*

"And the woman?" Dering said. "Has she anything to win?"

"Does it matter? But if she stays the course until I

declare the game at an end, she will certainly have endured enough to merit a thousand pounds. That way, my wager and yours will equal out. Does that satisfy you?"

"In fact, I'd rather you gave the thousand pounds to me." Dering lifted himself from the railing, tilted his head, and examined her from head to sandaled feet. "But I'll console myself with other pleasures."

"You agree, then?"

"It seems that I do. Ennui must be contagious. But let us be sure there is no misunderstanding. If you have other rules to lay out, do so now, before these witnesses."

"No hidden traps, sir. We understand each other perfectly well." With the slightest of bows, Carrington stepped away from his position next to the musicians' pit. "Take her."

Dering tossed back the remains of his drink, set the glass on the railing, and ambled to the place Carrington had surrendered.

The theater was silent as a mausoleum. No one had ever seen anything quite like this, and with the drama at its turning point, attention arrowed to Kate. Frozen on the narrow glass bridge over the musicians' heads, she awaited Dering's next move.

It came with a single, graceful leap that carried him onto the bridge, just at the point where it was supported by the rail. Then, like a leopard stalking its dinner, he moved forward.

Kate held her ground. Pride would let her do no less. Under the added weight, the glass bowed dangerously.

"Pick it up," he said, pointing to the coin at her feet.

Her first act of obedience. She might have defied

him, in part for show, and on her own behalf because he had replaced Carrington as the most dangerous male in the theater. But the sooner they both left the bridge, the better. The musicians nearest the glass, sensing trouble, were moving to the edges of the pit. Bending her knees, she scooped up the guinea and held it out to him.

"Keep that," he said, "until I ask you for it. And when I do, be sure you can give it to me straight-away."

He took another step forward, and now she had no choice but to retreat. His cool gaze held hers implacably. She might ought to assert herself now, for the crowd's entertainment, giving promise of defiance to come. But he held her in his grip, more firmly than she was clutching the coin with which he had sealed her to him.

Then she was off the bridge and standing beside Fidkin, who smiled broadly as Dering came onto the stage.

"Congratulations, my lord. You have secured for yourself a prize, and at a bargain price, which will be added to your account. Here is the contract of terms."

"Indeed?" Dering took the folded parchment, dramatically festooned with seals and ribbons. "Restrictions, are they, on what I may do with my property?"

Fidkin's plump face reddened. "Minimal restrictions. More like suggesti—"

Fragments of wax and bits of ribbon fluttered to the stage as Dering ripped the contract in half and flung the pieces away. Then, with the crowd cheering his audacity, he seized Kate's wrist and pulled her across the stage, into the wings, and out of sight.

Chapter 8

With a half moon sailing overhead and a cool breeze floating off the lake, Kate and Lord Dering rode side by side in an open gig, her blood pulsing to the rhythm of the clopping hooves. Since leading her from the stage, he had not spoken to her except to say, as she climbed onto the bench, that Sheffer would more than likely have made her walk behind the vehicle.

The gig, along with the driver, had been waiting for them just outside an obscure door at the rear of the Dome, enabling them to leave the compound without drawing attention. She wondered if it was Dering himself who had made the arrangements.

When they arrived at the cottage, Dering swung down and strode immediately to the door, leaving the driver to hand her out. It was exactly the right thing for his lordship to do, she had to admit, but the anger bunched up inside her began to unravel itself. She willfully let it go free. Even rage had its uses, if only to drive out the more dangerous emotions.

He wasn't in sight when she came through the door he'd left open. A pair of Argand lamps glowed from the mantelpiece, lighting a pleasant room furnished

with a Grecian couch, two wing-back chairs flanking
a small table, a sideboard spread with decanters of
wine and brandy, a writing desk, and a nest of plush
furs laid out in front of the hearth.

It seemed to her a great luxury. Everything one
could wish for comfort, touches of beauty here and
there, never a shortage of candles and coal.

A sound behind her. Startled, she turned to see the
cottage door swing shut with Lord Dering's hand propelling it.

"Now then," he said, resting his shoulders against
the wall. "Who the devil are you when you're not
pretending to be an actress, and what precisely are we
supposed to be doing for Black Phoenix?"

She held her ground. While he had been crossing
the glass bridge to claim her, she'd looked into his
eyes and been struck by the arrogance he made no
effort to hide, by his satisfaction at having her in his
power. It had not been an act. "We cannot discuss
this at present," she said. "The driver has gone to
fetch my dresser, Mrs. Kipper, who is bringing my
portmanteau. A few drunken louts might follow along,
hoping to witness an epilogue."

"Shall we provide them one?"

"I've endured enough bad theatrics for tonight."
The Greek patrician, what little of her remained after
the auction, had by this time entirely evaporated. Kate
was herself again, but at her terrible worst. She had
restrained herself for too long, had stood motionless
on that stage for an eternity, had sat quietly in the
carriage for aeons. Her feet started moving, carrying
her with them.

"Do you understand how near we came to losing
everything? Oh, I cannot deny you did well, the grand

entrance and the rest. But it didn't fadge, not until
Carrington took a hand. And then you *refused* him!
You threw it all away. What if he had not pursued
you? What then?"

"Then I would have been proven wrong. You are
wearing a rut on the carpet, my dear. If you must
pace, vary the route."

His amused calm scratched on her nerves. "I'll not
be here long enough for ruts. Wrong about *what?*"

He looked resigned, like a man forced to teach the
alphabet to a fish. "About our benefactor's intentions.
Carrington intervened for a purpose of his own, and
after some thought, I believe it comes down to exactly
what he said. With an agile mind, too much money,
and somewhat twisted sensibilities, he enjoys manipulating others and proving himself superior. But there
is no satisfaction if the prey is weak, or if it surrenders
too easily. He relishes a challenge."

Dering frowned. "I am oversimplifying. I have not
deciphered his character. But even a man of supreme
self-control, which Carrington possesses, cannot help
but hint at what he wishes to conceal. A gambler, a
good one—and if nothing else, I am that—learns to
recognize the signs. A blink. A slight flush across the
cheekbones. The feigned dispassion. The barest twitch
of a muscle in the jaw. No. Not really those things,
which are too obvious. Perhaps this is purely a matter
of instinct. But I have come to trust mine, and I made
a decision, and it paid off. So why are you curling
your fingers? Because you still wish to scratch my
eyes out?"

"I shall attempt to restrain myself," she said, "until
the seven days have passed."

"Make it six. Whatever Carrington has planned for

his unholy sabbath, I don't intend to be around to see it. Meantime, I require a name to call you. Have you a preference?"

"I am known as Gaetana."

"Too many syllables, especially if I need to shout a warning. We'll make it Kate, which is near enough your stage name to catch your attention. In return, the usual forms of address for a viscount will suffice. Come look at this."

Had Black Phoenix discovered her real name? He couldn't simply have guessed. Or was he thinking of the role she had played with him that night—Kate the shrew?

She followed him to the writing table, where he took up a pamphlet contained in a plain brown cover. Opening it to a page marked with a strip of paper, he put the book in her hands.

A poem, she saw, and not a very long one. She was about to ask him why he'd given it her when she glanced at the first lines.

> *In Xanadu did Kubla Khan*
> *A stately pleasure-dome decree:*

"Good heavens. Someone wrote a poem about Paradise?" She looked to the front of the book—*Christabel; Kubla Khan, a Vision; The Pains of Sleep*—and saw the author's name. "I've heard of him. He wrote a play we acted. Are there more references to Paradise?"

"I thought so at first. The yacht that ferried me about this morning was named Mount Amara, and I fancied it had been mentioned as well. But the reference in the poem is to Mount Abora." He moved closer and ran his forefinger down the poem, stopping at a line not far from the end. "See there?"

She did. Sure enough, Mount Abora. As if it signified. She'd never heard of a mountain by either name.

"This as well." His finger went to the last lines.

> *And all should cry, Beware! Beware!*
> *His flashing eyes, his floating hair!*
> *Weave a circle round him thrice,*
> *And close your eyes with holy dread,*
> *For he on honey-dew hath fed,*
> *And drunk the milk of Paradise.*

"That's very odd," she said.

"Indeed it is. When I arrived here, Fidkin mentioned the poem and I said, only to be saying something, that I should like to read it. The book was here when I returned from my ride this afternoon."

"Express an offhand fancy, and Paradise will grant it. But what is the relevance of all this? Did you imagine that reading poetry would calm me?"

"It would probably require a mallet upside the head to do that. In fact, the poem is likely irrelevant, at least for the purposes of Black Phoenix. But there is a slight chance it holds a clue to the owner of Paradise. This is a first edition, published on the twenty-fifth of May, 1816. Barely a month ago. Do you know when Paradise was constructed? When it opened for business?"

"In the spring of 1814. Perhaps Mr. Samuel Taylor Coleridge has been a guest here, and when he wrote his poem, decided to incorporate Xanadu and the Pleasure Dome. I've heard any number of songs and parodies that make reference to Paradise. It has become a landmark here in the north."

"I heard Coleridge speak once," Dering said. "Charming, brilliant, a trifle radical, and his eyes looked something like mine after I've used your infernal eyedrops. I doubt he has any connection to Paradise, or to any other profitable endeavor. He's almost certainly never been here. Now look at the preface to the poem. He says that it was written in the summer of 1797."

"Oh. Well, that explains it. He gave copies to people, or recited it during one of his appearances. I'm not so uneducated, sir, that I've not read about Mr. Coleridge. I understand that he is a great friend of Mr. Wordsworth, who is famous in the Lake District. The manager of the company I was with before coming here once took tea with Mr. Wordsworth. And Mr. Southey, the Poet Laureate of England, lives in Keswick. So you see, almost anyone might be familiar with this poem."

"More than likely the road leads nowhere, as you say. But I'll take it nonetheless. The clue one ignores invariably points to the answer. Besides, I noticed that the publisher is John Murray, who happens to be Byron's publisher. That reminded me of an advertisement I recently saw in the *Morning Chronicle*. It contained Byron's recommendation of another poem in this book, 'Christabel.'"

"Now you are linking Lord Byron to Paradise?" She threw up her hands. "I think you have been taking the opium after all."

"A little more time in your company will almost certainly drive me to it. In fact, had he two crowns to scratch together, Byron would be a good candidate for owner of this place. He was known to be planning a revival of Francis Dashwood's Hellfire Club on his own estate in Nottingham and had taken to calling himself 'Pontifex Maximus,' of all things. I expect Byron's club would have attracted the usual fellows who like to dress up and pretend to be friars or knights or other such nonsense. Much like the original, which was little more than fabricated rituals and lavish orgies cloaked in bits and pieces filched from secret societies. Despite the rumors Dashwood liked to encourage, it was fairly harmless stuff. Had to be, with members like the prime minister, the Archbishop of Canterbury's son, the Lord Mayor of London, the Prince of Wales, and their ilk. It's all about being in fashion, really."

"You appear to know a good deal about the Hellfire Club. I thought it disappeared a long time ago."

"Half a century at least. Byron used to talk about it rather a lot, though. He wanted to re-create the statues and whatnots Dashwood had accumulated, and some of the rituals as well. Now I wish I'd paid more attention."

"You are acquainted with Lord Byron, then? Might he have information of use to us?"

"If he does, he carried it with him to the Continent a few weeks ago, just ahead of a pack of irate creditors. I doubt we'll see him again on this side of the Channel. There is someone else, though, who may be able to help. Is it possible to dispatch a letter without putting it into the hands of Paradise servants?"

"Mrs. Kipper could take it. She has a cousin in Hawkshead she sometimes visits, although I'm not sure what will become of her now. Since I no longer require a dresser, she might be dismissed."

"Can she be trusted?"

"She is one of us. There is another member of Black Phoenix on the property, a servant, but his identity has not been told me."

"I see." He took the pamphlet and returned it to the drawer. "Shall we prepare ourselves for company? I propose we begin as we mean to go on. Come here, Kate, and remove my boots."

She stared at him, three backstage oaths lodged in her throat, and as she watched, one corner of his mouth turned up. It shocked her into outrage. "I will *not!* I am not your valet."

"You are whatever this endeavor requires you to be." An icy undercurrent in his voice. "It's only a role, Kate, except you can't put it off after a few hours on stage. And you have to play against the nasty piece of work I am supposed to be, which won't be pleasant for either of us. Fight me, yes, even in public. But under no circumstances should you dishonor me. Never force me into a position where I'd be expected to correct you with a display of violence. If I am able to retaliate, I must. Otherwise, I lose all credibility with my fellows, and if that happens, we may as well call off the mission and toddle along home. Do you understand what I am saying?"

"Certainly." Sounds rose up in her memory— sounds that had stayed with her long after she'd buried the rest. "You're a brute who gets his way with his fists."

"Not if you're clever. But you are missing the point. I'm surprised."

"Do not forget, sir, that we are partners in this enterprise. I am not your servant. And I shall not"—she pointed at his feet—"remove your— Oh." She looked back at his face. "You're not wearing boots."

"That's right. Perhaps you should undo the buttons on my waistcoat instead. Over here by the window, where we can be seen."

"You are playing games with me." She dragged herself over to where he stood, aiming all her attention at his waistcoat. It was a work of art, white satin embroidered with metallic gold thread, the buttons wrapped with the same gold thread, all perfectly fitted to his broad chest and slim waist. The waistcoat must have cost a year's worth of wages in the Pendragon Theater Company. His shirt was fine cambric, open at the neck. She wondered what had become of his collar and neckcloth and coat.

Her fingers felt like sausages as they fumbled with the buttons. It would be easier going if his chest didn't keep moving up and down. The man had to breathe, she supposed, but not while she was wrestling with his tiny stitched buttonholes. She didn't dare look up at his face. Or at his neck, not since she'd found herself distracted by the pulse beating there.

Coxcomb. Probably accustomed to females falling all over him, or not being able to undo a simple button because she couldn't make her fingers work properly. But in her case, his attractions were nothing to the point. It was exhaustion made her inept. Humiliation that made her angry.

"They're here," he said softly. "Continue on. When someone knocks, I'll direct you to admit them. Do so. Then follow my lead."

"Aye, aye, sir," she said between her teeth.

Jarrett, looking down at her bent head, could practically see the steam rising off her. Could an explosion be far behind? He hoped it wouldn't take place in front of witnesses, but tonight, raw as she was in the aftermath of the auction, she was capable of a serious misstep. She had to learn, and quickly, how to play the dangerous game they had undertaken.

When the knocking came, he waved a hand and went over to the sideboard to pour himself a drink, fairly certain he was going to need one.

The disturbing sound he had noticed when the gig pulled up quadrupled in volume as Kate opened the door. Pretending disinterest, he watched her step aside to admit a plump, well-groomed woman with smoothly coiffed gray-white hair and a cheerful expression on her face. She looked to be in her fifties and was carrying a lidded basket that seemed to have a lot to say for itself. Behind her stood the driver, a large portmanteau in one hand, a good-sized parcel in the other, and an aggrieved look on his face.

Jarrett turned, scowling. "What the devil is that racket?"

The woman—Mrs. Kipper, he presumed—set down the basket and raised the hinged lid.

Immediately a small, wiry, furious creature sprang out, took a quick look around, homed in on Jarrett, and scooted in his direction. It stopped about three feet away, front legs stiff and hindquarters sloped back, as if gathering leverage for a jump. The mouth opened, exposing sharp, pointy teeth. A snarl began low in its throat, got progressively louder, and erupted into an ear-rattling bark.

"He doesn't appear to like you," Kate said sweetly.

"The feeling is mutual. Get it out of here."

"*It* is a dog, sir." Her lips turned down. "The last gift my father gave to me."

"Not a gesture of affection, then. And if that wretched creature is a dog, I'm Marie Antoinette. It's a barking rat. A bristle brush on four legs. And it's not staying here." He removed his gaze from the scrawny beast long enough to catch Mrs. Kipper's bland smile. "Take that thing away."

"I cannot, my lord. My new duties will not permit me to care for him. But I assure you that when he calms himself, you'll scarcely know he's around."

"That's right. He'll be somewhere else."

"My lord," said the driver, "there is a smaller residence set back a little way from the cottage, suitable for a valet or other servants a gentleman might bring with him. The offending dog could be confined there."

"There's also a lake. He could be confined there with a lot less trouble."

Rushing over, Kate scooped up the rat and held it to her chest, her eyes afire with defiance. The bark subsided to a constant, throbbing growl. And she, blessedly, said nothing irretrievable. She simply gazed at him, pitting her will against his.

The driver, who couldn't see she meant to win this round, had to be got rid of before she made it crystal clear. "I do not intend," Jarrett said firmly, "to squabble with a servant. In fact, I really ought to be celebrating." He caught the driver's eye. "Fetch me a bottle or two of iced champagne, a dish of strawberries, and a platter of shortbread, will you? I've a particular fondness for shortbread. Meantime, this woman can unpack the portmanteau while I come to terms with my new toy about her intensely irritating pet. Well, get moving. All of you."

They did, although Kate moved only to the opposite side of the Grecian sofa, as if she thought he might be planning to rip her pet from her arms. His fault. He'd spoken to her of violence when there was no opportunity to finish the conversation. And he'd been deliberately provocative, which he thought at the time to be essential. He still thought so. It was the timing he'd got wrong.

"We have perhaps twenty or thirty minutes," he said, "before the driver returns. I need to write the letter for Mrs. Kipper to post, and I expect the two of you have information to exchange. It might be your last opportunity for a while. Run along, Kate. And don't worry. I probably won't drown your rat."

Chapter 9

Kate closed the door to the bedroom, set the dog atop Lord Dering's bed, and used the candle on his night table to ignite a pair of lamps. When she'd last seen it, in moonlight and shadows, the room had appeared much smaller. But then, all her attention had been on the imposing canopied bed and the formidable male sprawled there, sleeping the sleep of the unrepentant.

"He is impossible," she said to Malvolio, who was trying to dig a hole in the counterpane.

"Put him on the floor, dear." Mrs. Kipper had set the portmanteau on a cedar chest and was examining the contents of the armoire.

"I was referring to the lord and master."

"Well, I doubt *he'll* agree to sleep on the floor. Or in company with Malvolio. Will he permit the dog to stay, do you suppose?"

"I don't know what he'll do. He is entirely unpredictable. It's maddening."

"I expect so." Mrs. Kipper found an empty drawer and left it open. "But he has managed fairly well so far, wouldn't you agree?"

"He has stumbled into good fortune, that is all."

Kate opened the portmanteau, removed a dressing gown, and tossed it over a chair. "Without Carrington's intervention, we'd be in the soup."

"Please observe the contents as we unpack, my dear, so that you can tell me what you wish me to bring on my next visit."

"You are permitted to remain, then?"

"I am to serve the . . . *ladies*"—Mrs. Kipper tossed her a wry smile—"who sometimes accompany gentlemen to Paradise. This will give me a degree of freedom to move around the estate, and I shall try to come by every day to attend your wardrobe. But you'll not be assured of finding me if I am needed. Instruct Lord Dering to take a meal at the Dome as soon as may be. There, my associate will identify himself and establish a means of communication."

Kate grabbed her night rail from the portmanteau and flung it after the dressing gown. Dering was to know the identity of the other Black Phoenix spy, which had been kept from her all this time. Did they not trust her? For that matter, why was she even here? So far as she could tell, the three of them could proceed nicely on their own. They appeared to be doing precisely that.

Malvolio, abandoning his plunder of the counterpane, had got a tassel from the canopy curtains between his teeth and was chomping it into submission. Fine with her if he ripped the entire bed into rags. She had no intention of sleeping there.

Anger and fear gnawed at her the way Malvolio was going at the tassel. She took a deep breath, and then another. She oughtn't to sharpen her temper on Mrs. Kipper, who had been kind from the moment they were introduced. Taking up an armful of undergarments, she carried them over to the armoire. "He cares nothing for our mission. He means only to indulge himself."

Pale blue eyes lifted to hers. "Have you had the opportunity to explain why we were sent here? What Phoenix believes to be occurring?"

"Not yet. Since Fidkin ruled that I must be sold or take my leave, I have been entirely consumed with the auction."

"And now the wind has gone out of your sails." Mrs. Kipper folded the last chemise, placed it in the drawer, and took the stockings Kate held out. "It is only natural, my dear. I have been worried, too. But we've come about, or nearly so. Will your concerns about Dering prevent you from staying the course?"

"I . . . I'm not sure." There. She'd said it aloud. The secret she had been keeping from herself until this very moment. "I can scarcely believe it. You know, better than anyone, that I want nothing more than to accomplish what I was sent here to do. It means everything to me. But how can I put myself into his hands? I did everything I could to make it possible, and now that I am here, in his cottage, in his bedchamber, I want only to flee."

Mrs. Kipper, her plump face flushed with concern, inclined her head. "Tell me, then. And be perfectly straightforward."

"Forgive me. I am letting you all down. There's just something about him—I can't say what—that makes it impossible for us to work together. In part it is my own obsession with the charge and his indifference to it. But I might be able to let him get on with his drinking and gaming and do the job myself, except that he fancies I have become his plaything. He'll not free me to work alone."

Kate looked down and saw her hands clutching her

skirts. She felt like the schoolgirl she had once been, stifling her temper as she confessed a misdemeanor to the headmistress . . . a rather frequent occurrence during her years at St. Bridget's Academy for Young Ladies. With effort, she loosened her fingers and let her hands drop to her sides. "I beg your pardon, ma'am. I do not mean to insult the gentleman. Black Phoenix selects its emissaries with care. You have told me so."

"Generally true. But on this occasion we were rather scrambling for a candidate." Mrs. Kipper went to retrieve slippers and half boots from the portmanteau. "It is hard going to find a dedicated, trustworthy man with the sort of reputation needed to operate here without raising suspicion. And Phoenix has peculiar requirements of which I know nothing. At the end, it was a stroke of luck and a little manipulation put Dering in our grasp. I am sorry you find him unsuitable. He certainly cannot be replaced this go-around."

"If we fail, you will try again?"

"That is not for me to say. But given what we suspect, it would be surprising if Phoenix abandoned the project altogether. However, to arrange another deception would take time, and in the interim . . . well, who is to say what might occur here?"

"You needn't be concerned," Kate said stiffly. "I have no intention of leaving my post."

"But you must," said Mrs. Kipper, arranging the shoes on a low shelf in the armoire. "Unless you are able to carry on without reservations, you will become a liability. There is no shame in withdrawing if you do so in the best interest of our mission."

"There is shame, then. The best interest is my own."

"Might I ask what that is? You needn't tell me, but perhaps I can be of assistance."

Embarrassment sent heat galloping up Kate's body

to her face, where it settled in to burn on her neck and cheeks. "He intends to . . . Well, he hasn't said so, but I'm fairly sure—"

Her gaze went to the bed, where Malvolio was burrowing under the sheets.

Mrs. Kipper closed the portmanteau with a snap. "You believe he means to become your lover? *That* is your concern?"

"He takes it for granted. As if it were necessary, and it isn't. Who would know? And I don't wish to."

For the first time since Kate had known her, Mrs. Kipper looked stern. "Then you need not. So long as it doesn't compromise our reason for being here, I have nothing to say to it. Nor, for that matter, does Lord Dering. The decision is entirely yours."

"Do you imagine he'll settle for that?"

"He does not appear the sort to force you. But one can never be sure." With a little sigh, Mrs. Kipper lowered herself onto a chair. "Last night, when we discussed what might happen at the auction, you refused to consider withdrawing. Whatever the outcome, you insisted on following through, even if it meant putting yourself into the hands of a beastly winner. How is it, my dear, that you would accept any other man, and not this one?"

After a time Kate sat as well, on the same chair she'd used the previous night. "The others are different. Some can be controlled, some must be endured. I have learned to deal with either sort."

"And Dering is unknown territory. How unfortunate that I am not half my age and invited, as you have been, to explore such a remarkable landscape." Mrs. Kipper gave a rueful smile. "I've always had a weakness for charming men. My Charles was much like Dering, a handsome man and a rogue, and while

I loved him dearly, it was as well he spent more time at sea than in my company. I'd have tried to shape him into a purely domesticated spouse and spoiled the very things that made him what he was. Or I'd have slit his throat for the infidelities, which broke my heart a hundred times. Oh, my. What sent me off on this lark?"

"Do you regret marrying him?"

"Certainly not. But given another chance, I might choose a calmer, more settled fellow. Never mind all that. You will be in Dering's company no more than a week. If he makes things too difficult for you, by all means take your leave. Terence Pendragon will have you back, if you wish to rejoin the company. Or you might prefer a London theater. After the success you have made here among influential men, it should be easy to find you a place at Drury Lane or Covent Garden. Whatever you decide, Black Phoenix will assist you."

"Even if I walk out on this mission?"

"Even then. We all have boundaries, and if Dering is the other side of yours, there is no more to be said. Simply let me know your decision, when you are certain it is final."

"Perhaps I am mistaken. He has not said I must lie with him. He might not wish it."

"I shouldn't count on that." Mrs. Kipper rose and took hold of the portmanteau. "Shall we go see what the troublesome young man has got up to?"

He was at the writing table, Kate saw as she closed the bedchamber door behind her, holding a stick of red sealing wax close by a candle flame. A moment later he dropped molten wax onto the folded parchment paper, removed his signet ring, and impressed it onto the seal. Only then did he look up.

Even from a distance, Kate could see from his eyes that he had used the drops. But for what reason? No one of significance would see him tonight. He grinned at her and returned the writing materials to the drawer. Then she noticed the brandy glass nearby, along with an array of items she could not identify. Well, she knew a mortar and pestle when she saw them, and something that looked like a snuffbox. A tinderbox as well, and some sort of apparatus that, in a larger form, might have been found in a stillroom. Just near his elbow, the table was smudged. She took a step closer, and another. Powder, she thought. Spilled powder.

Opium. Not the eyedrops. He was taking the opium! If she'd had a poker in her hand, she'd have bashed him with it. But it was a warm evening, and the hearth as empty as her heart.

He stood, with more grace than a man in his condition ought to possess, and carried his letter over to Mrs. Kipper. "I am told, ma'am, that you can see this posted without drawing the attention of anyone at Paradise."

Trying to look unhurried about it, Kate put herself at Mrs. Kipper's side just as he handed over the letter. The name inscribed there was impossible to mistake. *Her Grace, the Duchess of Sarne.*

"Is it urgent?" Mrs. Kipper slid the letter into a pocket. "I can have this privately delivered."

"That won't be necessary. No reply is likely to reach me before I leave here, which—you should know—I intend to do before the end of the week. Whatever we can accomplish together will have to be finished before then."

He went back to the writing table and retrieved his glass of brandy. "I have asked that any response be directed to one of your associates, Major Lord Blair.

His is the only name I have been provided. My queries relate to the ownership of Paradise, but I confess there is little chance they will pay off."

"Nothing ventured," said Mrs. Kipper. "We have attempted to penetrate the legal shields surrounding the purchase of the estate without success, although we continue to try. I suspect the present owner is a puppet—someone's aged relation who scarcely recalls his own name, let alone what the property is being used for."

"Might I ask a service?" he said, his tone impeccably polite. "Last night in the theater, seated in a box near the stage, I saw a woman of my acquaintance. She was accompanied by a gentleman I did not recognize, nor could I make out his face in the poor light. He was about my height, I think, light-haired, slender, and his garb appeared to be of an outdated fashion. I should like to know his identity and whether or not they are still in residence."

"A simple matter, there being so few ladies here to choose from. Is the one in question redheaded?"

He nodded.

"Ah, yes. The lady did not provide a name, but her escort was surely the Comte d'Arvaine, who owns an estate not far from Carlisle. He has long interested us, although there is no evidence he is other than he purports to be—a French aristocrat who fell out with Bonaparte and led a ragtag troop of *guerrilleros* against his countrymen for several years. With the peace of 1814, he was invited to the Victory Celebrations and permitted to set up residence in England. This morning he left for his estate, and the lady departed at the same time."

Dering seemed relieved to hear that, Kate thought. But angry, probably because the Frenchman had replaced him as the lady's lover. So many of his women present in this room—the one he had asked about, the one he'd just written to, and the one he'd purchased. Oh, and Mrs. Kipper as well, who would not have minded being asked to stay with him for the night. So far as Kate was concerned, she was welcome to do just that.

Mrs. Kipper was starting to say something when Malvolio, enclosed in the bedchamber, set to barking.

"What the devil?" Dering stomped to the bedchamber door and wrenched it open. "Shut up, you mangy hairbrush."

Malvolio shut up long enough to chomp into Dering's trouser leg and begin shaking his head back and forth, which resulted in his own stubby legs lifting off the floor.

Kate, afraid Dering would hurt the dog to be rid of him, rushed over, dropped to the floor, and wrapped her arms around his scrappy little body. "Stop it. Hush. Please."

"Oh, that will help," said Dering, holding his leg still.

"Is he biting you?"

"He's biting an expensive pair of—" Another oath, barely smothered. "Never mind. Get him off me."

Mrs. Kipper joined the party. Bending down, she massaged the dog's stubborn jaws until he relaxed his grip, at which point Kate snatched him away. A chunk of black broadfine came with him.

"Malvolio doesn't care for gentlemen," said Mrs. Kipper, rising. "He began barking because he heard one of your sex approaching. Then you opened the door, and a man in the mouth is worth two outside the cottage. I believe you will hear the driver knocking very soon."

"So every time I come near him, he will attack?"

"Not if you woo him with his special treats. Kate will show you how. The men in the Pendragon Company had to learn as well, after I brought him to her. By now you will have worked out his purpose."

"I gather he is meant to be a sentry. Can he be trusted to raise the dead whenever a man comes near the cottage?"

"Without fail. I trained him myself. Is there anything more I can provide you?"

"Information about the Marquess of Carrington. He— No time. I hear the pony trap pulling up. Back to work, ladies."

He was refilling his brandy glass when Mrs. Kipper opened the cottage door, sending Malvolio into a frenzy until Kate towed him over to his basket and closed him inside. The barking continued, the basket bouncing with the force of canine indignation.

The driver, who had brought another servant along to help with the refreshments, stepped inside and bowed.

"Put all that on the sideboard," Dering said, crossing to the hearth and picking up a sheepskin rug. "And uncork the champagne." He tossed the rug over the dog's basket.

"You'll smother him!" Kate dropped to one knee and took hold of the offending rug.

A loud crack as the back of his hand flashed by her face. She screamed. The servants looked over at them, wide-eyed, and quickly returned to their work.

When the shock passed, she realized he hadn't hurt her. Not at all. She had felt only the air as his hand swept past her cheek. How he'd produced the sound she didn't know, but it had been effective enough to scare the devil out of her.

As if he'd forgotten the incident, Dering wandered

over to the sideboard. "I've a fancy to go climbing tomorrow," he said. "What does one wear to ascend the heights?"

"Will you join the climbing party, my lord? If you are unfamiliar with the area—"

"Yes, yes." Dering took the flute of champagne offered him by the other servant. "I'm not gudgeon enough to brave the wilds on my own. I'd as soon not brave them at all, but I'm courting a young man with money to lose, and he's an outdoorsman. Can you provide what I require? See me awake, fed, dressed, and at the boat in time for departure?"

"Indeed, my lord, if you will loan us a sample of your footwear for sizing. We have special boots for fell walking."

"The Gypsy will need clothing as well. I'd intended to keep her free of it—clothing, I mean—but if I have to tramp the hills, she can damn well come along to carry my gear."

"I'll see she has what she needs," said Mrs. Kipper.

Dering drained his glass and held it out for a refill. "Have you a leash that will fit her?" He seemed boneless, relaxed as floating seaweed.

"That can be arranged," the servant said. "Along with any such items that please you. Simply make your wishes known, my lord."

My Lord slumped onto a chair, lids drooping. "I wish you gone now, I think. Take the rat with you."

Kate let out a squeal.

"Not her," Dering said. "The rat in the basket. And the other female."

Mrs. Kipper went immediately out the door, leaving the servants to handle Kate and her dog. They approached gingerly. The basket protested loudly.

Dering slid off his chair to the floor.

Thump. The sound of his glass shattering. An oath.

The servants swung around. Kate grabbed the basket, dashed into the bedchamber, and latched the door. They could break it down, of course. She was not safe here, nor anywhere else in Paradise. She would never be safe.

The dog kept barking, but she could scarcely hear it over the blood pounding in her ears.

She didn't know, even yet, if Dering would let her keep Malvolio. If he'd even understood why it was necessary. She could not bear this, his drunkenness and the opium, the uncertainty of his wits. Above all, his amusement, as if they were all engaged in a meaningless game.

She went to her chair and sat with her arms around the basket, rocking back and forth. Malvolio had quieted, except for a low keening noise.

No. The sound was coming from her own throat. She made it stop.

Later—she didn't know how long—there was a rap on the door. "You can come out now," said Dering. "I've sent them off."

She felt attached to the chair, glued there by exhaustion. "Let me alone," she said, not sure he could hear her, not caring.

"Give in with good grace, Kate, or I'll raise the lantern and have them back to remove you forcibly."

She knew that. It was futile, defying him. She had no more power than Malvolio barking in his basket, all sound and no teeth.

She set down the basket and went on shaky legs into the parlor, where Dering, his back to her, stood with his palms braced against the sideboard. From the slumped shoulders and lowered head, she thought he might be close to falling again. Perhaps he'd wind up spending the rest of the night on the floor, a prospect that raised her spirits a notch.

Stopping just inside the room, she watched him become aware of her presence and take a deep breath, as if dreading the next few minutes as much as she was. But when he straightened and turned, he had a glass of champagne in his hand. "Shall we have our discussion over there, at the table?"

It wasn't really a question. Kate went to the bay window that overlooked the terrace and, beyond it, the lake. There were two chairs set across from each other on either side of the small square table. She chose the one farthest from the light and perched herself on its edge.

Dering put the flute of champagne in front of her. "Not the best I've ever had, but it will help you sleep. Drink it slowly." Then he went back to the sideboard.

Suspiciously alert for a man well gone on drink and opium, she thought, watching him approach again. He'd brought strawberries in a bowl, a platter of shortbread, two saucers, and the ice bucket containing the bottle of champagne. His own glass was balanced atop the saucers.

She took hold of it before it could fall. "Must we do this now? It must be nearly dawn."

"Perhaps two hours," he said, laying out the dishes before refilling his glass and settling opposite her. "But I believe we must get a few things straight before venturing out in public."

"Yes. I am supposed to tell you what Black Phoenix has learned about Paradise, and what Mrs. Kipper and I have discovered since arriving here ten days ago." On safe ground for once, Kate spoke matter-of-factly. "She says that you were provided little information before leaving London."

"Almost none. But since there's precious little I can

do to advance the investigation tonight, we'll leave that for another time."

"But that's why we're both here! Don't you care the least little bit about what we are to do?"

"Not at the moment." He was carefully selecting strawberries from the large bowl and placing them on a saucer.

"Then why did you agree to come?"

"If you must know, for the expense money. I'd hoped to parlay it into *more* money at the gaming tables, keeping the winnings for myself." He examined a strawberry, seemed to find it unworthy, and dropped it on the other saucer. "But mostly, I think, it was for the horse. And then all the money went to buy you, and now the horse is gone as well, in exchange for Carrington's contribution. So at this point, damned if I can scratch up a good reason to be here."

He glanced at her face. "No insult. I still have you for a short time, unless you mean to use that cunning stiletto you put to my throat last night. Be sure you wouldn't be sitting alone with me now if I thought you were carrying it. But you aren't wearing anything beneath that blue silk, as every man could see tonight. Did Mrs. Kipper smuggle the knife inside the portmanteau, wrapped in your underthings?"

She ought to have changed clothing when she had the chance. Suddenly, with his gaze exploring her, she felt as if she were wearing nothing at all. "If I need to make use of my knife," she said, "you may be sure it will be within reach. But I see little purpose continuing this charade. If you have no interest in our investigation, then we should both abandon the field before we make an irrevocable error, one that would betray the intentions of Black Phoenix. Someone can be sent to replace us."

"But no one better suited, I think, to the task. Or are you seeking an excuse to escape *me?*"

"Certainly not." A frail protest. To cover it she took up the champagne, which she'd meant to leave untouched, and drank a good long swallow. Compounding her troubles, she realized even as she was doing it. The combination of champagne and this man—she was beginning to suspect he had not taken opium after all—could be lethal. "Escape never crossed my mind. I simply dislike wasting my time on a futile endeavor."

"Is there any other kind?" He set a dish of strawberries, red and plump and perfect, in front of her. "I imagine you've eaten very little today, Kate. Oblige me in this. And have some shortbread as well, if I leave you any. It's frightfully good."

The thought of eating put sawdust in her mouth. But he was right, blast him. She'd touched nothing since a sparse breakfast, and her mind felt stuffed with feathers. With an overacted shrug of resignation, she picked up the smallest strawberry and nibbled off the tip.

Oh, my. The juice, blending with the tang of the champagne she'd just drunk, sent all her troubles to a corner while she enjoyed the taste.

Smiling, his smug lordship dropped two strawberries into her glass and topped it off with more champagne. "Try it this way as well."

"Are you entirely devoted to pleasure?" she couldn't help asking.

"Are you entirely devoted to penance? In all my life, I have never met a creature so determined to deny herself what she wants. I hope that one day you will explain it to me."

"I shouldn't count on that." She was glad that Mrs. Kipper had provided her the line. With a quick memory for dialogue, she often used other people's words because her own might wander too near the truth.

He bit into a square of shortbread and sighed his pleasure. "I, on the other hand, think of nothing but getting what I most want, however small my chances of succeeding. The anticipation of good things is to be preferred—is it not?—to the sour certainty that no blessings will ever fall one's way."

Until you discover that what you wanted never turned out to be what you'd expected. Kate remembered the one other time she had felt akin to the way she felt this night, tempted beyond reason to cast herself over a cliff in the embrace of the devil. And she had done so, joyfully, only to plunge into an abyss that she was, even at this moment, trying to pull her way clear of. But there were new devils near the top, it appeared, devils like this aristocrat with narcotic eyes and a ready laugh who was now holding a fat ripe strawberry to her lips.

To prove she wasn't the shriveled prude he thought her to be, she bit off half of it and took the rest between her fingers to feed herself the second bite. She wished he wouldn't bother playing the role of a gentleman in company with a favored lady. Few men—and certainly not any of his rank—troubled to properly seduce an actress. In her experience, they flatly offered money in exchange for her favors and went off with fleas in their ears. But she wasn't fooled. This seducer would put down coins as well, except that he had more silver in his tongue than in his pocket.

"You cannot accept that our present circumstances might prove a blessing in disguise?" said Dering. "Perhaps you have been too often disappointed. But even when it seems that nothing will ever change, a surprise could be waiting in the next hedgerow. A week ago I could never have imagined you. And now here you are in my company, in my possession, and very soon to be in my bed."

Cold slid down her back. With care, she put down the champagne she'd just picked up. That she had known his intentions to be inevitable had not, after all, prepared her to deal with this moment. She thought of Isabella in *Measure for Measure,* a role she had played in Lancaster only a month earlier, and how the virtuous woman had been coerced by the villainous Angelo. A martyr in temperament, Isabella, but lucky as well. She'd had a powerful duke to rescue her.

There were no powerful dukes in the wings for Kate Falshaw. Only one bed in the cottage, one man who expected her to join him there, and her commitment to follow through with the auction and its consequences. Also her wits, flagging now and muddled with champagne. Perhaps she could appeal to his conscience.

Perhaps it would snow in July.

"Nothing to say, my dear? You have had a difficult time of it, I know, but if left to your own devices, you will create in your imagination a far worse situation than any reality could measure down to." He sat across from her, arms folded on the table, eyes locked on her face. "Despite my lack of enthusiasm for Black Phoenix and secretive investigations, you and I are in this together. We are to be lovers. Why must you fight me? It's not as if we don't wish to take pleasure from each other."

"But that's exactly how it is. Oh, I've no doubt of your own wishes. Men always want to. Any excuse will do, and any female. Or do you restrict yourself to females?"

"For the most part. There is, of course, the occasional sheep."

She stared at him, appalled. Farm boys, perhaps, but an English aristocrat? Then she saw his mouth quirk. "I'm surprised a self-respecting sheep would have you," she fired back.

"That's my girl. Are you a virgin?"

She choked on a swallow of champagne. "Good heavens," she said when the coughing subsided. "Let us by all means practice good manners and tact. But why do you ask? You persist in thinking yourself able to read my thoughts and my . . . my feelings. Cannot you tell?"

"I believe so, but in this matter, to be wrong would lead to some degree of awkwardness. A straightforward assurance from you, one way or another, would ease our path."

His, perhaps. "You assume I am not, because a woman in my profession must, by nature or circumstances, whore herself."

"Not at all. But I have drawn a few conclusions based on what you told me—that you had come to Paradise prepared to whore yourself. And you must agree that a member of a traveling company of players necessarily sees and experiences far more than any sheltered, gently bred young woman has occasion to. You may be physically innocent, my dear, but you cannot have remained ignorant. Or naive."

"I know about vegetables, at any rate. But what is this to the point? We are alone here, and Malvolio will keep us free of spies. There is no need to maintain a pretense. No one will know what we do in private."

"I was wrong," he said. "You *are* naive."

"Are you saying you cannot restrain yourself?"

"I'll have no need to make the effort." He regarded her steadily. "Listen to me. Men can tell, most of them, when a woman has been satisfactorily tumbled.

There is a change in her complexion. The slight abrasion of whiskers on her skin. Lips swollen from kisses. Sometimes color on her flesh where he has left his mark. Even if she has bathed, there is no mistaking the scent of lovemaking. She moves differently. Her eyes are shadowed with awareness. She feels, everywhere her lover has been, the echo of his presence."

Memories, like echoes of her past, reverberated to the sound of his voice. Just listening to him describe the aftermath of lovemaking in that silken voice sent pleasurable sensations rushing to places they ought not to go.

She wrestled herself free of them. "But everyone will presume you have . . . What I mean is, people don't go looking for what they are already sure is there. We can easily provide a few visible signs." She took another drink of champagne. "And I'll behave as they would expect me to. They will be convinced. I am an actress."

"But not a good one. Oh, draw in your claws, my dear. We're not speaking of a stage performance. For all I know you'd make a splendid Ophelia, or Rosalind, or Beatrice. I should very much like to see you play Beatrice. But you are not adept at concealing your own emotions. I find it exceptionally easy to know when you are trying to hide something, although I cannot always be sure what it is. And all unaware, you sometimes reveal secrets you are attempting to hide even from yourself."

"Rubbish! That is your arrogance speaking, my lord. You have no idea, none whatever, of my secret thoughts and feelings."

"But I do. As useless as you think I am—not without reason—I have trained myself to be attentive to the ways an individual's body discloses what he would keep private. Women especially interest me, and I have some experience with them at close range. Grant me this one skill."

"If it pleases you. But you are not the enemy. Your interpretation is of no consequence. And I can fool the others."

"Most of them, yes. And had I been able to purchase you in a straightforward transaction, there would be no need to insist on bedding you, although you may be sure I would have tried to persuade you by other means. But now we have Carrington, whose insight into the darker corners of human nature far surpasses my own. There will be no escaping his scrutiny. Nor that of the men who place wagers on the outcome of this absurd game, and most of them will. When we are in public, Kate, theatrics will not suffice. We must *be* what we want them to think we are."

"Which is why you will strike me in front of them? To demonstrate your control of me?"

He passed a hand wearily across his forehead. "On this subject, I spoke too soon and not clearly. I did mean that you should fear me, more than a little. It is the law of nature, male over female, not to mention my rank. Fear will put an edge on your performance. But you must defy me as well, to make the game exciting for Carrington and the rest. Only, when you do so in front of witnesses, make sure I am unable at that moment to physically punish you. Every man will expect me to strike back, and it won't always be possible to fake a blow, as I did tonight."

"Insult you from a distance, then?"

"Or be sure the witnesses are at a distance. Use your imagination, Kate. I don't want to hurt you."

"Comforting, to be sure." He was saying that if it came down to violence, the fault would be hers. She knew exactly how that scene played out. "Have you any other instructions, my lord?"

"Oh, a great many. Some of them you will enjoy. But I think we understand each other well enough for now."

"If you say so." She downed the last of her champagne, pink from the strawberries. "Shall we get on with it, then? The bedding, I mean. Will it take long?"

His eyes widened. She thought he was going to laugh.

"How long do you want it to take?" he said.

"The beat of a bird's wing. The blink of an eye. Can you manage so much?"

"Probably not tonight," he said, grinning, "despite your prodigious efforts to seduce me. Trot along to a chaste bed, my dear. I shall join you later, inoffensive as an octogenarian monk."

Relief flooded through her, salted with . . . she could not be sure. It felt, impossibly, like regret. He didn't want her.

"Before you go to ground," he said, "I need to win the affections of that yappy rodent. Will it be a difficult courtship, do you think, or might there be a shortcut?"

"He is easily won, but only if you know the trick." She went to the bedchamber, removed a packet from its hiding place, and returned with the dog at her heels. When he saw Dering, Malvolio dropped to his belly, growling and vibrating like a bowstring.

Prelude to an attack, she knew, stepping between dog and viscount.

"This is dried venison, his favorite treat. Feed it to him and he will thereafter know you for a friend. But first you must identify yourself and seal the bond." She tore off a bite-size piece and put it in his hand.

"When I move out of the way, you are to place this on top of his nose."

"Not anytime this year," said Dering. "I've suddenly developed a taste for barking."

"I don't understand." She was beginning to enjoy herself. "Are you afraid he'll bite you?"

"There is precedent." He gave her a penetrating look. "The trick here is being played by you, on me, with the rat as an accessory."

"Calling him names won't help your cause," she said. "But perhaps you'll not be so fearful if I show you how it works."

An indecipherable response from his lordship, who rose and took refuge behind his chair.

"Malvolio," she said in a chipper voice. "Who's a good dog?"

He was still eyeing his lordship and emitting a rumbling growl.

"This is the code," she said to Dering. "I'll be revenged on the whole pack of you."

The dog perked up. He sat neatly, his little tail whipping back and forth, and fixed his bright eyes on her face.

She put the bite of venison atop his muzzle and stepped back. "He will hold there until I give him the code to proceed, but I never keep him waiting. Malvolio?"

The dog looked like a Congreve rocket, fuse sparking and an instant from flight.

"M," she said. "O. A." A tiny pause. "I!"

On "I," the dog flipped his muzzle, sending the venison spinning into the air. When it came down, his open mouth was waiting.

"Impressive," Dering said. "But he likes you. What's to stop him from taking a chunk out of me?"

"The code. Really, my lord, he cannot be an effective sentry if *your* appearance sets him barking. Will you give it a try? Wear gloves, if you like."

"Unless you have a pair of steel gauntlets I can borrow, I don't expect gloves would stand proof against those fangs." He came out from behind the chair, which set Malvolio to barking again. "Oh, very well, you wretched creature. The venison, please."

She gave him a piece and moved out of the way.

Dog and man faced off. Dering took a wary step closer. Malvolio started pronking up and down, legs stiff as pipes.

"I'll be revenged," said Dering, "on the whole pack of you."

Malvolio barked and pronked.

"Say it with more conviction," Kate advised. "You have to get his attention."

"Everyone's a critic." He fixed Malvolio with a lordly glare. "Listen here, you dyspeptic hound. I'll be revenged on the whole pack of you!"

Looking startled, the dog folded himself into a sitting position. This time, his tail was ominously still.

Dering came forward, holding the venison between thumb and forefinger. Malvolio gave him a malevolent growl, but didn't move as the dried meat was put—with a watchmaker's precision—on his nose.

Straightening, Dering held in place as well. "M. O. I. A."

Nothing from the dog.

"You got it wrong," said Kate. "It's—"

"I know what it is. I'm avenging my ripped breeches. M," he said. And, slowly, "O. A." Finally, "I."

The venison was quickly snapped up. Malvolio

looked over at Kate, still holding the packet, with a hopeful expression. She broke off a segment and tossed it to him.

"No question about it," said Dering, brushing off his hands. "That dog has you thoroughly trained. Maybe he can devise a trick to get you under me with your legs open."

Caught off stride, she made a high-pitched sound of indignation.

"Would you fetch the leash?" said his lordship blandly, as if he hadn't just made an incendiary remark. "I'm going to take my new friend for a long, restorative walk."

"I can see to that." She felt that she ought to make a gesture of . . . what? Cooperation, perhaps. Besides, Malvolio was her pet, in a way, until the mission ended and Mrs. Kipper took him back. "I know the area and can navigate it in the dark."

He gave her a slow, heated smile. "You don't appear to understand the purpose behind my sudden need for exercise. Bring me the leash, my dear, and then to bed with you. We'll make a new start tomorrow. Meantime, there's no need for you to lie awake, fretting that I might decide to pounce after all."

She expected she would. It was an old habit, in suspension these last many years but rearing to life again.

When she returned with the leash, he attached it and led the unprotesting Malvolio to the door. "Good night, Gypsy. I'll try not to wake you when I come back. But if you find yourself preferring the man to the monk, by all means give me a shake."

Chapter 10

Morning entered the bedchamber with a pale shaft of light that slowly made its way from the foot of Jarrett's bed to his eyes. With a groan, he let them open and looked over to the rumpled covers where Kate had been sleeping. She wasn't there now.

He was shivering on top of the counterpane with a single blanket covering his goose-bumpy flesh. On a typical morning after a dissipated night, he'd have dived under the covers and slept until the air was warmer and the world a more welcoming place. But today a gruesome fate awaited him. It was probably on its way at this very moment, because he had invited it.

The climb. In last night's champagne-fuzzy state, fell walking had seemed a good idea for several reasons he couldn't now recall. But in the cold light of actually having to do it, he didn't want to.

Cursing himself, he staggered upright, pulled on a dressing gown, and padded on slippered feet into the sitting room, wishing a cup of hot tea would materialize in his hands. His tongue felt as if he'd spent the night licking sheep. But there was no tea, nor fire, nor breakfast waiting for him.

No Kate, either, and the dog had gone missing as

well. He went to the window and gazed blankly into the pale dawn. Once he got over the shock of it, perhaps a walk in the frigid air would blast the cobwebs out of his head. And he wanted to assure himself the Gypsy hadn't run off.

What he wanted even more was to spend the entire day in bed with her. Which would be, he had no doubt, at the very bottom of any list she might put together. Her pride had locked in, and despite the undeniable attraction humming between them, nothing was likely to change until he compelled it.

Dragging her up a hill was hardly his best seduction plot, but he'd set the plan in motion and couldn't very well cancel it now. Kate, already resentful of his authority, would pounce on the smallest sign of weakness like a dog on a pork chop. And, too, there was some advantage to removing themselves from Carrington's scrutiny while they plotted strategy. Not a bad idea, that, and it seemed familiar. Maybe that was the reason he'd called for the climbing in the first place.

Feeling more sensible than he probably was, he went through the French windows that led to the terrace, wrapped his arms around himself against the damp air, and looked out through the break in the trees to the lake. A low mist hovered over the smooth water. The rising sun streaked the pale blue morning with apricot, pink, and gold, colors he never saw in the grubby London sky.

Near the shoreline, the dog bounded out of the woods, streaked across the open space, and disappeared into the trees again. No barking, Jarrett couldn't help but notice. Either the dog had got used to his company, or it couldn't be relied on to sound a warning.

Kate must be in the vicinity. Jarrett set out for water's edge, enjoying the scent of wet leaves and the feel of springy moss under his feet. Birds chirped from the tree branches. Flowers were opening practically before his eyes.

And then a dark shape appeared in the water, rising up like a specter.

Like a witch.

He came to a halt, stepped sideways into the trees, found a sight line, and looked out at the figure emerging from the lake.

Kate had been for a swim. When her feet found purchase on the lake bottom, she stood and walked toward the shore, disclosing a little more of herself with each step. Mist swirled around her like gauze, reminding him of the way he had first seen her in the theater, separated from the audience by a screen. This time, nature was her protector.

He would honor it, and respect her solitude.

But neither could he turn away. She was like a character materializing from the old myths, born of the sun's rays and the water, her chemise clinging transparent to her perfect form. She paused, the stirred water lapping at her thighs, and gathered her wet, tangled hair between both hands to wring it out. Then she let it go and shook her head, sending droplets like a spray of gold to form a nimbus around her.

He wasn't sure any longer what he was seeing. A vision from a dream, perhaps. Nothing he could claim or hold on to. A lonely woman, isolated by her beauty and her iron will, on some sort of crusade in which he, for his sins, had been enlisted to carry a spear.

Or perhaps more than that. Whatever his Gypsy's real name, whatever her reasons for being here, she had walked out of the lake and, astonishingly, into his protection.

The decision, made without conscious thought, felt

absolutely right. Irrevocable. On the bones of the defenseless women who had died in Herne Water, he took a silent oath that for so long as she was in danger, he would make her safety the grail of his own crusade.

He remained a few moments longer, sealing the lady of the lake in his memory. Then, taking care not to be seen, he went back through the trees and was in the cottage, shaving, when she arrived.

The dog came with her, barking, and shortly after a pony trap pulled up with a servant and Mrs. Kipper aboard. Kate, still wet and wrapped in a pelisse, flounced into the bedchamber and asked for privacy while she dressed.

Gathering up his bowl of cold water, bar of soap, mirror, and razor, he went into the sitting room in time to admit the servants. As crusades went, this one was not featuring him as a knightly hero.

"We won't be going to the Roman fort at Hard Knott after all," said Mr. John Gilliam, arriving at the spot near the yacht's capstan where Kate and His Arrogance had taken refuge from the other climbers.

He was a nice enough young man, and she resented Dering for taking advantage of him at the gaming tables. Why not target someone who deserved a little bad fortune? But of course, Dering's sole concern was for himself, when he was sober enough to concentrate at all. At least he'd had the kindness to pass out on the bed last night, not stirring even when she left him to take her swim.

"One hill is much like another," Dering said with a shrug. "All I ask is a tavern at the top. Or at the bottom, where I can stay while the rest of you exert yourselves."

"Lord Parton is an avid climber," said Mr. Gilliam, "and business is calling him away tomorrow. He doesn't want to leave without ascending Sca Fell Peak."

Kate gasped. "That's the highest mountain in England."

"Not by much, really," Mr. Gilliam said. "I've been up once, by a far more difficult route than we'll use today, and it wasn't so bad. We're taking the easier ascent because the weather is uncertain, but you needn't join us. Most of the others will turn back if the going gets rough, and there are plenty of servants to escort them down again."

"Well, I've no doubt the Gypsy could romp right up to the summit, but I am an indolent fellow." Dering turned to Kate. "Let's just stay on the boat, shall we, until it brings us back to Paradise? Then home to bed."

Her stomach tightened. She didn't wish to climb—far from it—but the alternative was far more hazardous. She tried to look humble. "I shall never have another chance, my lord, to stand atop all England."

"If you mean to climb, Dering, I wish you will exchange your belt for this one. It's a good deal more substantial, with proper fittings, and I've had years of experience—"

"While I am likely to fall. If you wish, Gilliam. You know I have a vested interest in pleasing you."

They both laughed, which made no sense to Kate. And neither of them was the least concerned about her own belt, which was too large and had no metal devices for attaching lines. Not that she minded. Her dislike of edges would keep her as far from them as possible.

A line of pony carts waited near the dock to convey

the climbers, eighteen in all counting the guide and servants, to the place where they were to begin their ascent. It seemed unfair that she would have to wrestle with skirts when she had a usable, if scandalous, pair of trousers better suited for climbing. At least her sturdy half boots had been designed for rough terrain. Itinerant players did a lot of walking, what with most of the space in the caravan wagons taken up with props, scenery, and costumes. Like all the members of the company, she helped with packing and lifting, which had given her more physical strength than most females possessed. Dancing helped as well, and she expected no difficulty keeping up with the gentlemen.

It was easy going for the first two hours, with stone bridges to take them across the rushing streams, and wide, rock-strewn paths that required a degree of alertness or she would trip herself up, as did one of the servants. The wind, flowing in from the Irish Sea not far to the west, had a chill on it in spite of the late-morning sunshine. Clouds, white at first but increasingly tinged with gray, scudded overhead.

Three keen mountaineers had moved ahead, determined to reach the peak before bad weather forced them to leave the fell. The guide, Mr. Cobbe, paused frequently to examine the landscape with his spyglass, and once, when she chanced to be close by, he offered her a look. "Each dale has its own weather," he said. "A storm can be just the other side of where you are, especially this year. A volcanic eruption, so they say, has changed the climate for the worst."

She had read of it, and later Mr. Gilliam told her more as they walked side by side. He also explained the geological formations, the colors—red, pink, and green—and how they came to be, the minerals mined in the area, all with the fervor of a lover describing his lady. She wondered at the vivid contrasts of scenery, the commons where sheep were brought to graze, the craggy peaks and deep chasms, the razor-edged ridges like the one they were not going to cross, the buttresses and ghylls and long slopes covered with broken rocks. *Scree,* he called it.

After a short rest and refreshments laid out by the servants, they struck out across a high sheepwalk and from there onto the prow of a ridge. The path was wide enough, but Kate's fingers dug into her skirts as she lifted them. This close to an edge, she abandoned her enjoyment of the scenery and kept her gaze on the next place she would step. Sometimes she thought about Dering, who had left her to herself since the ride in the pony cart. He walked in a group of gentlemen who appeared to be wagering on how many sheep would be around the next curve, or which of their party would first spot a golden eagle.

"I don't care for that sky," said Mr. Gilliam.

She glanced up to see a roiling mass of clouds. And as if it had been waiting for its target, a fat raindrop splatted on her forehead. Others quickly followed, sending up little clouds of dust from the path, creating black splotches on the gray rocks. She glanced over her shoulder. The others had stopped perhaps twenty-five yards away, where servants were unpacking squares of oilcloth. Each had a hole in the center for a head to go through, and there were floppy-brimmed oilcloth hats as well, in bright colors for visibility.

"We'll go back now," Mr. Gilliam said. "The guide must surely insist. But I had hoped we would make it far enough to ascend Lord's Rake."

Two servants approached and helped them don the oilcloth and hats before going on to fetch the gentlemen who'd got ahead of the party. The beautiful day was over, and now they all faced a long walk in the rain. And the wind. It whipped at her clothing, snapping the oilcloth, twisting her skirts around her legs.

A shout from behind her. Whirling, she saw a man just fallen from the overhang. He hit the scree-strewn ground about ten feet below and slid, along with an avalanche of rocks, toward a precipice. But just at the edge, where the ground sloped a little upward like a shallow saucer, the man and the rocks beneath him ceased rolling as though an invisible hand had lifted to prevent him from going over. To his right and left the landslide continued, the rocks slickened with rainwater washing down and sweeping off into the chasm.

The man hadn't yet donned the oilcloth before he fell, and even with rain pelting her face, she could make out the rich brown of his leather climbing jacket. But she had already known it was Dering.

Mr. Gilliam dashed back to where the other men stood, shouting as he ran. "Don't move, Dering! Don't move! Don't move!"

She could not take her eyes from the limp figure sprawled inches from certain death. He lay on his side facing cliff's edge, immobile. Perhaps unconscious. Perhaps dead. He'd landed on stones. The wind lifted his hair, teased at his coat, created the illusion of life.

She wanted him to move, if only a finger. But he was, after all, a useless man, a care-for-nothing. Who would miss him? Only the people he owed money to.

Not her, to be sure. She would work better on her own.

It wasn't that she wished him ill. But there he was, and what could be done for him? Surely, if he must fall, it was better that he be unconscious. Better yet that he be already dead.

Her thoughts changing direction like the winds, she

made her way to the men, most of them silently looking down at Lord Dering. Mr. Cobbe and Mr. Gilliam spoke rapidly together, but she couldn't hear what they said. Then Mr. Cobbe began issuing orders, and three of the servants took off at a run. The other four pulled coiled ropes from wicker baskets.

Mr. Gilliam turned to her. "Cobbe has sent for a physician, and for men with a litter, and for transportation to be waiting. Also for a shepherd who lives not far away. He knows, better than anyone, how to conduct a rescue on the fells. I'm going down to see if I can reach Dering, but I doubt it will be possible. At the least, I'll come close enough that if he starts to go over, I can toss him a rope. There is little else we can do for now."

While he was talking, Mr. Cobbe had attached two ropes to his belt and given the other ends to a pair of servants. Mr. Gilliam draped a coiled rope over his shoulder and led them to a spot about twenty feet away, where the overhang was narrowest. The servants lowered him over the side.

No sooner had his feet touched ground than the dislodged rocks began another landslide. He waited until it subsided before picking his way slowly along the path the rocks had taken, parallel to where Dering had fallen.

She couldn't bear to watch, could not stop looking.

"Don't move!" Mr. Gilliam called again. "If you feel the ground going out from under you, shout and I'll throw the rope."

From Dering, not the slightest response.

She crouched down, arms wrapped around her knees, watching the rocks where Dering lay. If they moved, if she saw them move, she could call to Mr. Gilliam. Dering might be unable to do so. But in that case, neither could he catch the rope and hold on to it. *Dear God.*

After some time, she couldn't guess how long, a barrel-shaped, bearded man in a sleeveless coat made of patched-together sheepskins came along the path, followed by two of the servants. They were carrying what appeared to be the vertically sawn half of a long, straight tree trunk. At each end, two spikes had been affixed. She couldn't imagine how it might be of use. Rising, not wanting to interfere, she drew as close as she could to learn what they were planning.

Whatever it was, they all found reason to turn and look at her at the same time.

Clearing his throat, Mr. Cobbe stepped forward. "Miss . . . I do not know your name, ma'am. But I am told you are . . . that is, you belong in some fashion to Lord Dering. May I present Tom Brumby, who has a plan that might succeed if you are willing to help us."

"Of course," she said, knowing she would eventually agree no matter what it was. Expiation took many forms.

Tom Brumby, bluff and practical, set his plan in motion even as he described it. The log, flat side up, was anchored to the path by pounding down one set of the spikes and by asking the four heaviest gentlemen to sit on the land-side end. About eight feet of the log hung out over the ridge, directly above where Dering lay. He was more than twenty feet below and a little way beyond the end of the log. Beyond reach, it seemed to Kate.

But Mr. Cobbe was already removing her oilcloth cloak, and then her belt. In its place he wrapped a wide canvas sling. "They use these to lift animals," he said. "I hope you will not be terribly uncomfortable.

From the top, we shall keep weight on the log and work the ropes to lower and raise you. With luck, to raise Lord Dering as well. We'd not have asked you do this, but you are not so heavy as the rest of us, and Gilliam, who is also light, is making himself of use where he is."

"I don't mind," she assured him, her heart pumping with fear. Over the edge, dangling midair. She had never swooned, but if she were ever to do so, these would be the circumstances.

She'd thought they were to send her down straightaway, but Mr. Cobbe took a long time making sure she understood how to work the clamps, and how to attach them to the metal loops on Dering's belt. Her hands were strong, but even her kidskin gloves could find little traction on the metal. The clamps were difficult to wrench open long enough to hook them to anything. She practiced on Mr. Cobbe's belt with infrequent success, and finally decided her hands might seize up if she continued. Better she preserve her remaining strength for when it counted.

There was also a heavy rope with a noose for her to carry. Once she had secured Dering with the clamps, she was to spread the loop and try to thread it over his head and arms until it was wrapped around his chest.

At last, Mr. Cobbe judged her ready for the descent.

She wasn't at all confident of that, especially when she was directed to crawl out on the log, taking care not to get her skirts hung up on the spikes, and sit on the very end. Tom Brumby would direct her from there.

She looked up into the shepherd's brown, sympathetic eyes. "It'll keep well enough," he said. "We use the logs to cross becks when they be running fast. I'll have hold of the lines to your sling. We'll not let you fall, m'lady."

"Thank you," she said, knees shaking as she stepped up onto the log.

"Miss?" It was Mr. Cobbe. "If he's . . . if there is no reason . . . wave your arm and we will pull you up. The winds are growing fierce. Do not risk yourself unnecessarily."

If he is dead. But she didn't say it, couldn't face it. Nodding, she practically rushed to the end of the log, sat herself down, and felt two enormous hands at her waist.

"I'll upend ye now, m'lady. You're to go down face-first. Remember what Cobbe told ye. Try not to move, because it will set you swinging and ye'll hit the cliff. But swing if you must, only a bit, to reach him. If he be conscious, give him the noose to hold while you work the clamps, unless he would have to move overmuch. Aye . . . call it as ye will. He'll be in your hands now, as you be in mine."

And with that, she was suddenly suspended midair.

The wind caught her and her skirts. She reacted by flailing, and next thing, she hit hard against the side of the cliff. Rain beat against her head and face. She had to close her eyes, force herself to go limp until the swinging subsided. Then she felt the slight jolt each time Tom Brumby let go a bit of the rope. On her way again. She risked swiping her face against her shoulder, the one without the rope slung around it, to clear her eyes of rainwater.

When she opened them, she was only a few feet off the ground. The slope had looked greater from above. In fact, Dering lay almost directly beneath her, limp and unmoving, so close to the edge that one bent knee stuck out over the cliff. She dared not look beyond that, to the emptiness.

Instead, she held as quietly as she could and tried to tell if she had come to him too late. Mostly she could see a hunched shoulder, clumps of wet, matted hair, and long limbs precariously balanced among stones with rivulets of water undermining the soil beneath them. At any time, the stones could let go and carry him over.

Was he breathing? She couldn't tell because of the wind. Rain pounded against his heavy jacket. His left arm was thrown forward, and the jacket had got twisted during his roll down the hill, exposing a small section of his belt. She saw one of the metal hooks. If she could secure the clamp on it, the rope would hold him long enough for her to finish the job.

Each careful motion caused her to swing as she withdrew one of the rope ends from where Mr. Cobbe had attached it. Then she scrunched forward in the sling, tilting her body at a downward angle. Tom Brumby let her slowly drop another foot. Any closer and one of the ropes she carried might brush against Dering. Or one of her limbs could strike him, if the wind kept buffeting her as it was.

"The Angel of Death, I presume."

His voice, soft and thready, startled her into a wild rocking motion. When it subsided, she glared at the side of his face and the one eye, now open, that she could see. "A tempting thought," she told him. "But there are too many witnesses. Don't move."

"Yes, I've taken that message."

She'd forgotten the noose. *Damn.* She stowed the rope with the clamp between her thighs and unwrapped the rope from around her shoulder. "I will put a lifeline near your hand, if the wind doesn't take it off. Should you start to slide again, grab hold of it. I'm going to try to hook a clamp to your belt. Are you injured? Broken bones?"

"I don't know. Can't move to test them out."

All the gear she was carrying weighed her down, and with the wide cinch pressing on her lower chest and belly, she was having trouble drawing breath. She managed to place the noosed end of the rope within his reach and retrieved the rope she had stashed between her legs. Now for the hard part.

As they had done when practicing, her fingers kept slipping whenever she tried to open the clamp. If she managed that much, she couldn't keep it open long enough to slip it over the U-shaped hook protruding from his belt. She tried and failed again and again.

"You shock me, Miss Kate. Where did you learn such language?"

She hadn't realized she was muttering aloud. "From rakes and wastrels," she snapped. Did he not understand the danger— Ah! There! The distraction he'd provided, or perhaps good fortune, had turned the trick. The clamp was secured. Her eyes burned with tears of relief as she wrestled to pull loose his jacket from the rest of his belt.

"Whoa!" He seized the noose with both hands. "The rocks beneath me are itching to travel."

She found the other hook by touch and applied her dwindling strength to the clamp. It seemed forever before it caught, and then it did, with a satisfying clank.

Rain hammered against her back, streamed down her face and arms, washed over the man lying beneath her. She looked at him, at his face now turned to her, at the curve of his lips. At the dark streaks mingling with the rainwater.

"There is blood, sir."

"The stones objected to my head bashing against them. It's as well. Listen carefully."

Conversation *now*? Was he mad? The bleeding must be stanched. They must lift him out immediately and tend to his wounds. "Give me the noose, sir. We must widen it and pass the rope around your chest."

"I can do that." He took the noose between both hands and expanded it. "Listen to me. I'm telling you this because there is yet another charade for us to play. While it lasts, you must keep your eyes and ears open. And tell no one."

The men holding the other ends of the ropes she had been carrying had tightened them. Lord Dering was in their grasp now. Mr. Gilliam, seeing it, had begun making his way over the unstable ground to be of help.

"Safe and sound, my angel," Dering said. "I hope you'll not regret saving me today. And now you must go." He waved an arm and pointed at her. Almost immediately Tom Brumby began drawing her up.

"But what am I not to tell?"

"Shhh. Not even Gilliam must know. This wasn't an accident, Kate. I was pushed."

Chapter 11

A clicking sound, soothingly regular, penetrated the fog in Dering's head. He had been floating in and out of sleep, or of consciousness, for what seemed a year. The *out* intervals had not been pleasant, as he recalled. That was about all he did recall, but since he appeared to be in a bed at the moment, someone must have fetched him down from Sca Fell Pike.

He remembered trying to walk. Insisting on it. But somewhere along the way, he awoke in a litter being carried by a large man wearing a sheep. And another man in back, he supposed, holding up the other end. Oh, and there had been a vehicle of some sort, not well sprung. It had bounced and swayed, shocking him from intervals of pleasant oblivion into longer intervals of being poked at by devils with pitchforks.

This was the first time he'd awakened and not felt as if he was moving. And before now there had been no clicking. He wondered if it was worth opening his eyes to find out what caused it. Perhaps later, when the horse stopped kicking the side of his head.

A long time later, or it might have been a few minutes, he wandered out of the fog again. The clicking persisted, and he thought this time he'd discover the source. But first there was himself to contend with. Most of him hurt, some bits more than others. Already aware his head hurt worst of all, he started his inventory with his toes, checking for the ability to move them, testing for the feel of bandages or splints as he advanced upward.

Pain with the slightest motion, but nothing that couldn't be accounted for by a fall onto rocks.

Needle. He remembered someone sewing up his forehead, just above the temple.

Buttery sheets against naked flesh. Nothing restraining him except his unwillingness to move.

He told his eyes to open, and kept telling them that, and after a time, they did.

He was looking up at the wooden canopy over his bed at the cottage. The room was mostly dark, except for a circle of golden light to his left.

His heart gave a small jump of anticipation. Kate. All he had to do was turn his head, and he would see her. His angel of death and salvation. The witch from the lake.

In a moment of acute clarity, he realized that for the better part of a decade, he wouldn't have greatly minded a plunge over a cliff. Even while he had been holding himself motionless on the rim, fairly sure he was experiencing the last moments of his life, he had felt nothing. A sense of inevitability, perhaps. Salvation ought to be reserved for better men than Jarrett Dering. But now he was wildly glad to be alive for at least another day or two, because he'd be spending that time in company with the most fascinating creature he'd ever met.

Definitely worth turning his head for, in spite of that horse still kicking at it. The slight motion felt like trying to push a boulder, but at last he could see the woman seated on the chair beside his bed, her smooth, pudgy hands twisting yarn around a pair of long knitting needles. Mrs. Kipper.

She looked back at him, her expression placid. "Good evening, my lord. How are you feeling?"

"I cannot answer that in language fit for a lady," he said, wincing at the sound of his voice in his ears. "There was a doctor, I believe. What was his verdict?"

"Nothing broken. Left ankle strained a bit. Mild concussion. Assorted cuts, the one on your temple requiring to be stitched up. You are like to feel as if cattle had stampeded over you, but he thinks no permanent damage has been done." She smiled. "We are all greatly relieved."

"No more than I. But we're left with the fact that anything I might be able to accomplish must be done before Saturday, and I don't expect I'll wish to move between now and then."

"You'll not be required to. As soon as it can be arranged, we'll see you comfortably transported to London, or wherever you wish to go."

"I am to leave Paradise? Am I not meant to mingle and observe? Perhaps I won't feel up to the sporting events, but drinking, gaming, and selected debaucheries are surely within my power. I practically do those things by rote."

"Nonetheless, you have been found out. There is nothing more you can do, except to free us of concern for your safety. It would be of use, though, to learn how your purpose was disclosed. Has anyone quizzed you, or regarded you with untoward suspicion?"

"It has seemed to me, from the first, that everyone knew exactly why I had come here. But I have no reason, beyond my own uneasiness, to believe that to be true. Why do you assume otherwise?"

"Because you were pushed off the cliff. Or did you imagine that?"

He should have realized Kate would pass on the information. "Two hands thrust hard against the small of my back, low enough that the movement would not have been noticed. I nearly caught my balance, but then a boot swiped against my leg and I was gone. There is no mistaking what occurred. And no, I did not see who it was. A group of us—climbers and servants—had gathered around while rain cloaks and hats were being distributed. Cobbe, the guide, was announcing that we would turn back. I looked to see where Kate and Gilliam had got to, and that's when I was pushed. Except for Cobbe and one or two others standing near him, the culprit could have been anyone in the group."

"Kate has provided the names of the climbers and described the servants. Had you a quarrel with any of them?"

"Save for John Gilliam, I was unacquainted with the gentlemen before we met on the yacht. They seemed decent enough fellows. The servants I paid no attention to. In any case, we can't be sure that anyone associated with Paradise knows of my intentions here. The attempt on my life was almost surely personal, and I expect I know who set the plan in motion. Although how such a thing could be arranged on short notice—"

"Oh, that is simple enough." The knitting needles had stilled. "Do you suspect the gentleman you asked me about, the Comte d'Arvaine?"

"The female who accompanied him. She has long wished me to the devil. While I continue living, she remains plain Mrs. Dering, and should I ever decide to marry, her own sons stand to be pushed back in the line of succession."

"The lady is your brother's wife? What a troublesome complication."

"So I thought at the time. But she was here for only one night. Is it so simple a matter, in Paradise, to arrange a murder?"

"We believe such arrangements have been made on several occasions, although the inquests invariably ruled death by accident or misadventure. There are five such cases we know of. Was Mrs. Dering informed you would be coming here?"

"Not by me. Since I left Dorset we have spoken only once, and that was about five years ago. I take it you, like every man, woman, and hedgehog in England, are acquainted with my family history?"

She nodded. "So it was pure coincidence, the two of you here at the same time? That seems unlikely."

"To me as well, but such things happen. I know that given the chance to explore Paradise, she would leap at it."

"D'Arvaine is a frequent guest," Mrs. Kipper said thoughtfully. "He is known to break his journey here for a night or two when he travels, and since Paradise opened its gates, he has on seven occasions spent longer periods of time in residence. But Kate will tell you more about that. Is there anyone else we should be considering?"

The icy-eyed Duke of Sarne popped into his thoughts. "I have run afoul of jealous husbands from time to time. Perhaps one of them seized the opportunity to repay me. In any case, this event changes nothing. I have no intention of abandoning the field."

"That is your decision to make, my lord. But we cannot protect you."

"I understand." He let his head roll back on the

pillow and stared again at the dark canopy above him. Like a starless night, it seemed to capture his life and show it back to him, blank and empty of meaning. "Kate must leave," he said, with more difficulty than he could remember saying anything, ever. "She will not be safe in my company or even in my vicinity. Will you make arrangements for her to go? Today, if possible."

"It is well after midnight," said Mrs. Kipper, rising. "And the decision will be hers. If you can rise, I believe you would do well to immerse yourself in hot water infused with salts. Shall I order the bath for you? And a meal?"

"Yes." God, he would have to move. But there was little time left for him to accomplish his purposes. Almost none. "Thank you."

"I've brought pistols, one for each of you, and a walking stick, which no one will be surprised to see you employ. It holds a blade." At the door, she paused and turned. "Even if Kate goes, I shall remain to be of what help I can. It won't be the same, I know, but the choice must be hers. Don't bully the girl."

He was thinking more along the lines of pleading. But that would be a form of bullying, he supposed. He wanted her safe, which meant wanting her gone, and he'd hoped that Mrs. Kipper would arrange it before he was tempted to be selfish. He let his eyes drift shut. Nothing ever came easily, did it?

When the servants arrived with a large copper tub and a wagonload of kettles filled with steaming water, Kate put the yapping Malvolio on his leash and led him onto the terrace. The storm had blown through not long after sunset, leaving behind a winter-cold night. She tugged the quilted dressing gown more closely around the flannel night rail she wore beneath it.

After the long, rain-drenched walk down Sca Fell Pike, she had thought she would never again be warm. Servants had brought wood to the cottage and built a fire, and once Lord Dering was settled in his bed and everyone but Mrs. Kipper had left, she'd curled up on the fur rugs by the hearth and fallen almost immediately asleep.

Now she must decide whether to go or stay. While they were waiting for servants to respond to the raised lantern, Mrs. Kipper had given her a good idea of what to expect. Males often found it difficult, she had said, to abandon a battlefield even when the war was lost. Females usually had better sense, and Kate must not consider staying from pride or obligation. Better she clear the field for another effort by Black Phoenix.

In her way, Mrs. Kipper was hard as the spikes in Tom Brumby's log. Kate had always thought the same about herself, but just lately, weaknesses were sprouting from every vulnerable spot she had. There appeared to be a great many of them, including the one that had created all her real troubles—her susceptibility to handsome, charming men who made her treasonous flesh go on fire.

As it was right now, merely from the prospect of imagining Lord Dering in his bath. To her own chagrin, she had deliberately chosen a position where she could watch him emerge from the bedchamber and take his place in the copper tub. But she hadn't accounted for the steam. As the servants carried container after container of hot water from the wagon to the tub, the window glass began to fog over.

Just as well. She had no right to intrude on his

privacy. Then again, if she was expected to accept him as a lover, she deserved an advance look—wouldn't you think?—at the goods.

Or perhaps she just wanted to make sure he was all in one piece. What she had seen when suspended over him, and later, when he was being transported here, had not looked promising. He'd rarely been conscious, and never lucid.

Through the misted French windows she saw three blurred figures, two of them clad in Paradise's maroon livery supporting a figure clad in nothing at all. Although she could see little, she had no difficulty following their movements. Soon Lord Dering was settled in the tub, and not long after, one of the servants opened the French window and stepped outside.

Malvolio lunged in his direction.

The young man leaped back inside and pulled the window nearly closed. "I beg your pardon," he said, somewhat breathlessly, "but we are departing now. Within a short time a hot supper will be delivered. Mrs. Kipper is leaving with us. She asked that you tend to his lordship."

He immediately closed the window the rest of the way, probably unwilling to deal with the possibility of a refusal.

She stayed on the other side of that closed window until the others had left, probably unwilling to deal with Lord Dering clothed in nothing but hot water.

But it was cold where she was, and warm where he was. Grumbling under her breath, she slipped inside, let Malvolio off his leash, and finally brought herself to look in the direction of the fireplace and the copper tub.

Again, clouds of steam obscured her vision. The tub was perhaps five feet long, with high sides and a pillowed headrest. She could see Dering's hair and the bandage on his forehead, held in place with a gauze wrapping. And the tops of his bent knees, and his upper arms, which were resting on the curved rim of the tub. He was utterly still.

"Is there something you wish done for you?" she said, more harshly than she'd intended.

A chuckle, annoying her even as it assured her he hadn't gone faint again. "You may be sure there is. But we won't want to be interrupted by servants bearing sandwiches. Come talk with me, Kate. We seem rarely to be alone together."

"I can talk from here."

"Don't be obstinate, my dear. Pleasurable as they were, we have been catapulted beyond the games we had been playing. It is time for plain speaking, and that is best done face-to-face."

"You will tell me to leave," she said, slumping in the direction of the hearth and settling herself on a sheepskin rug. From this angle, she could see only his upper arms, shoulders, and head. Safe enough, one might have thought.

"Yes. For everyone's sake, you must go." He made a little sound, suspiciously like a sigh. "Be sure this is not what I would have wanted. But it seems that someone unconnected to the mission is making use of Paradise's more disconcerting resources to eliminate me. You mustn't be in the way."

"Don't worry," she said. "I'll be to one side, pointing to where you are."

He started to laugh, brought one hand to his head with a groan. "Sorry. Your company makes me forget how rotten I feel. Mrs. Kipper believes that under the circumstances, neither of us can be effective. I know you have felt an obligation to this mission, Kate, but that is now lifted from you. You can best serve by leaving. Will you consent to do so?"

The mist had dissipated. She could see him clearly now. The gray-green eyes framed with long, water-clumped lashes, the tousled wet hair, the serious expression on a face lined with weariness and pain. "Of course not," she said. "How could you think I would even consider it?"

Another groan, this one sheer theatrics. "Why do females never understand when a battle has been lost? When it is time to leave the field? You are always trying to prove something."

She nearly laughed, hearing the backward echo of what Mrs. Kipper had told her. "I doubt you have the slightest idea of what is going on here, or what our mission truly is. What use would you be without me? You couldn't even get into that tub without assistance."

"Oh-ho. So you were watching, were you?" He grinned. "Are you impressed?"

"With what?" She felt like a drop of water landing on a griddle. "I saw the servants practically carry you in. Then I walked Malvolio into the woods and waited while he relieved himself. Don't tell me I missed something spectacular?"

"Not tonight, I fear." His eyes shone with amusement. "But before you take a decision your pride will not allow you to withdraw, consider this. If you remain, your life will be in constant danger from sources no one anticipated until the events of this morning. That is over and above the threats we accepted by coming here."

"Yes, yes. All that is perfectly clear."

"The risk of death may not trouble you, but I wonder if you have yet resigned yourself to what will be required if we proceed. We cannot remain at odds, unless we are staging a public scene. Because we are under intense scrutiny, we must become what we are pretending to be. There is no time for leisurely seduction, flirtatious rejections, mistrust, or anger that should properly be directed elsewhere."

"I doubt anger can be banished, my lord. It is entrenched in my character."

"Oh, feel free to sharpen your claws on me. I've got used to it. How is it you came to be part of this, anyway? A letter out of the blue? A meeting at a chophouse?"

She wrapped her arms around her knees. "I was on tour with a theater company, and when our seamstress abruptly resigned, Mrs. Kipper was hired to replace her. Later I learned that had all been prearranged. She sought my company rather too often, but I couldn't help liking her. After a fortnight she asked if I would agree to keep a secret, no matter what I thought of the subject or how I chose to respond. I gave her my promise, and she gave me a letter."

" 'You are summoned,' " he said.

"That is how it began. Mrs. Kipper was to explain the task and direct the next stages of the operation. They are exceedingly well organized, Black Phoenix. Once she had assured herself that I was a good candidate, which she said she'd done straightaway, plans were laid as if I had already consented. Not long after, we played out my quarrel with the manager of the company, and I was offered a position here. Then I waited for your arrival."

"And what a disappointment I have proven to be. Why did you accept the invitation?"

"That, my lord, is none of your concern. It is past time that we discuss what is known about Paradise and devise some means to gather evidence. If you truly mean to leave on Saturday—"

"I do. But so that potential murderers don't go hurrying up their plans, let's keep my imminent departure to ourselves. Meantime, on the chance you will reward me for good behavior, I shall force myself to concentrate."

At last. She rose and went to Malvolio's basket, lifted the false bottom, and removed a sheaf of papers. The coded information, mostly lists of names and dates, was to be destroyed after she had made Dering familiar with it, but she had not anticipated having this conversation with a wet, bare male. This was serious business, and he was immensely distracting.

Keeping her gaze on the papers, she returned to the rugs and sat cross-legged. "I shall give you the general picture first and then reply, if I can, to your questions. One subject—murder for hire—you have briefly discussed with Mrs. Kipper. Of the five deaths that occurred while the victim was a guest at Paradise, two were shot while hunting, one drowned when his sailboat capsized, one fell off his horse during an improvised race, and one fell into a quarry."

"These are not uncommon accidents," he said, "when gentlemen engage in sporting activities. Here, where they are likely to be drunk or suffering the aftereffects of being drunk, one would expect more than the usual number of mishaps."

"There have been more accidents than the five I mentioned, not all of them fatal. Phoenix examined only those incidents where a motive could be inferred, in most cases an inheritance at stake. In two of them, a title as well. One gentleman, the one who stumbled into the quarry, had accumulated a number of enemies who might pay to have him eliminated. Naturally, Paradise does not openly advertise this service, but Phoenix is persuaded they offer it."

"But only, I expect, to regular customers trusted

by . . . well, by the owner, don't you think? The staff wouldn't let just anyone rent a killer."

"I doubt most of them know anything of this," she said. "In my time here, I've observed that the servants are much like servants everywhere, average people busy earning their wages, gossiping about the peculiarities of their superiors, and hoping for advancement."

"While the guests," he said, "are the same chaps I'm likely to meet in a London ballroom, a gentleman's club, or a gaming hell. They come here to escape their domestic trials, indulge their weaknesses, and enjoy the sports. In great part, they come because it is the fashionable place to be seen. Wives and families may not regard Paradise as harmless, but it seems that way to me."

"Excepting the murders."

"Unless they are, as the authorities have deemed, accidents. This will seem heresy to you, but I think Black Phoenix is speculating on remarkably flimsy evidence."

"And investing a great deal in the search for more reliable evidence."

"Ah, yes. The money. It passed from my thoughts almost as fast as it slipped through my fingers. Very well, then. What else besides the murder scheme? We are not, I take it, delegated to punish moral turpitude."

"The other matter of speculation is less easy to explain. You mentioned, when we were talking about Mr. Coleridge's poem, that Lord Byron spoke of reincarnating the Hellfire Club. Phoenix believes that something of the kind has occurred here, and that a select group of gentlemen gathers several times a year for secret rites that include . . ."

She could not bring herself to say it. With no illusions about the cruelty human beings could inflict on one another, she still found it difficult to accept what Mrs. Kipper had told her.

"Kate?" Concern in his voice, surprising her. "I take it this goes beyond the usual costumes and orgies. You needn't be specific."

"Children," she said quietly. "They use them in sacrificial rites. Perhaps. There is no proof. One boy was found dead on the property, apparently of drowning, but no one came forward to identify him. He was buried in a paupers' field near Lancaster, and Phoenix later saw to it the body was examined. There were indications he had been tightly bound. Little enough, I know. Authorities in Lancashire, Cumberland, and Westmoreland have been questioned about the disappearance of local children, but that trail led nowhere."

"One unknown dead boy, no missing children . . . is this all?"

"Records of guests and the dates of their visits have been examined by the other Black Phoenix emissary. I don't know his identity, but his job is to make certain that incoming guests find everything arranged according to their preferences. He noted that several gentlemen, ten or twelve of them, come together in the spring, summer, autumn, and winter, always at the time of the solstices and equinoxes. Seven of them are here now, and the summer solstice is Friday night."

"I gather we were sent to discover what, if anything, these gentlemen get up to when they meet. May I have their names? Carrington for one, I would guess."

"Yes." She knew the names by heart. One was Lord Sheffer, who had so nearly bought her services. Another regular participant, although not here at present, was the Frenchman who had interested Lord Dering.

When she'd listed them, Dering was silent for a time. "At least four rotters," he finally said, "counting

D'Arvaine, and I'm including him only because of the company he recently kept. Two of the others are inconsequential, except for their wealth and a tendency to toad-eat. Three are men I have encountered from time to time, not always in high places. The others are unknown to me. So what do you think, Kate? Assuming they mean to gather for perfidious rites, am I supposed to get myself invited?"

"Do you think you can?"

"In fact, I'm thinking that Carrington has been evaluating my suitability. Little else explains his interest in my sexual practices, which—now I think of it— began when someone mentioned my rather public affair with the wife of a dangerous man."

"The Duke of Sarne."

"I forget how much you know of me, which seems damnably unfair when I know nothing about you. But yes, Carrington came to attention when he heard I had defied Sarne for no better reason than to bed a female. I later concluded that was the reason he took a role in the auction. He is interested in power, and wishes to discover how far I will go to bend a woman to my will. Or so I had thought, but obviously the situation is more complex than I had imagined. Especially since one of their company may have paid to have me pushed off a mountain."

"It seems unlikely they'll welcome you," she said, discouraged. "Unless they decide you'd make a good sacrifice."

"Not my first choice of plans, but we'll keep it in reserve." He stretched his arms overhead, wincing at the results. "In fact, about all I can do is make myself visible, available, and patently bored with the usual fare of entertainment. Not easy to make that convincing, being—as I am—in possession of you."

"A mere woman, of no account whatever, any one of us being much the same as the others. Isn't that what Carrington said?"

"Something of the kind. He may be right."

She shot Dering the glare he must have been expecting, because his smile was waiting for her. "How do you know Carrington is engaging in a display of power?" she said. "This might be, for him, an elaborate courtship. Perhaps he fancies you."

"That is possible as well." Dering seemed untroubled by the prospect. "But again, it all comes down to power. I am notoriously—and exclusively—fond of women. To imagine he has seduced me away from them would be a coup of sorts, in his own obscure reasoning. I may have to let him succeed."

Realizing her mouth was hanging open, she snapped it shut.

"An absolute last resort," he said, "right after handing myself over as a human sacrifice. Don't worry, Kate. It's only playacting. But you won't mind if I flirt with him a bit? You never permit me to flirt with *you*."

"There is no time for flirtation. You said so yourself."

"Flirtatious *rejections,* Kate. At the least, will you do me the service of locating some bath sheets? This water is growing cold."

The servants had left a stack of thick towels on a stool. She pulled it within his reach and went to the bedchamber for his dressing gown, arriving just as Malvolio, who had been napping atop the bed, lifted his head, perked his ears, and sprang barking to the floor. Supper must have arrived.

Chapter 12

"This cottage has more traffic than Piccadilly," Dering grumped. He was standing in the bath, a towel secured around his waist and another draped over his shoulders, trying to dry his hair without disturbing the bandage. "Let them in, will you?"

Kate opened the door, surprised to see Mr. Fidkin standing there, flanked by a handful of servants.

"My apologies for intruding," he said with more deference than she had ever heard in his voice. "I wish to assure myself of Lord Dering's health and to ascertain if he requires anything for his comfort."

"I have the Gypsy for that," Dering said. "But come in, Fidkin, and help me climb out of this contraption. I'm still a trifle muddleheaded."

Fidkin glanced over at a servant, appeared to think better of it, and crossed to offer his own arm. "I am distressed beyond words at the accident that has befallen you, my lord."

"*Befallen* is one way to put it." Leaning heavily on Fidkin's arm, he sat on the rim of the tub, swung a leg over the side, and after some maneuvering, got himself standing in front of the fire. Despite the towels, bandages, disheveled appearance, and mostly naked flesh, his posture bespoke lord of the manor. "Of course, no tale with me at the center of it has ever remained in the vicinity of the truth. By the time this one reaches London, God knows what exaggerated reports will be snaking through the drawing rooms."

Fidkin made a disparaging gesture at the still-yapping Malvolio. "Shall I dispose of that disturbing animal for you?"

"I'll see to him, sir." Kate scooped up the dog, took him into the bedchamber, and held him until he'd calmed enough to be left alone. When she returned, Fidkin was mopping his forehead, his color high.

"Was there some dereliction by the staff during the climb? By the guide?" His voice was high as well. "On your word, they will be dismissed."

"No, no. Cobbe and the others did all that was proper. They must have, or I'd not be standing here. But when the inevitable rumors appear in the news rags, do not be overly concerned about the reputation of Paradise. Upon my return to London, I shall set the story straight."

"Is it your intention to depart soon, my lord? Will your health permit the journey?"

"Well, that's the problem. I'll not go before my lease on the Gypsy expires, although given my present physical limitations, she will have to be amazingly inventive. And when I am sufficiently recovered, I wish to engage in a little boating, shooting, and . . . well, anything not involving fells and peaks. A fortnight, at least, I should think, to regain my usually hearty constitution. Will that incommode you?"

"You are most welcome," said Fidkin. "I shall extend your hold on the cottage."

While the men were speaking, servants had laid out

a meal on the table, hauled away the tub, and replen-
ished the supply of firewood. Lord Dering didn't appear to notice, but then, a man of his class would
take fine service for granted. She felt, as always in his
company, like a rustic bumpkin.

When the door finally closed behind Fidkin and the
others, Dering stumbled to the nearest chair and sat,
lowering his head between his knees. "Don't worry,"
he said. "It will pass."

But not quickly, she realized after a time, and not
without help. She went to the table, dished up a bowl
of thick stew, and knelt before him. "You'll feel better
if you eat, sir."

To her surprise, he didn't argue the point. Still leaning over, he swallowed each spoonful she offered him.

She was sitting on her heels between his bare legs,
far too aware of everything she could see and even
more aware of what the towel concealed. She tried to
concentrate on his face, on the stubble of beard, the
damp ends of his hair. But her gaze soon drifted down
to where the towel had slipped off his shoulders, and
to the sprinkling of wiry hair on his chest. Wholly
inappropriate images cartwheeled through her mind.
Her hand shook. A dollop of stew plopped onto the
floor.

"That will do it," he said, planting his hands on his
knees. "If you'll fetch my dressing gown, I believe I
can totter over to the table like a proper gentleman."

While she got rid of the bowl and gathered up the
heavy brocade robe, he came to his feet and shucked
off the towels. She turned just as they were falling and
immediately closed her eyes. "Here," she said, tossing
the robe in his direction.

Soft laughter and the rustle of brocade. "You may
safely unseal your shocked eyes, my dear. Can I have

been wrong after all? Are you, devil help us both, a dewy virgin?"

"No!" Spoken too enthusiastically. Her cheeks burned.

"Well, that's good news. Will you put out the lamps, please? While we are dining, I don't care to be looking at an apprehensive face."

She was beginning to recognize when he wasn't saying precisely what was on his mind. Not that it helped her to know his real thoughts, but she no longer took immediate offense at his teasing. She thought she might even like it, under different circumstances. And from a different man, of course. This one would be gone within five days—none too soon for her—and their paths would never cross again.

When the room was lit only by firelight, she sat across from him at the table where they had shared strawberries and champagne only the night before. It seemed much longer than that. He was making inroads into a slab of cold roast beef, apparently recovered from his fainting spell.

"Were you threatening Mr. Fidkin?" she said, to steer the conversation in a safe direction.

"After a fashion. Also misleading him, you will have noticed. With any luck, the Paradise assassin squad won't try to kill me within the next few days."

"What do you intend to do, then? What do you wish *me* to do?"

He waggled his eyebrows.

"I'm *serious*," she said, reaching for a carrot and taking a bite. It was a mistake. No one could retain any dignity crunching on a carrot.

"Far too serious, Kate. Whatever else I think of Black Phoenix's theories, I must credit their splendid casting. Here I am, masquerading as a man who cares for nothing but his own pleasure—close enough to the truth—while you play a tempestuous beauty fallen into my wicked clutches. The beauty's pride compels her to defy me, even as she submits from fear and, more profoundly, from desire. That, you must admit, is no reach at all."

She put down the carrot. "I haven't submitted."

"But you have. Your will is mine, and your desires. Only your pride stands in the way, and if you force me to, I will break it down."

A blow fell, invisible but sharp, like a stone dropped onto her heart. "I force you to *nothing*! If you are a brute, it is because you choose to be. Or because you are a brute by nature."

Silence. And after a time, a large, gentle hand against her cheek. "You didn't speak that to me, Kate. I am not that man."

She looked up, into the shadow that was his face, into the darkness where his eyes reflected the glow of moonlight through the window. "I know. I'm sorry. It was . . . I am tired, that is all."

Another long silence. She studied her hands, rough and scratched from wielding the ropes. She heard the crackle of the fire, the soft exhalation of his breath, the ragged voices calling her away from him. From life. From happiness. They would never release her, she already knew. Not willingly. And to escape, she would have to be far braver than she was.

"Ask me something," he said.

"I . . . What? Ask you what?"

"You choose. Whatever will allow you to trust me for a little. Only a few days, Kate. And nights . . . it is the nights you fear. But I will take nothing that you do not want to give."

"That's what you keep saying. But how do you

know what I want? How can you be so . . . so arrogant as to imagine you have divined my thoughts? My secrets are my own."

"It is my one useful skill," he said. "But my sensibilities are confined to the present, to how you feel or are likely to respond at this moment, or the next. Beyond that, past or future, I cannot guess. And by the way, despite my vaunted gift, you surprise me more often than not. Most disconcerting. I become unable to rely on my own instincts."

"Rubbish. You are manipulating me, the way I have watched you work your alchemy on others. Carrington. Fidkin. Even Mr. Gilliam, who admires you."

"Good God. And with all that talk of rocks and geological whatnots, I thought him a bright fellow." The gleam of white teeth. "Kate, I cannot remember the last person or supposed truth I could embrace without the anticipation of betrayal. We walk on quicksand. Things are not always what they seem. But if you ask me a question now, I will answer it without guile."

To name the hundred things she wanted to know about him would be to disclose an interest she ought not to have. "But what is the use," she said with a commendable degree of indifference, "if I have nothing of substance to wonder about?"

"Think of it as an experiment. You know what is said of me. Are you not the least bit curious? Wouldn't you like an explanation?"

"But I don't know anything about you, except that you were recruited in a hurry and chosen because you would fit in among the other guests."

He regarded her, speechless, for a time. Then, shaking his head, he began to laugh. "By heaven," he said at length, still choked with laughter. "I am in company with the only person in England unacquainted with my reputation."

"Well, I do know you are a rake, a gambler, and a wastrel."

"True on all counts. But Paradise is crawling with those." He propped his chin on folded hands. "How lowering. I'd thought your immediate disdain for me was rooted in the usual causes. Instead, you dislike me for myself alone."

She fumbled for a response. "My only concern has been for our investigation, and for your lack of dedication to it."

"We have already plucked that crow to the last pinfeather," he said, beginning to rise. "I believe I am in need of wine."

"I'll fetch it," she said immediately. When she returned, he was staring out the window. A waxing moon cast a ribbon of light over the black lake. She filled a glass for him, poured a little wine for herself, and placed the decanter where he could easily reach it. "Very well, my lord. What are the usual causes for people disliking you?"

He turned to look at her. "Where shall I begin? At the end of the tale, I think, with what I have come to be—an impoverished viscount, banished from my home, repudiated by my family, stripped of my inheritance. All but the title and the entailed land, which belong to me in name, although the estate is held in stewardship by my brother. He has preserved it reasonably well under the circumstances, while I scratch my own living at the gaming tables."

After a sip of wine, he went back to looking out the window. "This is certain to sound as if I blame everyone but myself, which is not the case. My own faults led me into trouble, and if there was an alternate path, pride blinded me to it."

He might have been talking about her. She took a piece of bread and spread butter on it, to give herself something to do besides stare at him. He seemed to have retreated into his own world, and while he might describe it to her, she was not invited there.

"My father was a devoted accumulator of land," he said. "When he was in funds, he immediately bought more of it. Above all things, he wished to acquire an extensive parcel of grassland adjacent to our estate, but our neighbor would not sell. The neighbor bred horses, and for that reason I spent more time on his property than on our own. I'm . . . partial to horses, have been all my life, and his daughter was a spanking rider. It had long been agreed between our parents that we would marry, but for me that remained a distant prospect. There was Eton, and Oxford, and after that, when my grand tour was forestalled by Bonaparte, I thought only of joining my friends in London. Home visits were few, and while Belinda and I still went riding, it was the horses that had my attention."

Kate would have wagered her life savings—eleven pounds—that Belinda's attention had been on him.

"Then, about four months after a Christmas visit, Father came down to London with fire in his eyes. And, I later realized, a good deal of satisfaction as well. As soon as a license could be procured and arrangements made, Belinda and I were to be married. The settlements had already been drawn up. The bride was chomping at the bit, not without reason. She was, by her account, four months gone with my child."

Heart sinking, Kate reached for her glass. At the same moment, Dering reached for his, and their hands brushed lightly together. The touch resounded through her like the tolling of a great brass bell. *His child. His child. His child.*

"To bring this tiresome recital to a close," he said, "I declined to wed her. Father went wild, primarily because the land he coveted would have been his under the marriage settlement. He threatened to do precisely what he later did—repudiate me—but I would not be moved. All my family, all her family, all the neighbors and all their cows were up in arms against me. The scandal consumed northern Dorset and spread, naturally, to London. I ceased receiving invitations. Friends turned their backs to me. With my allowance cut off and my reputation in shreds, I could neither pay nor borrow."

He was looking at her now. Although she couldn't see his eyes, she felt his gaze seeking hers, a darkling union she wanted without understanding why. And then she did know.

"Belinda was lying!"

He didn't speak for a long time. Then he made a harsh sound, almost a laugh, and took a long drink of wine. "Even I am not cad enough to reject my own child and its mother. But I'd never touched Belinda, except to hand her onto a saddle. She had been clever, though, making sure we were inappropriately alone, and—did I mention my naïveté?—I thought nothing of keeping company with a childhood friend. More than likely my father and hers, and most of our families and neighbors as well, had guessed I was not responsible for her condition. Even so, they thought I should spare them the trouble and the scandal and just have her. A long-standing arrangement, the alliance of families and property, the reputations of everyone concerned—what were my reservations against all

that? And what of the unfortunate child in need of a
name and a father?"

How much easier it was, she knew, just to give in.
To go along with what was asked, do the expected
thing. How she envied him the courage to refuse.

And where was love? she kept wondering. Children
sold off for land, or to pay debts, or simply to be rid
of them. Neighbors who closed their eyes because they
feared the consequences of seeing the truth.

"The babe was born in wedlock after all," he said,
"placing him third in line for the title. My brother,
younger by a year than I, had been persuaded to fall
on his sword for the family honor. In exchange, everything not mine by entail was willed to him. George is
a quiet fellow, easily influenced. I expect he sought to
please Father, who had rarely paid him any attention
before then.

"These events took place a dozen years ago, and in
the interval, there have been sufficient regrets to go
around for everyone. Father managed to hold Belinda
on a tight financial leash, but since his death she has
depleted George's fortune and presented him with
three more children, none of them apt to be his own.
Our mother devotes herself to their care. Belinda's
parents, shamed by her behavior, live in solitude. The
neighbors have ostracized both families."

"And you have disavowed them as well?"

"Rather the other way around, although I did have
one opportunity to mend fences. After a few years I
received a letter from Father. He wished to speak with
me about a reconciliation, dangling the prospect of
financial inducements and the alteration of his will. I
naturally leaped at the chance to restore my fortunes
and galloped *ventre à terre* to Dering Park."

A grim laugh. "At first it appeared we would come

to terms. He required that I remain in Dorset and devote myself to the estate, which I willingly agreed to do. In my life, I have never wanted more than to do precisely that. But there was another price to be paid for his forgiveness."

Anger, simmering since he began his story, now burned in her. "What in creation had *he* to forgive?"

"I asked the same question, in less genteel language. That enraged him. He demanded I accept full responsibility for everything that had gone wrong, make abject apologies, do public penance. Only when I had humbled myself to the population of southwest England would I be taken in like the prodigal son. As a bonus, I would be permitted to wed the bride he had secured for me. What followed was a rather ugly scene with Mother weeping, George wringing his hands, and Father and I trying to outshout each other. Not long after, I rode off again, and that was that. My obstinacy cost me everything."

"But you weren't responsible! How dare he lay this on you?"

"My dear Kate. Have you wandered over to my side? You ought not to be so impulsive. What harm would a false confession have done? I had nothing left save a few tattered threads of pride, and against all reason, I turned away my inheritance and clung instead to them. Pride, I assure you, pays no bills, and the satisfaction quickly evaporates. Without question, Father was wrong. But he was also desperate. It took me years to understand that behind all his bluster, he had come to me seeking absolution. And being the man he was, he could do so only by making demands and asserting his own pride. I shall never regret turning Belinda away, but I wish that on the day my father offered a thorny olive branch, I had accepted it."

"And married to please him?"

"Not that, unless his judgment of women had considerably improved. But the bloodline should be preserved, even when it is passing through an unworthy vessel like myself. Given time to polish up my reputation, I would have found a suitable wife."

"You still could. If you married an heiress, you'd have the funds to take your proper position and manage the estate. It's done all the time."

"You'd have me become a fortune hunter?" He sat back, as if to get a better view of her in the firelight. "I wouldn't have thought. . . . What is that in your hand?"

She looked down. As her anger had grown, her hands had fisted, and now five of her fingers were wrapped around a balled-up lump of buttered bread. "Oh, fustian!"

To the sound of his laughter, she took herself into the bedchamber—Malvolio scampering by her when she opened the door—and cleaned her hands. Washed her face as well, so long as she was there, and gingerly allowed the implications of what Lord Dering had told her to sink in.

All her certainties about this man were dissolving. With confidence in her hard-won ability to evaluate the male character, she had judged him to be clever, self-absorbed, a sybarite, an exploiter of others, charming, an indolent and useless specimen of the aristocracy. The very sort, in fact, that gave the aristocracy a bad name. Had she been born into his class, she would have done a great deal more with her opportunities.

He might, in fact, be all those things. But he was other things as well, although she'd not quite pinned down what they were. Nor was she going to try. They

might cause her to like him overmuch, to become concerned for him, to infuse already treacherous desires
with more complex longings. She had quite enough
troubles already.

Still, she might allow herself to enjoy his company.
He was undeniably amusing, and he challenged her,
which she resented even as she gleefully took him on.
It didn't bother her that he won nearly every
engagement.

Returning to the sitting room, she saw Dering hand-
feeding bits of roast beef to Malvolio, who had required no coaxing to accept this particular male into
his pack.

"Kate. Come look out the window and tell me what
you see."

She did, leaning over his shoulder. "Moonlight reflecting off the water. Outlines of hills on the other
side of the lake. What am I looking for?"

"Wait just where you are. Or draw nearer, if you
like, and continue to watch."

"Is this a trick?"

"Well, I am taking a little advantage," he said as
an arm wrapped around her waist. "But no tricks."

She felt the rise and fall of his chest as he breathed,
the texture of his robe, the warmth radiating from his
body. "Seduction, then?"

"Oh, I do hope so. But at the moment we are com-
bining pleasure with business. Watch the lake."

She forced herself to concentrate. And then she saw
it, a light where there had been none before, and it
was moving. "A boat lantern, just now unshuttered."

"Partly unshuttered. It's the third I've seen. Unless
they have just changed course, I'm guessing they set
out in darkness from the island, and when they arrive

at a point where their origin is no longer traceable, they become what most observers would assume them to be—night fishermen. We need a spyglass, Kate."

"I'm sure Mrs. Kipper can provide one. What do you believe is occurring? Smuggling?"

"Given the quantity of wine and spirits consumed here, I wouldn't be surprised if Paradise was buying under the table. Does Phoenix care?"

"About the purchase of smuggled goods? I shouldn't think so. But the evidence might be useful on other counts."

"We need to inspect that island, Kate. Not tomorrow. I doubt I'll be up to an excursion. A picnic on Wednesday will do, and I've already had a dinghy brought over. Can you row?"

It occurred to her that she was still pressed against him, unnecessarily so. "I have rowed," she said, retreating to her own chair, "but not for a long time. Are you so impaired that you cannot manage a dinghy?"

"I might wish to give that impression. Or I may not have any choice." He gave her a suspiciously earnest look. "To be truthful, my dear, I am devilish sore and tired."

"I am sorry to hear it." She kept all traces of sympathy out of her voice. "It's a puzzle, though. You did land on hard ground, and you did roll down a short way. But from then on, I cannot recall the slightest exertion on your part. Two men carried you off the fell, and you were transported here in a carriage. Before that, I was the one slung up like a smoked ham and sent to secure you to the lines. I did all the work, my lord. You simply lay there."

A slow, mischievous smile curved his lips. "Not my

usual preference, but in more comfortable circumstances—say, with a soft bed at my back—I should be glad to simply lie there while you do all the work."

"Oh, for pity's sake. Is there never another thought in your head?"

"While in your company? Almost never. Would you rather I did not desire you?"

"It would make our task a good deal less . . . less agitating for me."

"But a good deal less pleasurable, especially when the real agitating begins. Have I not been exorbitantly patient? I have played opium eater and drunkard to give you time. To give you more time, I got myself pushed off a cliff."

"Ha!"

"But we cannot continue in this fashion. Servants are in and out of this cottage. They see what is disturbed, and what is not. They change the sheets. They gossip among themselves, and some are paid for information. The time for discussion and delay has ended. Tonight you will sleep in my arms, and when my body catches up to my will, I shall make you glad my patience has run out."

Along with her willpower, now teetering precariously on the edge of a cliff. She could have continued to resist him, if she'd put all her strength into the effort. But the risk of giving their game away was real. Or real enough to give her the excuse her flesh was clamoring for.

As the fire dwindled, she could see less of his face. Of his expression. That made it easier, what she had to say. And who could have thought, after the life she had led, that she could feel such embarrassment? "I am a dancer," she said. "An actress and an entertainer. When this week is done, I shall return to my trade. Nothing must prevent that. Will you . . . take care, my lord?"

"I always do. You must help me, Kate, but yes. So long as we are both heedful, there will be no consequences." He began to rise, with apparent difficulty. "Go on to bed if you wish. I'll take this hound"—Malvolio was lying at his feet, snoring—"for a walk in the direction of the island. I don't expect to see anything, but I'd wager more than smuggling is going on there."

"Very well, except you have it backward. I'm already familiar with these woods at night, and I have the black garments that will keep me invisible. Not to mention that if one of us has to take a runner, you'd be brought down straightaway."

"You needn't spare me the walk," he said. "Or is this another of your delaying tactics?"

"A right good one, sir. I'm glad you thought of it."

Chapter 13

Kate decided to leave Malvolio, more likely to betray her presence by barking at a vole than he was to be of use, tethered to a tree in the garden. He flopped down on his little belly, rounded with an excess of roast beef, and rested his snout on his outstretched paws. So uncomplicated, the life of a dog. Adjusting her knit mask, she struck out to the east.

The moon, now floating low in the west, gave little light. She followed the shoreline, but kept herself well within the protection of the woods. Sometimes, through a break in the foliage, she glimpsed the island, sprawled on the dark water like a sleeping animal furred with trees.

Locating a small rise that provided her a better view, she went partway up a tree and watched for . . . she didn't know what. If another boat left the island, it would probably do so from the other side, beyond her view. She waited nearly an hour, measured by her mental clock, and saw nothing more than an owl hunting among the trees. Then, just as she was about to give it up, light flickered near the center of the island.

She climbed higher. The light, vanishing and reappearing according to the density of the woodland, was moving steadily to the east. She slithered to the ground and headed in the same direction.

Walking parallel to the island, she came to realize how large it was. From ground level she could no longer see the light, but she reckoned the bearer had a boat tied up on the eastern peninsula, a spit of land that stuck out into the water like a bent elbow. Anyone leaving from that point would find himself within easy reach of the Paradise gatehouse.

When she could make out the peninsula, she found another well-branched tree and climbed higher than before. Sure enough, the light had continued in the same direction and was approaching the water. Then it disappeared. Not long after, visible only as a dark shadow against the starlit lake, a small craft pulled away from the island.

Her first instinct was to follow, hoping to see the boat land. But she had no spyglass, and unless the oarsman made sure to carry his lantern so that it illuminated his face, there was little chance of learning his identity. Never tolerant of failure, she expended part of her frustration by running most of the way to the cottage.

Dering had built up the fire and set out a lit candle for her to use. She removed Malvolio's leash, gave him the remains of the roast beef on a saucer, refilled his water dish, and began quietly stripping off her trousers and knit tunic.

She felt as if a storm had blown by without touching her. Years of discipline and control had so nearly run aground, and for a brief time, a shameful time, she had been glad of it. But the long sprint in December-cold air had smudged the sharp edges of her desire. She was safe again, in control of her unruly passions.

Logic began ticking off the arguments she wanted

to hear. There was no reason to wake his lordship. She'd learned nothing that could not wait the telling until morning. The bed was enormous. Perhaps she could slip in unnoticed. And he did need to rest.

Her night rail and dressing gown were on the Grecian couch where she'd left them. By necessity she had learned how to undress silently, how to move silently, how to enter a bed without disturbing its occupant. How to be aware of the hour and the minute, so that she could take herself away before he woke up. It helped, of course, if the man was deeply drunk.

Leaving off the dressing gown, which tended to rustle, she extinguished the candle and tiptoed into the bedchamber. Ambient firelight marked out the long, blanketed form of his lordship, conveniently turned away from her on the other side of the bed. She closed the door against Malvolio, who would join them if given the opportunity, and slid inchmeal between the sheets.

Stillness from the other side of the bed. She dared to make herself a little more comfortable, luxuriating in the soft linens, their fresh scent, the warmth coming from the body lying perhaps a little too far away. Why was it so much easier to risk her life side by side with this man than it was to lie beside him, fearing his touch and craving it?

She closed her eyes, willed herself to relax, listened for the sound of his breathing. She could hear only the pulse beating at her temples. Every muscle in her body had stiffened with foreboding. She should have stayed in the other room with Malvolio.

A sound then—a body moving against the sheets—and a large, warm hand on her waist. "I thought I heard an intruder," he murmured. The hand moved along her hip and to her thigh, where it closed on a fistful of fabric. "What's all this? Armor?"

"Flannel."

"An effective barrier nonetheless. Are you planning to remain all the way over there for the entire night?"

"As you are proving, my lord, I am within arm's reach."

"But you will be more comfortable closer to me," he said. "No need for panic. I am going to turn over and draw you nearer, that is all."

"Do you not wish to learn what I saw on the island?"

"Were it important, you'd have told me already. Come along, Katie. Keep me warm."

He had no difficulty dragging her right up to him, her back to his front, nested together like a pair of spoons. He was, as she had expected, wearing nothing.

His forearm lay across her breasts, his wrist near her chin, his hand curved around her neck. Once settled, he ceased moving . . . not at all what she had expected. The undemanding embrace, at once possessive and protective, slowly melted her taut resistance. Little by little, the bonds of dread and longing slipped away. And still he didn't move. Didn't despoil everything with his rough passions.

After a time, transported beyond desire to a place of tranquillity, she drifted into a twilight of sensations. His breath stirring her hair. The pulse at his wrist throbbing against her throat. The blessed conviction that for a brief time, she was entirely safe.

Her dreams, when they came, were of feathers. She floated on a cloud of them, soft as thistledown. She was a thistle, but there was softness inside. Or weakness. They were the same.

Thistles, nettles, thorns. She had not been born quilled like a porcupine. She didn't want sharp things protruding from her flesh, rooted in her heart. But they were necessary.

Why wasn't she falling? She ought to be falling now. Every lovely thing, like her cloud of feathers, got ruined when she came near it. Torn to rags. But still the feathers cradled her, and a breeze carried her over the grassy fields. Then she was suspended from a tree, looking down on a fallen man, and she held out her arms, and he floated up to her.

She was at the top of a staircase, looking down on a fallen man, and her arms were held out, and she ran.

Shshshsh, said the feathers, enfolding her like angel wings, lifting her back to the sky.

When she dreamed again, it was of water. She floated in a warm pool, the water tickling at her nape, dampening her hair, ebbing and flowing over her belly and her breasts. It stole into the secret places and bathed them with water that was also fire. Light. Rain-soaked earth. She sent forth green shoots and they opened to the sun. Blossomed. She was a flower. A thorn. A thistle.

Her eyes flew open.

Warm lips were nuzzling at her neck. Warm breath teased at her hair. "Sometimes I think you are awake," whispered a deep voice. "Then I lose you again."

"Were you touching me?"

"A little. Here"—he brushed a kiss on her nape— "and here"—his hand settled on her waist and moved along her hip, along her thigh—"and here." The tip of a finger teased at her breast, at her nipple. Her breath caught in her throat.

"Stay with me now, Katie. There is nothing to fear."

Her heart thundered in her chest. He must feel it. His hand was spread over her breast, as if he would calm the rage inside her. She let herself breathe again, slow, deep breaths that found an echo against her back. His chest rose and fell in cadence with her own. He was tuning himself to her rhythms, finding her moods and soothing them.

Simply holding her now, just as she needed him to.

And she began to accept that the white heat in her had not been rage. Not this time. It was habit that made her think so. Fear and anger were what she expected when a man was on her, were nearly all she remembered of a man's possession. Of his dominance.

Like tendrils of vapor rising from deep in the earth, the memories stirred. A young girl concealed behind a tapestry fire screen, gazing on the elegant English gentleman who had come to call. Her shy curtsy on his next visit. The flattery, the ready smile, the strength as he lifted her onto a wagon seat.

She was lost from the first, lost with her desperation to escape and the promise of a refuge in his arms. So when he stole away with her into empty rooms and sheltered alcoves, when he taught her how a man could make her feel, desire swept her into madness.

And now another elegant English gentleman was bent on seducing her, and yielding to such a man was the last thing she ever meant to do again.

"Have you left me?" His voice, soft as thistledown, feathered against her ear. "How can I bring you to trust me for this little while?"

She put her hand over his hand, the one that lay against her heart. "Do not ask for trust. But for this time, I will go with you wherever you take me."

"And you will let me go everywhere? Touch you everywhere?"

"Please. I cannot *think*. I cannot *decide*. I—"

A finger put itself against her lips. "You needn't, sweet Kate. I will give you what you need. Come with me now. Do nothing more than feel."

Before she could draw a second breath, he had found his way under her night rail, lifting it until the flannel was bunched around her waist. She would have let him remove it, would have sat up to help him do so, but he'd got access to where he wanted to be. His hands burrowed under the soft flannel to cup her breasts, stroke them, fondle her nipples.

Swathed in fabric where he touched her, bare and open where he did not. The sensations, unexpected and contradictory, set her legs to moving. Rubbing together. She was suddenly in a great hurry.

But he was not. "I am your lover," he murmured, "in the dark safety of this night. Another time you may demand more of me. You may demand everything I can give you. But you are not prepared for that now. We shall be gentle, Kate. We shall remain in the shallows of passion, where you needn't fear whatever it is that enchains you."

The fingers of one hand trailed along her stomach, slipped maddeningly by their natural destination to the delicate spot behind her knee, and started to work their way up again. Like an artist, he knew just where to paint his strokes. She never guessed where he would touch next. It was the anticipation made her squirm, the near-satisfaction that made her grasp his wrist and urge it forward.

He ignored her direction. "Just imagine," he said, his voice husky with restraint, "what we shall do some other time, when I can kiss you, and press against you, and put all my body to pleasuring all of your body."

We can do that now, she wanted to tell him. But

this was better. He knew it, knew what she needed. One large, warm hand still toyed with her breasts. A finger grazed her inner thigh. And against the back of her leg, a hot, swollen presence made itself known.

Her head fell back against his shoulder. His tongue pushed against her neck, as if seeking entrance. Teeth followed, gentle but firm, and lips as well, all leaving their mark. He was moving his hips, letting her feel the size of him, the hardness of him, letting her imagine how it would be at the moment of penetration.

She had thought it impossible to be unchained, to be fearless, but his body was powerful, his hands infused with magic. They freed her entirely. When his finger reached where she had longed for it to be, she made a little cry of wonder. It felt so good. He felt so good.

He stroked upward, through the moist welcome to her swollen nub, and almost she blazed off like fireworks. He must have sensed it, chose to delay. She didn't mind. More than anything else, she wanted him inside her. Her hands were fisted now. She was curled in a position to receive him. His manhood pulsed against her buttocks.

He sent a finger into her. Only that, but she cried out again.

"More?" he whispered.

His head was against hers. He must have felt her nod. Another finger joined the first, and his tongue slipped into her ear, wet and warm.

He surrounded her. It felt as if he touched her everywhere. His fingers moved in her, he pressed at her from behind, his hand caressed her breasts, his mouth played on neck and shoulders and in the whorls of her ear.

"One more," he said, "to be sure you can take me entirely."

Another of his long fingers, hurting a little when it pressed through her opening, but too soon, it was not enough. She writhed against his hand, against his chest, against the need building in her. So long alone and empty. So long aching for what she had refused to allow herself. "Please," she said. "Oh, please."

"Yes." He withdrew his fingers. Adjusted his position. "Bring your knees up. Let me in, Kate, deep as I can go."

She raised her knees until they nearly touched her breasts. He put a hand between her thighs and made a space.

"Hold here for a moment." The hand went elsewhere, and then he brought himself against her open body. Prodded for entrance.

Achieved it.

Thick and relentless, his manhood pushed inside her by slow degrees. He pulled back a little, made another adjustment, and drove deeper. "Nearly there."

He took hold of a fisted hand, opened her fingers, and brought it to the place where they were joined. "You can't see," he said. "But you can imagine. Put your thumb and forefinger around my cock. Like that. Move them down to where I disappear inside you."

Her fingers could not encompass him. She could scarcely believe anything so large had managed to get so far into her. And now he meant to keep going. "Surely you cannot—"

"But I can. We both can. It would be easier with me on top of you, with your glorious legs thrown up over my shoulders. Another time, we'll do it that way. And several other ways you'll like even better than you are going to like this. Hold on, Kate. I can't wait any longer."

She felt him push past her encircling fingers until she had to open them and permit the sealing of his flesh against hers. The joining complete, he held in place for what seemed a long time, breathing heavily, stretching her beyond anything she had ever experienced or thought possible.

"Am I hurting you?"

"Oh, no." She moved her hips, not much because they were staked with a large pole, but experimentally, to see what was possible. Movement without pain. That was possible. It was also becoming essential. But as they were, he would have to do the moving. And she wanted him to.

She told him so.

"Ah," he said on a long sigh. The hand that had cradled her breasts moved to her waist and tightened, keeping her in place as he withdrew partway and went back again, the prelude to a leisurely motion that let her feel every inch of him each time he repeated it. There were many times, a hard, steady stroking that made her want it to last forever, just as it was, even as she needed him to go harder and deeper than ever before.

He sucked at her neck, used his hand to direct her hips in a clockwise motion for a time. Now she really felt him, their movements complementing each other and creating sensations that radiated from the friction of their genitals to every part of her body.

"I need more," she said on a gasp. "More."

"You need this." He brought a finger to just above where he plunged in and out of her and began rubbing the place where excitement had come together in one quivering bit of flesh. "And this." His thrusts matched the build of pressure that drove her higher and higher.

And then the burning became a conflagration. She pressed her face into the pillow to keep from screaming.

When her pleasure peaked, he stopped moving on a downward thrust. Still pressed inside her, he waited until the pulses of heat and miraculous sensation ran their blissful course. Only when she'd gone limp, satiated past coherent thought, did he move again.

But it was to pull out of her, still hard, shocking a protest from her lips. "Will you not—"

"I will keep you safe," he said. "As I promised. Sleep now, my Kate. I'm leaving for a short time to do what is necessary. Then I will come back and hold you through the night."

Jarrett woke shortly before noon, surprised to find Kate still snuggled alongside him. His first thought, which met with applause from below his waist, was to get the day off to its best possible start. But it diminished as he sensed the profundity of her sleep, the exhaustion that wrapped her in its embrace. No room for him there, not now.

He gathered some clothing, dressed in the sitting room, and after tending to the dog, set out with walking stick in hand for the Dome. On his first night there, Meacham had shown him facilities for hot and cold bathing, grooming, rubdowns, and physical exercise. He required all of those, and his duty—the word felt alien to him—directed that he spend the afternoon making himself visible and available.

When he'd been washed, boiled, steamed, iced, and shaved, he submitted to a punishing rubdown from a Turkish madman that left him in rags. "You be happy," said the madman with a last pummel. "I promise." And sure enough, after a leisurely meal in the Dome's restaurant, he was able to move with little of the stiffness that had impeded him since the fall.

Just as well Kate was sleeping late, he reflected, anticipation stirring in his loins. There would be no rest for either of them tonight.

Throughout the afternoon, which seemed to him endless, his thoughts kept circling back to his Gypsy tyrant. She reminded him of a birthday gift he had received from his grandfather, one box inside of another until the last tiny box was revealed. Its contents—an emerald stickpin—had been of little interest to an eight-year-old boy, although many years later he escaped eviction from his lodgings by selling it. What he recalled was the mounting excitement, the pleasure of curiosity, the wonder of complexity. After that gift, he began to take an interest in his studies.

If the mysterious Kate could be unwrapped in seven tries, what would he find?

Good weather had sent most of the guests out-of-doors, so he had to make do with a few sluggards like himself for company and managed to win a little at whist. Every penny counted. By the end of this week he would be on his own again, back where he'd been for the last dozen years.

Every minute counted as well, and he had squandered precious hours learning nothing of value until a servant delivered a note inscribed on Paradise stationery. At his lordship's convenience, Silas Indigo would be pleased to offer the demonstration of fishing tackle his lordship had requested.

After making his apologies for leaving the game, Jarrett followed the servant to a grassy slope overlooking a stream that fed into the lake. There, a man of late middle years with white hair and side-whiskers was laying out a series of fishing rods and other implements that were, for the most part, a mystery to Jarrett.

"Not a fisherman, I can tell by your expression," said Indigo softly. "Until the servant is out of earshot, feign interest in my demonstration."

The other Black Phoenix lackey, Jarrett had realized when he read the note. He took a rod and made a show of examining it. "The fishing is poor in London. Do you have news?"

"I meant to ask the same of you. But yes, I can add a little to what you already know. We have learned of Lord Carrington's connection to a charitable foundation for abandoned children, located not far from Cartmel. Saint Swithin's provides a smattering of education and work skills, after which the residents are apprenticed or put into service. Carrington is reported to be a generous benefactor who makes himself especially useful by ferreting out positions for the children."

"Positions that you are able to trace?"

"We have not yet gained access to their records, although we did locate and question a few boys and girls who secured employment in the immediate area. They spoke well of conditions at Saint Swithin's and appeared to be thriving. But some of them mentioned that Lord Carrington and one or two other gentlemen paid calls from time to time, bringing treats like oranges and gingerbread and inquiring about their health. And from the children's accounts—anecdotal at this time—the most beautiful of the boys and girls were set apart for special grooming and training. Not long after, positions had been found for them. We believe most were taken to London."

Jarrett did not fail to grasp the implications. "And sold to brothels."

"Attractive children are often favored for other reasons. As tigers or pages, for example, or playmates for a family's own brood. But I fear your conclusion is on the mark. What we lack is evidence of a link between the sale of children and the Cartmel foundation, and it will not fall into our grasp. Can you provide us some direction, my lord? If Phoenix were to go looking for these unfortunates, where might we find establishments that—"

Jarrett cut him off with a slashing gesture. "I regret to disappoint you, Indigo, but I am an exceedingly commonplace reprobate. You should have chosen a more depraved fellow."

"A man beyond the reach of his conscience would not have accepted our invitation. Still, we had reason to believe you could supply the information we need. Whatever the truth of them, your name is connected to rumors of unnatural practices."

A cramp gripped Jarrett's stomach. "Old stories, spread far and wide by a woman I famously rejected. Believe what you will, but I cannot help you."

"You must hear rumors as well, about other gentlemen. We needn't approach them directly. If we had someone to follow—"

"Understand this. I know what it is to live under suspicion and condemnation. You will have to do your fishing elsewhere. But on the possibility that children are endangered, I suggest you seek out Blossom Cottle in Half Moon Street. She knows as much as anyone about the sexual trade in London, and if your emissary is neither insulting nor officious, an extravagant bribe will loosen her tongue." He tossed the rod he'd been examining onto the grass. "Is there anything else?"

"One thing more. We have received word that on his recent travels, the Frenchman about whom you

inquired purchased several horses at a property near
to Dering Park. The woman he brought here came
north with him, but did not accompany him to Carlisle. We believe she hired a post chaise the night they
left Paradise. Nonetheless, we cannot rule out the possibility she arranged the attack, or had D'Arvaine do
so on her behalf."

Nodding, Jarrett strode past him and walked along
the lake to let his temper cool. If nothing else, Belinda's coincidental appearance had been explained, although he wasn't yet ready to hold her accountable
for the attempt on his life. She certainly wanted him
out of the way, but there were other candidates as
well. Sarne, for one, or someone connected with Black
Phoenix who had a reason to scuttle this endeavor.
Every camp had its traitor.

Visible and available, he reminded himself after a
considerable time. Returning to the Dome, he joined
a desultory game of hazard. Later, John Gilliam
stopped by to lose the second installment of his father's money at piquet, after which they dined on the
terrace with three harmless chaps and enjoyed a startlingly red sunset.

Eight hundred pounds richer than he had been a
few hours earlier, Jarrett was more than ready to go
in search of Kate, and would have done so had not
Carrington's lavish coach turned up the hill. With keen
loathing, he resigned himself to remaining available
awhile longer.

Chapter 14

The message from Dering arrived just as Kate, frustrated at being left alone most of the day, was about to boil over. He'd left her that morning without a word, without asking what she'd learned in her surveillance of the island, not bothering to let her know when to expect him. Even the two solitary hours she'd spent on the stage of the theater, exercising and practicing her routines, had failed to lure him away from his loutish friends. And now, not very long before midnight, he'd scrawled a letter that sent her temper soaring.

"Come to the Dome. Bind up your hair and dress plainly. Keep quiet."

While the servant waited to drive her there, she took her time changing from the flattering dress Mrs. Kipper had pressed for her into a dark green gown with only a simple ribbon tied beneath her breasts for adornment. More time to scrape back her hair, wrap it into a tight chignon, and secure it with pins.

Each disappointment stung. He needn't have pretended to develop an interest in their mission, or in her. She had never asked for his confidences. And she'd nearly accepted his argument that they must provide evidence he was making use of her, which effectively removed her last excuse for fending him off. If nothing else, the good of the mission would have laid her out under him before very long. He didn't have to lure her into wanting him.

But she mustn't keep reflecting on what had occurred last night. She had reviewed the scene a score of times, and her conclusion remained the same. He had awakened with the edge of desire on him, and she chanced to be conveniently in his arms. No more than that.

As the curricle navigated the narrow torchlit road, she drew in the reins of her anger. Probably Dering had sent for her because some of the guests were requesting a performance. Or perhaps he wished to demonstrate, by her subdued dress and demeanor, that she had yielded entirely to his mastery. She could scarcely deny it, could she?

How low she had fallen in only four days and nights. Protecting herself from men who assumed an actress to be common goods had never been difficult. The true challenge lay in the closeness, physical and otherwise, of her itinerant life with a theater company. Her companions, most of them, had been kind, but it was dangerous to want friends, or to imagine she could weave a family from unconnected strands. To be anything other than entirely self-sufficient weakened her. It threatened what little peace of mind she had cobbled together.

So after a decade of shielding herself, she had fancied herself invulnerable to temptation. And then a rascally viscount sauntered onto her ice floe and built a fire. Built it inside her, and charmed her into not minding so much. He reached into the cold places and warmed them, into the dark places and illuminated them. Into the empty places, which he filled with himself.

And after slipping through her every defense, he blithely strolled away and left her burning.

It would not happen again, she had resolved during that long, empty day. She had relearned a lesson she ought never to have forgotten.

When they arrived at the Dome, a servant ran down to help her alight and escort her past the men relaxing on the terrace and in the entrance hall, nearly all of them turning to look as she was led by. She saw no other women, and there were none in the midsize gaming room where the servant delivered her.

Only one table was occupied. She recognized Lord Carrington, Lord Sheffer, and Sir Robert Wylie playing cards. Behind Carrington, looking bleary-eyed, sat Lord Golsham. Dering, in his shirtsleeves, was slouched in an armed chair, legs stretched out under the table, a glass of what looked to be brandy near his elbow. He glanced up as she approached and went back to studying his cards.

From the layout, she could tell they were playing whist. And from where the markers were stacked, it appeared that Carrington controlled the game.

A shot of fear darted through her. Surely not! Even Dering wouldn't tender her as a wager. And yet, he'd done something of the kind before. When first she heard the servants gossiping about the newly arrived guest who had won a duchess in a game of chess, she hadn't credited the story. Then she met Dering and believed every word of it.

While she watched, the last tricks were played and a few markers went over to Dering's side. He took a long, slow drink of brandy, regarding her incuriously over the rim of the glass.

"Well, what do you say?" That was Carrington, a satisfied expression on his face. "It is an excellent arrangement, one thousand in markers against the demonstration. I fail to comprehend your reluctance. Whatever the outcome, you cannot lose."

"Indeed I can. I already have. Almost six hundred pounds." Dering shuffled with limber fingers. "How to account for that? My luck isn't out. The cards have run fairly evenly. I have played brilliantly, as always." He flashed a smile. "It must be my partners."

"Sheffer and Wylie changed places with every rubber," Carrington said. "As we agreed."

"But they play so well with you, and so badly with me."

Sheffer slapped a hand on the table, causing the markers to bounce. "Do you accuse me of cheating?"

"Dear me, no. If I thought you dishonest, I'd not play with you or against you. But confess it, you want Carrington to win, or me to lose, and your wishes cannot help but affect your play. Entirely without your volition, I am sure."

"And I am sure they'll try to do better," Carrington said. "The money is trivial, after all. A few hundred at best. It is the challenge that should interest you, the clash of wits."

"There you have it," said Dering. "For me, gambling long ago ceased to be a sport. It is common labor, as tedious as plowing a field. Except that if I lose, I could wind up sleeping in the field."

"But in this case, your loss would be everyone's gain. Unless you are concerned that observers might hinder your performance? Or is it that you've lost interest in bed sport with the Gypsy? Has she grown tiresome?"

Kate held in place with every grain of self-control

she possessed. Not that it signified. No one paid her the slightest heed. They cared as little for her as they did the thin ivory wafers on the table. One as good as another, of value only as a commodity of exchange.

"What is tiresome to me," said Dering, "is the prospect of tossing her on a communal bed where hundreds have been before, in a room that for all the labor of Paradise's excellent servants, carries the stench of my predecessors. Even in pursuit of my pleasures, I am invariably fastidious."

Carrington's brows rose like two birds lifting off a fence. "You appreciate order, then. Even ritual?"

"Sometimes. When it is carried out with a purpose that transcends amateur theatricals. I had thought we shared a preference for refined entertainment, which is why your wish to watch through a peephole while I toss the Gypsy astonishes me. I'd not have cast you as a voyeur."

A slight flush, the first hint of color Kate had ever seen on Carrington's ashen face, and then a laugh. "Oh, I like to watch, on occasion. But you are quite right. To observe you tupping a woman you've already had would be wearisome. Let us raise the stakes, shall we?"

Dering laced his fingers behind his neck. "What do you have in mind?"

"Some of my friends are to gather on Thursday night for a ceremony of sorts. Nothing elaborate— more of a preliminary event—but I should like to render it less routine than it might otherwise have been. For our amusement, let us have the girl."

Kate measured her breathing. Anchored her feet to the floor.

"*Have* in the usual sense?" Dering said. "Or is the prospect somewhat more obscure?"

"Not on this occasion. Ordinarily we satisfy ourselves with the whores, but it might be more diverting to have our turns, one after the other, with this particular whore. There are a dozen of us, more or less."

Dering rolled his eyes. "And what good would she be to me after such a night? You forget, Carrington, that I paid three thousand guineas to own her for a week. Never mind your contribution, nor that I was out of my head at the time. I paid, and I got her, and I mean to keep her to myself until the week is done. After that, of course, it would be my pleasure to turn her over to your compatriots. How about Saturday? The lease runs out at midnight, but until then I can compel her obedience. Have your ceremony at, say, ten o'clock, and we shall end this piquant adventure with a flourish."

Carrington frowned. "There is no meeting planned for Saturday. But I suppose our general enjoyment of the witch could be a prelude to my judgment of your stewardship. Or had you forgotten that?"

"In fact, I had. At worst, you'll rule me a failure, and I've been called that before. But you have not said what you are putting on the table."

"Two thousand pounds," Carrington said immediately. "On the condition you use it to continue this game. If you double it, you keep all the money. If you lose it, we take the Gypsy."

Dering appeared to think it over. Then he gave a lingering sigh. "But it's still *work*, my dear. More slogging through the fields. I don't live in your rarified atmosphere, where a few thousand pounds is a trifle. I stand to win the equivalent of wages, and that is not the purpose of my holiday in Paradise. You must excuse me from this game."

Kate, with the small part of her attention not directed to keeping herself silent, had expected Carrington to balk at the refusal.

Instead, he smiled. "I did not mean to patronize you. How if I add to my wager the horse that was formerly yours?"

Dering sat forward and propped his elbows on the table. "Now you interest me. I want the money, and as you are aware, I badly want that horse. But to get them I have to defeat you in a game of cards while being partnered by your friends. No offense, gentlemen. Although Carrington would not mind your playing splendidly on my behalf, I hesitate to put your loyalty on the table along with the other stakes."

"A turn of the card, then," said Carrington. "For variety, low card wins."

"But that is no challenge, and one of us will lose. Why not a simple trade, sir? Never mind the money or the game. I am willing to exchange the Gypsy for my horse. What do you say?"

"That's not in my contract!"

Kate realized, a second too late, that she had taken a step forward and spoken. Objected. She did not imagine, not for a minute, that these men would tolerate such insolence. But it was too late to back down now, even if she could have brought herself to do it. The marquess meant to pass her around among his friends? Dering would trade her for a *horse*?

"Another word," said Dering amiably, "and I'll give you to the servants as well."

Carrington templed his hands. "You already know the quality of the bay. It is only fair, don't you think, that before handing him over to you, I see what we'll be getting in return?"

Dering made a desultory gesture. "There she is."

"I meant," Carrington said, "a more thorough inspection. Sheffer, will you do the honors?"

"She's not yours yet," said Dering, beckoning to the servant who waited beside an array of decanters. "Close the door, with you on the other side of it, and admit no one."

Sheffer, who had begun to rise, sat down again. "You are protecting her?"

"Hardly. But Carrington is prepared to relinquish my horse, which he'd really rather keep, for your pleasure. Where is the cachet, gentlemen, if the rabble are given a free show?"

"Sheffer is consumed with punishment," Carrington said, "the less refined, the better. He shall have his opportunity, as he always does at our celebrations, but in the interim, permit us the delights of anticipation. Will you strip her?"

"Oh, very well." Dering rose, stretched, and ambled in her direction. "It's an exceptionally fine body, I must say. You will have no complaints."

She had thought nothing could shame her more than the auction had done, but as Dering had once told her, she was sublimely naive. The exhibition would have been infinitely worse than what was to come, to be sure. But since he'd meant to refuse the demonstration, he needn't have brought her here at all.

Stomach roiling, she fixed her gaze directly ahead, on a painting of men shooting birds. Dering came around behind her and began plucking the pins from her bundled hair. She thought of the last time he had been so close. The same heat had radiated from him, and the smell of brandy, and the scent that was his alone.

When the last pin hit the ground, he combed his fingers through her hair until it fell in coils and tangles around her shoulders and down her back. Then he untied the green ribbon and tossed it onto the card table.

He had undressed his share of women, she could tell. He knew where to find the slits in her skirts that gave him access to the tapes. They were swiftly untied, and he let the skirts slide down to pool on the carpet. The bodice with its short sleeves was soon unhooked and removed, leaving her in corset, chemise, stockings, and shoes.

She had been clinging to the hope that it would be enough, and when Dering went back to the table, she let her gaze follow him.

"I don't suppose," he said, "that one of you gentlemen is carrying a knife?"

Carrington reached to his boot and withdrew a slim blade. The jeweled hilt shone in the lamplight.

"Excellent. I've lost my taste for unlacing corsets." At her back again, Dering fumbled with the ties. "Hold still, Gypsy. My hands are none too steady."

Moments later she felt the pressure, but not the edge, of the blade as it sliced through the laces. The corset dropped to the floor. Then, reaching around from behind her, he slit the muslin chemise from neckline to hem.

Gasping, she felt the two sides separate, exposing her from neck to toes. Next he cut through the loops of fabric over her shoulders, and the entire garment dropped away.

Clothed only in her hair, dizzy with humiliation, she stared into a gray void. Pride kept her arms at her sides, her face without expression. She preserved what dignity she could.

She plotted vengeance.

"Turn, my dear. Slowly. As you see, gentlemen, perfect from every side, from every angle. Best of all, dancing has made her agile, flexible, and vigorous. You won't be disappointed."

"A good bargain," said Carrington. "Your horse is returned in exchange for two hours' control of the woman."

Dering went to the door, glancing at her over his shoulder. "Get dressed."

While she scrambled into skirt and bodice, he spoke to someone in the passageway. Ignoring the laughter and lewd speculations of the other men, she stooped to gather the rest of her garments and as many of the pins as she could find.

Returning, Dering put a hand under her elbow and drew her to her feet. "A servant will drive you to the cottage," he said, tugging her to the door and practically thrusting her into the passageway. "You know what to expect when I get there."

Chapter 15

For a time Kate moved like an automaton, pushing herself from one step to the next, her gaze fixed in the middle distance.

She endured the gauntlet of stares and laughter and ribald jests on her way to the curricle, and sat beside the driver with her chin raised and her undergarments clutched to her chest. The night, for a change, was seasonably warm.

She made plans.

At the cottage she took Malvolio for a short walk and fed him dried venison. She stripped again and washed every inch of her body, using her hairbrush to scrape away all traces of Dering's hands, of sticky male gazes, of her crushing mortification. She braided her hair in a single plait and pinned it in a knot at her nape. She put on a plain, long-sleeved dress, and over that a smock she wore backstage to protect her costumes while cosmetics were applied. Her sheathed blade was secured around her calf.

Whatever he had meant by his parting line, whatever it was she was supposed to expect on his return, she had no intention of gratifying him.

Finally, after closing Malvolio in the bedchamber,

she extinguished all but one of the lamps in the sitting room and placed it on the mantelpiece. Even covered from neck to foot, she could not bear to be looked at.

Taking a chair by the window, she focused her attention on the lake, watching for lanterns the way she and Dering had done the night before. Making the mistake, again, of bringing him into her thoughts.

Would she have minded so much, she wondered, had he not witnessed her shame? The risks were made clear enough to her before she accepted this mission, and they hadn't troubled her in the slightest. Not then, while they were theoretical and she was consumed with guilt. The chance to redeem herself, or at least to make a start in that direction, had overcome her apprehension. What did she care for humiliation and insult, even from men who generally behaved themselves? In Paradise, the worst elements of their natures were allowed free play. To impress one another, they would swagger and strut the way small boys did in school.

Dering was no different. Indeed, he had been selected precisely because he fit right in with the most reprehensible of the guests. And if she glimpsed in him, from time to time, a character quite other than the one he possessed, it only proved she had learned nothing from experience. When charm and good looks were painted over a black soul, she could still be fooled.

On this night, though, she'd seen beneath the paint. He had behaved just like the others, a vulgar boor. His opinion of her was of no importance.

But the question, once it had slipped through her defenses, would not leave her alone. The sad truth remained—she was an utter fraud.

Before the auction, as Mrs. Kipper had pointed out, she had declared herself willing to endure any ordeal. And so she was, right up until an ordeal presented itself. Then she balked, and complained, and felt sorry for herself.

Now Dering had seen her falter. When he touched her, she had quivered. Her pulse had raced. He knew she wasn't really dedicated or brave. And that, more than the rest, kept nagging at her.

As a performer, she had always been able to lose herself in the role she was playing, even if she had to make up a character for the occasion. But tonight, stripped by his hands, more than her body had been uncovered. She had felt entirely exposed to him, weak and frightened and worthless.

At least she hadn't run. Not from the room—she'd never have escaped those men—but later, when the driver left her alone at the cottage. Even now she could go. From the day she arrived at Paradise, she had plotted her escape and knew five ways to remove herself from the property with little chance of being seen.

She invariably arranged an exit from any town, any company, any situation she could not absolutely control. Meaning all of them, she supposed. Sometimes she required only the back way to leave an inn or where she might most easily steal a horse. But whenever Pendragon was to remain in a county for more than a few days, the schemes had to be more elaborate. Her profession exposed her to thousands of people, and someday one of them would recognize her.

She had always known her time was limited. It still amazed her that she had survived so many years without being discovered. But each morning might begin

her last day of freedom, and she always fell asleep
with the dread of sunrise. Fate had hold of her now,
or perhaps it was Retribution.

Then came the summons from Black Phoenix, and
she had recognized a crossroads, a chance to make
amends. Could Fate have done her a kindness?

But, no. It had given her Dering.

And he was on his way, she could tell when Malvolio set to barking. Shortly after came a banging at
the door, which she took her time opening.

There he stood, or, rather, slumped, with each arm
wrapped around the shoulder of a liveried servant, a
look of vacant cheerfulness on his flushed face.

"Where shall we place him?" said one of the
young men.

"Anywhere will do." She moved aside to let them
tow him in. "The Grecian couch, I suppose. Or the
bedchamber."

"See," said Dering. It sounded, in his slurred voice,
like *she*. "Can't wait to get me in bed. Tell 'em,
Gypsy."

"He's a regular rooster," she assured the servants,
who wore masks of patient experience.

Dering shook himself loose, staggered to the Grecian couch, and nearly toppled over when he tried to
give her a bow. In the effort to recover, he found
himself seated and smiled with delight.

"You may go," Kate said to the servants. "I'll see
to him now."

"See," said Dering. *She*. "Tol' you she couldn't
wait."

All this spoken over Malvolio's incessant barking,
which finally ceased when the servants had gone. Kate
looked at Dering with disgust.

"I have two things to tell you," he said, more distinctly than he had spoken before. "I am very drunk. Damned drunk. Drunk as a lord. All that was one thing. The other is, I am probably not as drunk as you think I am. Or even as I think I am. Which is, I c'nfess, damned drunk."

"Thank you for the information." To think she had been concerned that this . . . this *goat* had thought ill of her.

"You waited up," he said. "All dressed, with an apron to catch the blood. Means you want to ring a peal over me."

"I had hoped to speak with you, but clearly that is impossible tonight."

"Oh, 'speak the speech, I pray you . . . trippingly on the tongue.'" He preened. "Did I get it right? Anyway, have at me. Nothing to stop you. I'll even listen, probably."

She was standing by the mantelpiece, her hand perilously near a heavy candlestick. "I am in no humor for condescension, my lord."

"No humor whatever, I would say. Let us for pity's sake get on with it. Fire your weapons, my dear. Flay me with your tongue. Incinerate me with your basilisk stare." He frowned. "What the devil is a basilisk, anyway? And why does it stare?"

She had been primed for a quarrel, sure enough, but there could be no sense got from this drunken buffoon. Why didn't he fall senseless onto the floor like drunks were supposed to do? This one had propped his elbows on his knees and his chin in his hands, apparently contemplating basilisks.

"Well, it's Greek, that's certain," he said, verifying her suspicions. "You could be Greek, I think, except for the eyes. I don't know many Greeks. More likely you are Welsh, or Irish, or Scots. Not good country

English, at any rate. Where did you come from, Gypsy?"

Her heart sank. She had perfected a flawless accent. No one had ever suspected. "I was born under a toad-stool, sir, and I learned to speak from the magpies."

"Go on. I'm fascinated. Or change the subject, if you like. I can wait. Neither of us is leaving this room until you've loosed your arsenal on me, and your patience will run out well before mine."

That pronouncement had sounded perfectly coherent. Had he been playacting all along? Making fun of her?

Just then he lurched to his feet and bolted out the cottage door.

She had too much experience with drunken males to mistake his exit for anything other than what it was. *Repellent oaf.* With luck he'd pass out in the bushes and spend the night there, with bugs crawling over him. Which was just what he deserved for making her stand naked in front of those aristocratic vermin.

Her rage, shoved aside for a time when he might actually understand what she had to say, elbowed its way forward again. If he dared show his dissolute face in this room again tonight, there would be no stopping her. In fact, she thought a glass of brandy might suit her nicely. Everything else been stripped from her. Why not let go her inhibitions as well?

She was halfway through her drink, eyes watering, coughing and choking with every swallow, when he burst through the door. A good deal paler, she noted with pleasure.

"Well, that was inevitable, I suppose," he said, looking unrepentant as he made his way to the decanter and poured himself *more* to drink. "Don't look so censorious, my dear. Just enough to rid myself of the foul taste in my mouth. You needn't worry I'll try to kiss you."

"As if I would permit it!"

"I imagine not." He rested his hips against the sideboard. "Has it occurred to you that what I did tonight was necessary?"

She wasn't prepared to admit as much. "That would require me to trust your judgment, Lord Dering. Nothing I have seen has given me reason to do so."

"On the other hand, what is the point of continuing without a reasonable degree of trust between us? Might as well pack it in, don't you think?"

"You haven't wanted to be here from the first. You drink, you gamble, you whore, and when all that grows stale, you play despicable games."

"That covers it fairly well," he said. "Keep in mind I am trying to become one of the Inner Circle of Loathsome Louts, which requires me to persuade them I am one of their kind, albeit one with enough tricks and quirks to spice up their dull pastimes. Even absolute dissipation palls after a while, I would guess."

"Not purely guesswork, I think."

"You'd be surprised. It's not that I made lofty moral choices. I simply couldn't afford to buy my way into the halls of refined vice. But now, for the dubious purposes of Black Phoenix, I am attempting to weasel myself in with guile and charm, and by exploiting *you*. That is, you must admit, what you are here for."

"Not for what happened tonight!"

"For exactly that. Or worse. You were chosen from a third-rate theater company to seduce the guests with your beauty and, yes, your talent. But you weren't exactly playing Ophelia's mad scene when first I saw you perform. You set yourself to deliberately tease and arouse the men in that audience. Quite effectively,

I must say. And now you pronounce yourself shocked
because some of those men want more than teasing
promises, and are willing to use their wealth, rank,
and power to get it."

This confrontation was not going as she had
planned. "You are twisting everything around. They
could not have compelled you to put me on display,
in the exhibition rooms or anywhere else. *You* sent
for me. What happened was *your* doing."

"It's not so simple as that. Carrington, with the amateur assistance of his fellows, was putting me to the
test. The maneuvering had been going on for several
hours before you arrived, and it was clear the usual
drinking and carousing would not turn the trick. A
demonstration was called for, an unmistakable rite of
passage from potential evildoer to confirmed villain. I
count us fortunate to have eluded a more public
initiation."

He ran the fingers of both hands through his hair.
"Answer me this, will you? Had you been told in advance the price to take the next step in our plan,
would you have consented to it?"

Back again to her dilemma. She always consented
to the theory, recoiled from the practice. And back-
tracked from the truth, as she heard herself doing
now. "You might have explained in your note. I could
have prepared myself."

"For *that*? Look, never mind what led up to my
sending for you. The notepaper was brought to the
table. If they hadn't read the message as I wrote it,
do you imagine a servant would not have done so and
reported back? It was a *test*, Kate, devised by a man
far more clever than I. Forced to make a decision, I
guessed you would have agreed to play your part."

Anger vibrated in the air around him as he moved

in no particular direction. Expending energy, she thought. Restraining himself. Trying to reason with her.

No hope of that, with her being altogether unreasonable. But she couldn't stop herself.

He propped himself against the wall on the other side of the room, his face in shadow, his hands loose at his sides. "Could I have found some other way? Was there an alternative I failed to see? I honestly don't know. I accept responsibility for the choices I made, but that doesn't mean I defend them. It damned well doesn't mean I take pride in them."

"You didn't appear to be minding in the least. Yes, I take the point you were giving them what they wanted to see. But they recognized something in you, my lord. Tonight, I saw it for myself."

"I'm as leaky a boat as the rest. What I cannot understand is your loyalty to Black Phoenix. On their behalf you subject yourself to humiliation and abuse, and to my company, which appears to offend you more than all the rest. Why have you put your life into their hands? It is senseless. Unworthy of you."

"But people are being *murdered*. You nearly were. Children . . . we're not sure what is happening to them, but you have taken Carrington's measure. You know what he is capable of."

"Diabolical sexual practices, certainly. But Paradise is not the only spot in England where crimes are committed and aberrant tastes indulged. You can find most abominations flourishing in the average English village. So why would a . . . a confederacy of do-gooders spend a small fortune to discredit this inconsequential watering place?"

"You think such wickedness should be permitted to continue? That nothing should be done?"

"Phoenix has a right to its hobbies. And I don't object to playing the role of a tarted-up decoy. But I sure as hell mind their sending *you* into this swamp."

"Because I am incapable of doing the job?"

"Because they are throwing you against the enemy like cannon fodder. You have cast them as gallant knights, Kate, but they are on a mission to get something for themselves. Ownership, perhaps. The pursuit of a vendetta. Or Phoenix may be no more than a band of mercenaries, for hire to anyone who will pay their price. You can bet they have something to gain here. They have little enough to lose, since the dangerous work—as we both have reason to know—is delegated to flunkeys."

"I hope the day will not soon come, my lord, when I have grown so cynical as you."

"It won't. You have blinders on top of your blinders. Your judgment will never be wholly critical, and it will rarely be accurate. Until you trust yourself, Kate, you will not be able to discern the man or woman who merits your trust as well."

"Ha! Lectures from a scoundrel. One who knows nothing about me. You said so yourself."

"Hoping to elicit a few confidences," he said with a dismissive gesture. "I even bared a little of my own black soul. But nothing has penetrated your battlements, and we remain at odds. There is danger enough, Kate, without our tripping each other up. We must come to an understanding. So I will tell you what I know to be true, and if you cannot abide it, then the game is off."

"You haven't the right to end it. You keep making arbitrary decisions, like promising to give me to those men on Saturday night because you knew you'd be well gone by that time. But I never said I was leaving, nor will I until this mission is completed. You should have considered that before serving me up on a platter."

"Oh, you are leaving Paradise, my dear, if I have to drag you out by your hair. But do we leave tomorrow morning, or find a means of cooperating long enough to see what Carrington and his friends do at the solstice party? Whatever else I did wrong tonight, I managed to secure an invitation."

"For Thursday, I thought."

"Both. It took longer to winkle the voucher for Friday night. And yes, I got bloody drunk in the bargain, although the outward display was primarily for show. You caught the tail end of the performance and have been assuming I meant to trick you as well, which is not untrue. I couldn't resist."

So, then. All her efforts in this endeavor had ended in failure, humiliation, or general ineffectiveness. But his lordship had swanned in without the slightest regard to the outcome and swept off with the prize.

She ought to be glad. Only the objective signified, never mind how it was accomplished. But she envied his triumph, resented the ease with which he danced around every obstacle. Nothing in her life had ever mattered so much as succeeding here. And she must have a starring role, even if no one else learned of it. Everything depended on what she was able to prove to herself.

And now this man, without authority, right, or justifiable reason, meant to shut her out. Deprive her of the chance to complete her own mission.

She could barely see him, a dark figure slumped against the wall, elbows bent and hands knotted with his chin resting against them. He was waiting her out. Preparing to turn her arguments against her, mock her anger, deal patiently with her as he might a temperamental horse.

No. He liked horses. He had traded her for one.

If she ceded one inch to him now, she would never recover ground. "What is it, my lord, that you were going to tell me? The things you know to be true."

"Ah." Softly, as if he had not wished her to resurrect the subject. "One thing only, Kate. It is too deep-rooted in the both of us to be ignored, and if we cannot come to terms with it, none of the rest will make the slightest difference. I wanted to explain why you are so antagonistic."

"Dear heavens, we've been talking about that for an hour. I have a score of reasons to be angry, some less worthy than others. Some entirely misguided, I admit, but I have reasons good enough."

"After what you were subjected to this evening, nothing you have said to me or believed to be true was unjustified. But I am not speaking of what occurred in the gaming room. Your hostility isn't for me. It's not even for Carrington and his fellow lice. This is about what happened last night, in my bed."

"Rubbish." She said it without conviction, on a breath that caught in her throat. "I d-did what you said I must do, as part of our masquerade. Your arguments were persuasive."

"As you say. But not, it turned out, a factor in your decision. That had been made some time earlier, by the passionate creature you keep bound and gagged in the cellars. All I did was provide a way for you to rationalize your desire, to accept pleasure without admitting you wanted it. You dressed it up as duty and sacrifice, as martyrdom, and then the experience turned out to be other than you had feared. What we did together reached beyond every illusion you tried to construct around it. And that is what you find intolerable, Kate. You cannot pretend anymore. Tonight's events gave you an excuse to turn on me, but anger will not protect you from the truth."

"Was there ever a man," she said, "who did not fancy himself an irresistible lover? You mistake hostility, my lord, for disdain. But this needn't be a problem for us, not any longer. Now you have insinuated yourself into Carrington's circle, there is no longer any need—if ever there was—to be overconcerned about appearances. Of the sexual kind, I mean."

"I know what you mean." He had moved into the light, his gaze steady, his face unsmiling. "I quite agree."

The air deadened. She had not expected capitulation. "Good," she said too briskly. "I had anticipated another quarrel."

"You overestimate my interest in bedding an unwilling woman. But since I wish to preserve my reputation as a master swordsman, we shall continue our charade in public. In private, you needn't worry I'll try to seduce you. Unless circumstances change, of course. Or you decide you want me to."

She started to deny the possibility, but something about his face, about the look in his eyes, held the words in her throat. She nodded instead, aware of a deep sadness spreading through her. Only two more days, she thought, and three nights. She would not weaken again in so short a time.

"Take the bed, then," he said. "I'm still drunk enough to sleep on a thatch of thistles. Tomorrow, if you care to join me, we'll drop by the island. Go now. We're done for tonight."

She left without another word, although not before pausing by the door. Her curtsy began as a gesture of defiance, or perhaps of sarcasm, but as she rose from it she realized, astonished, that she had been honoring him.

The tribute, which he could not have recognized, stamped a seal on their relationship. What had never really begun had slammed to an end. In future she would keep her pride in check and her wits about her. The mission was everything.

For half an hour she sat on the bed with Malvolio in her lap, listening for sounds from the other room. When fairly certain Dering was dead to the world, she took the precaution of making sure. Opening the door a crack, she saw him lying on his stomach among the fur rugs near the unlit hearth, his face turned away from her, his breathing slow and regular.

She closed the door, quietly changed her clothes, and gave Malvolio a venison treat to keep him occupied. Then she lifted the window she had used to enter the cottage on her first visit, climbed out, and lowered it again.

The night was warm and exceptionally bright. A reddish moon, missing a bare slice, shone in a field of sparkling stars. She moved silently into the woods.

Chapter 16

When Kate opened her eyes the next morning, she saw a note propped on the pillow near her cheek. Not a helpful note—*Be ready to leave at twelve o'clock. Wear a hat.*—but she obeyed on both counts and was waiting when Lord Dering, trailed by a convoy of carts and servants, arrived at the cottage.

Unsure how she ought to behave, she kept out of the way while he directed all the preparations. Servants were put to cleaning and polishing the large dinghy that had been tied up for several days at the water steps, and when it gleamed in the sunlight they stocked it with food, drink, fishing tackle and bait, blankets and cushions, oilcloth cloaks and umbrellas in the event of rain, a gun and powder in the event his lordship wanted to shoot something . . . all the particulars a gentleman and his lady might require for an afternoon spent on the lake. Then his lordship took his seat in the prow, leaving it to a servant to hand her in, and after a good push, the boat was under way.

Comfortably seated on the pillow-strewn bench in the stern, she watched Dering pull the oars with long, even strokes, propelling the boat smoothly across the lake. Despite a sugaring breeze, the afternoon was exceptionally warm. He soon peeled down to shirt-sleeves, and she pretended not to notice muscles bunching and stretching under the white cambric linen as he rowed. Beneath the shadow cast by his wide-brimmed hat, a smile played on his lips. He looked at ease. At peace. Almost happy.

Not wanting to spoil his fine mood, she sat quietly, letting her gaze roam to the shoreline, and beyond it, to the hills rising in grassy folds. Hawks, looking small as sparrows from this distance, circled on the warm air currents. Directly ahead of the boat an assembly of coots, their foreheads and beaks as white as Dering's shirt, lifted off the water and arrowed to a safer spot.

"Miss Kate," he said, startling her, "since I am doing all the work, would you be kind enough to pour me a tankard of ale? There's a jug beside the picnic basket."

She found it, wrenched out the cork, and located a tankard wrapped in a flannel cloth. "You have long since put the island out of sight, my lord. Are we not to inspect it?"

"Eventually. But first, I shall fish." He raised the oars and aligned them inside the boat.

She passed him the mug, three-quarters full, and watched him down the better part of it. They were midlake now, in view of the Dome, which meant, she presumed, that he was staging another of his shows. "Do you enjoy fishing?" she said, making polite conversation for the first time since being taught the art at St. Bridget's Academy. In her experience, polite conversation had never been of much use.

"Not really. But after Silas chose a demonstration

of fishing rods as an excuse to talk with me, I decided to follow his theme to its conclusion."

"Silas?"

"Ask Mrs. Kipper about him. All this clandestine tiptoeing keeps tripping me up."

The other Black Phoenix emissary, the one she wasn't supposed to know about. Or perhaps they just never got around to telling her. "There are several rods. Might I fish as well?"

"You may fish *instead*." He held out his mug for a second helping. "Have you done it before?"

"Oh, many times, for salmon. But my experience is in rivers and streams, not on a lake. I don't know what is down there, or what might entice it to a hook."

"That basket contains everything you are supposed to need," he said, taking back the filled mug. "Load your hook and angle away. We are, as they say, killing a little time and satisfying the curiosity of those who might be keeping an eye on us. When we've bored them to tears, we'll proceed by slow steps to the island."

She was selecting a rod, rising long enough to check weight and balance.

"Silas told me that in this lake I could catch perch, trout, pike, char, and eel." Dering took another swallow of ale. "I've been thirsty all day. Why is the remedy for drinking too much a dose of drinking some more? Only ale, of course, but nonetheless. There's lemonade as well, being towed in the water to keep it cool, but I thought to save it for our lunch. Catch an eel, will you? I wouldn't recognize any of the others. Well, perhaps I'd know a trout, but only if it was served up with butter sauce."

Seated again, her chosen rod across her knees, she

took a chunk of bacon from the bait parcel in the basket and threaded it onto the hook.

"Do eels like bacon?" He leaned back against the prow, elbows resting on the sides of the boat.

A regular magpie, she thought, chattering away as if they were boon companions. She'd have liked to chatter back, but she no longer knew how. "*I* like bacon," she said, feeling dull-witted. Feeling dull in every possible way. Only last night he had told her that she lacked humor. But she didn't. She'd only misplaced it, and trained herself not to relax in company, or to laugh easily. People—well, men—took laughter as an invitation to more intimacy.

But there was nothing threatening about Lord Dering this afternoon. His good spirits flowed over the boat like sunshine. No teasing, no sexual innuendos, no superior lordly ways. Had they met on safe ground, she might have genuinely liked the man sitting across from her now.

"If the fish won't take the bacon," he said, "you can have it for lunch."

She stood and sent her line out a good distance from the boat. "And if they do, might we cook *them* for lunch?"

"Only if you perform all the nasty procedures between catching and eating. I'll build a fire, if you insist, but that's as far as my skills will carry me. Other than toasting bread or roasting potatoes over the hearth, I know nothing about providing for myself."

"Another helpless aristocrat." She smiled over her shoulder and saw his brows rise. Not because she'd insulted him, she realized a beat later, but because of the smile. Excepting the fake smiles during her performances in the theater, she probably didn't smile often. If ever.

"I am why God created taverns," he said. "And chophouses, and street vendors selling cheese pies. Also females who can fish."

"And in return, what do you contribute to society?" Not amusing, but for nearly the first time in memory, she was beginning to hold up her side of a conversation that wasn't a quarrel.

"Oh, dear." Then a throaty sound, as if he was stretching. "Let me see. I am indisputably decorative. Witty. Charming to the ladies. If I can be towed away from the gaming tables, I'm a passable dancer. And I'm a damned good horseman. On consideration, I expect the average chimney sweep contributes more to society than I ever have done. Then again, had the deity wanted me to make a better showing, He should have cast me in a more heroic role."

"Aren't you playing one now?"

In the silence that followed, she regretted the question a dozen times.

Then he said, "Not in the least. I don't seem to know my lines, or what I am supposed to do next. You could best describe me as a competent prop."

She felt a tug on the line, and then the pole, left to sag in her hands while they were conversing, nearly jerked itself free of her. She got hold of it just in time. "I have a fish! I have a fish!"

Planting her feet on either side of the bench for balance, she set about drawing in the line. "It's very big," she said, breathless from exhilaration. "It's trying to swim away."

"Wouldn't you? Ask if it will tow us to the island."

The rod, unlike the simple ones she'd used to fish the river near her home, had rings along its length and was fitted with a reel. Accustomed to the delicate manipulation of a long, supple pole, she was having difficulty managing the fancy equipment. "You might help, sir."

"Not today. I am here to watch and learn."

Insufferable man. But in the face of his relaxed amusement, she realized that she'd been treating this small exercise as a battle and the fish as her enemy.

No humor whatever, I would say. His words still rankled because—for all her denials—they were true, and because she didn't want them to be. Perhaps one day she would rediscover the young girl who used to get into trouble for laughing too often.

Calmer now, she applied herself to the reel and kept the line moving steadily. Dering was whistling softly between his teeth, deliberately trying to annoy her. She considered what it would require to drop the fish onto his lap.

Her catch came out of the water swiftly and much lighter than it had felt to her before. The change and the surprise rocked her on her heels, nearly sending her backward off the boat. Dering broke out laughing.

She'd let go the reel, sending the fish back down. Grabbing the handle, she turned with a fury and up popped the fish again. Then she swung the rod to her left, missing Dering's lap but landing the fish on his boot.

He flipped it off, and it began wriggling and flapping in the bottom of the dinghy. Both Dering's feet were lifted now, to keep them out of the struggling creature's way. "But it's a baby," he said, still laughing. "A fishlet."

"Seven pounds at least!" She was exaggerating only a little. "Don't insult my fish."

"Heaven forfend. 'Tis a fine fish indeed. But send him back anyway."

"Back? You mean, into the lake? Let him go?"

"He fought the good fight, Katie. He still is. A great will to live, that fish has, and we should honor it. Besides, he did no more than yield to the temptation of a bit of bacon. Surely all God's creatures deserve a second chance. Shall we give him one?"

She looked down at her one small accomplishment, the catching of a fish, and could scarcely wait to return it to its home. But when she tried to take hold of it, the fish naturally evaded her hands. She was no friend.

Nor was Dering, but his hands were larger and he was closer. They closed on the fish just as she made another grab for it, her hands coming down on top of his. For a moment . . . for much longer than that, neither of them moved. His gaze found hers and held it. She was still legs akimbo over the bench, off balance and teetering in his direction. The fish squirmed in protest, gasping for water, desperate to escape.

"Remove the hook," said Dering softly.

She let go long enough to put her right leg next to her left. Then, feeling his gaze on her, she bent her head and, clasping the fish's head with one hand, carefully slipped the hook from where it had caught on the side of its wide mouth.

Two flat fish eyes stared blankly up at her. The sun glinted off its scales. She let go its head.

"Together," said Dering. "Put your hands with mine, and let's send him off."

With their hands on the fish and touching each other's hands, she looked again into Dering's gray-green eyes and saw them looking deeply into hers. Then, following his lead, she lifted her arms the same time he did, opened her hands at the same time, and they watched the fish hover in the air like a diver before cutting neatly into the water. One silver flash just beneath the surface and it was gone.

The freeing of the fish had taken only a short time, but it had seemed an eternity. Nothing of significance had changed, and yet she felt transformed. She dropped onto the bench, took one deep breath after another, and watched golden sunlight dancing on the blue water.

"No point carrying on with the fishing," said Dering. "By now that fellow will have spread word of our treachery to all his friends. Shall we find a spot for our picnic?"

She looked up at him, a little disoriented. "If you like. But the island—"

"Can wait a little longer. We'll go back that direction now, but beyond it. More misdirection, in case anyone is paying attention to us." He picked up the oars, slid them into the water, and began to row. "Keep watch on the opposite shore for grass and shady trees."

"You never asked," she said, "what I saw the night I went to take a closer look at the island."

"Oh, very well," he said with a dramatic groan. "I'd hoped to put off business until the last possible moment, but go ahead. What did you encounter? Smoke? Eerie noises? Witchly incantations?"

"A light," she said, hearing the impatience in her voice. She hadn't learned much, but he kept dismissing it as not worth hearing about at all. "I first saw it near the center of the island, moving east. It went dark at the eastern shoreline, and then I saw a boat moving away."

"So, much the same thing we detected from the window."

"But those boats went to the west. And they left from a different place on the island. This one headed east."

"Still redolent of smugglers, don't you think?"

The oars went lax in the water, causing the boat to slow and begin turning on an invisible axis. She glanced up at Dering, who was staring at her with a frown.

"And just how do you know where the westbound boats left from?"

The information wasn't meant to be kept from him, but that didn't make the telling of it a pleasure. "Last night, when you were asleep, I visited the island."

"You . . . !" He shook his head. "What could you have been thinking? I . . . Good God."

Whenever had she seen him at a loss for words? "There was no danger. I'd watched for lights and seen none. And I was careful."

"Oh, indeed. Rowed yourself over, did you?"

"I swam. It is not a great distance, my lord, and I am a prodigiously good swimmer. Have you noticed that we are turning in place?"

"That's what always happens when I'm with you," he said, digging the oars into the water. "I find myself going around in circles. Will you now tell me you made a wondrous discovery?"

"No." How desperately she wished it had been otherwise. As she had made her way through the woods, moved silently through the water, come onto the island, her heart had pounded with anticipation. She would find something of importance. Her initiative would pay off at last. But it hadn't, and the journey back to the cottage had been made on leaden feet.

"I explored only the perimeter," she said. "Under the canopy of trees, the interior was too dark, but until moonset I could see quite well along the shoreline. To the east there is a spit of crooked land that forms a little harbor of sorts. It's evident that many boats have been there since the last rain. I also found coils of rope attached to trees and covered with fallen twigs and leaves."

"No casks of wine? No Belgian lace? No booty?"

"Goods might have been landed there and stashed elsewhere. There were track marks, as if heavy objects had been dragged. And after a time I discovered two paths leading to the interior, their entrances concealed with branches and the like. Had I not been looking, I wouldn't have noticed them."

He had got the boat steadied and, tight-lipped, begun rowing again. She thought that for once she had made a small dent in his poise, which ought to have felt more rewarding than it did.

"I kept going," she said when he failed to speak. "It took perhaps two hours, the walk back to where I'd begun. For the most part, the trees come right down to the waterline. I was often walking knee-deep in the lake, and along those stretches I saw no signs of paths, landings, or boat tethers. Except once, just where it appeared there could be nothing at all. I can hardly describe the site. It's as if someone peeled the edge of the island away from the body and concealed the wound with trees. Until you are on it, inches away, you don't see that if you tie back a few branches to clear a path, you can bring in a small boat. Several boats could be stored there, towed partly up onto land. I saw where that had been done. I also saw paths, not so carefully hidden as the others, leading inland."

"The place where the westering boats sailed from?"

"Possibly. There is a third spot, not well concealed, that I could show you from here with a spyglass. We are soon to pass by it."

"And keep right on going. We'll ignore the island

for now, and we certainly won't fix a spyglass on it. Watch the shore to our left, Kate, and find a location well beyond the island for our picnic. Did you discover anything else?"

"Nothing. On the side of the island closest to the cottage, there was no evidence of anything unusual. My exploration proved of little value, I know. But I had to try."

"To the contrary." He pushed back his hat and swiped his shirtsleeve across his damp forehead. "This is useful information. I don't know if the island is linked to Black Phoenix's suspicions, but you have narrowed our investigation considerably. This afternoon we'll make a landing not far from the most exposed point and wander inside from there. Good work, Miss Kate. Don't do it, or anything like it, again."

Her heart was practically bursting with delight. She had been praised, not for her dancing or singing or acting, not even for the usual reason—the curse of her beauty—but for an act of . . . well, she wasn't sure. But he hadn't dismissed the little she accomplished as of no significance. Wanting to please him again, she turned her attention to her left, to the landscape that bordered the northern side of the lake, and kept watch for trees, grass, and a stream.

"Since we are confessing our independent leaps into the dark," he said after an interval, "I should probably tell you that I have drawn John Gilliam into our company."

She gazed at him in horror. "You told him about Black Phoenix? But the penalty—"

"Would make the Spanish Inquisition look like a clatch of ducklings. Yes, I know. So I took care not to mention Phoenix by name and implied that I was here on my own, conducting an investigation on behalf of God, England, and Saint George. We need help, Kate. And he's a good man.''

"But we *have* help. Mrs. Kipper and your Silas.''

"Functionaries. Besides, I don't altogether trust them. Gilliam will be the card up my sleeve, to be played if needed. At present he is collecting rocks and fossils in places where he has a view of the island, mentally recording any comings and goings he might detect through his spyglass. He is also a cracking good shot, if reluctant to prove it. Do I have to tell you to say nothing of this to our official comrades?''

And just like that, she was expected to shift her loyalty from Phoenix to a rakehell and a young man he had only just met. "I cannot make such a promise.''

"At the least, then, hold off for a time. I'll tell them myself, if they are needed to assist with my plan.'' He gave a short laugh. "Assuming, of course, I succeed in concocting a plan.''

She looked up at a heron, blue-gray and white, its long legs javelin straight as it flew over the lake. Shifting sides, seeking new fishing ground, perhaps wanting a change in scenery. Who could say why a bird chose its direction? Or a woman her alliances? "Perhaps I could help you,'' she said.

"By all means. With the planning, that is. I won't put you at risk.''

"Only I,'' she said, "can do that.''

"Which is exactly what has me worried. You've a habit of taking the bit between your teeth and galloping . . . or swimming . . . into danger. I have visions of you charging into Carrington's solstice ceremony waving your little knife, all afire with heroic righteousness.''

"I'm not apt to do anything so foolish, my lord. But as we make plans, consideration for my safety should not affect our decisions."

"Who said anything about *your* safety? I have resolved to leave here relatively intact, and that means no fallen females for me to trip over on my way out."

"Now you are being absurd. You're worried about having to rescue me, but you needn't."

"And I wouldn't. If chivalry is not yet defunct, I'm more than happy to give it a push in that direction. I'm also willing to make it impossible for you to get in trouble. But enough of this." The oars picked up speed. "We'll squabble later, when I've been fed."

They had left the island behind and out of sight when the lake curved around a rocky promontory and carried them a little to the north. Kate spotted a thin waterfall bouncing its way down a steep hill toward a stream and called Dering's attention to it. Not long after, he had guided the boat to shore.

"Find a place to settle," he directed, "while I unload our feast."

She carried an armful of blankets and cushions to a tree-studded meadow near the stream and spread them out in a shady spot between two oaks. He soon arrived with a wicker basket the size of a large portmanteau in one hand and a jug in the other.

"Because I have labored like a galley slave," he said, "you may have the distinction of serving me."

"Gladly." She went to the basket he'd set on the blanket. "Good heavens. There's enough here for eight people."

"We have insulted Paradise by accepting so little. They wanted to set up a pavilion with a table and chairs, fine china, and two or three servants to cater our meal." He began stretching his arms, legs, and back. "When I told them I'd no destination in mind, they insisted on sending a servant to row and another to attend to us. At the end, I had to say you weren't worth the bother."

"I quite agree." She laid out plates, glasses, and silverware. "Has the exertion been too much for you, my lord?"

"Probably." More stretching. "I sometimes hire a boat in Hyde Park, but you could fit a great many Serpentines into this lake. Tonight, if I am not to stiffen up like a post, I'll have to subject myself to the ministrations of a mad Turk."

"I'm sure I don't wish to know what that means," she said primly.

Laughing, he went to the stream and crouched beside it, reminding her that like a delinquent schoolgirl, she had forgotten to wash her hands before dinner. She'd rinsed them in the lake, of course, but they still felt slippery and smelled a little fishy. Rummaging around in the basket, she located soap and washcloths and carried them to the stream. "Here you are, sir."

In response, he scooped up a handful of water and sprayed it onto her face. "Doesn't that feel good? Ice cold, clear as a quality diamond, and it tastes good besides. Nothing like this to be had in London."

She might have sprayed him back, but she had long since outgrown childish games. They shared the soap, laid out the damp towels in the sunlight to dry, and were soon munching on chicken legs, ham with mustard, a fruit compote, buns stuffed with roast beef, and wedges of cheese.

There was wine, too, but he declined to open the bottles. They drank the lemonade, and when it was gone, he filled the jug with springwater and they drank that.

Little was said little during the meal. Dering was eating like a starved bear, with slightly better manners, and despite everything they had passed through together, she had begun to feel unaccountably shy. Probably because they had not quarreled, which always made things easier for her. Or because she was alone with a man, unthreatened by him, and enjoying his company.

What could be more dangerous than that?

Dering, on a search of the basket, had uncovered lemon tarts, a jam roll, and squares of shortbread. He propped a pair of cushions between his back and an oak, spread a checkered serviette over his lap, and topped it with a plate of sweets. "I hadn't thought it possible," he said, "but today, Paradise has lived up to its name. If I had the funds, I'd spend a good part of the summer here. Except that I'd sail instead of rowing, and when the nights were clear and warm I'd sleep in a pavilion on this very spot."

"Would that not grow tedious? I have little experience of holidays, to be sure, but I cannot imagine being so long without something productive to do."

"Ah, but we helpless aristocrats can't be expected to soil our hands with trade." He consumed a tart in two bites. "And if I must live a useless life, God knows I'd prefer to be doing it in fresh air, surrounded by beauty. I've always been a country lad at heart."

"That is the very last conclusion I'd have drawn about you," she said, wondering at her boldness. "Had you no choice but London and the gaming hells?"

"Probably a hundred. But that's where I ended up. And because I did, I find myself here today. Not an even trade, to be sure, but at the moment I cannot be sorry for it."

"What a very odd gentleman you are," she murmured, unsurprised to hear another of his laughs. "More shortbread?"

Shaking his head, he put aside his empty plate and slouched lower against the cushions, folding his arms across his chest. "Your service is done, Miss Kate. Let us have another peaceful hour here, and then we'll get back to business."

She nodded, but too late. His eyes were already drifting shut.

While Dering napped, she silently gathered the dishes, rinsed them in the stream, and repacked the basket. Then she sat near him on the blanket for a time, cross-legged with her hands properly folded, and allowed herself the joy of looking at him.

No one would describe him as classically beautiful, not in the way of Roman statues or Martin Fellows, the leading actor of the Pendragon Company. But even with his mouth slightly open in sleep, Dering contrived to look . . . just as he ought.

And for a little part of one night, this dazzling, irresponsible, unexpectedly kind man had been hers. Or she had given herself to him. She wasn't altogether sure when her resistance had dissolved, but she would not undo what had happened between them. Nor would she regret it, although the price of that brief interlude would be paid again and again.

She was paying it now. The pain of loss had dug deep, curled itself around the other pains, and become part of her. She awoke with a tightness in her throat. Beauty made her sad because it could not endure. Pleasures like the day she had just shared with him made her want to weep.

I am sorry, she longed to tell him. *All I know is how to survive, how to protect myself, how to run away. One mistake and all the world caves in. You should not have made me want you.*

But how could she have stopped herself? He had given her dreams to replace her nightmares, good memories to hold off the bad ones. Gazing at him through eyes that burned with unshed tears, she knew that when they parted, he would remain for always in her heart.

Chapter 17

Kate put away her spyglass with a loud *humph*. "You act as though watchers are lurking everywhere, scrutinizing us at every moment. Who would go to such trouble? Surely we've done nothing to put ourselves under suspicion. We've done almost nothing at all."

"By 'we,' you mean me." Dering, again at the oars, had just given her a series of orders relating to reconnaissance and how they would be conducting it. Without spyglasses, for one thing. "We should assume the servants routinely gather and report information, especially if it relates to first-time guests. As a target for murder, I remain of interest to the would-be killer and those he, or she, paid to dispatch me. Some of the gentlemen laying wagers on Carrington's verdict may be on the lookout for an edge. And, of course, there is Carrington himself. If I can recruit John Gilliam as a spy, I don't see why he shouldn't hire some help as well."

"So our visit to the island is certain to be noticed?"

"We're making no effort to conceal it. As summer tourists following a spur-of-the-moment whim, we'll land, bumble around for a time, and claim—if asked—

that we got lost. More than likely I shall receive an admonition from Mr. Fidkin, and should anyone speak to you of our excursion, you will complain about insects and a tear in your dress. Remind me to tear your dress."

They had come to the eastern edge of the island, but were still hugging the opposite shore of the lake. "Shall I direct you to a landing spot?" she said, trying to pick out the site where she'd found evidence of boats being tied up. "We want to be near one of the paths."

"To the contrary. Let's keep a wide berth between ourselves and the landing places you discovered last night. As for paths, we'll make our own. This is the Lake District, not a jungle in Africa. I'm going to head over now, and on the way we'll perform a mime about you objecting to my plan. When we arrive, refuse to disembark. I'll haul you out."

"Yes, my lord. Very good, my lord."

He gave her a sharp look. "I'm well aware that these precautions are, for the most part, ineffective or unnecessary. But consider that in all this muddle, our own behavior is the only thing over which we exercise a degree of control. So imagine spyglasses fixed on us at all times, Kate, just in case. Let us not make the seemingly inconsequential blunder that could bring us down."

She lowered her head. All her experience affirmed what he had said. On the stage and off it, she had created a thousand illusions, drawn skeptical observers into her make-believe world, made a lie appear to be the truth. Her one talent, and she'd failed to recognize that it was needed. "I should have better understood," she said. "From this time on, I'll do whatever you say."

"*That* would be a change." Grinning, he put the boat on course for the island. "While you're feeling obedient, now would be the time to berate me for taking a detour."

The drama didn't play out for long, which was just as well, because she was having a hard time staying in character. When she demanded he take her back to the cottage, he replied with nonsense verse. She took to faking sneezes so she could hide her face in her handkerchief. Children would adore him, she thought as he sang, off-key, about the improbable adventures of a pig and a hedgehog. By the time he'd guided the boat into the shallows and jumped out to draw it onto shore, she had laughed behind her handkerchief more than she'd laughed since her school days.

"Come along, Miss Kate." He was carrying his walking stick, the one that held a sword. "We'll push our way directly through for a time and then go left or right, hoping to intersect one of the paths. How is your sense of direction?"

"Superb," she told him. "My sense of time as well, if that proves useful. What are we looking for?"

"Damned if I know. We've no interest in smugglers, you will agree, unless Phoenix is a revenue collector in disguise. I suppose we should watch for the source of rumored lights, smoke, and mystical folderol. Carrington hasn't said where his solstice celebration is to take place, but I'd wager it's somewhere in the neighborhood. The exact site is our primary goal, assuming we can recognize it. What is the time?"

"About four o'clock."

"Plenty of daylight, then, but we can't stay more than three hours. Even that is probably too long. In sum, we're looking for whatever we find, which includes paths, landmarks, and anything that strikes us as suspicious. Don't wander off on your own."

The island might not be deepest Africa, but it proved to be virtually impenetrable. After a while they were forced to return to the shore and pretend to discover the concealed path she had already discovered. In the spirit of it now, she mimed more reluctance before he seized her wrist and pulled her after him.

He had to release her because the rough path, dim and littered with stones and twigs, was barely wide enough to accommodate his shoulders. The air, musky with the smells of moss, lichen, and fallen leaves, grew warmer as they made their way inland.

It was as if they'd left the ordinary world behind and come into a fairy woodland. She saw hazel, white-flowered holly, crabapple, and wild cherry among stands of lovely silver birches. Insects and small animals rustled in the undergrowth. Overhead, birds came and went, marking their passage with song. And set like jewels among the trees and shrubs and ferns were wildflowers—violets and bluebells, wild strawberry, cow parsley, red campions and white ramsons, honeysuckle, yellow archangel, enchanters night-shade—all opening their hearts to bees and butterflies.

With Dering leading the way, she had only to keep pace with him and enjoy the beauty of this magical weald. It seemed impossible, even sacrilegious, that terrible deeds could be done in such a place. But she knew of a woman murdered while arranging flowers in the sacristy of a church, and of unwanted infants abandoned to die in the new-fallen snow. On all the earth, there was no safe place.

"Good God!" It was Dering, who had disappeared around a curve. "Come look at this."

When she caught him up, he was standing before
what looked at first to be an unbroken wall. But drawing closer, she realized that it was a hedge, eight or
nine feet high and extending as far to the left and
right as she could see. "How do we get over it?"

"This way," he said, striking out to the left. "The
undergrowth is not so thick."

Sure enough, at a point where little light reached
through the screen of trees overhead, an entrance had
been created, invisible until one was directly on it.
"Wait here," he said.

Despite her promise of obedience, she followed him
into what appeared to be a high-walled maze with a
narrow path, except there were no breaks in the wall,
nor any tempting side passages leading to dead ends.
They were walking parallel to the outer hedge, and
after sixty or seventy yards, a hairpin turn took them
back the other direction, now a level closer to the
center. This time the journey was longer, perhaps a
hundred yards, and when they made a turn at the
opposite end, what she saw took her breath away.

Sunlight, all but missing since they'd entered the
woodland, dazzled her eyes. The maze-hedge formed
an enormous square, and at the far side were trees
and flowers, marble columns, pedestaled statues, and
a large Grecian folly of some kind. A showy garden,
but she was more interested in what was spread out
directly in front of her. "What is this?" she asked
Dering, now standing beside her.

"A labyrinth," he said. "Sometimes called a turf
maze. I've seen one before, when I was a student,
near the village of Somerton in Oxfordshire. About
this size, a different pattern, but well maintained.
There's another in Dorset, not far from Dering Park,
but that one is much older. Centuries, probably. One

can barely discern the patterns, they are so worn down and neglected, but the local people make use of it for May Day celebrations and the like."

"Would witches use a labyrinth?"

"I have no idea what witches use, except for the bubbling cauldron recipe in *Macbeth*. Eye of newt, toe of frog, that sort of thing. Shall we see what's on the other side?"

They might have cut directly across, the graceful pattern being carved out from a lush carpet of grass, but by silent agreement they slowly meandered along the graveled walkway, back and forth in ever-narrowing arcs until they reached a marble sundial. The pattern repeated itself on the other side, and she thought how soothing it was, and how rhythmic, to traverse the labyrinth. A Celtic song, one of those taught her by the travelers, played in her mind as she walked. Its haunting simplicity suited this place. So would a lullaby, or a hymn, or a lament.

As they came nearer the garden, the shapes of the statues and columns began to distinguish themselves. She blinked and looked again. From a distance she had assumed them to be the usual gods, goddesses, korai, and kouroi. But they were quite . . . other.

And she was here with Dering.

Heat blazed on her cheeks. If he gave her one of those seductively amused smiles . . .

She couldn't help herself. She glanced back at him and there it was. *That* smile. She knew exactly what he was thinking, and of course, he nearly always knew what she was thinking.

Since the harm was done, she might as well be hung for a sheep. "Are those columns meant to represent what I think they are?"

"Let me see." He rubbed his chin. "According to

my instructors," he said, now using a pretentious, elder-emeritus voice, "classical columns are of three designs—Corinthian, Ionic, and Doric. But these, I must say, are decidedly out of the ordinary. One might describe them as . . . Cockic."

"That's what I was afraid of," she said, trying not to laugh. He always made her want to do what she had spent years training herself *not* to do. "And the statues are vile. All those bare, bent-over backsides."

"Now *that* I happen to know about, courtesy of Byron and his fascination with Francis Dashwood's gardens. It represents the practice of kissing Satan's buttocks. Not something I would be in a great hurry to do, by the way, but apparently a staple of witchly rites."

They wandered among the statues in the direction of the folly, marveling at sculpted knot gardens and rose trees studded with blossoms. "Those might not have been smugglers' boats after all," Dering said. "Perhaps they were carrying gardeners."

"Someone has gone to a great deal of trouble. I cannot judge how long the garden has been here, but that hedge wall has been growing for a considerable time."

"Indeed. The island must have been inhabited, or at least in frequent use, for centuries. I believe we have found our primary target, Kate. Look here." He pointed to a metal pole set in concrete. "These are used to anchor large pavilions. And all around us are torch stands."

They passed through a break in a low boxwood hedge and came into the area centered by the Grecian folly. The outer rim was formed by the lewd columns, with high-backed marble chairs set between them. Thirteen all, she noted after a count. Each chair had a marble footstool. On the ground, laid out in some sort of pattern, were round white stones. They glittered in the sunlight.

"Thirteen chairs in a circle," he said. "Those white rocks form a pentangle. And up there is the altar. Shall we go see?"

A circle of three steps was topped by a large slab of black marble about six feet by four feet and standing waist-high. There was also a smaller stand of marble, this one white, probably used to hold candles, offerings, and the devil knew what else.

Beyond the circle of columns lay a stretch of the maze wall. Left in shadow by the late afternoon sun, it looked perfectly solid to her. She was about to suggest they find out if there was an exit on this side when Dering seized her arm and swung her around to face him.

He looked savage. The whites of his eyes glittered like the stones. His fingers dug into her arm, his other hand gripped her shoulder. She let out a yelp and he let go long enough to take a swipe at her, another of those pretend slaps that failed to touch her. Then he seized her again and towed her to the altar, bending her backward over it. His body pressed against her. His hot breath burned on her cheek. Afternoon whiskers scoured her chin as his mouth came down on hers. Almost on hers.

"I saw two men looking through a disguised opening in the maze. They're directly across from us. We're being watched."

The rough whisper halted her struggle.

"Keep fighting me." He shook her. "Make it look bad."

She screeched a back-alley oath and began to struggle. He wasn't hurting her, but his urgency put anger

into her fight, and strength besides. She got free one
hand and struck out at his face, catching it solidly.

He swore and came back at her, but like the one
before, his blow was all sound and no impact. Then
he laid her out on the altar and climbed up with her,
planting his knees on either side of her thighs.

Imagine spyglasses fixed on us at all times. She gazed
up into his blazing eyes, beginning to understand. In
this place they could be killed with no one the wiser.
Deception might be their only way out.

She screamed at him in French, in Gaelic, in
Portuguese.

He swore at her in gutter English. Dug the fingers
of both hands into the top of her dress and pulled it
open. Without help to dress that morning, she hadn't
worn a corset. He brought his face to her breasts.
"Has to look real." His lips surrounded a muslin-
sheathed nipple, making her squirm under him.

She remembered to beat at his arms. Tried to kick
at him, but he dropped onto her to hold her legs in
place. His mouth went to her other breast. She
writhed against him, felt the strength of him, felt her
body readying itself to take him inside.

"More fight!"

She obliged by taking hold of his hair with both
hands and giving it a hard tug.

A shout of pain before he returned the gesture, not
hurting her but getting a good loud scream for his
effort. His chest rubbed against her breasts. His hips
rubbed against her belly and her thighs. It was strange.
Frightening. Wickedly arousing.

She had experienced violent sexual coupling many
times. Hated it. Hated the man. But this was different.
The man was different. She ought not to be able to
bear it, and yet she wanted it.

His restraint, as he pretended to master her with violence, was all the more exciting because he was aroused. Hard against her. His body felt it too, then, the wildness in them both, the call to mate, the primitive drive of their flesh to completion.

Only the fight was make-believe. The passion was real.

His hands were dragging up her skirts. His knee pushed between hers, parting her legs. Now his hands were under her knees, raising them. "Keep struggling, Kate. I won't enter you, but we need it to look authentic."

More cries from her, more oaths. Her fists pummeled his back. And between the fake screams and the blows, she whispered, "Do it. Make it real."

His head snapped back. She drew it down to her again, to her breasts, pretending to pull at his hair.

He was shaking. "Are you sure?"

"Feel me. Put your hand there."

He did, sliding it up her leg and between them to the moist welcome her desire had created. A groan from him. He knelt up to open his breeches.

She couldn't help him, had to continue the mock combat when all she wanted was to drag him closer and feel him press inside her.

And then he did, with a swift, powerful thrust that brought a cry of pleasure to her throat.

Their eyes met. He must have seen her acceptance, the intensity of her response. "Fight still, Kate," he said on a ragged breath. "I must seem to ride you hard."

Long and hard, she discovered. Her knees were pushed up and up, giving him greater access. His hips swung back and forth. His breath came in harsh gasps.

The pressure mounted against her core of desire,

driving her past thought. She felt white heat shoot through her, heard a long scream and knew it was hers. He held her legs up, concealing what he did as he withdrew himself.

Keeping her safe, as he had promised he would do.

Little whimpers she hoped would pass for weeping to onlookers. She lay there on her back, alone now as he climbed off her and off the altar as well, fumbling with his breeches. Her gaze went lazily to his face. His mouth moved. "Escape," he whispered. "I'll follow."

She started to move, felt an obstruction, and realized his walking stick lay alongside her. Grabbing it, she struck a harder blow on his shoulder than she'd meant to. He yowled and reached for her.

She went the other direction, swinging off the altar, leaping over the three steps, and striking out at a run through the garden, the cane still in her hand. She took hold of the other end as well. If one of the watchers chased her, she wouldn't hesitate to free the blade and run him through.

When she came to the labyrinth, she tore directly across it, achieved the shelter of the high hedge maze, and sped up during the long straight stretches. Anticipating danger when she emerged, she drew out the sword and had it ready, but no one was awaiting her. She sped along the path as it wound around trees, bushes, and limestone outcroppings, her skirts lifted, her eyes watching her feet to keep from tripping herself up.

Only when she saw light ahead and knew she was near the shore did she slow. This was the next, perhaps greatest, point of danger. If the watchers had seen them arrive, one might be waiting near the boat. More effectively, they might have removed the boat altogether.

She slipped into the trees, so close together that she could scarcely push between them. At least it was spring. No crackle of twigs, no crunch of brittle leaves. Finally a small break in the thick foliage gave her a view of the dinghy. It lay exactly where Dering had tied it up, apparently undisturbed.

Now the danger was behind her. She didn't let herself imagine what might be happening to Lord Dering. A determined enemy would have gone for him, figuring an escaping woman to be inconsequential, easily disposed of at a later time. She pushed herself through the thick woods and burst into lakeshore sunlight.

She blinked. Took a few seconds to catch her breath. Quiet water lapped gently at her half boots, the indifferent lake untroubled by small human dramas.

It occurred to her the next person to arrive might not be Dering. She unwrapped the tie rope, tossed it into the boat, and shoved with all her strength until the dinghy was bobbing in the shallows. She followed it there, got it turned around, and climbed inside. Settled on the prow bench. Took up the oars. And all the while her attention held on the opening to the path, to the place where Dering should have emerged before now.

Still he didn't come. Her heart pounded in her chest, just under the place where her dress gaped apart. He'd torn her dress, just as he'd said he would do.

The more time that passed, the less likely he would appear. He would advise caution, she thought. He always did, and pretended to practice it, but his concern was ever for her. Only because it was what he would have wanted, she took up the oars and paddled about thirty yards out.

The sun beat down on her bare head. She had no recollection of him removing her bonnet, but he had always been clever with those agile hands. She thought of the golden guinea dancing between his long fingers, the magic he worked with them on her flesh. Sweet memories, brushed off and polished, filed away to cherish. Even if he appeared the next instant, he would be gone again in two more days. Memories were all she would have of him to keep.

And then he did appear, disheveled and beautiful, one hand shading his eyes as he searched for the boat. Found it. Lifted a hand in a wave.

Or so she thought, until he pointed a finger in her direction. "Get the hell back here, or I'll beat the devil out of you!"

Stunned, she went weak for a moment. Sagged onto the bench. Recovered . . . in part. He might be acting again, to mislead someone who might be following him. Might, might, might. He was so good, so much better than any actor she had ever worked with, that she never knew for sure. She nearly trusted him, some of the time. Blamed herself when she lacked faith, knowing the source of her fearfulness. But it was so often beyond her power to determine his intentions.

His last orders had been to fight him. To escape. She'd stick with that. If he wanted something other, he'd damn well have to give her a clearer signal. She stood, an oar in each hand, and raised her chin. "Here is the boat, my lord. If you want in it, you will have to swim."

"If you want to remain intact, you'll come and get me."

He appeared to be looking past her and to her left. Glancing over her shoulder, she saw the Paradise yacht making its way in the direction of the Dome. A few men were standing at the rail, watching them.

Safe enough, then. Someone else would give him a lift.

She sat again and dipped the oars in the water. "One last chance, my lord. Swim or find yourself another way home."

"I *can't* swim! Get back here! Are you mad? Come back!"

She kept going, not quickly in case the yacht kept going as well.

He shook a fist at her. Pulled off his shirt and began waving it, now directing his attention to the yacht. "Ahoy! Ahoy there!"

Slowly, the yacht began to change course for the island. A man was descending a rope ladder, on his way to the dory.

Assured that Dering would soon be picked up, she applied herself to the oars. And began wondering if she had done the right thing, in front of so many witnesses, to defy him.

Chapter 18

Up to his aching neck in hot water, Jarrett sat on the bench attached to the inside of the steaming pool and considered which of his half-formed plans had better than a snowflake's chance on a skillet of succeeding. None of them, so far as he could tell, but he had to come up with something, and quickly. Kate was expecting at least a good-faith effort from him, and for her sake, he meant to provide it.

What in blazes was he supposed to *do*? *You will procure incontrovertible evidence for a trial,* Black Phoenix had directed with boneheaded impracticality. Not bloody likely. Just who would take the word of Jarrett Dering, ne'er-do-well gambler, over the Marquess of Carrington and the peers he'd line up to speak on his behalf? And that was assuming Jarrett survived long enough to bring evidence, a long shot that made the snowflake's prospects look bright.

No matter what took place at the solstice ceremony, it was clear to him the testimony of one ill-reputed eyewitness would not stand as evidence. And what other proof could he offer? There would be no written records. Stood to reason that if the partygoers were committing despicable crimes four times a year, they'd learned how to clean up after themselves. If the culprits were going to be brought to justice, the proper authorities would have to catch them in the act.

But how was he to arrange such a thing? An ambush would require a shrewd plan, stealth, and far more resources than he could muster. Not to mention he'd been wrong about the timing. The malefactors had to be caught just *before* the act, when their intentions were unmistakable but no harm had been done.

And the fact was, he'd not yet concluded that Carrington, admittedly a little queer in the attic, did more than host an occasional orgy and spice it up with a few spooky rituals. Violence of the sort Sheffer ran to was another matter, but what if the whores and catamites willingly hired themselves out to be abused? A not uncommon practice, and if illegal, it was insufficiently heinous to merit all this effort by Black Phoenix. Nothing he had learned about these men and their exploits justified the risks he and Kate were taking.

Abusing children or, God forbid, sacrificing them was in another realm of evil altogether. If it turned out that was what they were doing, he couldn't very well stand there and let it happen. But neither could he overcome a dozen men, even with John Gilliam backing him up from behind a tree.

No matter which direction he considered taking, the roads turned into circles or led nowhere at all. *You will do whatever is necessary to close the gates of Paradise,* Jordie had said. Fine talk. So why the devil hadn't Phoenix supplied him the means to accomplish it?

"I beg your pardon for the intrusion, Lord Dering, but might I have a few words with you?"

Fidkin, not to his surprise, standing behind him on the tiled edge of the pool. Jarrett didn't bother to turn. "Come on in," he said, waving a hand that probably sprayed water over Fidkin. "I've meant to tell you the mad Turk is well worth the fortune you charge for his services. This evening I thought he was beating the knots from my muscles with a sledgehammer, but already I discern a remarkable improvement."

"We are pleased to hear it. But it is my unpleasant duty to remonstrate with you about this afternoon's incident. The island is privately owned, and should any guest require the use of it, the tariff is, even by Paradise's standards, exorbitant."

"Nice place, a trifle oddly decorated in spots. Rent it out, do you?"

"Rarely. We act only as agents. The fact remains, my lord, that—"

"I took your point, Fidkin. You might have made it before I violated a proscription hitherto unknown to me."

"That information, my lord, is prominently displayed in the materials I gave you on your arrival."

"Then I must get around to reading them. Meantime, you have my apologies for trespassing. I view the island every day from my terrace, and when I happened to be rowing by, I took a fancy to have a closer look. It will not happen again."

"Thank you, my lord. Please continue to enjoy your evening."

Obsequious idiot. Jarrett rested his head against the side of the pool, his thoughts as murky as his steam-clouded vision. At least he hadn't been evicted, although a part of him would have welcomed the opportunity for a guiltless escape.

"I must confess," said Carrington from where Fidkin had been, "that your chances of escaping my censure have notably declined. How are you to recover from the humiliation of being stranded on a deserted island?"

"To begin with, I'd have to be experiencing humiliation. One cannot recover from a disease one has not caught." Jarrett was lounging in the baths to get these inevitable encounters out of the way, but that didn't make them any more bearable. "The Gypsy let her temper off the leash, is all. In good time she will pay for it. For my part, I found the afternoon a slice more entertaining than most."

"And yet it is evening, and she remains unpunished."

"You mistake me for Sheffer, who prefers swift, crude torture to slow, refined torment. In the heat of her anger and temporary triumph, my Gypsy felt a heady satisfaction. But not long after, the awareness of what she had done—and what I might do in consequence—settled over her. As the hours pass, her fear mounts. The anticipation of punishment will not let her rest. And when at last I come to her, she will crumble. It is only then, while she is begging my forgiveness, that I will make my displeasure known."

Two bare legs, white as porcelain, slipped into the water beside him. Carrington had seated himself at pool's edge and rested his feet on the bench.

Now was as good a time as any, Jarrett supposed. If the peculiar marquess harbored a fancy for him, he wanted to know about it before confronting a direct advance. Raising his elbows backward, he planted his hands on the tiles and hitched his unclad self onto the side of the pool.

To his relief, Carrington was wearing a belted robe. To his even greater relief, exposing himself did not appear to affect the man beside him in the slightest. No gaze ventured to below his waist, or indeed, to anywhere on his person. A complication Jarrett was glad to elude, although this test was hardly conclusive.

"I should like to know more about your tactics," Carrington said. "Delayed punishment, while delicious in its own way, is scarcely a novel concept. Have you developed any unusual techniques for managing difficult females?"

"Why? Have you one making herself difficult to manage?"

"No, no. I have neither a wife nor a mistress. My interest is purely theoretical now, but at one time I lived under the thumb of a tyrannical and quite probably insane woman. You will think me obsessed to dwell on the subject of punishing females, but generally speaking, it keeps me from actually doing so."

"Secondhand revenge?" Jarrett, astonished at the confidences being dished up to him, wondered if any of them were true.

"Not altogether. Vengeance never satisfies, not for long, because the crimes themselves cannot be undone. I have elected to conduct the orchestra and leave others to play the instruments, but I require to know, in detail, how they make their music. It enables me to refill the well, to keep alive the sense that I have not succumbed, not entirely, to forces once beyond my control." For the first time Carrington looked over at him, meeting his eyes. "Tell me, then, how you refine the punishment you inflict on your Gypsy. It will help me pass a fair judgment on you at our Saturday gathering."

"I care nothing for that, you know. But as one who lost my inheritance to a lying, scheming female, I have no objection to sharing with you my own particular music."

Jarrett was beginning to feel like a bad actor in

a worse play. The overwrought dialogue turned his stomach, but for some obscure reason Carrington had chosen to unburden himself to the very man sent here to bring him down. It was an advantage where no advantage had existed ten minutes earlier, and Jarrett had little choice but to feed and water it.

"The truly exquisite torture," he said, "is not to the body, but to the mind. And it must be specifically designed to flay not only the flesh, but the vulnerable places in a woman's heart. The Gypsy is accustomed to harsh treatment, and when she came into my hands, she accepted it with resignation. That gave me no pleasure, I assure you, so I probed for her secret hopes and fears, and it is those I play on. She hopes for kindness, even for rescue, so I am sometimes kind to her. I have led her to believe I might take her back to London as my mistress. This makes her almost painfully eager to please me."

"And her fears?"

"She fears to hope, of course. But I have seen to it she cannot help herself. She wonders if she can bear my cruelty if it comes with my protection, so I make it seem so, only to turn on her with even greater cruelty at the most unexpected times. I did so today, when we were exploring the island, and as you know, she retaliated by making off with the boat. The next move is mine, and so it goes. I always win, she always suffers. But no game absorbs me for long. I shall be pleased to turn her over to you on Saturday and go in search of a new challenge."

"By God," said Carrington. "You have made an art of pain."

"It requires patience to do so, and an interest in human nature. You, of course, will find satisfaction by means particular to your own needs. Before I could offer suggestions, I'd require a better acquaintance with them, and with you."

"That can be arranged." Carrington's feet, which had been—like the rest of him—nearly motionless, began to shuffle on the bench. "What did you do to her on the island?"

"You mustn't skip the prologue. I spent the entire day raising her hopes, investing her with confidence. The island was no part of my plans, but when a caprice led me there, we came upon the most remarkable scene. In the middle of a thick woodland, there is a maze containing a labyrinth and a garden with erotic statuary. Have you seen it?"

"Indeed. We shall meet there tomorrow night, and for the solstice as well."

"Then I've no need to describe the marble altar where I threw her down and ravished her." Watching the marquess's white hands on his white knees, Jarrett saw the blood pulsing suddenly harder through his veins. Was it excitement at hearing about sexual brutality, or gratification that his chosen recruit had confessed what the marquess's spies had already told him? No way to be sure.

"It was the unexpected brutality of it that pleasured me," Jarrett went on, his voice deliberately artless. "Her shock, her fear I was repudiating her altogether, the end of her hopes."

"And tonight? How will you repay her defiance?"

"With something new, I think. Restraints and . . . well, whatever takes my fancy. Implements can be procured here, I have been told."

"At Xanadu. There is a display not far from the show room. Inquire there." The marquess came to his feet. "Our weather has been unfortunate this summer," he said conversationally, as if they had not just left off discussing rape and torture. "Whatever it sends us on Friday night, the solstice festival will take place without fail. As for tomorrow's lesser celebration, I'll make my decision when I return in the late afternoon. For now, a matter of business has called me to my estate. It isn't far. Before you leave Paradise—a fortnight, is it?—I should like to welcome you there."

"My pleasure," said Jarrett, not sure what to make of all that. Probably no more than it appeared to be. Carrington seemed to believe they were forging a friendship of sorts, while Jarrett expected to spend the next twenty-four hours hoping for an orgy-preventing rainstorm.

Since he was already dry, or as near to as the steamy air permitted, he allowed an attendant to dress him and made the trek across the bridge to Xanadu. It was probably coincidence, or perhaps Lady Luck had taken him up again, but Silas Indigo was coming out of the show room just as he arrived there. Shortly after, they were enclosed together in what Paradise had labeled the Tack Room.

"Don't be shocked," Jarrett said. "I want shackles, harnesses, and assorted perverse instruments." He lowered his voice. "Can we be observed or overheard?"

"Not here, although it is always best to speak softly and appear to be engaged in a normal transaction."

"After five days in this place, I'm no longer sure what *normal* is. I'll explain a little to you now, but while I speak, select and package up what I requested. Later, have a servant deliver it to me in the smallest of the gaming rooms. I shall remain there until ten-thirty, accepting the jibes of my fellows. I should like you to make a number of other arrangements straightaway. If you have the services of a competent spy, set him to watching Lord Carrington, who is departing shortly for his estate. Or so he says. I should like to know if he pays a call at Saint . . . well, whatever the name is, and should you have another spy to hand, send him after any child who is removed from the orphanage before Friday evening. Find out where they are being taken. Can any of that be done?"

"On instantaneous notice? Not satisfactorily, but we will contrive."

"Send Mrs. Kipper to the cottage whenever she is free to come, but not before eleven o'clock. What else?" Jarrett mauled his hair with a shaky hand. He was setting a plan in motion, and he'd no very good idea what it was.

"You appear to have uncovered new information, my lord. May I have it?"

"Certainly. Ask Mrs. Kipper, after I have spoken with her. I've no time to spare now, and it would be conspicuous if all the little Phoenixes flocked together. I don't suppose you know where I might find John Gilliam?"

"Since you took to spending time with him, I have naturally traced his movements. He is at present in the library, reading the newspapers."

"I'm off, then. Don't forget to send me the packet."

Silas Indigo had been a bit put out at being treated so dismissively, Jarrett thought on the way to the library. For that matter, he was surprising himself, all this purposeful assertion when he was actually making everything up as he went along. But once he'd committed himself to the game, which happened at a moment he could not recall, his gambler's instincts had snapped into play. For now he was running a bluff, on himself as well as on his allies and opponents. Their reactions would guide him to the next play, and the next.

may contemplate their purposes while I affix the shackles to the bed and get myself ready to play my own part."

"It is unnerving, my lord, how well you do that. Sometimes I have feared the role is natural to you."

"I know. This time, at least, I had the opportunity to ask your permission before subjecting you to one of these displays. As for your fears, you will have to judge my character for yourself. I can only assure you that for all my many, many faults, I take no pleasure in cruelty."

He untangled the chains, shackles, and a gag from the other implements and saw her eyes grow round as dinner plates when she saw what those were. "Another thing, my dear. Your ploy with the boat was inspired. And as it happens, I *can* swim."

Twenty minutes later, Malvolio signaled the arrival of servants delivering the supper Dering had ordered. Kate, uncomfortable but not unbearably so, stood barefoot on the bed with her arms stretched over her head and her manacled hands attached to an iron ring implanted in the wooden canopy.

Dering, his pupils constricted from the eyedrops, his breath smelling of brandy, quickly secured the gag and gave her a wink before jumping down from the bed. "You can moan," he said, "but don't overdo it."

He closed Malvolio in the dressing room, mussed his hair, and checked once again the position of the cheval mirror. A servant would have to come near the open bedchamber door to have a direct look at her, but from several places in the sitting room he could catch her reflection. She was wearing her corset over a filmy chemise now missing the fabric that used to cover her legs, figuring the expanse of bare white skin would draw attention. It had that effect on Dering, at any rate.

A loud knock. Curtain time.

Dering picked up the riding crop, leaving the whip coiled prominently on the bed, and went to open the door. She heard male voices, his overloud and slurred, the others polite, and the sound of dishes being laid out. Then Dering said, "I want a fire."

That would put at least one servant at the hearth, and a glance to his left would give him a full view of her. She bent her knees, letting her wrists take most of her weight, and tried to look miserable. The young man, now hunkered down, was taking logs from the wrought-iron basket and laying them on the grate. After using a spill to light the kindling, he rose, turned in her direction, and froze.

Even from under her drooping eyelids, she could see his open mouth, the flags of color blazing on his cheeks, the effort to move away and behave as though he'd seen nothing. She held her position, and sure enough the other servant, somewhat older, found a reason to put something on the mantelpiece. No reaction beyond a raised brow from this one, but the work of Dering's latest charade had been done. Not long after, the cottage door opened and closed.

Dering waited a time before coming to release her, starting first with the manacles. "My reputation, what was left of it, is consigned firmly to the chamberpot. Will any heiress marry me now, do you think?"

She couldn't answer, and just as well. What was there to say? Since returning to the cottage that evening, he had been quite different from the gentleman she'd thought she was coming to understand. He still made outrageous remarks, of course. He would probably do so while being lowered into his grave. But there was new purpose in his eyes, determination in his bearing.

When her wrists were free, her legs gave out from under her. But he was there to catch her in his arms, carry her to the Grecian couch, and help her don her dressing gown. She glared at him, pointing to the gag.

"Must I? These last minutes have been so peaceful." Moving behind her, he undid the knots and tossed the gag into the fire. Then he dropped onto one knee and began massaging her wrists. "Very soon we'll have company, and I will start issuing orders as if I knew what I was talking about. You may correct me and even quarrel with me, but when a plan is under way, you will do as I tell you. Now let us have our supper. Later there will be work for the both of us."

Not long after, Mrs. Kipper arrived, bringing with her a letter for Lord Dering. "A servant in blue-and-gold livery carried it to the manor house," she said. "I told the steward I would deliver it here."

Kate watched him break the seal and scan the message, which caused him to frown. He slipped it inside his jacket.

John Gilliam was next, garbed all in black and arriving by way of the open bedchamber window, as she had done on more than one occasion. He carried a small portmanteau.

When everyone was seated and offered a glass of wine, Dering went to stand near the fireplace, his hands clasped behind his back. "I will keep this brief. Tonight, after a conversation with Lord Carrington, I am prepared to believe he may indeed be using his solstice rituals to perpetrate unnatural acts, possibly even murder. If such a deed is to occur, it will take place Friday night in the garden Kate and I discovered on the island. I am invited to be present, but one man cannot prevent a dozen from having their way. To catch them out at exactly the right moment, we will need allies, a plan, and the element of surprise. I have none of those in hand. However, there is a necessary first step, and it must be taken within the next few hours."

"Survey the island," said Kate.

He smiled at her. "She has already discovered the places where boats are landed, but we need a working map of the interior. Assuming no one is currently on the island, we have a few hours of darkness in which to explore. But that presents its own difficulty, because visible lights, such as lanterns, would draw attention to us. When I spoke earlier to Gilliam, he thought a partial solution might be devised."

Mr. Gilliam removed a small shuttered lantern from his portmanteau. "I have modified this to cast light directly down, but I could put my hands on only one."

"I'll see what is here," said Mrs. Kipper. "And there is the valet's lodging, if it is unlocked."

"Look also for something that will float," Dering said, "like the tray under those decanters. We can't risk taking the dinghy, so we'll have to transport materials on small rafts."

Kate had been keeping watch out the window since nightfall, save for the time she was strung up in the bedchamber, and had seen no lights. But they wouldn't know until they got there if other visitors were on the island as well.

A few minutes later, using a box of tools found in the valet's quarters and other items scavenged during the search, everyone but Dering adapted the lanterns and attached fishing line to trays. That was Kate's idea, when she remembered the poles and other equipment still in the dinghy. Was it only a few hours since the picnic? she wondered, nibbling on cheese as she worked. It seemed a month ago.

Dering was priming the pistols Mrs. Kipper had given them after the attempt on his life. He wrapped them, the lanterns, tinderboxes, and candles in squares of oilcloth cut from the tarps and hats she'd fetched from the dinghy, talking all the while of his suspicions, plans, and ideas.

Then he changed his clothing, as did she, and she couldn't help noticing the letter sticking out of an inner pocket when he removed his jacket. She looked up at him and saw him looking back.

"It is no great secret," he said. "I hadn't decided if I'd take you with me, but the journey will give us a chance to review our strategy. Can you ride?"

"Yes."

"We'll hire you a mount, then, but I don't know if the Paradise stables have sidesaddles. And you cannot wear those trousers, not where we're going."

"I'll manage," she said. "Where would that be, my lord?"

"A friend has arranged for me to speak with Mr. Robert Southey, who may have information relating to the poem I showed you. We are invited to pay a call at eleven o'clock tomorrow morning. I'll tell you the rest on the way there. For now, one mission at a time. Let us gather up Mr. Gilliam and steal quietly into the woods. You may lead the way."

She could not see the correspondent's inscription on the folded paper, if indeed there was one, but she had little doubt the letter had been sent him by the Duchess of Sarne.

Chapter 19

"Poetry must pay better than I had reckoned," Dering said, applying the brass knocker to the door.

Kate nodded, her gaze wandering from the gardens to Derwent Water and the surrounding fells. Although the house itself was unremarkable, the setting could hardly be bettered, especially if Mr. Southey, like Mr. Wordsworth, took inspiration from the beauties of nature.

When a servant appeared, Dering gave his name and they were admitted to a large room lined with bookshelves and display cases. Sunlight spilled through wide expanses of glass, causing her to blink. Then she made out the figure of a young woman, petite and fashionably dressed, seated on a cushioned bench in front of a bay window.

Dering made a sound of surprise, quickly cut off, and strode directly to her. "Your Grace. I was not expecting you."

"And neither, I must confess, was Mr. Southey." She rose and lifted a hand, permitting him to brush a kiss on her gloved wrist. "He will join us in a few minutes, but I wished to speak with you beforehand. Who is your companion?"

Dering, looking around at Kate as if he had forgotten her existence, beckoned her closer.

She approached gingerly, stopped a respectful six feet away, and made her curtsy to the duchess. To the woman he had won at the gaming tables.

"May I present Miss . . . um . . . Miss Kate Gaetana," he said. "She is an actress. Miss Gaetana, I have the honor to make you known to Her Grace, the Duchess of Sarne."

The duchess, bright-eyed, regarded her with a smile. "I once fancied going on the stage, Miss Gaetana. It seemed a vastly exciting notion at the time. One day, perhaps, you will describe to me what I missed by taking a husband instead."

Horrified at the prospect, Kate made another polite curtsy.

"But let us not stand on ceremony," said the duchess. "Indeed, let us not stand at all. Miss Gaetana, do select a chair with a view of the lake. Dering will sit here beside me and pretend not to be shocked while I explain my little deceit."

"I should like you to explain how it is you are here at all. It was only a few days ago I sent my letter. Have you learned to fly?"

"If only I could. The courier had been instructed to stop at Sarne Abbey on his way to London, and there I was, preparing for a journey to visit Sarne's grandmother, who is in poor health. But it is a long journey to the north of Scotland, and a duchess may go nowhere anonymously. Every stop is an occasion for flap and feathers."

"But fine service, I shouldn't wonder, and the best of everything."

"Of course. But a journey of a few days for you requires a fortnight for me. I was complaining of it to

Devonshire, who has developed the perfect solution. A britska. It is like my own little parlor and bedchamber on wheels. What with two coaches for luggage and servants, four outriders, and my britska, we take over the road like a circus parade. Oh, dear. I am rabbiting on. Let me hurry to tell you what I have learned."

"It cannot be much, if you were unable to make inquiries in London."

"I considered returning there, but I had already heard the latest news about Mr. Coleridge. His illness has worsened, and in a state of profound low spirits, he has taken residence in the home of a doctor, Mr. James Gilman, at Highgate. No one is permitted to see him. Since I could not question the author himself, I thought something might be learned from his friend of many years. And Mr. Southey is married to the sister of Mr. Coleridge's wife, who also lives here at Greta Hall. Perhaps you will meet her as well."

"Did he know anything of the poem?"

"Ah. We have come to my deception. When I sent my servant ahead with the letter telling you of this meeting, I hadn't yet secured Mr. Southey's consent. But he was kind enough to grant it, after I dropped myself on his doorstep this morning and pleaded with him. It was ill-done of me, especially at this time. I just learned from Mrs. Southey that their young son took ill and died only a few months ago. The household is privately in mourning, but she assured me that Lakers—that's what they called those who come to the district in summer—are so accustomed to paying calls here that they must be welcomed in the way they have always been. As a courtesy, though, I shall take myself off before other visitors appear."

"Dodging the flap and feathers."

"The perils of being a notorious duchess. Will you tell me, Dering, what this is all about?"

"One day, perhaps. Some of it. If you press me now, I shall be forced to lie."

"Then say nothing more. I am drowning in lies." She stood, brushed down her skirts, and looked over at Kate.

Caught gawping, Kate lowered her gaze and sprang off her chair, uncertain what to do next. Curtsy again? The only aristocrats she'd been in company with before today were male, and most of those had ventured backstage to give her a slip on the shoulder.

"I hope you don't feel we've been ignoring you," the duchess said with one of her friendly smiles. "After intruding on a houseful of strangers to beg a favor, I am in rather a rush to be off. But when we meet again, with your permission, I shall quiz you about life in the theater. My own existence is rather like that, all artifice and excess. I suppose Mr. Shakespeare had the right of it. All the world's a stage."

During this speech, she was crossing to the door with splendid grace. And Dering was watching her go, a frown drawing his brows together. Suddenly he came after her, took hold of the arm that was reaching for the door latch, and drew her to one side.

Kate, stranded in the center of the room, could not distinguish their words. They spoke softly together, the bond between them unmistakable. Dering looked intent, his head inclined to hers, and the duchess gazed up at him, her expression eager and curious. Once, she put a hand on his forearm. Only for a moment, but Kate felt the touch like a blow.

Jealousy, like a wolf's mouth, closed its fangs on her.

She had always accepted he could never be hers. It was unthinkable, a fugitive actress and an English viscount, although she could not help thinking of it anyway. To him, the notion would never occur at all. But knowing the divide impossible to cross and looking truth in the face were quite different experiences. As she watched him with a woman of his class, both of them attentive and charming, sophisticated and at ease in each other's company, a knife twisted in her chest. The elegant duchess made her feel inconsequential. Tall and gawky and common. Of another species altogether.

And such a short time ago she had been so happy. When the three conspirators set out for the island, towing their rafts, unsure what they would find, she had come fully, deliciously alive. She felt of value, working in a common cause with a viscount and the son of an earl. In return, they treated her ideas and her arguments with respect. And so they should. When it came to deception, she was the expert.

After leading Dering and Mr. Gilliam to the paths she'd previously discovered, she resisted only a little when they insisted she take for herself the easy one she had already explored that afternoon. Her task was to search the maze and the garden, where she discovered that what appeared to be large marble tiles were cleverly disguised trapdoors.

She could have used Dering's strength to raise them, but she managed, disclosing the concealed entrances to three underground cellars. Two contained wooden boxes, perhaps stored there by smugglers, but there were also torches, lanterns, and chests filled with what looked to be costumes and props. The third held more wooden crates and what appeared to be a cage for a midsize animal, but unlike the others, this cave narrowed to a tunnel. She followed the trail, bent nearly double, for several minutes before nearly butting heads with Lord Dering, who was coming from the other direction.

Too soon, the approach of dawn sent them all back to the cottage, where Mr. Gilliam put on the clothes he'd brought with him in his portmanteau and set out for the manor house as if he'd been enjoying an early-morning walk. She had fallen into bed beside Dering, where they slept for a short time in each other's arms.

Then came the long ride to Keswick, Dering on the horse he valued so much, a smile teasing at the corners of his mouth. He often smiled, frequently laughed, but the simple, quiet pleasure on his face that morning had resonated in her heart.

Now the inner glow she had been carrying with her like a magical candle had gone dark.

What could they still be talking about? The duchess had been on her way out, and he had, of a sudden, been unwilling to let her go. Kate didn't mind that they were ignoring her. In the circumstances, she was glad of it. But she felt like a voyeur watching two lovers sort out their past together, or their future, while she held still as a bootjack to keep from drawing their attention.

"But I wish," said the duchess, signaling the end of their confidences by raising her lovely voice, "that you would permit me to deliver my reply in person. I positively *long* to visit Paradise."

"Then do so after I am gone, Your Grace. The less attention called to me at present, the better. One thing more. Letters arriving at Paradise might well be opened or examined by surreptitious means."

"Have no fear," she said with a laugh. "I know precisely how to make something appear other than it is. Miss Gaetana, do pardon us for being so rude. I look forward to meeting you on a more sociable occasion."

Yes, indeed, thought Kate as the duchess swept out, arm in arm with Dering. *I am invited to all the best places.*

She went to a window and was standing there, seeing nothing through the film of moisture in her eyes, when Dering returned in company with a slim gentleman and a plump woman who was wearing, Kate could tell from experience, a wig. They looked to be in their forties and were smiling at her with a friendly, if detached, welcome.

Dering introduced her to Mr. Southey and Mrs. Coleridge, with bows and curtsies all around, and as if the library were his own, got everyone seated where they could easily converse. "I apologize," he said, "for intruding on your privacy about a matter of such little consequence. None at all, really, except that I am inordinately fond of puzzles. This one concerns the recent publication of a poem by Mr. Coleridge. I—"

"You are here," said Mr. Southey, his chest expanding like a bellows, "to question me about the work of another poet?"

"Only on account of the puzzle," Dering said quickly, color rising on his face. "I meant no slight to your own superior work, which was already a legend when I entered Balliol a few years after the college had been honored with your presence. Everyone tells me, sir, that I am an impertinent fellow."

"Yes, yes." Mr. Southey appeared mollified, to a small degree. "A Balliol man, are you? I suppose your inquiry cannot be altogether foolish. What is it, then?"

"I have for at least two years been familiar with several phrases clearly drawn from a poem, although

I could never recall the title or the author. Now I have discovered that the poem was first published last month." Dering removed the pamphlet from his jacket pocket. "The preface indicates that 'Kubla Khan' was actually written nearly ten years ago. I am wondering how it came to my attention, is all."

Mr. Southey shrugged, clearly indifferent to the mystery. "Perhaps you heard Coleridge recite it. He has done so on a few occasions, I believe, although he generally dislikes presenting an unfinished work. One such recital, at Lord Byron's house in Piccadilly, led to this publication. Isn't that right, Sara?"

"I was sadly vexed to read the advertisement announcing its appearance," she said. "Unwise of Coleridge to publish his *fragments*."

"The recitals are what I should like to trace," said Dering, steering clear of Mrs. Coleridge's remarks.

They had not been said unpleasantly, but Kate sensed a deep unhappiness in the woman. Or perhaps she was looking at the mirror image of her own.

"I cannot speak to those," Mr. Southey said. "If it matters, I once had occasion to recite the poem myself. It was in 1813, shortly after I was chosen Poet Laureate. Lady Willington, who has a summer house on Windermere, arranged a party in my honor. I was to speak, and Coleridge agreed to come up from Bristol and present one of his excellent lectures. But he must have failed to recall the engagement, for he neither appeared nor made his excuses to our hostess."

Mrs. Coleridge's moon-round face wore an expression of resigned forbearance. "Silence and absence. That has always been his way."

Mr. Southey nodded. "Lady Willington, distressed, sent a message asking that I expand my own presentation. I thought then to bring a little of Coleridge, if not his person, for the guests' entertainment, so that night I read 'Kubla Khan.' Not with the dramatic rendering Coleridge would have given it, to be sure, but the audience seemed pleased enough. One fellow in particular, who followed me into supper and asked permission to make a copy, which I naturally denied. But I let him hold the paper for several minutes while he committed his favorite lines to memory. A pleasant enough gentleman, if a trifle obsessed with a minor piece of work."

"Do you recall his name, sir?"

"I'm not sure I ever had it. No, wait. It started with a B, I'm almost certain. B and another syllable. Perhaps it will come to me. Did you wish to see the poem?"

"By all means, if you will be so kind."

Dering, following Mr. Southey to his desk, maintained his pose of whimsical interest, but Kate recognized the nearly invisible signs of alertness in his eyes, the subtle motions of his fingers that told of energy leashed. She should offer him his gold guinea to play with, as he'd done at the auction.

"Ah. Here it is." Southey held up a single sheet of paper, inscribed on both sides. "Coleridge sent me this many years ago. It is a copy, but written in his own hand, which is why I kept it. Although"—said with a smile, his first—"I rarely discard any book, pamphlet, or paper, as you can see by looking around you. Might I examine the published edition of the poem?"

"I hope you will keep it, sir, with my gratitude and regards."

While Mr. Southey studied the manuscript and the pamphlet, Dering sat himself across from Mrs. Coleridge and engaged her in conversation about places of interest in the vicinity.

Responding to his questions transformed Mrs. Coleridge. She spoke with enthusiasm and a good deal of wit, which Dering returned in kind. Another woman wrapped around his finger, Kate thought, fascinated by watching a master at work. She knew how it was to be the recipient of all that charming manipulation. Even knowing perfectly well what he was up to, you *wanted* him to be sincere, to be responding to you in a way he responded to no one else. Females were so susceptible, so easily deceived.

"He has made a number of modifications since inscribing my copy of the poem," said Mr. Southey. "No telling when, of course. Perhaps he revised it shortly before publication."

Kate and Dering joined him at the desk, one on either side of Mr. Southey as he pointed out variances in the two versions. None of the changes appeared significant to her, although Mr. Southey praised two of them as decided improvements.

"But *this*," he said, shaking his head, "is an abomination. Look here, how he first wrote 'Mount Amora,' only to strike it out and write 'Mount Amara,' which is surely the proper allusion."

"To what?" said Dering. " 'Amora' seems related to *amore*, to love. Is that not an effective reference?"

"But consider Milton, when he wrote of Satan's search for Eden. 'Nor where *Abassin* Kings thir issue Guard, Mount *Amara*, though this by som suppos'd True Paradise.' Does 'Amara' not suit a poem that ends with the word 'Paradise'?"

"Indeed." Dering glanced over at Kate, as if seeking the one person in the room who would understand its significance.

"And then, disgracefully, he alters the word to 'Abora,' unless it was an error of the publisher. I prefer to believe that. No poet in possession of his wits and his powers would willfully elect such a fall from grace."

"Even to my poor judgment, it seems an insensitive change," said Dering. "Might you recall, sir, anything more of the gentleman from the party? His appearance, perhaps, or his mannerisms?"

Mr. Southey visibly wrenched his attention from the poems and gazed out the window. "Very little. He was well mannered, not aggressive in speech or movement. Dark hair. A gentleman, Lord . . . Bee . . . no, it eludes me. I would say Lord Beacon, but that feels off. Something like it, though. If it comes to me, shall I let you know?"

"I should be glad of that."

While Dering provided Mr. Southey his direction in London, Mrs. Coleridge took Kate into the garden and proved herself an amiable conversationalist, even without Dering's encouragement. Finally, invited to return whenever they liked, Kate and Dering rode over the bridge that crossed the River Greta.

On the other side, waiting on horseback, was a young man in blue-and-gold livery.

"Shall we go into Keswick," Dering said to him, "and find a spot for a meal?"

In a private room at the Keswick Arms, Dering used the traveler's desk that had been attached to the servant's saddle and wrote page after page while Kate pushed shepherd's pie around her plate, wondering what he was doing. All day he had focused his resources on the next step and the next step after that, and in none of them had she played any part. Why had he even brought her along?

Guilt came out of hiding—it never stayed hidden for long—to gnaw at her. She ought to have known, when she had cared only for the mission and berated Dering because he cared nothing for it, what her punishment would be. Now he had dedicated himself to the mission, while she languished around him like a silly girl infatuated with the school's undergardener. At least she'd resisted nagging at him, demanding his attention, seeking reassurance. Out loud, anyway.

After a long time he put aside the pen, blotted the last page, and read through the entire letter. Then he folded it neatly, took up the pen again . . .

She couldn't help herself. Leaning forward, she tried to read the name of the recipient.

"The Earl of Kendal," he said. "I am begging him, in what I hope is a dignified manner, to assist us tomorrow night. It was Her Grace's suggestion, as this is her writing kit, and the young man who met us her servant. I have described to Lord Kendal what little we are sure of, told him what I expect to occur, and outlined what we hope he will provide. The duchess will, in her fashion, send us his response."

Dering applied hot wax to the letter, waited the proper time, and impressed his seal. "Of course, he may not be at his estate, but Her Grace says his brother is always up for a romp. If all that fails, she will apply to the Lord Lieutenant on our behalf."

"Why not go to him first? I thought you wished the authorities to bear witness."

"It is, in part, a matter of jurisdiction. The Sarne estate and the Lord Lieutenant of her acquaintance are both in Westmoreland, while Paradise lies in Lancastershire. Besides, the Lord Lieutenant rather disapproves of her. Kendal is our best chance of securing help, and his influence is far-reaching. Believe me, Kate, I did not wish to impose on the duchess. But where else could we turn?"

While speaking, he had packed up the writing kit. "Let me get the letter dispatched. Then I shall eat the rest of that pie and we'll be on our way."

She had thought he meant they would go directly back to Paradise, but his lordship had some shopping to do. Keswick was a small town, built mostly of local greystone roofed with shale. They wandered from shop to shop, choosing items that he explained only after he'd bought them. And even when he spoke with her, his true attention was elsewhere.

He'd bought her a dress as well, and undergarments he said were to replace the ones he had cut off her at the Pleasure Dome. But their real purpose was to be wrapped around items he wished no one to see.

It was midafternoon before they set off, their parcels neatly packed in a large tapestry bag, but Dering surprised her again by turning onto a narrow road that led to a moor set in a ring of hills above the town. There, a circle of standing stones surrounded a small rectangle of stones, all of them weathered by centuries of wind and rain.

"The real thing," he said. "An authentic Druid site, or perhaps it was built and used by some other ancient cult of worshipers. This is not an artificial shrine like the one on the island, not the product of a warped mind trying to cloak his rituals in primitive traditions. It is called the Castlerigg stone circle. Mrs. Coleridge told me how to find it."

"It's lovely." A halfhearted admission, although the scenery was spectacular. She was feeling like one of his parcels, carried along wherever he decided to go. "But why have we come here?"

"You must decide for yourself. I am here to let the fresh air blow the cobwebs from my head. To expiate my guilt. To recruit every power that may be to our side. And to pray for a storm to begin just when I need it, and to last for as long as I want it to last."

"You don't wish to attend Lord Carrington's . . . party tonight." She'd nearly said "orgy."

"If he has one, wherever it takes place, I must go to it. But I want the island clear for another invasion by our little army. When we meet with Gilliam, I'll explain what I have in mind. Can you be patient for so long?"

"If you promise I will not, for the sake of my *safety*, be excluded from the battle."

Lifting her by the waist, he set her on one of the smaller stones in the center of the ring. "It's true I want to keep you far from danger, but you are too greatly needed in the middle of it. We're all in this together now, and we'll each serve where we can be of most use."

Relieved, she watched him push back his hat and gaze at the hills rising around them. "Did you learn anything from Mr. Southey?" she said after a while.

"More about Milton than I cared to know, but yes, I think so. The timing of Southey's recitation, right here in the Lake District the year before Paradise was constructed, seems pertinent, as does the unknown gentleman's fixation on the poem. I know a man much like the one Southey described. Tonight I will convey my suspicions to Silas Indigo."

"You believe this man could be the owner of Paradise?"

"He is certainly worth investigating. Anyone who heard the poem recited might remember the Pleasure Dome, Paradise, even Xanadu. But only someone who had looked closely at the text of an early version would give the name of Mount Amara to the Paradise yacht."

"I think, my lord, that you have been exceedingly clever to deduce all this."

"Do you?" He looked absurdly pleased. "It is odd, how so many separate and apparently unrelated threads are coming together to form a picture. If my suspicions are correct, the owner is the same man who lost a large wager to me a fortnight ago. I wonder if he knows of my invitation to Paradise."

"Perhaps he arranged it."

"If he did, my little accident on Sca Fell may be yet another thread in the tapestry. I'd been assuming it a family matter, a murder for hire, but . . . Well, never mind all that. By tomorrow night our part in this will be done with." He stood on tiptoe, putting his head level with hers, and placed his hands on her shoulders. "Come give us a kiss, then, for good luck. We're going to need a devilish lot of it."

Chapter 20

The hoped-for storm swept in ahead of schedule. Forced to take refuge in a hostelry for several hours, Jarrett and Kate returned to the cottage at twilight and found two letters waiting for them on a table near the door. One was from the Marquess of Carrington. The other, its wax seal cleverly doctored, bore the inscription of Her Grace, the Duchess of Sarne.

"Someone has been at this," he said, showing Kate the evidence before opening the letter. It was long, several pages of flirtation, seduction, and disdain that might have convinced another man that Her Grace was in the throes of a passing obsession for him. Jarrett broke out laughing.

"Well?" Kate said with a touch of impatience. "Can we expect help?"

"I'll need to decipher the more subtle clues, but it appears Lord Kendal will back our play. He's sending someone here tonight for instructions. Blast. No way to prevent it, but I don't like strangers coming onto the grounds and drawing attention to us."

Kate extended her hand. "May I?"

Leaving her to read the duchess's letter, he scanned Carrington's brief message. Because of the storm, tonight's ceremony had been relocated from the island to Carrington's estate. Coaches would depart from the Dome at ten o'clock for those who wished to participate.

Jarrett had no intention of attending the orgy if he could credibly avoid it, but neither did he wish to seem unwilling. The clock showed just after nine-thirty. A man in a hurry might arrive on time, but a man well gone on opium—or using eyedrops to appear that way—could slog up to the Dome after the coaches had left and drown his disappointment in drink.

"You shouldn't walk," she said when he showed her the letter. "Not in this weather. Put out the lantern and request transportation."

"It won't get me there by ten." He gave her a considering look. "One might almost think you wanted me to miss the orgy."

"Nonsense. Mr. Gilliam and I have things well in hand. You may as well run along and enjoy yourself."

Kate had not been far from the truth, Jarrett reflected as the gig returned him to the cottage shortly after midnight. His sole responsibility now was to do what he'd been doing the last few hours, letting himself be seen as the deplorable fellow Carrington had taken up with and allaying suspicion—if there was any—about his character. By this time tomorrow, for good or ill, it would all be done with. He was looking forward to leaving Black Phoenix behind and coming to terms with his enticing, unbiddable Gypsy.

She was waiting for him, hair loose around her shoulders, wearing a dressing gown over her black trousers and tunic. She and Gilliam would be taking the supplies Jarrett had purchased over to the island.

"Everyone is waiting for you in the bedchamber," she said.

"Everyone" included John Gilliam and two men he didn't recognize, one of them small, thin, and missing his front teeth. He was sitting cross-legged on the floor, securing something in a length of oilcloth.

The other stranger, young, lanky, and blond, rose from the bed where he and Gilliam had been studying a hand-drawn map. "Kit Valliant, sir. Kendal's youngest and most amiable brother. He told me to give you a message. If I become a nuisance, you are to send me packing. Actually, he might have said *when* I become a nuisance."

Jarrett noticed then that all of them were wearing black trousers and shirts. "I seem to be out of uniform," he said.

"But you have no need to skulk about, while I have the proper costume to hand because I dabble in smuggling. Fergus there comes along to keep me out of trouble. He was the middle brother's batman on the Peninsula and got into the habit of looking after Valliant miscreants."

"We suspect that smugglers occasionally use the island to stow their goods. Would you chance to be one of them?"

"My own transgressions are confined to Morecambe Bay, but I know a chap who knows a chap. Are there inquiries you wish me to make? Or did you wonder if the smugglers would show up tomorrow night? Little chance of that, with a full moon. They might come in tonight, though, while it's stormy."

"What exactly do you mean to do for us, Mr. Valliant?"

"Whatever is needed. Gilliam and Miss Kate have explained everything. Fergus and I will go with them to the island, and he intends to remain until the business is done with. Fergus is used to wet bivouacs and can hide himself in a bathtub. No one will know he's there. I'll return tomorrow night for the party."

"Very well." Jarrett, becoming more irrelevant by the minute, dropped onto a chair. "Another of Carrington's crowd was at the Dome with me, too drunk for tonight's celebration. I managed to pry a few details out of him. There are generally twelve participants in the solstice rites, plus an odd fellow who claims to be a Druid priest. He performs a few magic tricks, most of them involved with making fire appear. You see the problem."

"If his fire tricks are visible to the men waiting in the boats," Kate said, "they could be mistaken for our signal to move in. But we already have a solution. Mr. Fergus thought we might have use for rockets, so he brought three of them along."

That explained the long, thin packet he was wrapping up. "Gilliam, do you know how they work?"

"I'll be managing the rockets," said Fergus. "Mr. Valliant will see to the fire arrows. Whichever of us gets the signal first will let go, and the other soon after."

Jarrett might have argued about sending yet another earl's son into harm's way, but he had been concerned about the signaling. Kate and Gilliam had no experience with a bow, and neither was strong enough to send an arrow to any great height.

"Unless Carrington changes the order of events," he said, "we'll arrive at the island in boats, five or six of them, shortly after eleven. Golsham didn't want to talk about the ceremony. Said it was tedious, except for the end, but that consists of exactly what we most feared. Each of us is expected to participate in the sacrifice, using a ceremonial blade, although the child usually succumbs early on. Golsham thinks the boy is drugged or given alcohol beforehand, because on arrival he is passive. Most of the men dislike the sacrifice, but Carrington demands it, and he's giving the party."

"Is the child transported in the boats with the rest of you?" Kate asked.

"I don't think so. If he can be intercepted along the way, all the better. Indigo has men watching the orphanage. But if the boy makes it onto the island, your first priority is to see him to safety. If possible, you should also disable the boats, except the one or two required to make your escape."

"How will you get away, then?"

"I shouldn't need to. Well, unless someone decides I am responsible for Kendal's invasion."

"Or takes the opportunity for a second try at killing you." Kate was at the dresser, making a list. "We'll hide a spare boat or mark the safe ones in case you need to take a runner. And fix you up with a weapon you can get to. Is there more to tell us?"

"I'm afraid not. I will spend most of tomorrow being conspicuously dissipated while keeping my ears open. The greatest problem is how to get the three of you onto the island without being seen. People are likely to be there throughout the day, cleaning up after this storm and arranging for the ceremony. It goes on, rain or no. Golsham said that if the weather looks bad, they'll erect a pavilion."

"Mr. Valliant and Mr. Fergus have given us some excellent suggestions," she said. "We'll choose times and methods of arrival after they have seen the island. It's late, Dering. We should leave now."

He nodded and helped gather the parcels they would be transporting. "Must you go?" he asked Kate when they had a moment alone. "Gilliam can show them around."

She gave him a sideways look. "We have scarcely enough people as it is. And if you are angling for a tumble, well, you should have gone to the orgy."

At eleven o'clock on the night of the summer solstice, five boats set out from a dock not far from the gates to Paradise, each carrying two oarsmen and two passengers bearing torches. Three invited guests had failed to appear, including the Frenchman Valery D'Arvaine, Belinda's sometime lover. Jarrett didn't know if that was good news or bad.

That afternoon, a package containing his costume had been delivered to the cottage. All the participants were provided white robes, white capes affixed with black hoods, and gold masks, Venetian in style. Even so, he had no trouble identifying the men whose acquaintance he had made. Carrington kept company with the celebrant, who wore only white and left off the mask. Golsham was drunk and boisterous, and Sheffer's vinegary cologne could not be mistaken.

Jarrett shared his boat with a man he didn't know and who had yet to say a word. That was enough to make him especially glad of the sling Kate had rigged to hold a pistol at the small of his back. His boot contained a sheathed knife.

The night, clear and rather cold, was bright with stars and a round moon as the procession of boats, torchlit and peopled with otherwordly figures, moved silently across the lake. They pulled up on the east side of the island, where a spit of land had created a shallow inlet that made disembarking easy, even for men wearing long robes.

Jarrett had worried about the oarsmen, whose presence would make it impossible to disable the boats, but it seemed Carrington wanted no witnesses roaming about. They all piled into a pair of the boats and set back the way they'd come.

So far, so good. Torch in hand, the mysterious stranger at his side, Jarrett joined the procession on the path that led to the maze garden.

Kate, wearing a brief costume contrived by Mrs. Kipper, entered the water as night fell and swam to the island, her clothing and weapons parceled atop the tray-raft she was towing. Fergus had advised against wet clothes and shoes, which could leave a noticeable trail. Concealing herself in the woods, she dressed quickly and hurried to the meeting place where Mr. Gilliam waited for her, full of news.

"There are more caves and tunnels," he said. "The island is riddled with them. The smugglers store their least valuable stock in the ones everyone knows about and hide their valuable merchandise elsewhere. Those locations are still a secret, but Valliant was told about a tunnel that connects with the largest cave. We now have a way in and out without being seen."

"What of the child?"

"No sign yet of anyone but servants and workmen, and nearly all of them left at sunset. Valliant thinks the child will be brought by boat, taken through the main tunnel, and placed in the cage we saw near the ramp. It's only a guess, of course. But we have to choose where to position ourselves, and that's as good a spot as any."

"Dering was unable to learn anything of use today," she said. "But he mentioned an odd joke someone made about a monkey in a cage. There might be something to that. So what do we do now?"

"If we have to pluck the child from the cage, he'll probably be least frightened by you. Would you be willing to hide yourself in the secret tunnel to receive the boy if we get our hands on him?"

"Just stick myself in a hole and wait?"

"You could conceal yourself behind the boxes, if you'd rather, but we need the passage opened so that the child can vanish. We think it better to take him to a safe hiding place than to try and get him off the island with rockets being fired and Kendal's people moving in. Anyway, you and I are assigned to that location. It's a hard go to the secret entrance. Are you up to it?"

They had to snake their way through close-set trees and tangled undergrowth to the trapdoor, which lay just outside the maze wall. Turf and bracken covered the wooden flap, rendering it undetectable to anyone who didn't know it was there.

Inside the narrow cave, barely large enough to let them stand upright, Mr. Gilliam partly unshuttered the lantern he'd left there earlier and led the way. "This is an escape route," he said. "Before Paradise was constructed, the smugglers had a fairly free hand, but at some point they dug a way out of the main cave to keep from being trapped there. We should whisper from now on."

At the end of the tunnel, which was about a hundred yards in length, a wooden frame marked the knee-level opening to the cave, with a hinged door large enough for a good-sized man to wriggle through. It opened inward. Kate cracked it about an inch, seeing nothing except boxes on the other side. There were lanterns as well, she knew from the flickering light overhead.

To conceal the entrance, the smugglers had attached something, perhaps papier-mâché sculpted and painted to resemble stone, on the cave side of the door. She widened the opening and slipped through, Gilliam following, both of them with pistols in hand.

Kate estimated the time to be within a minute or two of eleven o'clock. If the child was coming here, he must be on the way by now. The cage sat on a box, its hatch opening raised, and several lanterns lined the ramp leading to the garden. The trapdoor at the top was closed. She shrugged at Mr. Gilliam, who shrugged in reply.

After exploring their options, Mr. Gilliam chose a hiding place behind a stack of boxes near where the cave narrowed into the main tunnel. Kate stayed near the entrance to the escape tunnel, curling herself inside an empty box that let her see out where the slats did not fully meet. She had a fairly good view of the cage, but not much else. After some thought, she kicked out the boards on the side nearest the wall, very close to the fake stone door. The noise brought Mr. Gilliam, giving her a chance to practice a quick exit. It worked fairly well. He was unable to see her, even though he knew where to look. They both took up their positions again and settled in to wait.

The acolytes, as Carrington had taken to calling them, were seated on marble chairs set between the phallic columns that ringed the Grecian folly. The moon, almost directly overhead, cast a silvery light on the stone pentangle at their feet, on the statues populating the garden, on the folly and its black altar.

From atop the three steps leading to the altar, the so-called Druid had launched into his act, chanting in a language he'd probably invented. Periodically he lifted his stringy hands to the sky, a signal for them all to say, "So mote it be."

It was hot under the mask, under the woolen robe and cape and hood. Where the devil was Kate? Had they found the child? Jarrett kept looking to the sky, hoping for fire arrows.

Two men wearing brown robes and carrying large trays materialized near the maze wall and came forward. As they passed by him, he saw an array of knives on one tray and what looked to be smoking pipes on the other, along with items he could not identify. Golsham had said something about hashish. *Damn.*

The Druid blessed the contents of the trays. *So mote it be.* Then came the primitive magic show, which began with sparks shooting from the celebrant's fingertips.

By now Kendal's boats would have emerged from around the curve of the lake where Jarrett and Kate had shared a picnic. They would hold back, unlit, awaiting the signal.

The Druid had little up his sleeves, magic-wise. All too soon, Carrington and the servants descended the stairs with the pipe tray and went from acolyte to acolyte, igniting the hashish. A tube was inserted through the mouths of their carnival masks, allowing each man to inhale the drug. No one declined. It didn't seem to be an option.

Damn!

Kate and Mr. Gilliam had been in place nearly half an hour where she heard the sound of male voices. Two men emerged from the tunnel, moved past where Mr. Gilliam was concealed, and drew into her line of vision. She couldn't see above their shoulders, but one of them was carrying the limp form of a boy about eight or nine years old.

"Easy, there. Don't wake 'im up. His lordship don't like screamin'."

"He's swallowed enough laudanum to put a horse to sleep. Raise the hatch a bit. This one is bigger than most."

Kate would cheerfully have shot the brute there and then, except for the risk of injuring the boy. At least he was almost within her grasp. If the men left, she could have him away in a flash.

They got the child into the cage, not ungently. She supposed he wasn't to be marked before becoming part of Carrington's perverted rituals. He was lying peacefully on his side with his legs curled up as if he'd fallen into a natural sleep. Then one of the men sat himself on the box beside the cage, blocking her view of the boy.

The men were complaining about a bad supper and speculating on how soon the toffs would come for the lad. She wondered what Mr. Gilliam was thinking. Would he take some sort of action? Right now there were only two guards, which meant this could be their last, best chance. Once the door at the top of the ramp opened, the child was lost.

"I'm to watch the boat," said the man who was still on his feet. "But who's going to steal it? Too cold out there. What 'appened to summer?"

"You best go. If the marquess sticks his head in and sees you—"

"I'll be takin' me a bottle, then, and one for Will."

To Kate's horror, he came over to the stack of boxes and began poking at them, looking for one that contained wine or spirits. She was well back, but he came closer and still closer. An oath, and another one. Something about a splinter. Then a bark of success.

"Aye, good," from the seated man. "May as well give me one. Knock the top off, eh?"

Glass against stone as a bottle was opened the easy way. She hoped they both got splinters of glass down their throats.

Some whistling as the boat watcher took himself off. Where were Mr. Valliant and Fergus, to let these two land the child undetected? But that was unfair. Half their force was here, as it needed to be, and two men couldn't possibly keep watch over the entire island.

Between swallows, the man on the box was rumbling something like a song. The noise covered the small sounds she was making as she backed out of her hiding place and crawled between the cave wall and the boxes to a spot about ten feet behind the man and the cage.

Now what? She could shoot him, but a bullet might miss. Ricochet. Go directly through him to the child. Besides, a shot was bound to be heard, and a dozen men would come running down that ramp.

The box that had been ripped open to get at the wine lay just beyond reach. She would have to move within his line of vision, not that he was necessarily looking in that direction. Hard to tell from this angle. But the notion of a bottle upside his head had its appeal. She didn't much think she could bring herself to put a knife in his back, which was the safest, surest action available to her, and Mr. Gilliam couldn't get close enough to strike without being seen.

She edged toward the wine.

Jarrett had coughed, choked, and otherwise tried not to inhale the hashish smoke, but too much of it got trapped inside his mask and drawn into his lungs. Fairly soon, a sense of euphoria washed through him. The moonlight grew brighter. The sound of the Druid's infernal chanting became almost sweet to his ears. He looked around the circle of men, wondering if this might not be harmless fun after all. Why had he thought Carrington a murderer?

Feeling utterly relaxed, he slumped back against the marble chair and wished the Druid would send off sparks again. There was some reason he'd wanted fireworks. He seemed to be having trouble remembering things. Like why he was here.

One hand clutching the neck of a wine bottle, the other gripping her pistol, Kate crept up behind her target. He was tapping his foot and humming between swigs, a stroke of luck for her, and his attention seemed focused on the door at the top of the ramp. If it moved, she supposed he'd stash the bottle and come to attention in a hurry.

All this gave her a chance, better than she could have expected, to get close without being heard. Mr. Gilliam wisely kept silent as well. But nothing could stop the shadows. Flickering light from the lanterns sent them dancing over the walls and ceiling of the cave, and as she drew nearer, her own shadow joined the dancers.

Close enough. She raised her arm.

Something caused him to start a turn.

The bottle came down against the back of his head, a glancing blow that sent him off the box and to the ground. She heard Gilliam running toward her.

A hand closed around her ankle, pulled her off balance. She kicked out, freeing her leg, but couldn't stop her fall. When she landed, she kept rolling.

Instead of coming after her, he grabbed the cage and swung it at Gilliam, who dodged back and fell over a box. His gun, knocked from his hand, went somewhere out of sight. She raised her own pistol, but the man put the cage with the child between himself and the gun.

Mr. Gilliam was scrambling up. The man backed away from Kate, got hold of the bottle she'd dropped. The neck was intact, but the bottom was a jagged circle of sharp glass. "Come near me and I'll cut 'im," he said, swiping the weapon against the cage where the boy lay, still blessedly unconscious.

That was all it took. With moves she had practiced for years, Kate unsheathed her knife and sent it into the man's throat. He toppled, landing half on a box. Mr. Gilliam was in time to seize the cage before it could fall. The man slipped down, eyes and mouth open, blood pouring from his neck. He was dead before they got the boy out of the cage.

She thought they were home clear, then. The bottle had torn the boy's shirt, but not his skin. They had only to slip him into the escape tunnel, pull the surrounding boxes closer, and take him to the woodland exit. But when they got the boy into the tunnel, Mr. Gilliam went back to look for his pistol, in case they ran into trouble later. And while he was fumbling among the boxes, the other man emerged from the main tunnel into the cave.

Kate saw him at the moment he spotted Mr. Gilliam, who was bent over and unaware. The man still had his bottle. He threw it at Gilliam's head, missed, and leaped. Gilliam went down, tried to move away, but the man was on top of him. They were wrestling, rolling over and over, the man larger by half than his slender opponent.

Kate went for her own gun, which she'd laid nearby while moving the child.

The man had got his hands around Gilliam's throat and was getting ready to bash his head against the ground when Kate seized her pistol and raised it to fire.

Carrington descended the stairs for a second time, trailed by a brown-robed servant with a tray. Jarrett watched with desultory interest. The Druid had lit a lamp of red glass that looked like it had a snake wrapped around it. The lamp was hanging over the black altar where Jarrett had once lain with Kate, if so kind a word could be applied to that unpleasantness. He still had a bitter taste in his mouth, unsure if he'd done the right thing that day. Perhaps it had only been gardeners watching them through the maze wall. Perhaps there had been no threat to them, or to the mission.

At the time, with seconds to decide, he had refused to take any chances. Kate would understand, he had been sure. And she had seemed to. She had enjoyed a little revenge by stranding him on the island when it was safe to do so, what with the yacht within sight. They'd both got safely away and not been compromised, so he could say he'd made the best choice. But the outcome might have been the same if he'd simply taken her hand and led her away.

He glanced up to see Carrington standing over him and extending his hands. On them lay a knife with a jeweled handle.

Jarrett suddenly remembered why he was here.

He took the knife—what else could he do?—and Carrington moved on to the next acolyte, the stranger that set the hair at the back of Jarrett's neck on end.

Looking over at Jarrett, the man caressed the sharp edge of his knife with his thumb.

Where were the fire arrows? The rockets? Kate and the others? Where was the child?

As if in answer, a sound like a gunshot cut through the silence. It was muffled, seemed to come from beneath the ground, and startled everyone but Jarrett.

He knew it originated in the cave, knew why someone would be shooting off a gun down there. But he didn't know who fired, who was hit, or what had happened.

At first, the men seemed to consider it part of the show. They looked to Carrington, who was gazing at the trapdoor with its veneer of marble. The Druid had crouched down behind the altar. Jarrett glanced over at his procession partner and saw him looking back. He felt something like he'd done when a hard push sent him off the ridge at Sca Fell.

Carrington spoke to the servant, who set down the tray and went with the other servant to lift the trapdoor. A few of the men came to their feet then, recognizing a departure from tradition. Voices rose, asking questions.

When the door was up, the servants stepped onto the ramp and vanished from sight. A shout. Then another. Carrington went to the top of the ramp and stood for a moment, head bent as he tried to see what was at the bottom. Finally, slowly, he went into the cave.

Jarrett didn't expect him to be coming out. Not the way he'd entered. Whatever had happened down there, he would almost certainly use the tunnel to reach the boats. Some of the men were milling around. Others followed Carrington.

Dering broke for the far side of the circle, grabbing a torch on the way. At the spot where the servants with the trays had appeared, he found a small break in the maze wall. He darted through it, ran the double length of the course, and came out into the woods. Saw the path, hoped it led to the boats, and kept going.

That was when he heard the crunch of boots on the ground behind him. He was being followed.

They had crawled into the escape tunnel, pulled the boxes close in to hide it, and were just pushing shut the hinged door when the large trapdoor swung open. Kate hurriedly finished sealing them off while Mr. Gilliam gathered the child in his arms. The boy stirred. His lashes fluttered. But the narcotics had hold of him, and he sank back into sleep.

Bruised and battered, Mr. Gilliam still insisted he was fit enough to carry the child. There was no time to argue. She went ahead with the lantern, and soon enough they were at the opening that would take them outside.

"You should wait here," she whispered. "Leave if you hear sounds from the other end of the tunnel and hide as best you can in the woods. I have to find Valliant or Fergus and tell them to fire off the signals. Someone will come to help you." She raised the lantern to illuminate the boy's face. "Does he seem all right?"

"His breathing is steady. Hard to tell about his color. Anyway, there's nothing we can do except get him away and to a doctor." Mr. Gilliam sank onto the ground, the child on his lap. "No, you take the lantern. Drop the shutters and let the light show only on the ground. That will help you get to where Fergus camped last night. The rockets will be there. When you've climbed out, turn to the right."

Her sense of direction holding true, she arrived at the sheltered spot alongside the maze wall and saw the rockets, still encased in oilcloth, lying beside Fergus's kit. She unwrapped them and was trying to figure how to set them off when Fergus burst through the trees. He took over from her, working rapidly while he spoke.

Two more boats had come in, tying up at the hidden lagoon on the northeast side of the island. The oarsmen were now bound and gagged, but he and Valliant had got there after the boy was taken away. Valliant followed the path, hoping to catch up with the man or men who'd carried him off. Fergus had put small holes in the bottom of the boats and come back here to prepare the rockets.

She spoke just as quickly, telling him where the boy could be found while she helped him prop a rocket on a Y-shaped twig stuck into the ground. Fergus used her lantern to ignite a spill and applied it to the fuse. Seconds later, after some sputtering and sizzling, off went the rocket with a screech. The other two followed in quick succession, flashing across the sky.

When no fire arrows appeared, they knew Kit was busy elsewhere. What of Dering? Was anyone linking him to the disruption of the ceremony?

"Gilliam and the boy should stay where they be," Fergus said. "It's safer than any other place right now. You go back there and wait. I'll look out for Kit and Lord Dering."

She was having none of that. The minute Fergus disappeared into the trees, she headed for the place where anyone leaving the cave by way of the main tunnel would emerge. It wasn't far from where she'd seen the smuggler's boat the night she first climbed a tree to observe lights moving over the island.

As she came closer, she heard shouts and general disorder from inside the maze. Soon all the men would go looking for boats to take them away, only to be met by Kendal's men swooping in.

Reasoning that Carrington had brought his party into the little eastern harbor, she ducked into the trees along the shoreline and made her way that direction, almost colliding with Kit Valliant as she came around a large yew tree. He seized her shoulders and held her erect, white teeth gleaming in the moonlight.

"I'm going for the arrows," he said. "All hell is breaking loose back there. Only three boats tied up, all but one out of commission. They'll sink before they can get too far. I marked the other as we all agreed, with leaves in the bottom, but you can't get to it now. When I heard men running down the path, I took myself away. Come with me."

"Gilliam and the boy are in the escape tunnel." She was panting. "Fergus is looking for you. Go send off the arrows. The rockets made noise, but hardly any light. Let me catch my breath. I'll follow."

He looked unhappy about it, but left her in the shelter of the yew. She stayed long enough to be sure he hadn't changed his mind before setting out again.

Jarrett sped along the path, shedding torch, mask, and cape as he ran. The man coming after him had fallen a little behind, but not by much. He considered slipping into the woods and ambushing the man with his pistol, except that he couldn't be sure who it was trailing him or the nature of his intentions. Maybe the fellow was just making his escape and had decided to follow a man who looked like he knew where he was going.

Jarrett did know where, but not what he'd find when he arrived. If the oarsmen had returned with the other boats, he'd be pickled. But when he came out of the trees, he found only the three boats tied up and no one minding them.

"Marked with leaves," Kate had told him that afternoon. He found the safe boat, untethered it, and was about to push off when his nemesis came running toward him, knife in hand. The mask was gone, revealing a plain, vaguely familiar face. One of the Paradise servants, he thought as the man leaped for him. He threw himself to one side, reaching for his gun at the same time. The man whirled, clipping his shoulder with the blade.

With a yelp, Jarrett swung for the man's face and sent him over backward. But he wasn't down long enough for Jarrett to pull the gun from its sling. He went instead for the knife in his boot, getting hold of it just as the man jumped at him again. The weapon was knocked from his hand. Jarrett grabbed the man's wrist, just below where stubby fingers were wrapped around the jeweled hilt of the ceremonial blade. They wrestled silently, the man trying to drive his knife into Jarrett's chest, Jarrett holding him off. Blood was streaming down his arm from the wound, making his hand slippery.

Not much time now. He brought up a knee to the man's groin, eliciting a sharp scream. The man dropped the knife, fell onto his knees, and Jarrett knocked him out with a hard right to the jaw.

Back to the boat, dragging it into the water and climbing in. He'd just put himself on the bench and got his hands on the oars when several robed men came bounding out of the woods. He saw Carrington and Sheffer in the lead. Sheffer had a gun.

Overhead, fire arrows lit up the night.

Jarrett rowed for his life.

Kate rounded the curve of the shoreline and saw a boat casting off, one man at the oars. She knew the shape of his body, felt a desperate burst of relief. Then she saw men coming after him. Sheffer was aiming a pistol, seemed to think better of it as Dering opened the distance between them. The men got into the other boats and set off after him.

They were sure to catch up, with two men at the oars in each boat. And Dering seemed to be favoring his left arm. She'd have followed, but there were no more vessels. Other men could arrive at any time. She went back around the curve and scrambled up a tree that fronted the lake. From here she could see much of what was happening.

Dering rowed swiftly, but the others were closing the gap. There were five men after him, four of them plying the oars with a fury. They seemed to know that if Dering got away, his would be the testimony that would do them in. Carrington, now holding the gun, was standing in the prow of the boat closest to Dering's.

She looked beyond them, to the dark shapes in the distance. Kendal's boats, a half dozen of them, had spread out and were moving toward the island. Then a pair of them, the ones farthest to her right, broke away. She saw they were going after two boats crammed with men that appeared to start toward the island. The men must have spotted the darkened boats, because they made a quick turn back to where they'd come from. Kendal's allies followed, unshuttering their lanterns to reveal men holding rifles. There on the water, the fleeing culprits were taken into custody and guided to shore.

The distraction gave her a chance to breathe before returning her attention to Dering, now well within pistol range. Carrington, his feet braced apart for balance, was taking sight.

She couldn't bear this. So close to the end, to succeeding, and now she was going to watch him die.

Please God Please God Please God. But He wouldn't know her voice. She never spoke to Him. Why would He listen to her now? *Please God Please God.*

A cry from the men in the second boat. It seemed lower in the water. It *was* lower. She'd forgotten what Valliant said. He'd rigged them to sink. Carrington was looking back. The men in the other boat were shouting at him to come pick them up. Instead he pointed at Dering. His oarsmen picked up the pace, and Dering's was noticeably flagging.

The foundering boat reversed course as the rowers tried to make it to shore. Then, sensibly, they went over the side, overturned the dinghy, and used it to hold them up as they kicked their way to land.

Carrington persisted. She thought, could not be sure, that his boat was riding lower as well. Yes! The rowers began to come about.

But Carrington turned the pistol on them. One swung an oar in his direction, missing. It was every man for himself now. The man who had attacked Carrington slid into the water and struck out for shore, swimming strongly. The other—Sheffer, she thought— seemed to be pleading. It was clear to her that if they failed to leave the boat and turn it over, it would go down with them in it. Or perhaps Carrington could swim and just wanted to get in his shot first.

Now it was Sheffer who took up an oar and went at Carrington, trying to push him overboard. Carrington, turning, appeared to catch his feet on the long robe he wore. The gun went off, and Sheffer dropped like a stone.

The report was loud enough to reach Kendal's boats, which unshuttered their lamps and picked up speed. But they were still a considerable distance away, and Carrington's boat was rapidly filling with water. As she watched, it disappeared from under him.

He went down, as did Sheffer, but the limp body came up again, floating on its belly. Carrington appeared what seemed a long time later, flailing his arms, getting more and more entangled, she would guess, in the water-heavy robes. He appeared to be trying to pull them over his head, but the motions sent him underwater again.

She looked to Dering's boat. He'd turned it around and was coming back for Carrington. But when he reached the spot where Sheffer bobbed like a fishing cork, there was no sign of the marquess.

Dering got out of his robe, wrenched off his low-cut boots, and dove into the water. As she watched, he went down again and again, only to emerge for air with his hands empty. He was still trying to effect a rescue when the first of Kendal's boats arrived. Two of its occupants entered the water to resume the search, now a little easier because of the lantern light, but by now Carrington must surely have drowned. Dering clung for a few minutes to the side of the boat, looking around as if he might spot bubbles of air rising to the surface, some sign that Carrington could still be saved. Finally he allowed himself to be drawn into the boat. A man began wrapping a length of fabric around his shoulder.

He had been hurt. She watched a time longer, but he continued to sit upright and was speaking to the men. Another boat came up alongside.

It was over, then.

The fallout from this scandal would ensure the closing of Paradise and, most likely, a number of arrests. Prominent men would be disgraced. The child was safe and, with luck, would remember little of his ordeal. John Gilliam, Fergus MacFergus, and Kit Valliant would see him to safety. And Dering, indebted to the lady who had secured the help they had so desperately needed, would no doubt pay his warm regards to the Duchess of Sarne.

Moving with deliberation, Kate came to the ground and made her way into the concealment of thick vegetation. There was no hurry. She wouldn't be sought straightaway. They'd all assume she was with someone else, and by the time they realized she was missing, it would be too late.

So much easier to leave quietly, without explanations and farewells. She couldn't bear them, and someone might try to prevent her going.

But she had no choice. Everything she had done for Black Phoenix had led her to this moment, to the certainty she could gather courage when needed and take great risks when the cause was of significance. In this, the cause mattered only to her. But until she had overcome one last obstacle, she could not endure her guilt or begin to think of her future.

So never mind her planned departure and the arrangements she had made. She would go now, swimming over to land and getting on from there as best she could.

But she wept a little as she began the long journey, wept every day of it until she'd run dry of tears. What did it matter, really, that she would never again see Lord Dering? A creature of the higher atmosphere, he had flown into her intractable life and soared out of it again like one of Fergus's rockets.

The pain settled in, a tenant for life. And yet she could not be sorry that for a brief time, she had shared with him a bit of the sky.

Chapter 21

The parties of London in summer were few and flat.

Jarrett spotted his quarry at the third one he wandered through, his first without an invitation. But there was dancing, he could tell from the music and stomping overhead, and no unattached gentleman would be turned away. He ascended the staircase, slipped inside what was passing for a ballroom, and picked out a familiar back in a cluster of men.

Avoiding the handful of couples hoofing through a reel, he came up behind his target and tapped lightly on a blue-clad shoulder. "Care to dance, sweetheart?"

Scowling, Major Lord Jordan Blair swung around to face him. "By God, Dering. Have you no manners?"

"I have mislaid them." Jarrett smiled at the others in the group. "Will you pardon us, gentlemen? There is a debt to be negotiated."

"Owe him money, do you?" Sir Peregrine Jones applied a frivolous handkerchief to his forehead. "Never play cards with Blair. He don't cheat, because he don't need to."

"I owe him something, that is certain. Come, sir. We'll settle in private."

Maintaining a cool silence, they found a small, stuffy parlor and went onto the balcony, closing the French window behind them.

Blair, imposing in Hussar regimentals, medals, and lace, looked daggers at him. "Did I not warn you—"

"Yes, yes. Dire consequences and all the rest. But let us dispense with your theatrics and proceed directly to mine. My associate has gone missing. I located the Pendragon Theater Company from which you recruited her, but no one there had knowledge of her whereabouts. I have spent the last fortnight questioning innkeepers, coach drivers, farmers, herdsmen . . . you will by now take my point."

"With the mission completed, she was free to go. *Expected* to go, so as not to be associated with any subsequent unpleasantness. At some point you may be called to testify, but as a female, she will not. Have you taken *my* point? Phoenix has no further interest in the young woman, and I have no idea where she can be found. Are we finished, sir?"

"Only if you don't object to having Black Phoenix introduced to the world. Or to the portion of it wide-eyed at the fall of Paradise and the imprisonment of several notable personages, all of this under the fiery feathers of a secretive organization more dangerous than the enemies it chooses to pick on. Or perhaps it is not, but I assure you that the worst of whatever implications I wave about will be credited."

"You gave your word."

"You *asked* for my word. But we're quibbling. Had I sworn on my honor, it would mean nothing against what I now pursue. And you will provide that, my dear Jordie, because I have already stashed a provocative testimony with my solicitor. Should anything happen to me—even death by lightning strike—every name, fact, and exaggeration will be published far and wide."

Even in the sparse light from adjacent windows, Jarrett could tell that Blair had gone pale.

He kept a bemused, confident expression on his own face. It was all a bluff, of course.

There was no document crammed with awkward revelations, nor even a solicitor to publish it. His finances did not allow for a solicitor. And his conscience, that newly discovered annoyance, would not permit exposing Phoenix just because it failed to give him what he desperately wanted.

"What do you want?" Blair said with a snap.

"Every bit of information that might help me track her down. Her real name. Where she was born. Where her family lives. She is clearly educated, with more culture than one might expect from an itinerant player."

"You ask too much. Our arrangement did not include betraying her identity or her history, either of which she could have provided you, had she wished to."

"But it *did* include subjecting her to the worst abuses of Paradise, putting her at risk of her life, and when she had achieved more than all your fellowship put together, cutting her loose like a dog that had outstayed its welcome. What good is it, Major Lord Blair, to play Knights of the Round Table when you have no regard for the pawns you send into battle? If the people who work with you and for you are of no significance, then Black Phoenix has lost its moral compass. And yes, I understand that such high-minded concepts ring false, coming from me. But I have learned a little, since meeting Kate."

"I had nothing to do with her summons," Blair said at length. "I know nothing about her."

"Then get the information. And find out what it is that caused Phoenix to recruit her in the first place. I speak now of the guilty secret she hides. I know there is one, and I know someone in your organization sniffed it out. It is my belief she has gone to set it right. Should you withhold even the slightest clue to her location, I shall repay you by revealing every trifling bit of information I possess about Phoenix. That includes your name, sir, and the threats you made against me. In the event I meet with harm, you will be the primary suspect. Oh, and I want all of this information within twenty-four hours."

"You ask the impossible."

"I guard against false delays while you seek the identity of my solicitor and apply pressure to the poor fellow. *Make* it possible."

A long, angry release of breath from Blair. "If it is permitted, you will be informed."

That seemed a good exit note. With a not-quite-insulting bow to the soldier who clearly wanted to pummel him into oatmeal, Jarrett left the balcony and the party.

Early the next evening, a message was slipped under Jarrett's door. The large black seal—he now recognized it as a Phoenix rising from the ashes—the fine stationery, and the assertive handwriting were the same, as were the opening words

*You are summon*ed . . .

To the New Moon chophouse in Billingsgate, it turned out. Someone connected with Black Phoenix had a sense of humor. He set out half an hour later, carrying the bladed walking stick Mrs. Kipper had provided. Not much protection if he was being drawn into an ambush, but he didn't mean to give up without a fight.

The crowded chophouse, set on a narrow street between two taverns, smelled like mutton, ale, and sweat. He'd no sooner stepped inside than a servant collected him and played escort through a rabbit warren of staircases to a small, dim room fitted with a rickety table and two uncertain chairs. Seated on one of them was the clerk who, on their first meeting, had put a gun to his back.

He—Robin, if Jarrett recalled correctly—looked perfectly harmless on this occasion. He had a pair of plain-rimmed spectacles on his nose, a folder thick with papers open before him, and an untouched glass of wine at his elbow. When Jarrett appeared, he rose awkwardly and gestured to the chair across from him. "We have been in search of you, Lord Dering. There are many loose ends from the Paradise mission to be tied up."

"That is your problem. Let's talk about mine."

"Jordie said you would be difficult." With an indulgent smile, Robin shuffled papers and adjusted his glasses. "Very well, then. The young woman known as Gaetana was born Catriona Finnerty eight-and-twenty years ago, in Dublin. Her parents were of decent origin but feckless by nature, and in their greed to have more, they eventually lost everything. But while they were plying their schemes, a great-aunt took the child under her wing and saw her educated. She also willed her home, which sits on a respectable parcel of land, to Catriona. Will you have some wine, sir?"

In his galloping thoughts, Jarrett was already halfway to Ireland. "Go on."

"Hounded by creditors, the Finnertys scratched up

an English gentleman to marry their soon-to-be-an-heiress daughter, figuring he would provide a settlement they could pirate. But the gentleman, while eager to wed the heiress, had no funds to back up his promises. Not long after the wedding, the parents disappeared. We believe they emigrated, but we don't know where. That was a decade ago."

Wedding. Darkness wrapped around Jarrett like a winding cloth. She was married, then. He swallowed hard, waited for the sickness to pass. Reminded himself that she was in trouble, and that he meant to see her through it. All the rest, what he had hoped for . . . had he really thought it possible? It had been too late for him, even before he met her. Finally he looked up at the clerk. "And the husband?"

"Dead." A glint of what might have been amusement in Robin's eyes, as if he'd guessed the direction of Jarrett's thoughts. "He was Edward Falshaw. The great-aunt met her Maker shortly after the marriage, Falshaw was gone within the year, and his younger brother took over the property. Mrs. Catriona Falshaw took her leave."

"The brother threw her out?"

"Of these circumstances, I am not permitted to speak. And you needn't make a grab for my notes. I shall give them to you before we part ways, but the information you seek is not there. If you are to know the entire story, you must hear it from Mrs. Falshaw."

"Tell me now. It might help me find her."

"We will tell you where it occurred." Robin, lips taut as he spoke, appeared to wish he could say more. "Perhaps she has gone there to deal with unfinished business. You will no doubt wish to proceed on that assumption, so we have taken the liberty of arranging for you to do so."

Jarrett, who trusted Black Phoenix not at all, wondered where the devil they meant to send him. He'd probably find himself on a ship bound for Botany Bay. "Just give me the direction. I can bumble there on my own."

"To be sure. But the speediest way, not to mention the most comfortable, will be aboard a packet from Bristol. We are sending with you Mrs. Kipper, who shares your concern for the young woman. Silas Indigo is too engaged in the Paradise affair to be spared, but another gentleman will be more or less at your service. They will meet you aboard the packet."

Pride clamored for him to reject the boat, the assistance, and anything else Phoenix had to offer. But it was a long ride north to Holyhead, the usual port for a crossing, and he'd no idea what he would be facing in Ireland. What was pride, after all, when measured against Kate's best interest?

"Until this is done with," Jarrett said, "I require to keep the horse. The Phoenix money that remains to me will be used as needed, and if there's any left when this is finished, I shall return it. Is there nothing more you can tell me?"

"Very little. It's all in here"—Robin tapped the folder—"along with the location of the house willed to Mrs. Falshaw and a few tidbits about the current residents. I do have news on other subjects, although I must say you appear remarkably uncurious about what happened after the fall of Paradise."

Jarrett shrugged. "I was no more than a catalyst, or perhaps a crowbar. Something to pry open the top and let the vermin out. Their fate is of no concern to me."

"But one of them so nearly caused your death. Mr. Fidkin, who hopes a flood of revelations will buy him transportation instead of the noose, is wagging his tongue like a dowager's fan. I believe that you suspected your brother's wife of arranging the attack in the fells, perhaps through the patronage of her French lover. But if Fidkin is to be believed, it was Lord Beaton who asked him to provide for an accident. Only if a likely opportunity presented itself, Fidkin said, calling it a desultory request, not an order. There were two attempts, I understand, both by the same Paradise servant. No doubt Beaton was piqued after losing the chess game and the duchess to you."

For her children's sake, Jarrett supposed he ought to be glad to have Belinda's innocence confirmed. Which wasn't to say she might not, one of these days, give murder a try. "I'll have to swallow my disappointment," he said. "I was looking forward to visiting her at Newgate. What has become of Beaton?"

"Consigned to the Tower, by the skin of our teeth. Did you know he flies pigeons? Fidkin quickly sent word of the assault on the island, but as it happens, we fly pigeons too. Had you not worked out the clues to his identity and passed them on to Silas Indigo, we would have arrived too late to catch Lord Beaton before he fled. Phoenix commends you for the shrewd deduction."

"I am gratified, to be sure."

"There is news as well," said Robin, briskly changing the subject, "of Lord Carrington."

"Still dead, I trust?"

"Oh, yes. But when we recovered his body from the lake, we made rather a gruesome discovery. It was you, I am told, who recognized that he was mad. That is borne out by the testimony of neighbors and servants we have interviewed. His mother, widowed after five years of marriage, was reportedly insane. But since she all but confined herself, her son, and a handful of servants on the estate, there was no one who knew her well. Local rumor had it that she'd killed her husband, and that her son, when he came of age, killed her in turn. But in both cases, the ruling was suicide."

"Is there any reason I need to know this?" Jarrett asked, moderately curious in spite of himself. What could possibly drive a man to ritually slay a young boy, and repeat that iniquity four times a year? Which reminded him . . . "What of the boy we pulled from the cage?"

"An orphan who has been placed with a reputable family, along with funds for his schooling or an apprenticeship. As for Carrington, it seems that when he was about the same age as the boy is now, his mother used a knife to separate him from his masculine parts. Two women in service at the time verified the event and the consequent struggle to preserve his life."

Good God. "And they failed to report this to the authorities?"

"What can be said of that now? They were afraid, I suppose, and dependent on Lady Carrington. From all accounts, she appeared quite normal on the rare occasions she went into company. One must feel pity, a little of it, for the marquess. If he did not inherit her madness, his mother surely created madness in him with her knife. He has willed his considerable fortune to the orphanage from which he selected his victims, which may have been his attempt at expiation. Countless children will live far better lives than they could otherwise have hoped for."

"You were right to tell me," Jarrett said after a silence. "Is there more I ought to know?"

"A great deal of interest, but nothing directly pertinent to you." Robin closed the folder and pushed it across the table. "You may ask again later, if you like. And given your success in a virtually hopeless venture, we would not be reluctant to call on you for another service in future, should you—"

"I am not one of you." Rising, Jarrett snatched up the leather folder. "Her legal name is Catriona Falshaw?"

Eyes widening at the sudden question, Robin nodded. "But she won't be using it, I daresay."

"And I daresay you'd better hope I find her. If she eludes me, I'm coming after you."

Chapter 22

When the packet docked in Dublin Bay, the company of travelers, who had spent much of the journey laying plans, went in separate directions. Sir Peregrine Jones, accompanied by his valet, his auxiliary valet, and a giant manservant-of-all-duties, set off for the heart of Kildare, where he would pretend to be seeking an estate to buy. John Gilliam and Mrs. Kipper, who was playing the role of his mother, went in search of her runaway daughter.

Jarrett, after completing necessary business in Dublin, rode from inn to tavern to coach house on the outer edges of the county, expressing interest in purchasing horses while his gaze sought a familiar profile, a particular way of moving, a distinctive gesture. Kate would be in disguise, he was fairly certain, and if she spotted him before he recognized her, she'd go to ground. For that reason, his search area excluded any place within twenty miles of Greenwillow Manor, which Black Phoenix had targeted as her likely destination. Better if one of the others found her first.

It was Sir Peregrine who insisted they would easily locate the young woman. Only because he had never dealt with her, Jarrett was thinking on the seventh day of the search, when he came to the last unexplored tavern on the edges of Kildare and spent most of the afternoon brooding over a tankard of dark ale. Perry's manservant had delivered a message that morning with familiar, discouraging news—no sign of her.

Jarrett never considered giving up, even though they were only guessing that she'd returned to Ireland, or that her destination would be the place she had grown up. Perhaps it was a person she sought, one who had moved elsewhere.

Well, he couldn't know. He could only continue to look for her, and he might as well assume she'd not confine herself to Kildare. Rousing himself, he set out to the west.

The peaty odor of the Bog of Allen hung in the air as he rode through a nearly deserted landscape to the isolated village of Edenderry, a post stop along the coach road. Not worth the ride, he thought, looking around at the small houses and smaller shops. While he took supper at the post house, the bluff proprietor told him it would be dark before he could reach the next town, and beyond that, there was little for a gentleman of quality to trouble himself with.

Another day wasted. Another day in which Kate might have got herself into trouble. Worry burned in his stomach, pounded at the back of his head. He decided to turn around and try another direction in the morning.

A servant had led Banshee behind the post house and tethered him in the shade with plenty of grass to munch on. As Jarrett mounted he glimpsed a boy, rake in hand, mucking out a stall inside the stable. It was the black garb, much like the trousers and tunic Kate was wearing when last he saw her, that caught his attention. Caused his heart to jolt in his chest, the way it always did when he saw clothing like that, or a woman with abundant black hair, or blue eyes that could skewer a man like a roasting potato. Everywhere he looked, he saw ghosts of Kate. She was everyplace he went, if only because he brought her there with him.

He guided Banshee into a turn, saw the boy bend down to retrieve something on the stable floor. His black tunic pulled up, revealing the rounded shape of a female derriere.

Edenderry. It meant Paradise Grove, the proprietor had told him. For the second time, he had found his Kate in Paradise.

Inside him, cheers and huzzahs and silent prayers of thanks were carrying on. Profound relief engulfed every other feeling. *Dear God, look at her. Mucking out stables. How desperate she must be.*

His guts and heart in a turmoil, he guided Banshee into the stable, coming up directly behind Kate before remembering she was armed with a rake. He could imagine the story in the *Times*—"Noted Rake Dispatched with Rake."

When he drew up at the stall where she was working, she made a quarter turn, keeping her head low. "Ye be needin' stable lodgin', sir? The ostler's at his supper. I c'n hold yer nag for now. Ye'll find 'im in the kitchen."

"That must be," Jarrett said, "the worst combination of accents I ever heard."

At the first sound of his voice, she'd inadvertently looked up. The mask came down quickly, just as his own mask always did, but he'd caught the flash of . . . oh, he could not define it. Surprise, fear, relief . . . all those things. And unless he was very much mistaken, a trace of joy as well.

Because she was Kate, she immediately prickled, all

spines and claws and resentment. But it was too late for real conviction. He knew that whatever her intentions and misgivings, she was not displeased to see him.

"Go away." Her gloved hand was clenched around the rake handle. "You'll ruin everything."

"My dear, you are separating straw from horse droppings. Even at my most creative, I can find nothing here to ruin." He nudged Banshee closer to her, unsurprised when she held her ground. "Besides, how can I leave without what I came here to find? You have something that belongs to me. A golden guinea."

Color flagged her cheeks. "Y-yes. But it's in a place I cannot reach at this moment. Please, my lord. You must go."

"Very well." He took the rake from her hand and tossed it onto a pile of straw. "But you are coming with me. Don't fuss, please, unless you wish to draw attention. And I suggest, for the same reason, that you ride in back. I cannot, with any dignity, hold a stable-boy in my arms."

For a long, heated time, she glared at him. Then, lips drawn tight, she found a mounting box and used it to hoist herself onto the horse's croup. After another endless stretch of time, she wrapped her arms around his waist.

In its way, this was the most intimate embrace he had ever felt. An act of trust, given unwillingly and suspiciously, but *given*. For him, the unknown and impenetrable obstacles melted away at that moment. She had allowed him to enter, however briefly, into the quest that had brought her on this journey. All the rest was easily overcome.

"Thank God we're not going far," he said. "You smell like what you've been shoveling."

"Why are you here? How did you find me?"

"I will answer all your questions when you have been bathed and fed. Have you possessions we ought to retrieve?"

"There wasn't time. Truly, you should leave me off now. Leave me alone altogether. There is something I must do."

"I know. I'll be asking you—after the bath—what it is, and you will tell me the truth. Then, my lovely Catriona, I will help you do it."

Enveloped in Dering's dressing gown, Kate sat cross-legged on the bed while he lounged on an overstuffed chair across from her, a glass of wine held loosely in his hand. Servants had just finished removing the tub and the remains of their meal, most of which she had wolfed down while he told her a little of what happened at Paradise after she scarpered.

And through all the hours that had passed since he spoke them, she kept hearing the echo of four unimaginable words.

I will help you.

At some point he told her he had not come alone. Mrs. Kipper was here at the inn, along with John Gilliam. A gentleman described as not quite what he appeared to be was nearby, gathering information. They had been sent, he said, by Black Phoenix, on a mission to secure her well-being. She was expected to cooperate.

If what lay ahead of her had not been a dark pit, she would have been wildly encouraged. As it was, she felt a lingering warmth just to know she would not be facing it alone. And she was to have a little more time in Lord Dering's company, when she had resigned herself to never seeing him again. The pain of that, in a long and troubled life, had hurt more than anything she could remember.

Now she had to tell him a story that was certain to make him regret accepting this new mission from Black Phoenix. And tell him the truth, which she had never spoken to anyone. It was tangled up inside her, knotted in a hard lump she had carried around with her for what seemed like several lifetimes. She could not think how to unravel it.

"Are you deciding which lie to use?" he said with a half smile.

She met his eyes. Despite his relaxed posture and the off-hand tone of his question, his gaze was uncompromising. "I will not lie," she said. "I simply cannot decide where to begin."

"There is no prize for being logical," he said. "Why not start with the reason we are here?"

"Very well." Her heart was leaping in her chest. She swallowed hard, shifted her gaze to the wall behind him, brought it back again to his eyes. "When I was seventeen, I married. When I was eighteen, I killed my husband."

No shock. No outrage. One of his expressive brows lifted, that was all, as if he had been expecting something of the sort. "Were you compelled to wed him?"

She could scarcely draw breath, let alone speak her lines. "Not by force, if that is what you mean. But my alternatives were bleak, and he was beautiful and charming. Since childhood I had spent the greater part of each year in a school for young women, and except for a fancy I had recently developed for an undergardener, I knew almost nothing of men. Mr. Falshaw was presented to me by my parents. I was wary of their motives, but his attentions were ardent and flattering. I felt of significance, as I had never done before. Desire burned in me."

She gave a little shrug. "At the end, desire was my undoing. Although my great-aunt Maura advised against the marriage, even begged me to refuse him, I would not listen. Her health was failing by then, and I had always known she meant to leave me her house and land. I even knew that was why Falshaw paid court to me. But I was persuaded he had come to love me as well. I wanted so much to believe it that after we were married, when he began to show his true nature, I kept on trying to please him. I thought his cruelty was my fault. You must think me very foolish."

"Not at all." There was no sympathy in his voice, which would have been her undoing. Only a bare statement of fact.

"When Aunt Maura died and the house became mine, which meant *his*, Edward brought his mother and younger brother to live with us. Tom Falshaw was rather stupid, driven by superstitions and fear of his mother. Mrs. Falshaw took over the management of the household and drove off nearly all the servants. I did a good deal of the work, which I didn't mind. I was desperate to keep busy. But I did object to Edward spending his time drinking and gambling at the local tavern while the land was neglected. Tom had no interests except in contacting the dead. A fortune-teller at a fair once told him a great secret would be revealed to him, but nothing he heard from the other world ever suited his expectations."

"I believe you are avoiding the difficult part of your story," Dering said.

"I wanted you to understand *why* I did what I did."

"Come back to that when you are ready. I am not

here to judge you, Kate. No matter what you tell me, I will remain on your side."

"But why?" She was wringing the hem of the dressing gown with both hands. "What if it is too horrible?"

"It couldn't be. I already know a man treated you badly. There were signs of that from the first days we were together. I expect that if your husband still lived, I'd kill him myself."

It was another of those strangely cold nights in a summer like no other summer. A small peat fire burned in the hearth. But it felt to her as if the sun had risen inside this room at the Crock of Gold. That she needn't again fear the dark. That she would come out the other side of this long nightmare with her soul intact.

Courage, put there by this astonishing man, lit her from inside. She sat straighter, stopped worrying about crafting the story to justify her own actions, and sliced through to the heart of it.

"When Edward drank, he became mean. It also left him, most of the time, unable to bed me. For this he held me responsible, which meant I had to be punished. Although I was kept a virtual prisoner at home, he took care never to visibly mark me. His target was generally my"—she stopped her hands from moving to it, as they always did when she remembered—"my belly. I thought his blows would make it impossible for me to have a child, so when his temper was wild, I ran. I hid. Sometimes I fought him.

"On the night it happened, I had concealed myself in a room on the third floor. When he found me, he grabbed my wrist and pulled me down the first flight of stairs. On the landing, I began to struggle. He punched me, and I wrapped my arms around my stomach to protect it from the next blow. I was screaming.

I always screamed, but no one ever came. He reached
for my arms to pull them away, and I tried to push
his hands away. He must have been standing near the
edge of the staircase. He must have been off balance.
I don't know. It seemed he was moving because I
didn't get hold of him. Next I knew, he wasn't there."

Her throat burned from the telling of it. "I heard a
thumping, and he was crying out. It seemed to last a
long time. He landed in a heap on the first-floor landing. I closed my eyes, unable to look. Unable to move.
When I opened them, two servants had appeared. The
man, on one knee beside Edward, was pressing a finger to his throat and shaking his head. The housekeeper was looking up at me. I realized my arms were
outstretched with my palms flat against the air, as if I
had just pushed him. I might have done. But surely
I'd have known—don't you think?—if I had shoved
him with such force. I wasn't trying to strike him. I
was trying to keep him from striking *me*."

She had tried a thousand times to choreograph the
motions in her mind, the ones that caused Edward's
death, but they were never clear. Was she a killer?

Or did it even matter? She had wanted Edward
dead, which was the same thing.

"I turned and ran back up the stairs," she said, "and
came down again by way of a secret passageway. Before anyone knew I was gone, I'd left the house and
fled into the woods."

"Because you believed yourself guilty of murder?"

"From pure terror, I expect. Whatever the truth,
Mrs. Falshaw would see to it I was held responsible
for her son's death. What happened next can be
passed over. After a time I was taken up by a clan of
travelers who taught me to dance, sing, and separate
people from their coins. But I continued to wonder if

it might be safe to return home, so one of the lads who fancied me took work in the neighborhood to find out. He learned very little, except that Mrs. Falshaw and Tom still lived in the house, and that I was referred to by the local people as 'she what done in her husband.' After that, to make it less likely I would someday be recognized, I crossed to England and found work in small theater companies."

"Someone did recognize you. Someone who works with Black Phoenix."

"I know nothing of that. The letter of summons spoke of guilt, failures, and debts, all of which I have carried with me since that night. I wished always to do penance, to put something right in the world. Most of all, I thought that if I succeeded in performing one act of sacrifice for a good cause, I might find the strength to face the consequences of Edward's death."

"By mucking out stables?" His expression suddenly changed. "Don't tell me you mean to turn yourself over to the authorities?"

"If that is what it requires. I want to stop running. I want my name back, and my honor. Should God permit, my life."

A slow smile curved his mouth. "Well, then, let us get about it. What have you learned so far?"

And just like that, he dismissed the leaden history she'd carried like a boulder for ten years. Or perhaps he'd lifted it to his own shoulders. She felt lighter, in any case. She tasted the sweetness of hope.

"Almost nothing," she said, trying to sound efficient. "I have served in two taverns and worked in a stable, as you saw, but Edward's death and his wife's disappearance are no longer talked about. I do know that the Falshaws are still in residence at Greenwillow Manor. The house and gardens are in an appalling state. I forgot to tell you that when the banns of my marriage were cried, my great-aunt privately changed her will. The property did not come directly to me, as her previous will had stipulated. It is now held in trust for my firstborn child, which surely means that Tom Falshaw has no right to it."

"Then I wonder he is still there."

"If they don't hang me for murder, I will see him evicted. The solicitor who drew the will administers the trust, but I cannot recall his name. I had just turned seventeen, was swept away by passion, and could scarcely wait to become the envied wife of an English gentleman. Only because Aunt Maura made me promise, I hid my copy of the will instead of giving it to my husband, which had been my intention. It is in the library, because that is the last place any of the Falshaws were likely to go. If I am taken into custody, my lord, please make sure they are not permitted to keep the house."

"It won't come to that." He had the same look she'd seen in his eyes when he was planning the downfall of Lord Carrington. Only a little of his attention was on her now, she could tell. Wheels were spinning in his mind. All too soon, he would begin issuing orders.

"You did the right thing to flee ten years ago," he said. "You were young, female, and powerless. You had enemies. Now you have friends, and power will be put into your hands. As for strategy, I believe a direct attack, not a siege, is called for here. That means we move swiftly. Are you ready to proceed?"

She hadn't expected sympathy. Hadn't wanted it. But they might have been discussing the training of a horse. "Certainly," she said. "But I will need my clothes back."

"Mrs. Kipper is procuring something civilized for you to wear. We will set out as soon as everything else is arranged." He rose, clearly eager to be under way. "For now, I want you to call to mind everything you know about the two servants present during or just after your husband's accident. In fact, list every servant employed at Greenwillow. There are writing materials on that table. Describe the exact location of the will you hid. Draw a sketch of the room and mark the spot. Whoever goes there will have little time to secure the document. Questions?"

Now it was her mind doing the spinning, but in confusion. "Two," she said, stabbing at the first pair that separated themselves from the pack. "It is dark, or nearly so. Where are we going at night?"

"Dublin. And the other?"

Her second question lost out to a new one. "Why Dublin? What can we accomplish there?"

He was at the door, his eyes a little shadowed in spite of the grin on his face. "Shopping," he said. "You require to make a good appearance. Oh, and when we return to Kildare to confront the authorities and your late husband's family, you will be Lady Dering."

Chapter 23

"B-but I thought you meant *playacting*." Kate clung to the coach strap with both hands. "Surely you cannot mean to *marry* me. Not for real."

It was well past midnight and raining hard. The small hired carriage rocked from side to side on the rutted road. Kate, swaying on the bench across from him, had apparently just now understood what Jarrett had assumed was perfectly clear.

Very well, he hadn't actually *proposed* marriage. But it wasn't as if she had a choice, and asking her would have implied that she did. Besides, she might have refused. So he'd thought it easier to present the marriage as a fact, which it was, and gradually lead her around to his point of view. Better to act forcefully now and apologize later. Or that had been his theory.

It seemed the time for that apology had arrived. And he would make it, after his fashion, as soon as she let him get a word in edgewise.

Now she was telling him all the reasons a wedding was out of the question. And he was listening to them, even as a separate part of his mind wondered why, with Kate, everything had to be a battle. But she had been fighting, he shouldn't wonder, for nearly all her life. Probably she didn't know how to stop.

She'd already made her way through the difference-in-rank arguments, her possible condemnation as a murderess, her years as an itinerant actress, her provocative stint at Paradise, and was moving into a series of ruin-your-life objections when he looked more closely at her. This was not Kate in a temper. She was truly distressed. He had better draw in the reins before she ran herself over a cliff.

"There is, of course, another choice," he said, forcing the words through a clogged throat. "But it's not nearly so good an idea as the marriage. Listen to me. I dare not, *will* not let you face the authorities from anything other than a relatively unassailable position. Even the wife of a viscount might ultimately be condemned, but not without substantive evidence. More, for example, than the testimony of servants against you. It has been a decade since the event took place, and any good barrister could cast doubt on their memories of what occurred that night. Married to me, Kate, you will be safe. But without the protection of my name, which is the only thing I have to offer you, the outcome of a new investigation into Falshaw's death is uncertain. You ran away and have lived what many people would regard as a disreputable life."

"I know. What is my other choice?"

Stubborn female. "Come back with me to England," he said. "Take up your career again, if you like. Find a protector better able to provide for you, or a man you wish to marry. Why hand yourself over to an indifferent and probably incompetent system of justice in this backwater? The same mother-in-law who would have borne witness against you ten years

ago will do so now. Why must you pursue this? Can
the truth be found, after all this time? And are you
sure you want to know it?''

What seemed a long time went by before she responded, her voice barely audible against the rattling
of the carriage.

''I must do this, my lord. For all these years I have
been hoarding little scraps of courage until I'd gathered enough pieces to carry me here. I feel, always, a
crushing pressure in my chest. It is guilt, and fear, and
hopelessness. Better this be ended, whatever the cost,
than I go through the rest of a patched-together life
the way I have been doing. But I refuse to take you
down with me. Is there no third choice? A marriage,
perhaps, followed by an annulment? I could give a
false name.''

''It's too late for that.'' He had been saving this
news for when she'd accepted him. Now it would be
used as a weapon. ''I have a Special License from the
Archbishop of Canterbury, and a Marriage License
Bond from the diocesan court of the Church of Ireland in Dublin, both of them listing my bride as Catriona Falshaw. I have lodged a sum of money with the
court as a surety that there is no impediment to the
marriage. I am legally authorized to marry you in two
countries, Kate. For all I know, that may be redundant, but I was taking no chances.''

''You were planning to marry me before you found
me? Before you even left England?''

''There is a snake in every garden, my dear. I cannot
give you back your former life. No one can. But I can
free you of it and send you into a new life . . . so long
as you take me with you.''

Sitting forward, he unwrapped her stiff fingers from
the coach strap and took her hands between his. In

the golden lantern light, shadows played across her face. He could bring her to want him. He knew he could, if only she would take this one blind leap with him.

Again he was at the edge of a cliff, as he had been on Sca Fell, with this woman his only lifeline. He spoke softly so that she would lean into him, and watch his face, and concentrate on his words, not on the arguments she would later mount against them.

"Both of us," he said, "when we were young, made grievous mistakes. We were heedless and self-absorbed. We put our trust in the wrong people. Ultimately we were betrayed by our families, exiled from our homes, and deprived of our heritage. Your journey has been the more difficult, to be sure. Your character has been chiseled out by hardship. I can say nothing good of my own path or my character, except that at this time I am not in debt. You see how little I have to offer you."

"You are who you are," she said simply.

He didn't know what that meant to her. He could not measure up, he was sure, but with her to inspire him, he might become something better. To a small degree, he already had. "We are pilgrims," he said, "alone and lost until we found each other. Shall we not make the rest of our journey together?"

She was silent for a long time. He kept hold of her hands, felt the blood pulsing through them. Finally she said, "And what happens, my lord, when you regret being shackled to me?"

"I don't know," he said. "By that time I'll be ninety years old, drooling in a Bath chair, and probably enamored of someone's lapdog. All I can promise you is at least half a century of fidelity and, most likely, a hardscrabble existence. Especially if the authorities find you guilty of murder and we have to take a runner."

"I thought marrying you would prevent that happening."

"It will. But if it doesn't, plans are already laid for our escape. Whatever occurs, Kate, we'll deal with it. So what do you say?"

"That I do not trust myself. That I have not even begun to run out of arguments. That I fear, more than anything, coming on the one that will cause you to change your mind."

At first he could not believe what he'd heard. She must have misspoken, would take it back and trot out a whole new list of objections. She hadn't even got to considering that he might be marrying her for the estate—right in the middle of horse-breeding country—that their first child would inherit. He'd thought for certain she would throw that in his face straightaway.

"I won't, you know. Change my mind. But you will argue us both into knots if I let you continue. Come to me." Before she could resist him he tugged her off balance and brought her to sit across his knees, a little whelp of surprise her only protest. "Do you know that we have never kissed? I think about that all the time. Think about wanting it, think about doing it, and how you will taste, and what it will lead to."

"You cannot seduce me into marriage," she said, already leaning into him. "I've already tumbled into wedlock with one man just because I desired him. I'll not do that again."

"Of course you won't. You'll marry me for other reasons, and I don't care what they are. Meantime there is the passion we feel—don't pretend otherwise—and no sensible reason not to indulge it. Come on and kiss me, Kate."

"How is it you know the play so well?" she grumbled, even as she nestled into his embrace. "It is so maddening. Kate always did as Petruchio commanded."

"An excellent precedent." He untied the ribbons beneath her chin and removed her bonnet. "I'll memorize more lines to annoy you with."

She gave him a pert look. "If kissing you is the only way to keep you quiet . . ."

"Oh, it is." He drew her closer still, bent his head, and found her lips with his own. They were soft, lush, sweet as peaches. She made a little sound, female and welcoming, that sent his heart racing. Her hair, sleek and short, smelled of the soap he'd given her. Her mouth, when she opened it for him, tasted faintly of his tooth powder.

Everything male in him rejoiced at the small signs of his possession. At her yielding posture, her invitations to greater intimacy. But he knew, as he deepened the kiss, that it was she who held his being in her hands.

The rain had stopped and the morning sun was winking through the clouds when the carriage pulled up at a gracious hotel in Sackville Street. Kate, half-melted from the pleasures of the journey, leaned on Dering's arm as he led her to a suite of rooms that had been, she learned at the reception desk, reserved for them earlier that morning.

"John Gilliam rode ahead of us," Dering explained as she refreshed herself with warm water, soap, and soft towels. He was sitting on a leather wing-back chair with his feet propped on an ottoman, smug and relaxed, the pattern card of a thoroughly satisfied male. "About now he is alerting the vicar, gathering the witnesses, and procuring a bouquet of flowers for you to carry. We will receive word when they are ready for us at the church."

"I thought we were to shop."

"First things first, my dear. It would be inappropriate for me to purchase clothing for a woman who is not my wife."

"But what we did in the carriage *was* appropriate?"

"Certainly. God is well aware we are to be wed. Proper shopkeepers, on the other hand, wish to see a ring on your finger. And I'll not put it there until we are taking vows."

"You *have* a ring?"

"The jewel is unworthy of you, but yes. Everything has been arranged. What will happen regarding Falshaw's death and your inheritance hangs in the balance, but around this marriage I have built castle walls. Nothing will prevent it, or assail it."

"Unless I refuse to marry you. Was last night part of your effort to build walls around *me*?"

A flash of what might have been hurt in his eyes. He was breathing more heavily when, after a time, he responded. "In fact, I had planned a wedding night here." He gestured to the large platformed bed with its lavish canopy and brocade counterpane. "I had intended that we would, for the first time, truly make love with each other. What happened in the carriage was my ungovernable desire for you, and yours for me. Passion does not always behave itself."

She nodded, ashamed, and went back to washing her face. Every time she nearly trusted him, she panicked and lurched to the attack. He was not to blame. For all she knew, he truly believed everything he was saying to her now.

It was her own inadequacy she feared, her unsuitability to be his wife. Whatever would his aristocratic friends say when he returned to London with the likes of her in tow? She could never accompany him into society. And when he reentered his natural habitat, he would be with the women who were his match, like the Duchess of Sarne.

How could she endure the long nights when he left her at home to consort with his own kind? And he would. However fine his intentions, Lord Dering was heir to centuries of tradition. He thought he had left behind the legacy that had been snatched from him, but the absence of it ate away at his self-worth.

She could recite every word he'd ever spoken to her, describe every look on his face. She knew his evasions, his flights of fancy, the edifices he built to hide the truth, even from himself. There was much she didn't understand about him, contradictions that puzzled her, but of this one thing she was sure. Until he reclaimed what he was born to be, he would always be restless, dissatisfied, and empty of soul.

Would she, as his wife, be standing in his way? Or, because he had failed all this time to take action on his own, might she put him on the road to where he belonged? And would she find the courage to do so, even if it meant that he would, necessarily, leave her behind?

All these questions bouncing around in her head, and not an answer among them.

"How is it," she said, "that Black Phoenix took an interest in me? I was told that after the mission was done, Phoenix would help me secure a new position. Otherwise there was to be no further communication between us. Yet here is Mrs. Kipper, along with Sir Peregrine, whom I have not met. And Mr. Gilliam as well."

"And me."

"I'm not sure why you are here either, except that you have decided to be gallant. According to Mrs. Kipper, Phoenix concerns itself with crimes on the highest levels of society. Surely my sordid little history is beneath their notice."

"My dear Kate, you could never escape notice. And don't forget that for a time, you were one of them. Perhaps they take care of their own. As for John Gilliam, he is here because he greatly admires you. By his dramatic account of the events on the island, the ones I failed to see, you saved his life."

"I may have done. It was dark and a bit of a muddle." She didn't want to think about that. Examining her image in the mirror, she saw a ragged-haired urchin with whisker-burned cheeks, swollen lips, and eyes bright with awareness. A disreputable, wanton bride would stand before the altar today. She hoped the witnesses were nearsighted, and that their paths would never again cross hers.

Not long after, Kate and Dering made the short walk to Saint Anne's Church, where John Gilliam was waiting with a surprisingly fidgety minister and a distinguished man in his sixties. Dering presented her to Lord Whitworth, who had asked to stand witness to the marriage, and she managed a curtsy.

"We have an audience," said Lord Whitworth, offering her his arm. "In Ireland, when passersby spot a wedding about to take place, they troop in to enjoy the ceremony. A sentimental lot, the Irish. You wouldn't see this at Saint George's, Hanover Square."

"No, my lord." But she was pleased that the rear pews were filled with smiling, chatting people—her countrymen—and hoped they weren't too disappointed with her drab gown and bonnet. By way of consolation, Dering looked good enough for the both of them.

She supposed the enormity of what she was doing would strike her later, but as the minister proceeded at a fast clip, she wrapped herself in the role of a demure bride. Dering, at ease beside her, seemed perfectly content to wander into an unsuitable marriage, and no last-minute lecture from her would prevent him now. But when the minister asked if either of them knew of any impediment to their union, she bit her tongue and stared at the prayer book, rather expecting it to burst into flames.

Only once, when Dering slipped the ring onto her finger and squeezed her hand reassuringly, did she risk a glance into his eyes. *Mine,* they said. But she thought, too, that he looked happy.

In the vestry, they signed the parish register and a series of papers, two of them affixed with seals and ribbons. "No one," said Dering, "will question our marriage after setting eyes on one of these." Mr. Gilliam signed as well, followed by Lord Whitworth, who attached an even larger seal to the documents.

"Lady Dering," he said, startling her with the name. "Your husband tells me I cannot have the pleasure of offering hospitality until certain matters of business have been dealt with. As he knows, I stand ready to be of assistance if required. Meantime, I wish you great happiness and look forward to introducing you to our community of gentlemen and gentlewomen."

"Thank you, my lord." He must not know a single thing about her or her background, to say such a thing.

Dering and Mr. Gilliam had a great deal to discuss in private, but finally she was settled in the carriage with her husband and on her way to acquire a new wardrobe. Which, she quickly discovered, he had ordered soon after his arrival in Dublin. A half dozen gowns, a riding habit, a cloak and a pelisse, bonnets and gloves and underthings were all waiting for her to try on at the establishments they visited. Stunned into silence, she dutifully allowed hems to be measured and tucks taken, much in the way she had been fitted for costumes in the theater. It did not seem real that these lovely things, chosen by a man with a remarkable sense of what she would most like, were to belong to her.

"I must fatten you back up, my dear," he said. "On your travels, you have grown positively scrawny. But just as well, because the alterations will require us to delay our return. We can have our wedding night after all."

Hot from embarrassment, she heard the seamstresses tittering behind the screens.

In Dering's rush to sweep her into marriage, Kate had let herself float on the clouds of his assurances. But she came back to earth when they returned to the hotel, where wasps flew into her head with sharp, poisonous stingers.

What good, they buzzed, were a ring, fancy papers, and new clothes if she was condemned for Edward's murder? The two witnesses had not defended her during the original inquest, Mr. Gilliam had learned. Indeed, they failed to appear at all. What if, when they were found and brought forward, they testified that she had pushed him down the stairs? She couldn't deny the possibility. When all was said and done, what use was Dering's confidence against the truth?

There would be some relief, of course, knowing for certain what had happened. In the hundreds of times she had relived that night, trying to recall her movements and her intentions, she always ended by telling herself that whatever the circumstances, she could never deliberately kill another person. Then came the night on the island, when the child was endangered and she had killed without thought. Without regret. She had killed again to defend Mr. Gilliam.

Only God and the devil knew what she was capable of doing. She could not guess which of them would claim her now.

She was sitting across a small table from Dering, making a show of eating the lavish meal he'd arranged to be delivered to their bedchamber. Small lines at the corners of his eyes and mouth betrayed his weariness, although he seemed generally pleased with himself. And he spent a lot of time just gazing at her, which ought to have been bothersome, but wasn't. If he found pleasure in the way she looked now, all ragged and worried and sharp-boned from weeks of little food or rest, then she was a fortunate bride indeed.

"Lord Whitworth was very pleasant, if a bit stuffy," she said to keep from having to force another bite into her mouth. "He is a friend of yours?"

Chuckling, Dering topped off his wineglass. "The barest acquaintance. I looked him up first thing after docking, fairly sure he'd be useful. Most of the political British peers in Dublin relocated to London after the Act of Union, leaving him with a difficult job and few of the perquisites that used to come with it. Even the visit of a fellow English viscount, however disreputable, is something of a treat. And I assure you that his name affixed to those fancy, if unorthodox, marriage documents will be useful in the days ahead."

"He is an important gentleman?"

"Let us say, rather, that his position is influential

among those we will be dealing with. Did I not tell you? He is Lord Lieutenant of Ireland."

"Good heavens." A piece of roast beef fell off her fork onto the plate, followed by the fork. "*Of course* you didn't tell me. You rarely tell me anything. That will have to change, Dering. I like surprises, but only when I already know what they are."

"But I am trying to impress you. Believe me, when you see how I live in London, and how few resources I can dredge up in future, you will know me for the paltry fellow I am. Forgive me for indulging my vanity while I can. And speaking of vanity, we should, before leaving Dublin, see about procuring you a wig."

She felt a little stab of hurt. "Do I look so terrible?"

"No, indeed. But we mean to reopen inquiries into a possible crime, and shorn hair makes you appear as if you just emerged from a prison."

"But a bonnet—"

"Will do well enough. The wig is not important. If anyone remarks on your hair, I'll say it was cut when you became ill from a fever."

"I don't mind. Really. It's just a bit ironic, to buy a wig when I sold my own hair to create a wig for someone else."

"You *what*? I thought this shearing was in the interest of your disguise."

"Not that." She ran her fingers through her straight, boy-short hair. "I had a sudden chance to escape the island and Paradise without being observed, but it left me no opportunity to claim the funds I'd stashed away for the journey. My hair bought passage for the crossing to Ireland."

"But what of the guinea? You told me you still had it. Why didn't you use that?"

She hadn't meant to tell him about the hair. But it

had slipped out and, perniciously, he'd connected it to the guinea. She tried to make a jest of her plight. "You said I must have the guinea ready to give you when you asked for its return. Don't you remember?"

"That was a theatrical gesture for the audience. Did you think I would come after you to retrieve a damned coin?"

"I never thought to see you again, my lord." Heat flaming on her cheeks, she rose, slid a hand under her skirts, and dug into the small pouch attached to a band tied around her waist. The golden guinea shone in the candlelight as she offered it to him on the palm of her hand. "My hair will grow back, but this I could not relinquish. It was all of you I had to keep."

His gaze went to the guinea, paused, and rose to meet her eyes. She saw, then, that his own were glazed with moisture, enough that a tear gathered at the corner of one eye and slid slowly down his cheek. She watched it, mesmerized, moved beyond speech. The room filled with mist until she could see nothing more than his outline and the faint glimmer of gold in her hand.

Then he was standing in front of her. Candlelight shone golden on the track of the single teardrop marking his face. He looked to her as if he had appeared from some magical place, like a selkie come to claim a mortal bride.

His large hand slipped beneath her open hand and gently closed her fingers over the guinea. "Let this go," he said, "if ever it will do you good. But for so long as you can bear it, I hope you will keep me with you, in your heart and by your side and, yes, inside you. Will you come to bed with me, Kate? Let me love you all through the night, the way I have longed to do?"

She felt bathed in moisture, hot with desire, as if he were already joined with her. She might have taken hold of him and tugged him to the bed, as he probably wanted her to do. She wanted that as well.

But even more, she wanted a properly improper wedding night, with all the delicate ceremonies that had never been part of her life before. The small, attentive gestures. The tiny discoveries. She wanted to see all of him, and to give him all of herself.

He waited, still as glass and, she realized, apprehensive. It was new to them both, this voyage beyond desire, beyond pleasure, to the mysterious frontiers of love.

On this night, it began with the undoing of a button on his waistcoat.

He looked down at her, a smile teasing at his lips. "Are you planning to remove my clothes?"

"Indeed I am. And without cutting them off, and without an audience. Be grateful I am not seeking vengeance."

"What *are* you seeking?"

"I will let you know when I get to it." With the buttons undone, she slipped the waistcoat off his shoulders and applied herself to his cravat, which he had already loosened. The stiff collar was long gone. "Although I would have thought you'd guess."

Glancing below his waist, she saw her destination begin to make its presence known.

Her man. Her lover. Her husband. Plans of slow seduction dissolved in her urgency. She could not wait for him. She didn't think he could wait for her, either. Not from the lively evidence pushing against his breeches as she tried to tug his shirt free of them.

She paused, ordered her flesh to calm itself, and unhooked his cuffs. Then she lifted his arms, pushed down his shoulders, and pulled the shirt over his head. At every moment he followed her lead, did everything she told him by gesture to do. Straightening, he looked back at her, gray-green eyes molten with anticipation.

Her own gaze lowered to the powerful shoulders and sculpted muscles in his arms. To the broad chest, dusted with male hair, and the flat abdomen. "I row," he had told her, "to keep fit. How else am I to survive the drinking, gaming, and general profligacy that is my life?"

Had he not been so beautiful, her desire for him would have been no less. It was the intricacy of his character that excited her, his reluctant integrity, his humor, all the thousand strands of his personality that coiled around her and drew her to him. But her body, with a will of its own, rejoiced in his hard male strength and even—she couldn't deny it—in his confidence. He knew that he could, and would, please her.

"You must remove your own boots," she said, imperious as one of the queens she'd played on the stage. The role had never failed to suit her.

He went to the bootjack, and she enjoyed the play of sinew and muscle on his back while he obeyed her whim. "Will I get to undress you in return?" he asked, padding back to her on stockinged feet.

"Later," she said. "Perhaps. But first, this." Her fingers went to his breeches, loosing the buttons and lowering the flap. He wore silk drawers, which she had known without seeing them on him before this. Inside the creamy fabric, he rose like a tower.

Unable to resist, she put her hands on him, on his potent, silk-clad manhood.

"It has been a considerable time," he said in a raw voice. "Take care."

She relished her own power to arouse his desire,

the eagerness with which his flesh rose to greet her. Releasing the most impetuous part of him, she slid his breeches down his hips and thighs, put a hand against his chest as a command, and when he was seated on the bed, removed his drawers and stockings. Then she drew him to his feet again, naked as the day he was born and looking nothing like the way he'd looked then.

Letting him stand exposed, as she had done that night at Paradise, she walked around him thoughtfully, like an art dealer appraising a statue. Amusement danced in his eyes. He knew very well the appearance he made, and what women thought of it. He also—she could tell—enjoyed submitting himself to her as an object of desire.

Not that he would permit such games to last very long. Nor did he this time, but for good reason. "It is our wedding night," he said gently. "I am yours, always, to do with as you will. But on this night, unless it displeases you, I would ask that you give yourself over to me."

Fully clothed, she looked at her naked husband and didn't want to stop the game. She wasn't sure why, because they could, and probably would, replay something like it many times in the future.

And then, as he stroked his forefinger slowly down her cheek, she understood.

Earlier he had spoken of their wedding night in terms that frightened her, that implied an intimacy she feared. How could she give herself over to him? Yesterday at this time, she had been in a metal tub, scrubbing away the dirt and stench of her job in the stables. And today she was Lady Dering, transformed by a sorcerer into a creature she was never born to be.

Another role to play, another part she was acting.

She dared not imagine what would happen if she let herself care for this charming, impulsive scoundrel.

And yet, she could not deny him. Years of loneliness had stripped her past skin and flesh to the ice in her bones. She felt him possessing her with the smallest touch of his hand. And she—there was no accounting for it—she made him happy. His eyes were on fire with it.

Naked by her hands, he had freely offered himself to her, asking only that she give herself to him with equal abandon. She thought he might even know, a little, that what she faced from the authorities did not terrify her nearly so much as the prospect of opening her heart. But she must make a beginning, here on this night. She must try to become what he had called her to be.

"Yes," she said, answering a question he had asked a lifetime ago. "Because you wished it, by law and by name I am your wife. Now you must lead me to all the rest. I am willing, sir."

"It's a beginning." His smile warmed her. His hands rested for a moment on her cheeks. He looked deeply into her eyes, sealing a promise between them that required no words. And then, with gentle respect that flowered into passion, he began to remove her gown.

Chapter 24

L ord and Lady Dering returned to the Crock of
Gold late the next afternoon to find Sir Peregrine,
more flamboyantly self-assured than usual, waiting for
them in the private parlor reserved for their use. Sunlight glinted from the shiny brass buttons on his coat,
the startling white of his shirt and cravat, the many-
colored stripes of his waistcoat and the several watch
fobs dangling below it, not to mention a ruby stickpin
and at least seven beringed fingers.

"Oh, my," Kate murmured, squeezing her new husband's arm as she saw Sir Peregrine for the first time.
Clearly trying not to laugh, Dering led her forward
for an introduction.

By the time Sir Peregrine rose from an elaborate
series of bows and flourishes, she, too, was trying not
to laugh. It was impossible to tell if the gentleman
took himself seriously or was playing a joke on the
world, but she did recognize the patina of success
glowing on this performance.

"You have good news?" said Dering, who must
have seen it as well.

"Mostly good." Sir Peregrine could fashion a shrug into a dance. "But not altogether."

"There is a snake in every garden," she said, earning the expected laugh from Dering.

"The lady has an infallible ear for dialogue, Perry. Never say anything you wouldn't want used against you."

"I never regret what I say. But I might, on occasion, deny saying it. Shall we proceed with my wedding gift?" Sir Peregrine opened a leather satchel, withdrew a sheaf of papers folded in thirds, and gave the packet to Kate.

"Oh, my. You found Aunt Maura's will." She passed it to Dering, who had been leaning over her shoulder for a look. "However did you spirit it away, sir?"

"Inside my shirt, which was inside my waistcoat, which was inside my coat. A simple bit of thievery, perpetrated on a pair of simpleminded thieves. But if you wish to hear my tale, Lady Dering, please be seated in the audience."

Dering, preoccupied with the will, had moved to the window, so she took a chair across from Sir Peregrine, who had assumed a pose by the fireplace.

"While we were searching for you," he said, "I masqueraded as a foolish fellow out to snap up an Irish estate at a bargain price. By this time all of Kildare knows of me, and when I appeared at the door of Greenwillow Manor, Mrs. Falshaw practically dragged me inside. The house, I regret to say, is in poor condition. Most rooms have been stripped of paintings, adornments, and in some cases even the wallpaper."

"I expected that," she said. "Edward began selling things off soon after my great-aunt died. He swore he would use the money to buy livestock, but it got invested in brandy and gaming." She couldn't help glancing at Dering, overfond of both those things, but he didn't appear to have heard her.

"After a tedious exploration of the lower floors," said Sir Peregrine, "we arrived at the library, where I pronounced myself too fatigued for further exertion. After considerable persuasion, Mr. Falshaw agreed to escort my manservant around the estate while Mrs. Falshaw helped my valet create a floor plan of the house. I, of course, settled in with a bottle of claret and a good book. Despite the pillaging of the other rooms, the library shelves were full of books, all of them wearing heavy coats of dust."

She smiled her pleasure. Aunt Maura had lovingly collected books and maps since girlhood.

"There was no difficulty finding the secret panel you described. I whisked out the papers, stashed them next to my bosom, and was snoozing on a sofa when Mrs. Falshaw returned. Her fubsy son arrived not long after, dripping like a dish rag from the unprecedented exercise. To ensure a future welcome, should another visit be necessary, I gave them both reason for hope before taking my leave."

Sir Peregrine made a *tsk*ing sound. "Dering, you have failed to attend my story. Whatever are you doing?"

"Looking for loopholes."

Suddenly alarmed, Kate swept over to the window and snatched the will from his hand. "I have never read this. Is it other than what my aunt told me?"

"Unfortunately not. It appears the solicitor who drew it up locked her wishes into place with a score of legal clamps. I can't think how I shall wrest the property from our first daughter's clutches."

"A cold sentiment," Sir Peregrine said.

It required a deep breath, only one this time, before she realized Dering had been teasing her. "It is my own fault, Sir Peregrine. I advised him to marry an heiress. But . . . instead of the first child, the will now specifies *daughter?*"

"Unless you turn up your toes without producing any. Meantime, you hold the trust in partnership with the attorney, one Mr. Patrick Mahoney, whose offices are located in Kildare City."

"Actually," said the languid Sir Peregrine, "he has relocated to Naas and will be pleased to welcome Lord and Lady Dering at eleven o'clock tomorrow morning. Is that convenient?"

"You didn't explain—"

"Certainly not." Sir Peregrine contemplated the lace on his cuff. "My servant, pretending to be Dering's servant, delivered the request. No reason for the meeting was specified. Do you know the solicitor, Lady Dering?"

"Aunt Maura told me she trusted him, and that I should trust him as well. Naturally I was too excited about my upcoming marriage to pay her any attention. But why, exactly, are we to meet with him? Surely we cannot simply claim the property and evict the Falshaws?"

"I expect we'll be asking his advice," Dering said. "We shall require counsel to deal with the accusations against you. Any news on that?"

Sir Peregrine draped himself on a chair. "I regret to say that one of the witnesses, the young footman, was impressed into the Royal Navy during the unpleasantness with the Americans. When the conflict ended, he elected to remain in Ontario, where he was recuperating from a wound. We know this from his mother, who lives in Clare."

How could they could have accomplished so much in such a short time? She was about to ask when Sir Peregrine began to speak again.

"The mother is not well, and because a journey would be difficult for her, we have arranged a deposition. She will testify that her son, after being dismissed from Greenwillow Manor, told her that Mrs. Falshaw threatened to implicate him in the murder of Mr. Edward Falshaw. He said it wasn't true the young lady had deliberately pushed her husband down the stairs. But he was afraid to go to the authorities, and besides, the accused lady had already fled. If ever she returned, he would speak of what he saw."

At *it wasn't true,* Kate's heartbeat had set to thundering. "I didn't do it? Really?"

"You fancied that you had?" Sir Peregrine regarded her curiously. "The other witness, a maid now in service at Castleton House, did not see the moment Edward Falshaw went over the stairs, but she has much to say of his brutality. Like the footman, she was silenced at the time of the inquest by the threats of Mrs. Falshaw."

Sir Peregrine pulled a fan from his sleeve and snapped it open. "As you see, we cannot immediately produce an eyewitness able to say, with perfect accuracy, what caused the fall. If necessary, we'll attempt to bring the young man from Canada to speak for you, but I don't expect it will come to that. We are weaving a web of many strands, Lady Dering. None is strong enough of itself to contain the damage, but in the end I believe we shall prevail."

She had felt so alone for nearly all her life. Now, people she didn't know existed were rallying to her defense. "On my travels before leaving Ireland," she said, "I always tried—without drawing attention to myself—to locate the servants. How did you find them so quickly?"

"Reinforcements. Phoenix recruited help from the north and sent them over by way of Holyhead. You'll not meet them. We cannot be effective if all the world knows who we are and what we do."

"I would never tell. At the least, will you let them know how grateful I am?"

"Certainly. But for now, let us consider how to rid your home of the cockroaches. You are cursed, Lady Dering, with remarkably stupid relations. Falshaw struts like the lord of the manor, but he is entirely under his mother's thumb. She is a fool, but wily and mean-natured. Thus far she has held off her creditors, although we have reason to think they are growing impatient. Hence her eagerness to sell the property."

"She'll never pay them."

"The Falshaws would doubtless take the money and vanish. We want them gone, to be sure, but empty-handed and before a new inquiry into the death of your husband is called. Without Mrs. Falshaw's testimony, the case against you collapses."

"Even though I ran away?"

"You were young and terrified. We have two innocent witnesses so intimidated by Mrs. Falshaw that they fled as well. But your marriage to an English lord is the linchpin. Viscounts generally do not wed felons. Now I require to know the Falshaws' weaknesses. How can we persuade them to leave the field?"

The strategy meeting went on well into the night, part of it conducted over the supper table. John Gilliam had arrived, and for a time they were joined by one of Sir Peregrine's servants, who provided information about the frustrated creditors. By the next afternoon, some of them would be beating at the door of Greenwillow Manor.

When Dering brought up Tom Falshaw's superstitions, the ones she had told him about, Kate was struck with a brilliant idea.

Sir Peregrine shot it out of the sky. "You may not haunt Tom Falshaw," he said with uncharacteristic sternness. "That would be unseemly. And should you be recognized, he would sniff a plot. But playing on his fears is a splendid notion indeed, and I shouldn't mind dressing up as a specter. I wonder what a fashionable specter wears. Well, Mrs. Kipper will see to that. You may help, Lady Dering, by marking the location of servants' stairs and secret passageways on the floor plan my valet drew up."

"Since Falshaw was once obsessed with the prediction of a fortune-teller," Dering said, "perhaps he could be swayed by another."

She brightened. "I could—"

"No!" said both men at once.

"The intricate web," Sir Peregrine reminded her gently. "You must be, like Caesar's wife, above reproach."

"But I'm married to *Dering*. Reproach is inevitable."

They laughed, but it was because they recognized in her mild joke a reluctant surrender. These men did not want her meddling in manly affairs, even though it was her life at stake, her future, her inheritance. Her marriage as well, and her possible children, and, yes, her pride. She wanted to play the heroine, and they had cast her as a supernumerary.

Dering, seated to her right, took her hand between his hands. "On the island, I felt much the same. While I pranced around in silly robes, useless for anything except being seen to be there, you and Gilliam and the others took all the risks. It is difficult and maddening, I know."

She nodded, and smiled, and meant it. They were in a battle, only one person could be in charge, and for the time being that was clearly Sir Peregrine.

"Two nights ago," he said, "I noticed an encampment of what appeared to be Gypsies. If they are still in the neighborhood, perhaps we can employ a fortune-teller and provide her with details about Tom Falshaw that will astound him."

"This, at least, falls to me," she said. "I have lived among just such a band and speak the cant, which will identify me as one of them. Shall we go there now?"

"Perhaps tomorrow evening." Sir Peregrine refilled her wineglass. "Much of the day will be spent with lawyers, an ordeal that demands a good night's sleep and, I have always believed, rather a lot to drink."

Great-Aunt Maura's solicitor, Mr. Patrick Mahoney, rose when his clients were shown into his office, and properly acknowledged them by inclining his head.

Jarrett, whose last experience with a lawyer had brought the news of his disinheritance, regarded Mahoney with a jaundiced eye. He appeared to be in his sixties, of middle height and girth, with curly wisps of thinning red hair fluffed around his pate. Pale blue eyes, sharp with intelligence, met Jarrett's and held.

The clerk formally announced Lord and Lady Dering, at which point Mahoney shifted his gaze politely to Kate. Jarrett saw the moment he recognized her, astonishment passing across his freckled face.

She let go Jarrett's arm and approached the desk. "I remember you now, Mr. Mahoney. One afternoon you paid a call on Aunt Maura. She invited me to join you for tea and practice my company manners, but Catriona Finnerty could not be bothered with manners on a sunny afternoon. You must have thought me exceedingly ill-bred."

"I found you charming and wished for a share of your remarkable energy. But please, my lord, my lady, be seated and tell me how I may serve you. This call, I presume, concerns Greenwillow Manor?"

While they were settling on comfortable chairs, he opened a wall safe and returned with what looked to be another copy of Maura Coffey's will. His hands shook a little as he unfolded the papers and donned a pair of gold-rimmed spectacles. "Do you know what this contains?"

"Yes," said Kate. "Aunt Maura gave me the other copy."

"I have held her secret close for more than ten years. To have brought forward the new will at the time of your husband's death, to have sent it into probate, would likely have caused her intentions to be disregarded. Certainly the Falshaws would have pushed to overturn it. I continued to hope that when you left, you had been carrying a child who would one day claim her inheritance. Only my son, who practices in Dublin, knows the former will was made invalid by this one."

"There is no child," she said. "But I do wish to remove the Falshaws from the estate and see it properly cared for. That assumes, of course, that I have first overcome my other difficulties."

"Indeed. You will hardly be permitted to administer the property, or even to walk freely, with a charge of felony murder on your head."

Jarrett liked that Mahoney spoke directly with Kate instead of expecting her husband to speak for her. At the same time, he was itching to take over, especially when the subject became threatening. He unclenched his hands and tried to look at ease.

"Was a search mounted for me?" she said.

"None at all. The country was unsettled after the rebellion, and there were ongoing protests, some violent, against the Act of Union. Edward Falshaw represented the despised English, and he was more than a little unpopular on his own account. I doubt anyone believed Mrs. Falshaw's version of events, which she claimed to have witnessed, because her report was neither consistent nor in accord with the evidence. But there was no witness to counter it. The servants claimed to be elsewhere at the time, save for one who suddenly went missing, and some people thought he might have committed the crime. Others thought the two of you had conspired to murder your husband before running off together. At the end, without enthusiasm, the ruling at the inquest was handed down. Then it was all but buried."

"What happens if I come forward and ask for a new investigation? Would it be granted, do you think, or might I be clapped into irons?"

Mahoney's head tilted to one side. "It is usual, Lady Dering, for an investigation to originate with the victim or his kin, not with the accused. Are you certain that reopening this case will clear your name? Or is that even your objective?"

"I cannot breathe freely, or restore the inheritance due to my child—should God grant us children—unless this is resolved. We have found witnesses, sir, who will testify that Mrs. Falshaw was not present when the accident occurred."

"She perjured herself?" Mahoney didn't sound surprised.

"And intimidated the servants who would have contradicted her story. I do believe that we would prevail in a fair hearing, although I regret that the scandal will devolve upon my husband and children. Even so, Lord Dering supports my decision, and whatever the risk, I stand willing to take it."

"Were you aware, my lord, when you married her, that your bride stood accused of murder?"

"She had told me, yes. I believe her guilty only of marrying a brutal man who was so intent on beating her that he lost his footing and tumbled down the stairs."

"Is that the accounting she gave you?"

"Not exactly." When had *he* gone on trial? "From her words, I apprehended that she was unsure precisely what had occurred. It all happened quickly, while she was trying to protect herself from his fists. She had no recollection of striking him, or even of touching him, but couldn't swear that she had not. In the circumstances, what could she do afterward but flee? What chance had she, an Irish girl suspected of killing an English gentleman, in a trial?"

"I ask these questions now, Lord Dering, because the authorities will ask them later. Is it so unreasonable to believe that in a rage, or from hatred of her violent husband, she deliberately seized the opportunity to push him to his death?"

"Any human being has the right to fight back in self-defense. And Lady Dering would fight at the risk of her own life to protect a helpless victim from attack. But deliberate murder? Never." Jarrett glanced over at Kate, her face calm as a marble saint's. "It is because she fears her own strength of character and the force of her courage that she has never been sure it didn't explode on that night. A girl of eighteen has no great experience of her own nature, Mr. Mahoney. And she had no one on her side."

"Well, she has now. Let us hope it is not too late. What would you have me do, Lady Dering?"

"We hope you will help us navigate the legal procedures necessary to reopen the investigation or appeal the findings of the original inquest. Can you recommend a barrister with experience in such matters?"

"My son—if you will pardon the favoritism—is highly regarded at the Dublin Inns of Court."

"He will do very well," said Dering, unable to resist taking a hand. To him it seemed that Kate, behind her mask of cool poise, was about to dissolve with relief. Another obstacle overcome, by a woman who never dared to hope beyond the next small step. Each time her foot landed on solid ground, she was astonished. Then she regathered her strength and moved forward again. He hoped that soon he would learn when to let her walk free, when to take her arm, and when to sweep her off her feet and carry her over the next barrier.

"So," he said, leaning back in his chair and folding his arms. "How do we begin?"

Chapter 25

In the following week, a dozen spiders wove strands into the web that was to protect and free Catriona, Lady Dering.

Jarrett had little to do but escort her from solicitor to barrister to coroner to magistrate, his designated task to impress them all with his rank and breeding. At long last, he couldn't help thinking, he was getting some practical use out of being a viscount. When the actual interrogations got under way, he remained quietly on the sidelines, warm with affection and pride.

The nights, when they finally retired to their bedchamber, were for them alone. Refusing to allow discussion of what had passed, or what lay ahead of them, he made sure her worries were forgotten.

Now and again, the main conspirators joined up to compare notes. Over a supper at the Crock of Gold, Sir Peregrine was in full flight as he described the haunting of Tom Falshaw. "All too brief, my darlings," he said after reenacting the scene. "The poor fellow began screaming straightaway, and I had to vanish before the servants arrived. But effective nonetheless, and most entertaining. Truly, I am wasted on practicalities. In future I shall request more imaginative missions, like this one. My Cadaverous Specter deserves an encore."

The next morning Jarrett rode out with John Gilliam, who had been keeping an eye on Greenwillow Manor. It was the first time he'd seen the property, and it was, as Kate had told him, in poor repair. A few sheep grazed in the extensive pastures, but otherwise the house stood isolated atop a hill, the outbuildings shabby and the gardens untended.

If they got possession of the estate, what the devil would they do with it? He was paying expenses for Kate's rescue and defense with Black Phoenix funds left over from the Paradise gambit, but the balance had to be returned. He'd given his word. And while he retained most of the money Gilliam had eagerly lost to him, it wouldn't go far.

Always he ran up against his own impassable barrier—empty pockets. Used to living one day to the next, never mind the wolf lurking the other side of the door, he was unaccustomed to planning ahead. For now Kate walked in hope because he devoted himself to creating it in her. But he walked in despair, because at the end, he would let her down entirely.

Meantime there were more strands to weave, the most unruly of them an encampment of perhaps four dozen Gypsies clustered on the banks of a stream while their livestock—mules and goats—were let to eat their fill on someone else's pasture.

The sun was setting when Jarrett and Kate arrived, traveling alone, although two of Perry's servants, armed with rifles, had concealed themselves within firing distance. The protection was not unwelcome. Their sullen hosts tried to shoo them away until Kate spoke in what she had described to him as the cant, which sounded rather like English stirred in with gibberish.

The effect was immediate. While he stood apart, several glowering fellows escorted her out of his sight.

A few minutes later, bouncing with excitement, she returned. "A girl from the clan I traveled with has married the son of this clan's leader. We were friends. She and her mother are eager to lead Tom Falshaw wherever we wish to direct him, so I am going to tell her everything I can think of that might help. It will take awhile, but the leader will not permit his women in your vicinity. Do you mind waiting here?"

Now completely and officially redundant, he smiled at her pleasure and sent her off again. Then he settled by the campfire, where he was eventually served a mug of tea strong enough to grow hair on his teeth. Clumped in groups, the men and boys regarded him with wary interest. Then some of the younger ones began moving closer, sitting cross-legged around the fire and talking among themselves in their odd language. A boy shyly offered him a hard biscuit studded with caraway seeds.

After eating it and managing not to wince, Jarrett slipped a few coins from his pocket and startled the boy by reaching out an empty hand and plucking one of them from behind his ear.

Fairly soon he was surrounded by youngsters, each happy with a penny and trusting him enough to return the coin so he could make it appear again. After a time, he asked one of the older boys about the mules and got a lesson that included a field trip to the pasture.

All the while, he was imagining Kate living among a clan like this one, sleeping under the stars or a makeshift lean-to, and felt a profound affection for the strangers who had taken her in and protected her.

She returned in company with a burly, mustachioed

man who gave him a formal welcome to the camp even as their horses were being brought forward for their departure. His words were polite, but his expression said, *We've locked up our daughters.*

"Pay?" Jarrett whispered to Kate when the man wasn't looking.

She shook her head, gave the leader a smile and a curtsy, and led Jarrett to the horses. "His hospitality was granted because I am a friend of a family member," she told him as they rode away. "It would be rude to offer money in exchange, but naturally they will expect payment. One day, when we are established at Greenwillow, they will offer to sell us some mules and we will buy them."

He was glad he'd paid attention to the lesson in the pasture.

Three days later, Kate received a message from her Gypsy friend. It said only, in unschooled handwriting, *The word was dilivered.*

"That's all?" Jarrett rubbed the back of his neck. "Are we supposed to assume the mission was successful? How do we get details?"

"To ask would be insulting," she said with the patience that had been growing in her while his own was declining. "They gained access to him, which is something. I expect they did well. But we cannot say what effect they had unless the Falshaws leave, and even then, we can never be sure which of our ploys drove them off."

"The aggregate of them all, I suppose. But we're running short of ploys, and there they still squat. I'm tempted to flush them out the old-fashioned way, with beaters and guns."

The day, their first free of meetings, brought a series

of unpromising reports. The petition to reopen the case would be heard, but the appointed magistrate was a man notorious for strict interpretation of law and intolerant of accused criminals who did not conduct themselves properly.

"I guess running away wouldn't qualify as proper conduct," said Kate, buffing her nails as if a life-or-death sentence didn't hang over her head. "And I'll bet that being married to a viscount won't help me, either."

"You are becoming too fatalistic about this," he informed her, pacing the way she used to pace when she was the one in a temper. "We cannot simply give up."

"As you very well know, we haven't. Everything that can be done has been done. The review of the case might have been declined, meaning that constables would have been sent to take me into custody. Instead, we have a chance to present our evidence. Five servants have been located, and all agreed to speak of conditions at Greenwillow and the behavior of the Falshaws. Mrs. Aherne from Clare insists on coming all the way to Dublin to make her son's report available. I am content, Dering. But I wish you would take yourself off before you start punching at the walls."

A knock at the door woke Kate from her nap. It was Mr. Gilliam, who flushed to see her with mussed hair and wearing a dressing gown.

"They're going to bolt," he said the moment the door closed behind him. "Today a constable appeared at Greenwillow with official papers, which were almost certainly a summons. Shortly after, the servants—

there are only three now—were offered an extended holiday. The Falshaws said they had received an invitation to a house party and would soon depart. The servants were asked to go immediately."

She sank, weak-kneed, onto a chair. "How do you know this?"

"One of them was approached by one of us. The maid said that yesterday, after a visit from a veiled woman, the Falshaws closed off several rooms on the ground floor and appeared to be gathering their possessions to be packed."

"They won't appear at the inquest, then."

"It seems not. The house is being watched, and when they leave, they will be followed. Then, as soon as their direction can be worked out, riders will go ahead to determine their ultimate destination. And since they are undoubtedly pillaging the house, arrangements will be made to separate them from your property."

"Oh, please, do nothing that would cause them to change their minds. Let them take everything, so long as they *go*."

"Sir Peregrine has a plan. He is hard to persuade, in the throes of a plan, but I shall tell him what you said. The creditors, you know, would be glad to sell what you don't want in exchange for what they are owed."

"Yes. We mustn't leave them empty-handed." She could scarcely take it all in. The prospect of confronting the Falshaws had burned in her throat since first she resolved to return home. "Well, do as you think best, sir. Mr. Mahoney should be informed."

"If you will write to him, I'll hire a courier to take the letter. In half an hour?"

*   *   *

About an hour after the messenger had gone, Dering returned, soaking wet from his ride.

"The heavens opened," he announced, "just when I was in sight of the inn. By God, what a horse. Probably I should send him back to England with Sir Peregrine before I altogether lose the will to return him. You must be my conscience, Kate."

As he spoke, he was stripping off his wet clothes. She was about to say something when he pulled his shirt over his head, and again when he applied his boots to the jack. She did not want to tell her news to his backside. Then he vanished into the dressing room, returning not long after wearing his dressing gown and rubbing at his wet hair with a towel. "The bed is rumpled," he said. "Did you take a nap, or are you having an affair?"

"With the undergardener."

For the first time, he looked directly at her. The towel settled around his neck as he let it go and dropped to one knee in front of the chair where she was seated. "What is it? What has happened?"

"It's good. I simply can't get my mind to accept it. Mr. Gilliam brought news that the Falshaws are preparing to depart."

"But this is excellent!" He scooted forward and folded his arms across her lap. "It's over, then. We've won."

"Perhaps. The will can certainly go into probate. But we still have the inquest appeal to face, and even without opposition from Mrs. Falshaw, we have no proof that the decision reached at the first inquest should be overturned. We need to be prepared for that, Dering. We need to make plans."

"That is simple enough. If the inheritance can now be secured for our daughter, let's go somewhere safe and see about producing one. There is no reason to proceed with the inquest. There's nothing for us here in Ireland. We haven't the money to restore the house, which I'm told is barely livable. Mahoney can oversee the property, lease the land for grazing . . . he'll know what to do."

"And where would we go? How would we live?"

"Why not London? Or Canada. India. The Americas, North or South. With the war ended, Europe is open to us. Wherever you like, Kate. I've enough for transportation and a new, if meager, start. So long as you are with me and safe from prosecution, I'll be content."

"I knew you would want this," she said. "It is what you've wanted from the beginning. I'd wager the minute I told you the news about the Falshaws, leaving was the first thing popped into your head."

"Why not? Everyone who matters knows you are innocent. All the testimony will be held by the Mahoneys for our children to read. The inquest is too great a risk. Poor judgment by one narrow-minded magistrate could do us all in."

"The way your father's bad judgment did you in?"

He blinked. "If you need an example, that will do. You have the answers you needed. The Aherne boy witnessed the fall and said you did not cause it. Do you require some sort of official declaration to free you of the guilt you have felt? Some public display to polish your reputation with all the people who really don't give a damn what happened ten years ago?"

"It seems that I do," she said. "For all of those ten years, I woke to the fear someone would recognize me, that I would be carried off to face trial. I could not acknowledge my birthland or use my given name. I had no place of my own."

"Your place is with me now. And you carry my name."

"Those things make me happy, Dering. But they are not enough. I must reclaim myself. You'll call it unreasonable pride, and perhaps it is. And still, I know that if I am to be a good wife and, God willing, a good mother, I have to become whole again."

"You are, I think, the most completely *whole* person I have ever known. There are scars, my dear, and regrets, and longings, but they will fade over time. We will replace the bad memories by creating new lives for ourselves. I don't understand why you cannot be satisfied with that. Wherever we go, however we contrive to live, it will be more than enough for me."

"No, my love. It will not. It won't fill the emptiness in you. A new life will not replace the one you were born to lead. You cannot change who you are." She smoothed his messy, drying hair with her fingers. "I have accepted this truth for myself, and you must accept it as well. Neither of us will ever be truly happy until we have walked into the fire."

Their eyes met. Locked together. He understood, she thought, what she had just asked of him, but she didn't expect an answer. Not yet.

After a time, he came to his feet and went to the tray of decanters and glasses. "Are you wishing me to address you as Catriona, then?"

Men always changed a subject they found uncomfortable to something entirely ridiculous. "If you like. For myself, I prefer Kate. I've been called that since I was sent off to school. It gave me a start, I must say, when you plucked it out of nowhere when we were at Paradise."

"I plucked it out of *Shrew*," he said. "You'd planted the idea, and hence the name, in my head. No mystery about it."

"And I, of course, am a perfect shrew."

"Not yet." He brought her a glass of wine. "But you're getting better at it."

She smiled. The teasing was his way of avoiding a decision he was unready to make, but she had planted the seed. It would open when it could, and send forth shoots. And when the time came, she would stand by him as he was standing by her now.

Sitting, really, since he'd drawn up a chair and settled where he could see her face. He raised his wineglass. "To Catriona Kate Finnerty Falshaw Dering, which is a lot of names for a female who claims to have no identity. Shall we move over to Naas tomorrow and settle in? The weather is uncertain these days, and I shouldn't like us to miss the performance. Oughtn't we to rehearse my lines?"

Because her legal identity had been absorbed into his when they married, he would be required to present her testimony. It rubbed against her pride that with her life at stake, she was nonetheless forbidden to speak for herself. Dering should go into Parliament and see the laws changed, that's what. "You know the story as well as I," she said. "And you are the last man on this planet who requires rehearsal for a speaking part. There is no thought in your head, I hope, of abducting me and carrying me off before the hearing?"

"Not while you still own a knife. But perhaps I can get Sir Peregrine to do it."

Presided over by a magistrate who looked as if he'd eaten bad mackerel for breakfast, the hearing got under way in a large, overcrowded room used for assemblies. The citizens of Naas, Kildare's county town, squeezed themselves onto narrow benches like kernels of corn, while those who couldn't get a seat lined up along the walls.

Kate, wearing a subdued blue dress and a plain bonnet, wished she had thought to bring a fan. She and Dering had been placed beside each other on high-backed chairs in the section set apart for witnesses, a concession by the magistrate that he was not happy about. He'd wanted her in the makeshift docket, or set apart in some way that marked her as the accused. But Mr. Dennis Mahoney charmingly cited obscure precedents relating to unorthodox inquiries such as this until the magistrate gave in, probably to silence him.

All that took place before the audience was admitted, so as they came through the door, they saw only a demure young woman seated next to a handsome man with the distinctive composure of an English peer. His Excellency the Lord Lieutenant was there as well, ensconced in the first row of observers on a fancy carved chair and surrounded by prosperous-looking gentlemen and what looked to be bodyguards.

At the meetings with her barrister and his assistant, Kate had been told what to expect. She'd read the report of the original inquest, including the signed testimony of Mrs. Falshaw, and learned what the witnesses assembled on her behalf would say. Everything was going just as Mr. Mahoney had predicted.

Servant after servant testified to Mr. Edward Falshaw's maltreatment of his wife and the maids. The housekeeper swore that Mrs. Falshaw had not been present when her son fell down the stairs, and that when the housekeeper went to give her the terrible news, she had been asleep in her bed.

On and on it went, the room growing hotter, the magistrate's voice increasingly edged with annoyance. But things livened up when Mrs. Aherne was brought forward, only to hear the magistrate refuse to admit her statement on the grounds it contained no more than a secondhand report of what her son had told her. Chin quivering with outrage, she hobbled on her cane directly up to the table where he was seated and gave him a piece of her mind.

"My Kevin is a good lad, Your Honorship. I know he ought to have spoken up hisself, and it were wrong to run away. But he were only a boy when he worked for them devil Falshaws, and the mistress said she'd see him hung for helping kill the master. He would be here to speak for hisself this day, Kevin would, but he got pressed and fought in the war for the king. And then he got wounded in Canada, and . . . well, it's not his fault. I'll sell me cottage to buy him passage if you wait this trial so he can get here. He wants his truth said, because he has the worm of guilt at his stomach for what happened to this one." She pointed to Kate. "Hear it now from me, or let me bring him home to say it."

Every eye in the room pinned the magistrate to the back of his chair. Mrs. Aherne, frail but fierce, held her ground. At just the right moment, Dennis Mahoney came forward and quietly reminded the magistrate that this was not a formal trial, and that he had the power to waive the usual procedures.

So Mrs. Aherne got to speak, and Dering, for his sins, had to follow her performance. He related simply and clearly what Kate would have said, were she permitted, and retained his calm in the face of a harsh interrogation by the magistrate. Throughout, Kate was careful not to look at Dering's face or to draw attention to herself.

The only surprise came when The Honorable John Gilliam arrived and spoke, during a recess, with Dennis Mahoney. Throughout the morning, several references had been made to Mrs. William Falshaw's failure to answer her summons. Mr. Gilliam brought news of that, and when the hearing reconvened, permission for him to testify was reluctantly granted.

Mrs. Falshaw, he reported, accompanied by her son, had traveled to Cove and taken passage on a merchant ship bound for several ports in North America. It was not known where they meant to disembark. During the hurried preparations for sailing, a mishap occurred. Because the harbor was not deep enough to sustain large vessels, passengers, luggage, and freight had to be rowed out to the anchorage. Mysteriously, nearly all the boxes the Falshaws brought with them failed to be transported. Mr. Gilliam, who was returning to Kildare, offered to convey them back to Greenwillow Manor. Perhaps their contents could be sold to repay the Falshaws' creditors.

The magistrate, rightly suspicious, sniffed his displeasure. "Just how did you come to know all this?"

"I made it my business when I chanced to see them on the road, heading south with a wagonload of goods. Knowing they were expected at the hearing, I decided to follow along."

"And saw to it their possessions did not make the voyage with them?"

"I had nothing whatever to do with that," Mr. Gilliam said. "My involvement began when I elected not to leave the boxes sitting on the dock and ended when I stashed them in the barn at Greenwillow."

Beside her, Dering was vibrating with suppressed laughter. Kate was not so amused. If the magistrate asked the right questions, Sir Peregrine's little scheme would surely be exposed. Mr. Gilliam wouldn't lie under oath.

But the room was hot, and even the magistrate must realize by now that the only evidence against Catriona, Lady Dering, was the decade-old perjured testimony of an absconder from justice. Mr. Gilliam was instructed to stand down.

"Have you more witnesses?" the magistrate said to Mr. Dennis Mahoney.

"Oh, indeed," said the barrister cheerfully. "Also financial accountings, a review of the recently discovered and final will of Miss Maura Coffey—"

A gasp from the audience.

"And, of course, my summary of the considerable evidence that proves Lady Dering's innocence. Did you wish to declare a recess for luncheon, sir, and continue later in the afternoon?"

Rumbles of protest from the audience. They had been entertained, but the benches were hard and the prospect of Mr. Mahoney's financial accountings did not appeal. The Lord Lieutenant, who had thought to bring a fan, waved it with the impatience of a man ready to have an end declared.

Kate saw the magistrate look in His Excellency's direction, wrinkle his nose, and heave a sigh. "Is anyone in possession of information that might cause us to question the evidence we have thus far been presented? Rise and declare yourselves now."

Silence fell. She felt her body go stiff with apprehension. Dering's thigh, pressed against hers, was rock-hard with his own tension.

No one moved. No one spoke.

The magistrate waited for a time beyond endurance before rising. "In light of revelations unknown at the time of the original inquest," he said with the tone you'd expect from a Roman senator, "I declare the determination of death by intent, perpetrated by one Catriona Falshaw of Greenwillow Manor, County Kildare, nullified and voided. A new declaration reflecting the ascertained facts will be drawn up and submitted to the several parties required to sign their acquiescence. Furthermore, I direct that charges of willful perjury be pursued against Mrs. William Falshaw, and that if found within jurisdiction of our laws and rulings, she be taken into custody. Be it so ordered."

The cheers from the onlookers, who ignored the bailiff's efforts to silence them, showed whose side they had been on. They were clapping shoulders, shaking hands, celebrating as if they—all strangers to her— had harbored a stake in this hearing. And perhaps they had. The authorities had proven capable of retracting errors and restoring justice. No small thing, in a country that had seen too little justice for hundreds of years.

Her knees were shaking as Dering helped her stand and held her arm while she accepted congratulations and good wishes. Then she went from witness to witness, thanking each of them for coming forward on her behalf. She thanked the coroner as well, and Mr. Dennis Mahoney, who had manipulated events like a magician. Then she came to Patrick Mahoney, who had told her of falling in love with her great-aunt, only to have his proposal rejected.

"It means the world to me," he said softly amid the

jostling crowd, "to have done a service for the girl Maura loved as her own child."

Kate nearly wept then, from the relief of her freedom and the kindness of so many people who had made it possible. She wanted only to leave with Dering and be silent for a time, to let her new life put down roots. Until this moment, she had never been sure of a future with him.

Mr. Gilliam approached, a grin wreathing his face. "Do you know, Sir Perry has asked if I might accept an invitation from Black Phoenix should there be a mission that suits my talents. I told him yes, with great enthusiasm. He also asked me to convey his regards. This morning, he departed for England."

"He was so sure of the outcome?"

"I think the gentleman is never unsure of anything. Quite a remarkable fellow, if a little exhausting."

"And your own intentions, sir? Will you return home straightaway?"

"I am never in a hurry to go home," he said, a little sadness in his eyes. "Lord Whitworth has offered me the hospitality of his residence, so I shall enjoy Dublin for a time and then explore the countryside." After a moment he offered his hand to Dering, who took it immediately. "I must thank you, sir, for inviting me to share your adventures. The confidence you placed in me has changed my life."

Men could never endure sentiment for longer than a remark or two and a handshake. The back of his neck crimson, Mr. Gilliam quickly moved away.

She looked over to see Lord Whitworth approaching, his starched face crinkled in a smile. "A great triumph," he said as she curtsied.

"You have given valuable support, my lord. I am sure your presence here was of significance."

"Who can say? But this particular magistrate and I have crossed swords on a number of occasions, and he knew very well that any slip on his part would not pass unnoticed. I can say only that it has been my pleasure, Lady Dering. To honor this triumph of justice, I have planned a celebratory supper at the Castle tonight, not at all formal, and it will be a crushing bore if you decline to favor us. Even Mrs. Aherne will be there, for I am carrying her back to Dublin in my coach."

More public display was the last thing she wanted, but of course she must accept. "We would be delighted, my lord. You are very kind."

"And selfish. You will not make your home here, what with Dering's chief property being in Dorset, so I must secure your delightful company while I can." After a bow, he made his way to the door, collecting Mrs. Aherne on the way.

"Did you tell him to drop that lead ball?" Dering said, frowning.

"Don't be absurd. Do you imagine I would put my words in someone else's mouth?"

"If you think it might be effective." His gaze softened. "Trust me, seduction works much better. Apply yourself to it and you will almost certainly have your way."

"Even in this?" Riding the warm current of her success, she could not help trying to tow him along with her. "You will walk into the fire?"

"I expect so. I, too, am weary of running the other direction. But it is no small thing to throw a brother and his family out on the street, not to mention the several thousand complications that will follow. Give me a little time, will you?"

Chapter 26

"He's a popular chap," Dering said. "Honored in battle, dashing in his Hussar regimentals, witty conversationalist, all that nonsense. One hears nothing to his discredit. Yet I cannot be in his company thirty seconds before wanting to plant him a facer."

"In such cases, it is often similarity of character that causes unprovoked dislike," Kate said with the equanimity she had been preserving since their arrival in London. Until then he had kept up his good spirits, but the closer they came to the return of his horse and the confrontation with his brother, the more irritable he grew. Now, as he led Banshee through Hyde Park to the meeting place with Major Lord Jordan Blair, Dering's temper could melt nails.

"Your theory fails," he said. "The other Black Phoenix fellow—calls himself Robin—might as well be a bank clerk. Dull as dishwater, no resemblance to me. And I don't like him, either."

"Perhaps they'll sell you back the horse. I know you don't wish to ask, but—"

"I am tempted, of course. But the last few weeks at Greenwillow must have convinced you that every penny we can scrape up will be required to make it

livable. Before I could weaken, I swore a solemn oath
not to purchase Banshee even at a bargain price. A
hack will do me well enough for now."

That morning at dawn, he'd left the hotel for a long,
last ride, and groomed the horse himself on his return.
Her heart ached for him. They were approaching
Hyde Park Corner, and he pointed out the entrance
to Tattersall's auction house, where he had first seen
Banshee. She deduced that Blair, having reclaimed
Black Phoenix's property, would march the horse
across the street and put him on the block again. Why
else call the meeting for this location?

Shading her eyes against the September-afternoon
sun, she spotted a dapper gentleman in a blue uniform
leaning against a tree. Dering had seen him, too. She
heard the hiss of breath between his teeth.

"There you are," said the man who must be Lord
Blair as he broke loose of the tree and strode jauntily
in their direction.

Dering had halted, forcing Blair to come to him.
"Did you think I wouldn't appear?"

"Not at all, old lad. You have grown startlingly reliable. I expect the change is entirely due to this lovely
lady, to whom we are all in debt. Lady Dering, I am
entirely at your service."

"Let's get this over with," said Dering before she
could respond. "Here is a bank draft for the unspent
funds provided me by Phoenix. If you want an accounting, you're out of luck. I didn't keep records."

"And how could you, in the circumstances? We
have no reason to doubt your word, sir. This, I presume, is the horse. Splendid animal. I could quite
fancy him for myself."

Tight-jawed, Dering handed over the reins.

She knew what it cost him. Wanted to slap Lord Blair, who was being unnecessarily provocative. Yes, indeed, the two men facing off at daggers drawn were very alike. That much was perfectly clear. But she didn't sense rancor in Blair. She thought, instead, that he wanted something, or was putting Dering to the test. As if Dering had not already achieved far more than what Phoenix had asked of him.

"Now that you have returned the horse," Blair said, "do you wish to buy him back? We'll make you a good price."

"No." Dering's voice was flat.

"You may name it yourself."

"Is it a game you are playing with me? I've come all the way to London for this. Let it be. I'm done with the horse. Done with you. Done with Phoenix."

"Well, not quite." Blair sounded almost apologetic. "We have provided you a service, and if called upon, you must provide a service in return. How else could we accomplish what we do, if those who benefit did not pass on the favor to others?"

"I thought I already did."

"Ah, Paradise. But you were summoned for that mission. A horse of a different color. Of course, you can always decline our request."

Dering, hands clasped behind his back, looked over at Kate and then up to the trees, their leaves already beginning to turn as the cold summer melted into autumn. "I have responsibilities now," he said. "But I take your point. Call on me when you will, and if I can, I shall do as you ask."

Kate, astonished, longed to know if she would be called upon to do a service as well. Who had received more from Black Phoenix than she?

"Are you sure about the horse?" Blair said, without the taunting edge that had been on his words until now.

"I am," said Dering. "But I hope you will make every effort to place him with a decent owner."

"How much?" said Kate.

Dering made a slashing gesture. "I told you—"

"How much do you have?" said Lord Blair.

"Almost nothing at the moment. Might I pay on credit?" She reached inside the pocket slit of her skirts for the small pouch she always wore. "You may have this as surety that I will honor the debt. It is the most precious thing I have ever possessed."

The golden guinea flashed in the sunlight.

She felt a jab of pain. To let it go, to make it impossible for Dering to come to her and ask for the coin, seemed a breach of trust. Once it had represented all she had of him. Now it was, even more than her wedding ring, a symbol of their union.

Lord Blair looked pleased. "Why, a guinea is the exact price I was hoping to get. Have we a deal, then?"

"We do, sir." Tears burning at the back of her eyes, she dropped the coin onto his white-gloved hand. In return, he gave her Banshee's reins.

Dering put himself in front of Lord Blair. "Why are you doing this?"

"We pay our debts, sir. As the scripture says, 'Though I have all faith, so that I could remove mountains, and have not charity, I am nothing.' Black Phoenix, entangled in plots and schemes, was so busy removing mountains that we lost sight of why we came to exist. Our priorities had got skewed. It can be said, I think, that you restored to us our soul."

Dering, searching his face, was clearly at a loss for words.

Blair, grinning now, dodged around him to favor Kate with a gallant bow. "Your husband is a fortunate man, my lady. I only wish I had made your acquaintance before he did." And off he went, his fur-edged pelisse fluttering in the light wind.

Dering, rooted in place like a tree stump, gazed after him.

"Whatever was that about?" she asked.

"Nothing that signifies. He's a blowhard, is all, trying to impress a beautiful woman. Speaking of which . . ." His arms went around her, and next she knew, she was being deeply, thoroughly kissed. As a distraction, it was more than effective. She forgot where they were until a child's voice caught her attention and drew it to the passersby who were pausing to enjoy the show. "Dering!"

"What?" Not letting go of her, he set her back just a little. "Is it Banshee? I'll hold the reins."

"It's the *people*. We are creating a scene."

"Dear me. Such a scandal." His thumb caressed the swell of her breast. "A man in love with his own wife. I'll never be able to show my face in the clubs."

She looked up at him, searching his eyes. "Do you love me? Truly?"

Surprise furrowed his brow. "How can you doubt it? Was it some other woman in bed with me these last two months?"

"Passion is not love. In all this time you have never said you loved me."

"But it was obvious. Wasn't it? I mean, I never talk about breathing, either, but I do it all the time. I love you like the air, Kate. You are essential to every moment of my life. I thought you knew that."

"It is what I have *wanted* to believe. But when a man of words never says the ones I long to hear, I find myself questioning everything. Which is absurd, I know, because words are so often lies."

"Not between us. Not now. But we are both in need of reassurance, I think. Happiness came on us by surprise, and we fear it will vanish as quickly as it appeared."

"I have felt that, too. And it has made me behave foolishly, just when we should be celebrating. The audience is becoming restless, my love. Shall we treat them to another scene?"

He kissed her again, with convincing devotion, but as they set out for the hotel, she remembered a bit of unfinished business. "Are you displeased with me for handing over the guinea? I meant to keep it always, but you did tell me to let it go, if ever it would do me good."

"Planning to keep Banshee for yourself, are you?" He didn't sound worried. "The devil of it is, that was my lucky coin. Not that it always lived up to the role, given how many times I rubbed it and proceeded to lose everything except my underdrawers. But it had just redeemed itself by securing for me a wife and a horse, only to find itself banished into the pocket of that upstart Hussar. I don't mind losing the coin, Kate, but damned if I like knowing he's got it."

She grinned up at him. "In every garden—"

"—there is a snake," they said at the same time, laughing.

The weather was kind as they traveled from London to Dorset. More often than not, Dering left Kate inside the hired carriage and took to horseback, sometimes disappearing for hours at a time.

She worried about him, but said nothing. Since asking her to help compose the message he'd sent ahead to his brother, he had closed the door on where they were going and why. And because it had taken her almost as long to return to her own home and confront her own demons, she could scarcely complain. It wasn't as if she had invited him to her own trial by fire. And she knew he welcomed her company, even needed it, in spite of the distance he sometimes kept.

In fact, their only quarrel had concerned the wording of the message. His version had been so conciliatory and apologetic that anyone reading it would have missed the point altogether. "It's perfectly well," she said, "to tell your brother that you wish the family to meet your new wife. But that is not why we are going there, and the true kindness is to help them prepare for a complete change in their lives. Give them the truth. You are coming to Dering Park to claim what is yours."

So he did, writing words that had been difficult to inscribe in a letter and almost impossible to think of enforcing in person.

It was late morning when the coach slowed and edged onto the verge. Dering handed her out and led her to the lip of a ridge that overlooked a valley rimmed with rolling hills. The wet summer had turned the landscape intensely green, from the dark foliage of the hedgerows and trees to the bright blades of grass rippling over the pastureland. A silver-blue ribbon of a river curled around copses and under little stone bridges. Her breath caught at the beauty of it.

"The Blackmore Vale," he said. "That's the River Stour, which floods the bottomland and keeps the soil rich. Mostly small dairy farms there. The larger properties are along the hillsides. Dering Park is to our right, about five miles away."

If he had been speaking an obscure Asian language,

she would still have recognized in his voice the love
he cherished for this beautiful landscape. It was in his
blood, pulsing through him like the river that nour-
ished the valley. She had worried that she was doing
wrong by urging him to return to his home and heritage, but her concerns vanished in the sun-drenched
air. He belonged here, just as she belonged at his side.

His own worries were weeds that had taken root in
his kind nature, which he would probably have said
didn't exist to any great degree. Displacing his family
seemed to him a great crime, especially because his
brother had nurtured the property, so neglected by
their father, back to good order. Once or twice a year,
Dering had told her, he'd come to Dorset and quietly
surveyed his land, noting through his spyglass the improvements that followed one upon the other. The
tenant cottages were repaired, the outbuildings replaced, and the house itself given a badly needed new
roof. He'd not set foot inside it since his father's
death, but he expected the interior had been seen to
as well.

"George has been a good steward," he said, leading
her back to the coach. "How can I evict him? Not to
mention the four children. Where will they go?"

"I thought he'd inherited the family fortune."

"From what I can tell, he has put a good deal of it
into the estate. Dering Park is more his than mine
now."

The large manor house, constructed of Portland
stone, was approached by way of a circular drive lined
with rose trees. Two servants were waiting to take the
horses, and as Kate and Dering mounted the steps,
the door opened to reveal a slender young gentleman.
Dering's brother, Kate knew immediately. He stood a

head shorter, his gray eyes lacked the touch of green, and his hair was clipped shorter, but the cheekbones and jawline were precisely the same. He looked apprehensive and a little sad.

Beside her, Dering halted, his arm tightening around hers. "Jarvis is no longer here?" he said.

"He will outlast us all. But I've been watching for you and wished to be the one to greet you." He stepped onto the landing and moved aside, gesturing to the open door. "Welcome home, Jarrett."

Kate, listening hard, could detect no trace of resentment. Only sincerity, like a warm stream flowing beneath the formal words. Dering glanced over at her, puzzlement in his eyes, as they entered the house.

No one awaited them there. The entrance hall, with its marble floor and double-arc staircase, had been polished until it shone. In the eerie silence, their footfalls sounded like an army on the march.

George Dering paused at the foot of the stairs. "I thought the upstairs parlor, but if you would prefer—"

"Will you permit me, George, to make you known to my wife?"

George flushed as his brother made the introductions, and bowed gravely when the moment came. "I hope you will approve your home, Lady Dering," he said with a shy smile. "Did you wish to be shown to the master's chambers?"

"I'll withdraw, of course, if you and Dering wish to converse privately. But I'd rather not. At the pace the two of you are setting, I might be waiting there until I'm toothless."

"As you see," Dering said, "my wife does not hesitate to speak her mind. Shall we take a lesson from her and stop dancing this awkward minuet?"

"Gladly." Relief lit George's gentle face. "Be

warned, though. I've been preparing a speech. It isn't a good one, but it covers much of what must be said to you. Will you permit me to deliver it?"

"By all means."

They all trooped up the stairs, a little more at ease with one another, and settled in a bright, airy room with lacy curtains fluttering at the half-open windows. A tea tray had been laid out on a low table between two sofas, and beside it, cut-glass decanters filled with wine and brandy glowed red and amber.

"George," Dering said, settling beside Kate, "you look like you need a drink. I know I do."

"Yes." He took the brandy Dering offered him and raised the glass. "To your homecoming. I only wish it had come long before now."

Dering, taken by surprise, sloshed brandy onto the tray while filling his own glass. "There's no need to say such things, you know. With little notice, I am disrupting everything and everyone here. Attila and his Huns would have been a more welcome sight."

"Mother appears to think so. Convinced you meant to toss us, she had our luggage packed and removed to the dower house, where she is waiting with the children for word to leave."

"Good God."

"She has always been fearful. Father made her so. But it is her guilt driving her now, as it drives me." George, still on his feet, took a sip of brandy. "I seem to be wandering into my speech. May I say it, before I lose the courage?"

"Certainly. But you owe me no explanations. We'll do better to start from here and continue on, don't you think?"

"How can that be possible? I betrayed my brother and my friend, to please a father who cared only for his newest parcel of land. And, in part, for Belinda. You had always been the golden son, but she said I had replaced you in her affections. I took foolish pride in that. It sickens me to think I believed her, and continued to believe her when all evidence bent to the contrary."

"She is a chameleon, George. I was fooled as well. You did me no harm to wed her. And you could not prevent Father from leaving his fortune as he did. I've never resented you for that."

"It should have gone to you, and there was nothing to stop me from handing it over except my own weakness of character. I had wanted, all my life, to manage an estate. There was no need for university, only for tending the land and keeping the records. And suddenly, with you gone, Dering Park fell to my care. I told myself you were content in London, that you would never abandon the gaming and the women for a quiet life here. But you should have been given the choice. Perhaps you'd even have hired me as your steward."

"No one could have done better. I did keep watch, you know, after a fashion. Had you let the Park run down, I should have been on you like all nine Furies. But I'd not have taken your money. My pride would not, and will not, permit that."

"It's gone, anyway, most of it. I put a great deal into the estate, and while it soon began repaying the investment, Belinda . . . Well, I lacked the courage to deny her. I've hidden some, bought shares on the Exchange, made sure the children are provided for. Belinda's parents tell me they will leave everything to their grandchildren, but I dare not rely on that altogether. In any case, the estate, properly managed, will continue to sustain itself and return a profit."

"You should know that I intend to manage it myself. You may, of course, remain here, and the children as well."

"It is better if we do not." George sank onto the sofa across from his brother. "Belinda rarely comes to Dering Park these days, but so long as her parents live nearby, there can be no escaping her. And she never fails to disrupt the children's lives. I wish to remove them from her influence. They are not mine, you know. Not by blood. But I love them as my own, and in future, my concern must be entirely for them. Which leads me . . . Oh, I cannot think how to say this."

"With complete honesty," said Dering. "It spares a lot of confusion."

"I wish to separate from her legally, and keep the children, and make sure she receives no more than a frugal allowance. She has already made off with too much of their inheritance."

"A divorce?"

"I've no wish to marry again. But even a separation from bed and board is a terrible scandal. I'll quite understand if you do not wish me to undertake this. Perhaps I can settle in a remote place where she'll not bother with us, and—"

"Of course you must proceed. I'll help you. We'll hire a good attorney straightaway. And never mind public opinion. My own reputation is tiptoeing through the gutter, and my lovely bride came to me directly from the stage. I promise, your puny scandal will pass virtually unnoticed. Kate, you are bouncing. I intended no insult about your former career."

"Not that. I have an idea. May I speak?"

"Could I stop you? George, you are looking at a force of nature. Whatever her idea, you needn't pretend to like it if you do not. She'll soon come up with another."

"Greenwillow Manor. It requires a manager, one who can develop the land and restore the house. We'll not be living there." She looked at George, who was regarding her as if she'd just flown in from heaven. "I'm afraid, though, that it's in Ireland."

"But that is ideal. Belinda will never come so far."

"Greenwillow is held in trust for my first daughter. Until she is born and comes of age, you can remain there as long as you like. Dering, have you objections?"

"None, except that it's a long way to travel for a visit." He smiled at George. "I was hoping to renew our friendship."

"The separation will take considerable time to wind its way through the Ecclesiastical Courts," George said. "And I must make you familiar with every inch of Dering Park, not to mention all the records and accounts. You'll wish me gone soon enough."

"Then several problems are willy-nilly resolved." Dering brushed a kiss on her cheek, rose, and stretched. "I feel as if I have passed through a door I thought sealed, only to find it standing open for me with my brother waiting on the other side."

George, also coming to his feet, closed the short distance between them and offered his hand. Through tear-blurred eyes, Kate watched Dering take it. And then he moved closer and wrapped his brother in an embrace.

When they separated, two pairs of eyes were suspiciously wet.

"You have been, beyond reason, generous and kind." George's voice broke. "I hope that one day you can forgive my depriving you of your home for so long."

"Say, rather, that I must thank you." This time it was Dering who held out a hand . . . to his wife. She rose and let him draw her into the circle of his arm. "I cannot regret the last ten years, or what brought them to pass. They were the journey I had to take, the path that led me to Kate. Nothing else signifies."

Awash in happiness, she heard little of what followed. Dering suggested his brother retrieve the rest of the family from the dower house and set them to unpacking. He wished to meet his nieces and nephews. George said the master's suite of rooms had been prepared. There was talk of baths. Dinner. Plans to be made.

When George left them in the master's bedchamber, Dering sank onto the large bed and buried his face in his hands. He was shaking.

Leaving him to wrestle with his ghosts this one last time, Kate went to one of the tall windows and gazed out over the terraced gardens to the grasslands beyond. Not long after, George strode, light-footed, along a path and disappeared over a hill. Off to fetch his mother and children, she supposed, realizing of a sudden they were now her family as well. And this beautiful place, her home.

To be sure, it was Dering who would always be her true home. Whatever befell them, they would meet it together. But for now she'd a new role to learn—Lady of the Manor—and prayers to say, for the blessing of children.

She watched a marmalade cat stroll along a low stone wall edging the garden, its tail pointing to the sky. Mrs. Kipper had not permitted her to keep Malvolio, as she had asked, because he was needed for Black Phoenix missions. She had been sorry for it, even knowing she had no secure place to take him, or even to lay her own head.

But dreams she had not dared to imagine had come true. And like Dering, she was finding it impossible to stop looking over her shoulder or watching her next step. They were so accustomed to adversity that to simply accept happiness seemed beyond them both.

She turned, and saw him looking up at her.

"I cannot seem to believe what just happened," he said. "Or much of anything that happened since I got that dreadful summons from Black Phoenix. What a grace that turned out to be."

"Yes. For the both of us, and for your family as well. But it's made me prodigiously greedy. I still want children. And I want you to take your place in Parliament, and in Society, as is your due. I won't even be jealous when you're gone, not too very much, when I can console myself in this beautiful place."

He opened his arms and she walked into them, settling across his lap, warm in his embrace.

"Where I go," he said, "you go. Well, not into the Lords, I suppose, not straightaway. But if only for our children's sake, we should begin reconstructing the Dering reputation, which was fairly tolerable two or three generations ago."

"You cannot take an actress into Society, my love. Your friends would be insulted."

"I will have no friends who do not welcome you. But let us negotiate our next difficult mission at som future time, because right now I'm starting to rat like this whole business of being happy. I coul used to it."

"I'll see that you do," she murmured, drawir his head for a kiss.

Author's Note

The autographed manuscript of "Kubla Khan" that Robert Southey showed Lord Dering came to light in 1934 when it was loaned from a private collection to a Lamb and Coleridge exhibit in the National Portrait Gallery. According to scholars, who scurried to trace its history, Coleridge had sent a copy of his poem to Southey several years before Lord Byron, impressed by the poet's recitation of his own work, caused it to be published in 1816. The handwritten manuscript and several variants between the earlier and later versions of the poem are briefly described in this book.

After Southey's death in 1843, his wife gave the manuscript to an unknown autograph collector. It was eventually sold at an auction house for a paltry one pound, fifteen shillings to Monckton Milnes, father of ~~~ later created Marquess of Crewe. The Mar~~~ without an heir, and in 1962, what had ~~~ known as the Crewe Manuscript was ac~~~ his widow by the British Museum.

~~~riting *Dangerous Deceptions*, I remembered ~~~f this "discovered" copy of the poem and ~~~ Dering, clever fellow that he was, could ~~~ it a clue to the villain's identity. Just

another proof that majoring in English Lit can be useful in unexpected ways!

Read more about the background of this book at www.lynnkerstan.com.